DEATH
KNELL

By C. Terry Cline, Jr.

DAMON

DEATH KNELL

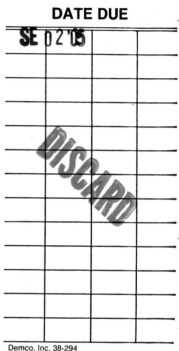

F

Cline, C. Terry
  Death knell, by C. Terry Cline, jr.
Putnam [c1977]
311p

ISBN 0-399-12010-6

Increasingly obsessed with her father's obscure life as a German refugee, Pamela Roth immerses herself in
the history and atrocities of the Holocaust until transformed by the spirit
of a Polish woman who survived Auschwitz but not the icy hands of Russell Roth

  I T

DEATH
KNELL

C. TERRY CLINE, Jr.

G.P. PUTNAM'S SONS, NEW YORK

SBN: 399-12010-6

Library of Congress Catalog Number 77–6935

PRINTED IN THE UNITED STATES OF AMERICA

To my mother:
MICKEY VANN CLINE
and sisters:
ELIZABETH ANN KRASHES
and in memoriam to:
CATHERINE (CAPPY) CASSIDY

CHAPTER ONE

SOMETHING WAS WRONG, she knew that. As though the fetus took from, or added to, the blood that coursed their veins in common. From the depths of her womb, Janet Roth detected something beyond the baby that was to be born in her twenty-eighth year. She did not fear the birthing of this, her first child. Ultimately, her only child. It was not the act of birth, she was certain of that, but she *was* afraid.

"Are you sure there's nothing wrong?" she'd questioned the doctor.

"You're in perfect health, Mrs. Roth."

"The baby. The baby seems all right?"

"Strong heartbeat, everything fine so far as we can determine. Do you have reason to believe otherwise?"

"No." Not really. Morning sickness had passed quickly. No symptoms of disease in dormancy. No fever. Fluid retention was easily controlled. Everything normal.

"Then why worry yourself?" the doctor had reasoned.

Yes. Indeed. Why worry? But she did. She lay awake nights with Russell's even breathing pulsing in the dark, his hirsute body radiating warmly against her. On her side, abdomen propped against two pillows, one hand on the cocoon of her belly, she felt for movement. It was there. A pushing kick as the infant stretched in the amniotic fluids, relieving muscles cramped by this natural confinement. Sometimes, through the walls of her taut flesh, Janet could detect a heel or an elbow, as though the child within were trying to communicate by touch with the mother without.

"Don't be puerile," Russell scolded. "All mothers fret for naught. It is a normal thing. Recognize it so, and put your mind at ease."

But some fears are without rationale, some anxieties defy logic. Russell's Prussian mind relied on the mathematics of thought as surely as he depended on the computers upon which his business was built. To him, all things had an orderly progression. Russell epitomized organization and the science of universal geometry. There was no place in his thinking for "fancied" ills and "imagined" woes.

"Worry about whether a boy or a girl this is," Russell counseled. "Worry that we buy too much blue or pink. Otherwise don't worry. Worry is a cause for worry. Simple?"

Too simple. Too orderly; regimented. That was Russell. Always in control. Emotions checked. Even conception had been deliberate and with forethought "at the appropriate time." Financially, chronologically appropriate.

Exacting in all things, was Russell. Precise in every way. His blue-gray eyes and expression a calculated mirror of those inner thoughts he wished to reveal. "But of course I love you," was his response to her question. "If I did not love you then why should I have taken you as my wife?"

Logic. His mouth producing a programmed response to a properly worded question. The key to eliciting information from Russell was to be certain the question *was* properly worded.

"Are you happy with me, Russell?"

"Certainly." Without emotion, casually respondent.

"Do you think you would have been happier married to some-one else?"

"There is no way to know that, of course."

Logic. Russell Roth had grown wealthy from logic. Their thirty-eight-room marble-halled mansion had been built on logic; the rose gardens, flowered terraces, swimming pool and patio—all by-products of logic.

"If the human mind can be surpassed in a single function by the machines I employ," Russell had once remarked, "it is by avoiding the complications of emotional response. That is what disturbs the human equation always, illogical obfuscation caused by emotional involvement in any question. Thus a computer reaches a conclusion based on hard data only, a feat quite beyond the human brain."

Of course, Russell had been right. There had been nothing to worry about. The baby was perfect.

If one of Russell's computers had been instructed to produce a child perfect in his eyes, Pamela would have been the result. Her face was a sculptor's dream: she was her father in every aspect, but a miracle had honed the genetic influence that had formed her. Russell's masculine Nordic nose was a finely chiseled and delicate shape above lips hewn from her father's flesh. His blond hair was even more luxuriant and alive on Pamela. Well-formed teeth, and a smile that came rarely but with magnificent effect once bestowed.

Pamela's eyes were her most striking feature. Liquid, curious eyes with a peculiar ability to change with chameleonic ease, reflecting the hue of her clothing, an azure sky or her mood: one time slate gray, the next a stunning blue or as green as sea water, all in a given day.

From the beginning, the child had a sixth sense about Russell. She would walk into a room prepared to make a request, and at a glance determine his probable reaction. She would sit, silent, patient beyond her years, while Russell's mind wrestled with a problem known only to him. Then at that precise instant when he could best be interrupted, Pamela was likely to stand and soberly take his hand.

"Too much thinking, Papa. Come, let's walk."

Heads hung, with identical gaits, hands clasped behind their backs, Russell and his icon in miniature could be seen strolling the grounds. Such moments were, to Janet, vaguely disturbing while at the same moment these were the very things which bonded father and daughter ever closer.

"She is truly the blood of my blood and flesh of my flesh," Russell had commented.

That she was. A somber, pensive, moody infant always slow to cry, Pamela evolved into a child cast from the matrix of her father. Beautiful beyond belief, a feminine version of all his most masculine attributes, Pamela *was* Russell. If he wished to perceive himself in the opposite gender he had only to gaze at his child.

But the likeness was more intrinsic, more inherent than first glance revealed. Pamela was nature's replica of her father to the very marrow of her bones, and through the child Janet caught glimpses of the boy Russell must surely have been. The configuration aside, it was the mechanism of the mind that proved conclusively and without doubt that Pamela was the perfection of her sire.

"That is not logical, Mother." This spoken when Pamela was two.

"Logical or not, I wish to have it my way," Janet had replied.

The issue was forgotten, but the exchange burned in Janet's mind. Logic. The cornerstone of the thinking process with both of them.

It wasn't natural for a child to reject playthings. It wasn't normal for a preschooler to speak of "microseconds" and "transistorized capacities."

Russell took pride in her exceptional vocabulary. Whether the child comprehended or not, she would sit for hours listening as Russell expounded as though speaking to a fellow craftsman.

When Pamela was scarcely three, she was enrolled in the Atlanta Montessori School.

"She will have no childhood!" Janet protested.

"When she complains," Russell had retorted, "then I shall consider the point valid."

Rarely, there were glimpses of the child within the adult that was Pamela and it always surprised Janet. One does not expect an adult to weep over a nightmare, or stomp in frustration. Pamela was self-assured, composed, seldom given to childish artifice or juvenile tantrums. She walked with her head high, steps deliberate, with the poise of a debutante.

"Mommy!" A shriek—not "Mother" but *Mommy!*

Janet had run down the length of the hallway to Pamela's bedroom. Russell was in Washington that week.

"What is it, Pamela?"

"Mommy! Mommy! Help me!"

"Pamela? You're dreaming, baby. Pamela! Wake up, Darling."

She found a switch and lamplight softly illuminated the canopied bed and its four-poster supports. Pamela was drenched with perspiration, face pale, sitting up, shivering.

"Did you have a bad dream, my baby?"

"I did, Mommy."

"There now, it's gone." She had dabbed the child's face with tissue, mopping away moisture.

"It scared me."

"Do you want to talk about it?"

As though coming from afar, her mind returning to reality, Pamela had looked at Janet with an expression infinitely sad. "No," the child said, voice low. "There's no need to discuss that. It's gone."

For the moment it was. But when Russell was out of town on business, the episode was repeated time and again.

11

"Mommy!" Screaming. "Mommy! Help me!"

"Here I am, Pamela."

Breathing heavily, her pajamas soaked with sweat, lips discolored, Pamela was sitting up in bed.

"Don't you want to tell me about it, Pamela? It might keep it from coming back ever again."

"No. It would serve no purpose."

Serve no purpose! As though the infant had somehow penetrated an adult facade only to be reenveloped when full consciousness returned!

"I don't mind listening," Janet urged gently.

"No. I'm all right now."

"Pamela?"

The child had snuggled back under the covers. "I'm all right now. Thank you, Mother."

Formally. Dismissed. *Thank you, Mother.*

Any attempt to discuss these events in the light of day was futile. Pamela professed not to remember. Such happenings were immediately rejected by Russell so brusquely that Janet ceased mentioning them to him. Nonetheless, the dreams were recurring and the pattern was always the same, any time Russell left town. The child's subconscious reacting to abandonment?

Russell approached any irrational behavior with a similar evaluation. As, for example, an incident at the Montessori School when Pamela was exposed to languages.

On the theory that, at a given age, a child absorbs a new language as readily as English, a specified period of each day became a course in Spanish, French or German. These classes were "conversational" in nature. The teacher spoke only the language of the moment and any discussion in class must also be the same. It was a technique that had won wide acceptance and which normally gave the Montessori student a "speaking acquaintance" with the language before he or she was nine.

Pamela had no problem with Spanish or French. It was her first exposure to German that stupefied her teachers.

Russell had grown up in Germany. But after World War II he had come to America as a highly prized specialist in the developing computer sciences, and he dropped his native tongue and past with customary finality. Janet had never heard him utter a single German word. Over the years, except for a slight trace of "V" in his "W's" there was little to indicate that he had ever spoken the language.

"What happened to my little girl in school today?" Russell had asked at dinner that night.

"I don't know, Papa."

"Well, your mother has told me about it. Don't you think we should discuss it now?"

"I'm sorry, Papa."

"Sorry? For what? Tell me what has happened."

"It won't happen again. I promise."

"I see." Russell's voice lost some of its edge. "Everything is under control then?"

"Yes, Papa."

"Fine. That suits me," Russell concluded. "Pass the brussels sprouts, please."

"Pamela," Janet prodded, "wouldn't you like to tell your father what happened?"

"Please, Mother!"

Russell ladled food onto his plate. "If Pamela is satisfied to end the subject, so am I, Janet."

Between them it may have been "ended" but for Janet and Pamela's teacher the issue arose again and again.

"Mrs. Roth, I am at a total loss. In Spanish and French sessions, Pamela is fine. But that child during German! She shakes like a leaf, her hands become so uncontrollable she can't write. She seems terrified."

13

"I don't understand, Mrs. Jones," Janet confessed. "I've tried to discuss it with her."

"So have I," Mrs. Jones had said, tossing her head with eyes closed in long quivering blinks. When Mrs. Jones began a statement, she closed her eyes, the lids tremulous, until the comment was completed. Only then did she gaze at her listener again.

"Pamela says she doesn't know why the class disturbs her so," Mrs. Jones related. "In fact, she now denies that it does!"

Janet could well imagine this was true. The first time it happened, she'd been called to school to take Pamela home, the child's body racked with involuntary spasms of sobbing.

"What happened, Pamela?" Janet had questioned, after getting the faculty version.

"I don't know, Mommy."

"Can you tell me what you think happened?"

"No."

"You can't? Or don't want to?"

Pamela had developed hiccups from prolonged muscle contractions and tried to even out her breathing.

"Darling, how can Mommy help you if we don't talk about it? The teacher said you began screaming for no apparent reason."

"I'm sorry."

"There's no reason to be sorry. Just talk about it with me. Let's see if we can determine what the problem is."

"I'm sorry, Mommy. It won't happen again."

"Pamela, Sweetheart, I'm not criticizing. I'm not asking for reasons of punishment. I love you. I want to see if together we can find out what happened back there in school."

Pamela had fallen into a litany of apologies, declaring anew, "It won't happen any more."

"So what did occur?" Russell had demanded when Janet telephoned him at the office.

"The teacher said Pamela commenced to scream hysterically."

"Yes. You said that. Why?"

"I don't know why, Russell. Pamela won't discuss it."

A long silence from his end of the line, an electronic hum barely discernible over Russell's breathing. A rush of air in Janet's ear as he sighed.

"Then what do you propose I do?" Russell had asked. "Do you wish that I come home now?"

Janet had turned to look at Pamela; the child's eyes were huge, almost frightened.

"Your father wants to know, should he come home now?"

"No, Mother," Pamela whispered, "please."

"Pamela says no, Russell."

"Very well."

Long silence.

"Is there anything more, Janet?"

"No, Russell. I'll see you this evening."

The phone went dead in her hand.

"I'm sorry," Pamela parroted.

"There's no reason to be," Janet had said, too sharply. "But how can we get to the bottom of this, or any other problem, if we don't talk about it, Pamela?"

The child's luminous eyes were moist.

"Pamela," Janet had said, more softly, "do you love me?"

"Yes, Mother."

Of course, the tone implied, why else would I have taken you as my mother?

"We're removing Pamela from German," Mrs. Jones announced, meeting Janet after school in an empty classroom.

"All right."

"I have tried to question the child, digging for the reason, and there is no reason she can or will reveal. Mrs. Roth, you say you never had a German-speaking servant who might have hurt or alarmed Pamela as an infant?"

"Never."

"Can you recall any association whatsoever which might have influenced the child?"

"No," Janet said. "I've thought about it, trying to remember every little thing. My husband was born in Germany, as I told you, and lived there until the end of the war. But to my knowledge he has never said a word of German. I hardly think it is anything like that. Pamela and her father are very close, in fact."

"Then I admit defeat," Mrs. Jones commented, her eyes fluttering closed. "Believe me, there is nothing worth what that child endures during the German-class session. When Mrs. Hoffman enters and begins to speak, Pamela undergoes the most unbelievable metamorphosis imaginable! Well, you saw it."

Yes, from behind a one-way mirrored glass where parents were allowed to observe classes in progress, Janet had watched with alarm. Unknown to Pamela, Janet had come on the invitation of the principal and Mrs. Jones to see for herself.

"Guten morgen!" Mrs. Hoffman's voice came through an overhead speaker in the insulated cubicle.

The reaction was immediate. Pamela, at a desk readily visible to Janet, had been sitting with her hands clasped atop the writing board. Mrs. Hoffman's voice seemed to shatter the child's calm.

The teacher went directly to the green slate "blackboard" and began writing German words, her voice rising as she turned her back to the class. Janet had watched spellbound as Pamela began trembling. Pamela's head started to shake, the tremor spreading until her entire desk shook and other students were turning to stare. Huge tears formed in the child's eyes, dislodged by blinks to roll down her cheeks.

"Pamela?" Mrs. Hoffman questioned kindly, *"nochmals?"*

"I'm sorry," Pamela cried. "I'm sorry, Mrs. Hoffman."

That evening, when she and Russell were preparing for bed, Janet casually mentioned, "They removed Pamela from her German classes."

She was aware of Russell's penetrating gaze at her back. She continued brushing her hair, using peripheral vision to gauge his response in the vanity mirror. After looking at her a very long time, almost accusingly it seemed to Janet, Russell neatly folded his trousers and hung them where the maid could take them out for cleaning in the morning.

"I went over to the school and observed the German class. It is a wise decision to remove her."

Russell was abed now, hands behind his head, staring up at the ceiling.

"For some unfathomable reason, the class seems to cause her great distress. She begins trembling—"

"It is the teacher then," Russell stated.

"No. I don't think so. She says she likes Mrs. Hoffman, her teacher."

"Then what?" Russell demanded.

"I don't know what, Russell. We can't figure it out."

"Does it matter, truly?"

"I guess not."

Russell cut out his bedside lamp and turned on his side, back to Janet. The subject was closed.

CHAPTER TWO

THERE HAD NEVER BEEN, even briefly, a time when Pamela doted on dolls and little-girl things. To the contrary, the child gyrated to interests which closely paralleled those of her father. For her seventh birthday, Pamela delighted Russell by requesting a "broad-band international shortwave radio . . . with directional antenna."

"For this you need a license to operate, Pamela," Russell warned.

"Oh, I don't want to talk," Pamela declared. "I want to listen."

And listen she did. For hours at a time the child would sit at the controls, delicately tuning knobs, her ears covered with a headset, or the room squawking with the static cacophony of foreign voices.

Janet complained bitterly, "Russell, this is not normal for a child Pamela's age! She sits up there in the attic from sundown to midnight sometimes! She defies me, getting up after she's supposed to be in bed."

Russell met this with his usual nonchalance, "The teachers say Pamela excels with language, do they not?"

"Yes, Russell, but that isn't the point here!"

"I believe it is the point precisely," Russell said curtly. "Pamela is intrigued with language; how better could she learn than to listen?"

"Russell, that child is not quite eight! She should be playing with dolls and prams, for God's sake."

"Is her schoolwork suffering for this time at night?"

"No, but—"

"Then why worry yourself?" Russell asked. "Always you are the worrier, Janet. Things do not become bad merely because they are enjoyable. Pamela is having fun and while she does this, she learns. What more could parents ask than that?"

So Pamela listened. Sometimes until shortly before dawn when the rising sun dissipated the signals from far stations, the girl sat in solitary confinement, hunched over a speaker, making notes.

"She is a natural with languages, Mrs. Roth," the teachers reported. "Pamela has an uncanny ear for inflection and dialect. We had a foreign-visitor's day here last week. The school invited guests from various corporations which have made Atlanta their headquarters. One of them was Señor Ramos. Pamela informed Señor Ramos that his childhood had been spent in Sonora, Mexico; he'd lived a while in Mexico City, then Yucatan, and later in life he went to Madrid; but that the American influence was diluting his speech! It was phenomenal."

"I find that difficult to believe," Janet confessed.

"So did Señor Ramos! He said she pegged him right down the line."

Confronting Pamela about this, trying to sound proud despite an unreasoning distress, Janet asked, "How do you know these things, Darling?"

"The same way you know a man is from New Orleans," Pamela primly replied. "Or The Bronx in New York. The two sound very much alike. The Bronx has certain speech characteristics that are similar to the Cajun influence in Louisiana. But the difference is—"

Calculated. Cold data. Logic.

At age nine, Pamela underwent a dramatic reversal of her earlier reaction to German. She requested that she be allowed to take remedial German classes at the school. Tentatively, the school concurred. Pamela absorbed German with the same ease with which she'd conquered Spanish, French and English.

"You see," Russell chided, "nothing to worry about, Janet."

Too much worry, Janet. Fret for naught, Janet. Always the worrier. Thus tagged, it gave Janet secret pleasure to see the roles turn about when Russell found Pamela inquisitive concerning her father's part in World War II.

"Papa, how old were you when you came to America?"

"Twenty-five."

"The Americans brought you over?"

"Yes."

"Why?"

"Because they felt my knowledge would be valuable."

"And it was?"

"Yes. You know that, Pamela."

"Yes."

"Then why do you ask questions to which you know already the answers?"

"I just wondered."

"Umm," Russell sipped his wine, gazing at the child, his thoughts veiled.

"What did you do in the war, Papa?"

"You have a reason for asking this?"

"I want to know." She met her father's eyes levelly.

"For what reason?"

"Because you are my father."

"I was responsible for the inventions of and construction of the circuitry which was used to guide pilotless aircraft."

20

"V-one and V-two aircraft."

Russell's expression altered, almost imperceptibly. Pamela persisted with questions that Janet had never dared ask.

"What was your rank in the German army, Papa? Was it army?"

Russell carefully placed the goblet beside his plate and rested his fingertips on the rim, peering at Pamela in the flickering candlelight.

"Might I ask a question?" Russell queried.

"Sure, Papa."

"Do you wish to cause me pain?"

"No."

"Then you must know, all that period of time is like a bad dream to me. It is something I would rather never think about again. I am an American now. I do not think of those days ever. If you would please your papa, do not force me to talk about it."

"Yes, Papa."

But it didn't end there. Pamela shifted from the direct to the oblique, posing artful questions which related to the war years but involved Russell only indirectly.

"We have been studying Germany," Pamela commented, again at the dinner table. She turned to Janet. "Why did the Germans follow Hitler? Could they not see he was mad?"

Russell's fork slammed his plate and he glared at Pamela.

The meal was completed in silence.

Later, at bedtime, Janet tucked a comforter around the child's shoulders. "Pamela, you love your father, don't you?"

"More than anything in the world, Mother. And you, too."

"You see that talk about German war years is upsetting him, don't you?"

"Yes. But how else can I learn?"

"Perhaps you could ask me, Darling."

"Do you know?"

"That which I know I will say, and that which I do not know, I will also say. Fair enough?"

"Yes, Mother."

Janet kissed the child lingeringly on the forehead. She sat up, rearranged the bedsheets, and Pamela's expression stayed Janet's hand on the lamp switch.

"What is it?" Janet asked.

"It would be better," Pamela said, "if Papa would tell me himself."

"Tell you what?"

"About—things."

"Yes. Well. It isn't always easy for a person to reveal painful experiences to others, Pamela."

"Yes," Pamela's eyes were distant, "I know."

All children have fears and fantasies. Some can be readily traced to a specific origin, others elude victim and observer. The child that nearly drowns could be expected to suffer hydrophobia. Similar "unreasonable" fears without apparent basis might almost all be logically explained away. An infant in a crib suddenly startled by a stranger in a large hat may to his dying day detest hats with wide brims. A cat leaps into a bassinet and the infant becomes an adult with an unyielding aversion to felines. Pamela too suffered certain fears. They seemed to fascinate her. She dwelt on the mechanizations of her own mind.

"Am I so serious, Mother?"

"Serious?"

"A boy at school said that. Teachers have said that, also."

"I would suppose it is due to the fact that there are no other children in your life," Janet explained. "You have been under the constant influence of two rather serious parents. Does that sound reasonable?"

"Yes."

"Then that must be it."

"What about showers?" Pamela asked.

"What about them?"

"I am required to take a shower after physical education classes at school. When I get in there with all those naked screaming girls, I become afraid."

"Like claustrophobia?"

"No. I don't think so. The room is not that small."

"Perhaps it is the act of undressing before others? Being naked?"

The child pondered this so long, Janet added, "I always hated to undress in front of others even though they were all females."

"I don't like that," Pamela admitted. "But that isn't it, really. Dislike is separate from—afraid."

"You become afraid? Actually?"

"Yes. It takes great effort not to yield to it."

"Would you like a note asking that you be allowed to skip these showers?" Janet questioned.

"I considered that. But I won't do it. I got over German classes. I'll get over this."

Janet could recall very few mother-child chats with Pamela. Born old, that was Pamela. The students and teachers were correct—Pamela was a serious child. Not child. A nine-year-old adult.

From the age of toddler on, Pamela had distinct and sharply defined likes and dislikes. If she liked/loved, it was undying, or so it seemed. If she disliked/hated, no argument, threat or punishment could alter her stand.

"I do not like orange marmalade, Mother."

"Please do not speak to me in that tone of voice, Pamela." She had been three at the time.

"Take it from my plate, please."

"Pamela, if you refuse to eat the marmalade, ignore it. But let's not discuss it at the breakfast table."

Back rigid, hands clamped to the seat of her chair, Pamela had stared at the jelly, face wrinkled.

"Take it away."

"Eat your breakfast."

"Take it away!"

"You are very near to a blistered bottom, child," Janet snapped. "You are not required to eat it, but you are required to be polite."

Pamela had seized the plate and thrown it to the floor. It was one of the few times she had been paddled in anger. Throughout, Russell had continued eating, reading the morning newspaper as though he were dining alone. Janet's administration of corporal punishment was ignored and never mentioned. But thereafter, orange marmalade was never served.

Efforts to force Pamela to "eat what's on your plate" had met with equal obstinance. In the beginning, Janet had pursued the matter to the point of "eat or stay there until you do." Pamela thwarted this by gagging and vomiting. With this, Russell intervened.

"Your mother made you do such things?" Russell had inquired of Janet, quietly. "She made you stuff foods in your stomach which you did not wish to eat?"

"Yes, she did, Russell. It's the only way to develop proper eating habits."

"I think not," Russell said. "Because of the millions of hungry mouths in the world, is that the reason your mother made you eat such foods?"

"That was part of it."

"Not a good reason," Russell concluded. "I would suggest you avoid such encounters hereafter."

Janet watched him fold his napkin, leave the table and go into the hallway. Later, she heard Pamela and her father talking in conspiratorial tones. Angrily, Janet had gone out for a day of shopping. She had bought nothing.

Never once could Janet remember Russell complaining about anything relating to himself personally. She had a vague idea of what his business was about—computers. But if business was good, or bad, she'd never known from Russell. He was quiet,

24

aloof, self-assured, a reclusive man by nature and unaccustomed to giving of himself without calculated forethought.

Janet learned more about Russell's work from Pamela's scrapbooks than any other source. Over the years, Pamela had collected copies of *Computer Science Digest, Electronics International,* newspaper clippings, trade-journal articles, and an interview which had appeared in *Fortune* magazine. Russell was, obviously, a leader in his field. He was (as though Janet did not know for certain) a very wealthy man. Worth millions of dollars. When Russell spoke, learned men listened. He was described by *Time* as "the single most important component in the computer sciences . . . since his break with IBM and with the advent of INTELCON, a solely owned corporation which controls most or all of the Roth patents."

When Janet considered her life, her married life particularly, she had contradictory thoughts: on the one hand she had anything and everything anyone could possibly want. On the other hand, she had never been especially happy. She ignored the latter because the former was, *logically,* enough.

Yet she was not a happy woman. She *was* a worrier. She was dimly aware of a niggling in her brain, a discontent akin to yearning for food when one is not truly hungry. At no time would she be prohibited from doing anything she desired to do. Go to Europe, shop in London or Paris, join a women's social club, she could do any of these and more. But she didn't.

She plodded her foggy course from day to day with the coming of dawn and setting of sun like a mule circling a cane press that turned as the creature walked. She had the maturity to recognize this as immaturity. For the most part, she successfully put such thoughts aside.

Now and then, though, she began to dwell on her existence. "Without karma," a college classmate had once accused. "Janet will go through life surrounded by luxury, suffer little or no discomforts and—I predict—even less passion."

25

The girlish comment had struck to the quick and hurt Janet deeply at the time. Now, in retrospect, the observation had been prophetic. She neither wanted nor enjoyed; she had no burning desires, no seething ambitions. She existed, that was all. She ate for fuel, without savor; she dressed modestly, without vanity; she oiled the day-to-day existence of them all but without joy. Sex? Yes. That was a prime point which typified it all: she made love when Russell wished, *submitted* was a more accurate term for it.

She had no friends. Had never had, truly. People came and went and the tide of human relations swept her along for a while only to deposit Janet in a backwater somewhere along the way. There, going nowhere, she ebbed and flowed and the world rushed past in the mainstream. She was dimly aware of tragedies and elations, wars and treaties, but only distantly.

"How'd you get to this specific point in life?" Janet once questioned her image in the bathroom mirror.

She knew how. She just didn't know *why*.

She had left Mercer College, in Macon, Georgia, the daughter of a successful milling family which produced fine linens, towels and bedspreads as well as carpeting. When her uncle casually offered her a job in Washington where he was serving his third term as senator, Janet had accepted with typical nondirection.

She'd been there less than a year when she met Russell at a semiofficial social-business Pentagon thing, stuffy with brass and men like her uncle—and Russell. He had consummated a lucrative deal for a new weapons system, it seemed. He was rich, successful, debonair, single, and introduced to her at his insistence after making Janet acutely uncomfortable with prolonged stares for most of the evening.

She didn't like him. She didn't dislike him. She accepted his proposal of marriage a year later because she could not think of a single reason why she shouldn't. They'd been married, without event, for three years when Pamela was born February 12, 1963.

Her life had been programmed by a force outside herself, it

seemed to Janet; an idle exercise culminating in nothing. No apexes, no nadirs—rolling gently over the hills of life, the calendar ticking away her youth. For what? For nothing.

"Mother? Are you all right?"

Janet had been staring out the bay window of Pamela's second-story bedroom, the veiled white curtain giving the eyes something to see, without seeing anything. She turned now, hearing Pamela's voice at the door.

"Are you all right?" Pamela asked anew.

God that child was beautiful! Her eyes reflected the predominant lavender decor of the spacious room. Golden hair, shoulder-length, two pale stripes of flesh that her bathing suit had left untanned showing beneath a see-through blouse.

"Mother?" Pamela's eyes darted, searching her mother's face, faintly distinguishable brows lifting, lowering, on a face remarkably mobile but always restrained.

"I'm fine, Pamela."

"Why are you sitting up here like this?"

"I don't know. I came in here for something—I forget—"

Pamela saw the books. "Oh," she said. "I see."

"I wasn't prying, actually," Janet said, without defense.

"I know that."

"Pamela? Why are you keeping those books? You know how upset your father would be if he discovered them."

"He won't. Unless we tell him. He wouldn't think of coming in here to search, Mother."

"Pamela, I was not searching—I don't know what I wanted."

Pamela put them away in her closet. "I told you," she said, unsmiling, "don't worry about it. If it concerns you that Papa might find them, I'll have them moved. But he won't. You and I both know he won't."

Yes, Janet knew. So why should it upset her? If Russell had no idea the books were here, he would not come seeking them. Pamela was studying Janet soberly.

"You could at least lock the closet door," Janet suggested.

"I'm not trying to hide them, Mother."

"All right."

"That one, Mother."

"What?"

"May I have the one you're holding?"

Holding one? Oh, yes. Janet closed the cover. *Life: A Pictorial History of World War Two.* A flicker of images crossed Janet's mind as Pamela put this book too in the closet and shut the door. The child locked it, leaving the key in place. Instant, burning, vivid black-and-white mental pictures of a tangle of arms and legs hardly distinguishable in a mountain of humanity piled before an oven in—

"Shall we go, Mother?" Pamela waited at the door.

"Yes. Of course."

CHAPTER THREE

"I WANT TO ATTEND the meeting, Papa."

"No."

Janet entered the den-study which Russell used as his office when at home. Father and daughter fell silent.

"Pamela, I'm going to Rich's. Would you like to come?"

"No, Mother." Then to Russell, "Please, Papa."

"I said no, Pamela."

"Are you two arguing?" Janet remarked.

"Papa's going to a seminar at Georgia Tech. It's after school is out, next week. I want to go."

"And I said no," Russell said, placidly.

"Papa, why?" Pamela shrilled. "I shan't be trouble. I'll stay out of your way. You don't have to take me, even. I can ride a bus."

"It is a meeting of dull people discussing a dry subject," Russell stated. "There's no point to your being there."

"But I want to go," Pamela stomped one foot, the quintessence of childish pique.

"Now for what purpose, Pamela?" Russell said, more sharply. "I have enough on my mind already."

"I told you I would stay out of your way!"

"And I said no."

"Papa!" Pamela tossed her head and glared at him. It was a rare occurrence to see either of them truly angry with the other.

"Why do you object, Russell?" Janet intervened, more from curiosity than to side with Pamela.

"Do I need a reason?"

"I suppose not," Janet said. "I was wondering why the big issue over nothing."

Pamela edged toward Janet, pleased to have an ally. Janet detected a rising anger in Russell and sought to dispel it. "You know how interested in your work Pamela is," she soothed. "You can hardly blame her for wanting to be there. She takes pride in your accomplishments."

Russell looked away, finally sighed, "Very well, my two women—how can I defy you both?"

"Oh, Papa!" Pamela ran into his arms. "Thank you!"

"One condition," Russell warned, "I take you at your word that you will not ask for even one second of my attention. Agreed?"

"Agreed," Pamela beamed. She kissed him quickly and ran from the room.

"What was that all about?" Janet asked.

"If you do not know, why did you persist in pressuring me?"

His tone stunned Janet. "I'm sorry, Russell. If you wish, I'll rescind my support and talk to Pamela."

"That won't be necessary now," Russell said, coldly. "Hereafter, however, should I make my wishes known as I was doing, I would consider it only proper for you to stay out of it."

"Yes, Russell, I'm sorry."

He turned to his desk. Janet stared at him a long moment, then went in search of Pamela. The child was in her room with the door closed. Janet knocked, waited for permission, then entered. She saw one of the books, hastily covered on Pamela's dresser.

"Pamela, why is it so important to you, this seminar? You must know how frightfully boring they can be."

"It's an international meeting of the top men in Papa's field," Pamela stated.

"But you see how it displeases your father. There is no place at such a function for a child, obviously."

"Nevertheless," Pamela concluded, "I want to go. Papa has no right to deny me that. It is open to the public anyway."

"What is this?" Janet uncovered the book. It was open to a double-page photograph of unsmiling men clustered around a transport truck. Houses burned in the background as a German tank passed troops who yielded way.

"It is a book," Pamela said.

"I see that, Pamela. The point is, why?"

Pamela's lovely eyes were darker now. "Why not?" she countered.

"Pamela"—Janet spoke more firmly—"I think you should get rid of these books."

"It is history, is it not?"

"For anybody else, yes. For your father it is a source of embarrassment. It would hurt him to know you were studying such unhappy scenes as this one—" Janet jabbed the picture.

"That is not logical," Pamela said.

"Logic be damned, girl! Are you trying to anger your father?"

"No."

"Then do away with these books and stop dwelling on something that hurts your father!"

"If he hurts," Pamela said, her tone shockingly frigid, "the pain comes from within, not without."

"Pamela," Janet said, hotly, "I shall not discuss it further. But you *will* get these books out of this house. Is that clear?"

"Yes, Mother."

Janet closed the bedroom door with more force than she intended and stood in the hallway, breathing hard. She heard something crash against the wall in the room behind her—Pamela venting her temper. Let it be! She'd had her say. Janet walked quickly down the long hall and descended the stairs.

For several days the incident disturbed Janet. With Pamela in the final week of school, Russell staying late at his office to prepare for the upcoming seminar, Janet did something she'd never done before. She entered Pamela's room with the purpose of searching it. What she discovered brought a shortness of breath.

She knew Pamela had collected books about Germany. What she had not known was the extent of her collection. In the closet, Janet found the overhead shelf filled with such books. Behind racks of clothing and stacked on the floor were hundreds of them! Political science documentaries: *The War Against the Jews 1933–1945; The Secret War Report of the OSS; The Game of the Foxes;* historical treatments of a tragic era. But by and large the books were picture essays—terrible visual depictions of atrocities, bland Aryan faces with arms stiff in salute, Hitler biographies and more. The stories of survivors from Treblinka, Auschwitz, Belżec, and Chelmno; verbal and pictorial accounts of man's inhumanity to man!

Was the child building some kind of fantasy around all this? Had Russell's refusal to discuss it fired Pamela's imagination? Or worse—was the girl assuming a connection between her father and his fatherland? What significance could Pamela possibly attach to these horrible scenes of Nazi crimes? Blame Germany? Russell? What?

Careful to replace the books as she found them, or as nearly as she could, and incensed that Pamela had not destroyed them as directed, Janet closed the closet door and locked it again. She debated whether she should confront Pamela or ignore it—either alternative was fraught with implications that were frightening.

Tell Russell about this? Let him handle it?

For some disturbing inner reason, Janet was afraid to do that. She didn't want to hurt Russell, she rationalized. Confront him with something uncomplimentary, derogatory, in the eyes of a child he adored? Unkind at best, cruel at worst. Better that Janet pretend not to know than to instigate a conflict between father and daughter.

How dared Pamela do this? The arrogance of youth! Condemning people from a time she'd never known. Keeping a few of these books would cut Russell deeply. But this many—dear God, that was a condemnation by inference alone!

Janet toyed with the idea of removing the books while Pamela was at school—destroy them herself! That would be neither wise nor final. It could, in fact, precipitate the very face-to-face situation she now sought to avoid. Why couldn't Pamela be interested in sex, like any other normal fourteen-year-old girl? At least that would be a healthy biological development which would soon enough attain perspective and pass. But this! Photo after photo of death *en masse,* individually, collectively, and starkly personal: an SS officer executing a row of people, several of whom were women and children with their hands bound behind them. God. God! God bless them!

"Is something on your mind?" Russell asked, mildly.

Janet's mind returned to the moment, the dinner table. "No," she said.

"You have seemed so preoccupied the last few days."

"It's nothing, Russell," Janet mustered a smile. "I was debating whether to plant camellias or roses beside the swimming pool this year."

"Too late for either," Russell said.

"Yes." Janet stole a glance at Pamela. "How was school today, Darling?"

"I made all A's again this semester."

"Good for you!" Russell said. "Dear child, you please me so! And did not mention it?"

"It isn't anything, Papa."

"Nonsense! It is not an easy school, true?"

"Well, they operate on the premise that a student should always be reaching, intellectually," Pamela noted.

Russell laughed, a rare and pleasant sound. "Soon enough," he said to Janet, "I will be attending her seminar somewhere, yes?"

"I am your protégée, Papa," Pamela teased. Russell took the child's hand, eyes filled with pride.

"You please me many ways, Pamela," Russell said, softly.

"And you me, Papa."

Janet systematically searched drawers, cedar chests and armoires. With a sinking heart she uncovered newspaper clippings, magazine articles, even 8-x-10 glossy photographs gleaned from God knows where! A compendium of printed materials which would rival a library collection: all about the Hitler years.

With only two days remaining in the school year, Janet extended her probe to other areas considered to be Pamela's private sanctums. She went to the dollhouse, given on the child's fourth birthday. The elaborate replica of the main house was a girl's dream for playing dolls. The gift was a failure. It had not kindled Pamela's interest in childish pastimes and served only as a retreat for the moody youngster.

In the dollhouse were more books, these hidden beneath Dutch window-board seats, even in the "attic" of the structure. But it was in the attic of the main house where Janet learned the full depth of Pamela's research.

Beside the radio transmitter, which was used after Pamela received her license to operate it, was a meticulously kept log of transmissions. In cryptic but neat scroll, the call letters of stations, the names of the operators and the points of origin. Janet scanned a clipboard: Berlin, Hamburg, Munich; on nails along one wall, neatly categorized by nations, hung extensive notes. On shelves, reels of recording tape, numbered, cross-indexed files to identify each speaker, date of conversation and additional comments.

"Born Austria, public school to age 16, rural culture, moved to Paris for further studies, degree attained equiv. to MA USA."

Pamela obviously communicated with many "ham" operators. Russell had once commented that it was an international brotherhood of people. People who, like Pamela, spent long solitary hours straining to hear weak signals. It was a hobby the appeal of which completely escaped Janet. But it was a pastime that had enthralled Pamela from the beginning.

There was more here than the intimacy of "pen pals" via airwaves. Pamela had compiled copious notes. Biographies? Points in common between an American teenager and foreigners? No, there was more here than that, Janet was positive of it! Standing in the attic, the air conditioner not turned on, perspiration traced her body, sticking blouse to flesh, giving a saline taste to her lips.

She examined broadcast logs on spindles. Above each was a neatly typed tag to identify the log below. Poland, Yugoslavia, France, Belgium, Finland, Germany, Austria, Czechoslovakia, Bohemia, Moravia, Slovakia—names and places that had been altered or absorbed in the tides of politics. Hungary, Rumania, Bulgaria, Greece, the Soviet Union, Latvia, Estonia—Poland.

She opened an index file of 3-x-5-inch cards. Alphabetically stored, it was not the name of the speaker, or even the subject of their conversations that interested Pamela. A series of small symbols filled card after card, pinned to cards upon which there were names—but the symbols themselves were the purpose of this index.

Pamela, the child with a "natural" bent for language, was not the least concerned with *what* people said to her—she was intent on *how* they said it.

"Gutteral R; diphthong slur, concurrent with elipsis vowels following . . . "

Legerdemain? Code? Only to an untrained eye. Janet realized the symbols were indications of inflections, accents, a visual record of what the ear perceived. Like the grooves in a recording, to

35

Pamela, these digits and swiggles translated into mannerisms of speech!

The span of her radio contacts was vast, varied and impressive. The work was that of an avid collector so engrossed she ignored time. An intellectual pursuit, a scholarly work that should be a source of pride to any parent. But Janet stood here with fear crawling over her body, tentacles of dread rising to choke her breathing. What possessed this child? Was she so hell bent to prove something that she would destroy the ones she loved? This went beyond a rational, normal quest for knowledge. This was not the idle curiosity of an inquisitive mind—not *this* coupled with the books and photographs Janet had uncovered! Pamela was brought to this garret not for some vicarious thrill through long distance communication. She was tracking something—as deliberately as a predator seeking prey by scent, sound and sight. She had slowly accumulated clues to lexicon, syntax and nuances of speech that betray an unwary speaker as surely as finger or voice prints.

"She pegged me right down the line," Señor Ramos had said.

Right down the line . . .

Janet pulled a knob to a cabinet and the clasp of a padlock stopped the door from swinging open. Pamela must have constructed this herself. Janet was seized with an impulse to rip the door from its hinges. With deliberate restraint, she resisted the urge. Wait. Be smart! Leave everything as it is until later. Leave it. It can wait.

A cooler flow of downstairs air chilled Janet as she descended the attic steps, then the wide oak spiral staircase to the main floor. The hall clock chimed four and she knew Pamela was home, or would be shortly.

"Eleanor," Janet spoke to the maid in passing, "the upstairs bedrooms are not as clean as I would like."

"Yes, Mrs. Roth."

"See to it tomorrow, will you?"

"I will, Mrs. Roth."

She found Pamela sitting at the kitchen table, a moustache of milk on her lip, a cookie in hand as she pored over a page of the evening newspaper.

"Hi, Mother!"

"Hi yourself. Wipe your mouth."

"You see Papa's picture?"

"No."

"Pretty good shot," Pamela noted, "but the photographer was too far back to do him justice. See?"

It was Russell at a podium, speaking. Behind him on the dais sat several men in poses suggesting stoic forbearance rather than keen interest. Pamela was right, the photographer should have been nearer.

"Say," Pamela said, brightly, "you're covered with dirt!"

"Dust," Janet acknowledged. "I've been upstairs and in the attic."

"Oh?" Pamela's expression denoted nothing.

"I'm not satisfied with the way the upper rooms are being cleaned."

Pamela took a bite of cookie, her huge haunting eyes following Janet from cupboard to counter.

"Pamela, have you done as I asked, about the books?"

"I haven't yet."

"You won't forget it?"

"No."

Keeping her voice casual, Janet persisted, "I wouldn't want your father upset over something that silly."

"No," Pamela said. "We wouldn't want to do that."

Janet turned from the coffee percolator. "Pamela, did I detect something in your tone?"

"Like what?"

"Like sarcasm."

"I don't think so. It was unintentional, if you did."

"I don't feel I'm being unfair about those books, Pamela."

"All right."

Janet subdued a surge of irritation. "Meaning you do," she said.

"Meaning nothing, Mother," Pamela swept cookie crumbs from the table into a napkin.

"'This and similar conversations on the subject have begun to disturb me, Pamela."

Pamela's eyes widened, "Then why do we continue discussing it?"

"Because I want those books out of this house, that's why!"

"I told you I would do it."

"Then do it!"

"Cripe."

"What?"

"I said, 'cripe.'"

"That isn't what it sounded like to me."

"Of course not," Pamela said, eyes flashing. "Why should it? You have managed to make something out of nothing, twisted everything out of proportion, I'm not surprised that 'cripe' sounded like 'Christ' to you, Mother!"

"Pamela!"

The child ran out the back door.

"Pamela!"

But Pamela was running down the terraced walkway toward the swimming pool. Janet fumed, standing in the door watching as Pamela crossed the patio, skirted the bathhouses and disappeared down the path toward her dollhouse.

Anger ebbed, Janet mentally recounting the preceding minutes. As always, where Pamela or Russell was concerned, she critically examined her actions and reactions—the first consideration being that she was somehow wrong and they couldn't be.

Perhaps she *was* blowing everything out of proportion. A childish curiosity about a period of history in which her father was at least alive, if not involved! Be sensible, Janet. Perhaps she was doing the very thing she had mentally attributed to Pamela, building a fantasy!

"You have certainly been withdrawn of late," Russell's voice made Janet wheel, gasping. Had he heard? How much?

"Have I?" she said. Russell poured two cups of coffee.

"Janet the worrier," Russell scolded.

CHAPTER FOUR

JANET PARKED HER CONTINENTAL, set the brake and sat staring at the building where Russell's seminar was taking place. What was she doing here anyway? It had been a spur-of-the-moment decision, made after Russell and Pamela left the house this morning. But here she was and having second thoughts. She glanced in the rearview mirror to check her hair and got out, locking the doors. Heat rose from the macadam lot as she walked unhurriedly toward the hall, seeking the shade of huge oaks shadowing walkways. Most of the students were out for the summer now, and this was the break between semesters.

Inside the huge double doors of the building, a hum of air conditioners, crowd noises and an amplified speaker lent the meeting that impersonal air of such affairs. Men and women wearing identification tags circulated, or sat, with varying degrees of attention to the lackluster proceedings.

Janet kept to the periphery of the crowd, along one wall, looking for Pamela or Russell. Russell she saw first, sitting on-stage, legs crossed, consulting his notes. Then on the front row she spotted Pamela. A portable tape recorder was capturing the monologue, Pamela sitting with head down jotting on a legal-sized yellow pad. Janet stepped back, watching, less likely to be noticed here.

" . . . size being the most formidable obstacle to such an undertaking, with the advent of Space-Age miniaturization developed by my colleague, Dr. Russell Roth," the speaker was saying.

Russell had been awarded honorary doctorates by several universities, usually as enticement to get him there for such activities as this one. He neither acknowledged nor cultured the use of "Dr." before his name.

" . . . transistorized high-speed components which have eliminated space and heat . . . "

Janet chanced to glance at Pamela and was captivated by the expression she saw on the child's face. Pamela stared at a man who was now whispering something to Russell, their heads close together.

" . . . pioneered in guidance technology making possible today's exploration of space, the ramifications of which have been felt in all walks of life, including medicine, research, computer sciences . . . "

On those uncommon occasions when Janet accompanied Russell to meetings like this, she had heard this introduction repeatedly.

" . . . gives me great pleasure to introduce at this time, a man *Newsweek* called the 'father of things small and indispensable,' Dr. Russell K. Roth."

A polite patter of applause as Russell approached the podium. He shuffled papers, putting them in some preferred order. "Honored members of the sciences, members of the board, fellow speakers, ladies and gentlemen, it gives me pleasure to welcome you to this two-day convocation of . . . "

Pamela sat, pencil poised, still staring at the gentleman who had been speaking to Russell. The intensity of the child's glare was discomforting at best. The gray-haired distinguished man could not help but notice—when he did, Janet saw him smile slightly and nod at Pamela, thereby breaking the spell. Pamela made a note on her pad.

Why Janet remained was a mystery to herself; she stood here listening to words which were either dull, as Russell prophesied, or beyond the ken of Janet's interest. Yet throughout, Pamela seemed to hang on every statement.

Then the conservatively dressed gentleman who knew Russell was introduced. "Dr. Hans Fiedler," the moderator said. "From Vienna, special representative under the auspices of the International Congress of . . . "

Pamela was diverted long enough to flip her tape cartridge, adjusting the volume, turning her pad to a fresh sheet.

"A man who excels in a variety of interrelated fields, adviser to NASA in this country, NATO in Europe, but fundamentally and foremost, a humanitarian whose devotion to the sciences has always been to the human element . . . "

Janet found an abandoned program and noted that the key speaker of the day was a former president of a company for which Russell had worked and the man was presently the administrative head of the U.S. space programs, recently concerned with the Viking I and II Mars shots. As Dr. Fiedler spoke with a plodding, heavily accented voice, reporters adjusted their lighting and cameras.

"Ve vill see the day when the vorld shall become only a vay station in space," Fiedler intoned.

But it was not the orator who mesmerized Janet. It was Pamela. The girl had slipped from her seat directly in front of the dais, moving to a more advantageous position, holding the tape recorder microphone in one hand now. Her expression! Like a teenager in the presence of a rock star! Russell, frowning, was quietly trying to get Pamela's attention to motion her back to her seat.

"Vhen shuttles ply corridors between terra firma and the firma-
ments," Fiedler said, his words infinitely more poetic than his
monotone. "Vhen man reaches for the farthest star in a final step
to galactic domination . . . "

What was that child *doing*? She was standing now at the edge
of the stage, pressing nearer so overtly and impolitely that even
Dr. Fiedler could not help but acknowledge her presence with a
lingering glance. Russell half rose from his chair, face flaming,
then sat back having thought better of his impending move.

Pamela inched ever closer, eyes unblinking, her face as bright
as a child on Christmas morning. Russell vainly glared at his
daughter in hopes of catching her attention. More people in the
audience were watching Pamela than were listening to the distinguished speaker!

"Closed circuitry plug-in components with a capacity for data
transmission in the millionths of one second, a 99.999 percent re-
liability," Fiedler said, now purposely directing his attention
away from the girl gazing up at him.

Well. Janet couldn't stand here and allow this to continue. She
moved along a wall toward the front of the audience. Just as she
prepared to walk out brazenly and collar Pamela, Dr. Hans Fiedler abruptly concluded his comments and returned to his seat as
the surprised audience came to life and sporadic applause rose
among them.

Damn that child! She stood staring! Russell was angry—very
angry—

" . . . brief break here . . . refreshments served in the lower
level . . . commencement of activities . . . films from unmanned Mars landings . . . "

Chairs scraped, a murmur of low voices, here and there something dropped, a short laugh and people stretched as they stood.
Janet pushed gently toward the stage where Russell and Dr. Fiedler were descending the steps. Pamela was waiting for them. They
converged as one, Russell, Pamela, Fiedler and Janet.

43

"Superb, Dr. Fiedler," Pamela was saying, shaking the man's hand. "Your article in the recent issue of *Computer Technology* was excellent."

"You read that?" Fiedler's bushy white eyebrows lifted.

"That and the book you wrote in 1949 in which you predicted many of the current developments in the field," Pamela expounded.

"Vell, vell," Fiedler turned to Russell. "So unusual for such a youngster to take an interest in our work, eh, Russell?"

"Yes, well," Russell's face was livid.

"I take after my papa," Pamela said. "I'm his protégée."

"Oh?"

"Pamela," Russell growled.

"You?" Fiedler looked at Russell, eyes sparkling. "I should have known!"

"This is my wife, Janet, Dr. Fiedler."

Janet saw Pamela touch the doctor's sleeve. Absolute adoration and Dr. Fiedler did not miss it. He acknowledged the introduction with one hand and reached out to pull Pamela to him with the other. Instantly the girl hugged him around the waist. Russell was slightly mollified, but only slightly.

"Pamela it is?" Fiedler asked. Pamela nodded, face radiant.

"Ve shall be friends, this I see," Fiedler chuckled.

"You lived in Munich, didn't you?" Pamela blurted.

The doctor darted a glance at Russell.

"Then Bremerhaven and for a while in Cologne. Why did you go to Cologne?"

"Pamela!" Janet took the girl's arm.

The smile was gone now and Fiedler spoke to Russell in a burst of German, a staccato of words unintelligible to Janet, but the tone was apparent enough.

"My daughter speaks German," Russell said, quickly.

"Oh?" Fiedler scrutinized the child with dawning wariness. "So smart so many vays, isn't she?"

"Pamela, I came to give you a ride home."

"I'm not ready, Mother."

"Yes," Russell said, voice ominous, "you are ready."

"I shall see all of you again I trust?" Dr. Fiedler inquired.

"Yes, Doctor."

"May I come visit you?" Pamela asked.

"Ah, how nice," Fiedler said. "But I am here at the hotel only for tonight and tomorrow. I'm sorry."

"At the Regency?" Pamela resisted Janet's pull.

"Yes, but—"

"Pamela," Russell spoke harshly, "you are being rude!"

Pamela's gaze fell. "I'm sorry."

"Vell, now, Russell, I am not offended," Fiedler said.

"I'm afraid Pamela becomes overly enthralled with people of your accomplishment," Janet explained.

"I am flattered, Mrs. Roth."

"It was nice to meet you, Dr. Fiedler." Pamela was the polite charmer now.

"The pleasure vas mine, Pamela."

"I didn't mean to be discourteous."

"*Es macht nichts*, Pamela. Someday if ever you are coming through Houston, Texas, then ve vill visit."

"How will I find you?"

"Oh! That is nothing! I am in the telephone book."

"You may live to see a day when she accepts," Russell cautioned.

Fiedler laughed. "Then I shall be fortunate indeed, Russell. Good-bye, Pamela."

"Good-bye."

Janet and Pamela waited a moment, watching the two men go toward the refreshment area speaking German in low voices. Then Pamela relented, sullenly.

"Get your pad and notes," Janet said.

"I have them." Surly.

In the automobile, driving out Peachtree Street north, Pamela peered stonily out the tinted glass window at the passing scene.

"What did Dr. Fiedler say in German, Pamela?"

"Oh." Long pause. "He said I was a pretty girl."

"That's the first time I ever heard your father speak the language," Janet noted, trying to alter Pamela's mood.

"Yes," Pamela said, softly. "He speaks it very well."

Pamela was to return to school on Thursday of the week after final examinations to get her report card. It was a nuisance factor to which parents submitted, the true purpose of the day being a convenience to teachers who had to have conferences with parents. No such meeting was requested by Pamela's teachers, so it was quickly accomplished. Pamela raced out the door of the building, hair flying, waving her arms.

"Mother can I go to Europe?" Pamela stood with the car door open, leaning in.

"Someday perhaps."

"No! I mean next week! Or the week after, I'm not sure."

"Pamela, there's more to going abroad than catching a bus or a train, you know."

"It's a class thing, Mother. They were oversubscribed until today and three kids dropped out. It's the seniors, really. But Mrs. Jones said they needed three more kids and *only* three can be chosen. She asked if I would like to go. May I, Mother? Please?"

"Pamela, I can't make a decision about something like this on such short notice."

"Mother! Tomorrow may be too late. Can I at least *say* yes, even if you change your mind? They'll only take three!"

"Pamela, baby, I would have to ask your father and he—"

"Let's call him. We can go into the office this minute and call. Okay?"

"Don't say 'okay.'"

"I meant, all right."

"Pamela, this is not an idle decision to make. There would be clothing to buy, itineraries to evolve—"

"Mother, please," Pamela's face was wrinkled, her voice intense. "If you say yes, I'll worry about everything else."

"Oh, damn, Pamela."

"Call Papa. Please. Right now."

Russell stunned Janet by listening to the request and then terminating the debate with a solid, "Certainly."

"You don't care?" Janet questioned.

"Why should I care? It is the school, is it not? She will be in good hands, Janet. Now don't begin to worry about this, all right? Pamela will learn much. She's never been abroad before. So certainly she may go!"

Pamela displayed an unusually girlish response shrieking down the hall, babbling to Mrs. Jones. "I can go! I can go!"

"Yes," Janet confirmed, none too sure, "and this is without knowing where she is going, Mrs. Jones."

The teacher's eyelids closed and she threw back her head laughing. "It's a cultural program, Mrs. Roth. Well chaperoned I can assure you."

"I'm not questioning that, actually," Janet explained. "But sudden changes tend to startle me until I can adjust to them. We came for report cards and abruptly my daughter is going to Europe."

Eyelids shut, announcing an announcement, Mrs. Jones said, "Pamela is very mature, very responsible. She will fit in nicely, even though all the others are upperclassmen. I think the trip might do wonders to extend her educational interests."

"It'll be fantastic!" Pamela emoted.

Fantastic? That was a new word in the child's vocabulary. It was, Janet now realized, the first typically teen-age thing she'd ever heard from Pamela's mouth. An exaggerated response. Well, well, this venture might produce some interesting developments in more ways than education.

47

"I suppose we'd better begin to begin then," Janet said. "What do we do first?"

"The office will need a check to cement the arrangements," Mrs. Jones stated. "The total cost including meals is nine hundred dollars. Someone in the office will give you a folder with tips and instructions about passports, clothing, spending money—that sort of thing."

Janet waited for the teacher's eyes to open. "Do this immediately? I didn't bring a checkbook."

"No problem," Mrs. Jones blinked. "State your intentions and take a check by the travel bureau tomorrow, if you wish."

They went to the school office, were given a folder with color photographs of Alpine mountains, mirror-reflective tarns and exotic scenes one might expect to encounter on the student trip. The brochure was an outright sales pitch, designed by the promoters of the tour. There were tips on clothes to take, cash money needed, traveler's checks, and throughout, in none too subtle script, the words told why this group plan was such a "fantastic" savings.

"Students will stay at specially selected resort areas combining adventure with safety, education with fun, and it is just adult enough to please such in-between young adults as these," the flier said. "Forty years of supervising such tours gives our guides and salespeople a unique advantage in which you the traveler can see more, do more, live more, and all for less cost!"

"Isn't it exciting?" Pamela marveled, reading the pamphlet aloud.

"It surely is, Pamela."

"Eurailpasses allow a maximum of freedom for the young travelers independent enough to venture off alone," the text stated.

"That's not you," Janet commented matter-of-factly.

"Well, I have to have one, according to this, whether I use it or not," Pamela continued. "The group travels by Eurailpass it says here . . . anywhere in the following countries . . . at no extra cost . . . unlimited number of rides within the specified period of time."

Janet wheeled up the long winding paved drive toward the house. "Let's have one thing clearly understood, young lady. You are going on a senior-class trip. But you are not a senior. You will comport yourself accordingly. Understood?"

"Of course."

Janet halted outside the side entrance. She turned to Pamela. "No independent trips. Stick with the adults and follow *them*, not necessarily the crowd. Do I make myself clear?"

"Absolutely," Pamela said, casually. "I wonder if we'll stay in a chateau like the one in this picture. See?"

"Yes," Janet glanced at the Swiss scene and got out. "Come along, we have a mountain of things to do, if we're going to get you ready for this."

"Yes, Mother." Pamela grabbed Janet's hand. The child's face softened.

"Mother, I love you."

They looked at one another a long moment, then Janet nodded. "And I love you."

"We don't say it very often, do we?"

Borrowing one of Russell's lines, Janet said, "Do we have to?"

"No. But I want you to know—I love you, Mother."

"Come on, Darling. We must make every minute count if we're going to see you off in style!"

The following days were exciting. They shopped according to the travel bureau's suggested list, from Davidson-Paxon to Rich's to some obscure shop in Hapeville which sold, of all things, ski equipment!

"Not snow, Mother!" Pamela screamed with laughter. "Water ski!"

"Oh," Janet felt her face flushing. "Yes, of course." She caught a knowing glance between the clerk and Pamela and, disturbingly, a glimmer of male interest which evinced itself more and more these days in Pamela's meetings with members of the opposite sex. The girl, if she noticed, ignored it.

"We need a warm woolen hat," Pamela said. "Preferably in hues of blue to match a coat I have already purchased. "

"Going to the Arctic?" the young man asked.

"Nope. Switzerland, France, Italy—mountains!"

He was digging in shelves filled with boxes, lifting tops, peeking in, and putting them back again.

"Yeah?" he said over his shoulder. "That's a great scene over there. You'll love it."

"You've been?" Pamela questioned.

"Few times. Take a look at these and see if they hit you."

"I like this knit," Pamela said to no one in particular, "but not the color."

"No sweat," the young man took the long hat and turned it inside out. Inside it was a completely different shade of blues and reds.

"Hey, cool!" Pamela exulted.

"No, warm," he grinned.

"I'll take it," Pamela said, then glanced furtively at her mother. "If you like it, I will."

"I like it."

"So be it then." The clerk put away the other samples.

"Hey, you know, you got to be sure to make it to Germany while you're over there."

"Germany?" Pamela said.

"Oh yeah, perfect time of year. You won't believe how beautiful that country is. Friendly natives too. Swift. Know what I mean?"

"Sure."

"She'll be in a group tour," Janet said, stupidly entering a conversation which didn't include her.

"Oh?" The clerk took Janet's credit card.

"I won't miss it," Pamela said. "We'll be in Germany seven days."

Janet's ears began drumming, like the aftereffect of ether in an operating room. Distantly, she heard Pamela say, "Munich will be nice, I know a ham operator there. Also Berlin, to the zoo which will be a drag, but then we'll be going to—"

Janet fumbled with her purse, replacing the credit card in her wallet. Nobody had mentioned Germany! Nobody!

A voice called from afar and Janet clutched at her senses, regaining composure. "Mother? Mother?"

"What is it, Pamela?"

"Are you ready, Mother?"

CHAPTER FIVE

A GUST OF WIND swept the concrete runways outside, lifting dust and litter in a swirl. Through the windows of an observation room, Janet watched the four adults and their sixty youthful charges file up the steps into the bowels of a sleek silvery jet. Mentally, even though now too late to do anything about omissions, Janet ticked off the indispensable items Pamela should have with her: American Express Card (with repeated warnings to guard it), passport, medical proof of inoculations, cash; she saw Pamela now, a new camera slung around her neck, tote bag in hand, ascending into the airplane.

A sudden surge of loneliness swept Janet and she had the empty feeling of being rejected, somehow. Nonsense! She watched until the mighty craft taxied out of her line of vision, then quickly walked back through the terminal.

She wasted the balance of her day in idle pursuits until Russell came home from the office. He asked if Pamela had gotten away all right, then retired to the den to read the newspaper. Dinner for both of them that evening was a mechanical chore devoid of conversation.

"She will be all right, Janet," Russell said, rising from the table.

"I know."

"So don't start your worrying!"

"I'm not worrying, Russell."

She thought she heard him laugh softly as he left the dining room. Twenty-one days. Three weeks without the child, for the first time in fourteen years. Already the house seemed to have lost something more than one child's presence. As though the building itself sagged slightly, pensive, withdrawn. What would Janet do with herself for three weeks?

She went to Pamela's room as soon as Russell departed the following morning. She had determined to clean Pamela's closets, remove all the books and destroy them. She was stunned to find them already gone. The shelves had been dusted, the armoire and cedar chests were empty except for clothing.

"I apologize, Pamela," Janet said aloud to the empty room. But rather than the relief she should have felt, having avoided the chore and conflict when Pamela returned, Janet had a worrisome sense that something was amiss. She had not seen the child take out any books—and what had she done with them? But of course, Pamela would have been circumspect for Russell's sake, so why should Janet have seen them removed?

She searched for the books nonetheless. Dollhouse, attic, even unoccupied and seldom used suites and bedrooms in the far reaches of the house. No books. It would have taken ten or fifteen trips with as many heavy boxes to cart out the publications. But gone they were, and if Janet could not now find them after so diligent a search, Russell never would! Therefore she reassured herself, the purpose was accomplished. So be logical, Janet. Stop worrying.

For several days she resisted the impulse to comb through the attic. She put aside thoughts of that one padlocked cabinet up there. But finally on the day Pamela's first postcard arrived from New York, she yielded.

"I need a small screwdriver, Harold," Janet instructed their yard man and gardener. When he brought this to her, Janet went into the attic, turned on the air conditioner and removed the hinges from the cabinet.

Inside, on various shelves, Pamela had sorted and filed newspaper clippings, photographs *of* newspaper clippings, all with a central theme: Russell. Janet carefully removed the contents off each shelf and turned the pages or pictures face down as she read them, thereby keeping everything in order.

Where in the world did the child get all this? Janet read a clipping from a 1946 newspaper. There was a three-line reference to Russell in the article on guidance systems. There was a series of glossy black-and-white photographs of men dressed in jodhpurs, wide black belts; officers in the German army. Janet thought it was army. Anyway in the background were several factories, a command car, in the distance a smokestack and on a far hill, barely visible in the shot, a convoy of trucks.

Resentment mounted as she pursued the contents of the cabinet. Where in God's name could that child have secured these photographs? Documents, letters in German, news stories—

"Janet!"

She froze. Russell's voice, somewhere afar.

"Janet, are you up here?"

She looked around furtively, seeking something with which to cover all this. No time to replace the door! She stood and with hammering heart listened, waited, holding her breath.

"Janet!" Farther away. Going down the north wing, probably, looking in the bedrooms. Janet cut off the air conditioner, doused the lights and crept down the narrow steep stairs to the second-floor level. She quietly closed the door behind her.

"Janet!"

She wheeled, inadvertently crying out.

"I'm sorry," Russell said, softly. "I didn't mean to startle you."

"You nearly gave me heart seizure."

He nodded, taking her arm, repeating, "I'm sorry."

She moved into the hall, away from the attic steps. "You're home early."

He glanced at his watch. "No. It's five o'clock."

"Oh? Time got away from me."

"Busy day?" He walked her down the spiral staircase.

"Cleaning the attic. The maid never goes up there."

"On strict orders," Russell said. "Pamela wants nothing disturbed. I hope you did not—"

"No, no. Everything will be as it was. Only cleaner."

They halted at the foot of the stairs and Russell studied her face in that disquieting manner he had, unsmiling, saying nothing, as though waiting for more information.

"Well!" Janet affected a smile. "How was your day?"

"My day?" the question seemed to surprise him. "You seldom ask me that."

"Today I asked."

Russell took a deep breath, exhaled. "As usual."

"Good," she said. "I guess."

"Yes," Russell affirmed. "Good." He was unaccustomed to trivial conversation. Janet knew idle chitchat irritated him. She clamped her jaws, smile set, and walked purposefully toward the kitchen, leaving Russell in the hall.

It took three days to go through everything in the cabinet. Endlessly boring, often technical articles with accompanying photographs of Russell and his various business acquaintances. If a scrap of material mentioned Russell at all, Pamela seemed to possess it.

Janet knew of the bulky scrapbook Pamela kept. This the child had begun nearly eight years ago. The neatly posted pictures and articles were a source of great pride to Russell, the surest tangible proof that his daughter doted on her papa. In fact, it had been Russell's doing as much as Pamela's. He had duplicated subscriptions of technical periodicals, the *Wall Street Journal* and two New York newspapers specifically so Pamela would have ready access to any probable source of stories about Russell and his work. If some obscure quarterly carried a blurb on Russell, he saw to it that his clipping service gave him an extra copy for Pamela.

Father and daughter seemed to derive equal pleasure from it, and until now Janet had not given it much thought. But the contents of the cabinet in the attic went far beyond the scrapbook itself. Possibly these were rejected items intended for the scrapbook, but not likely. For one thing, many of the photographs of articles seemed to have nothing to do with Russell's work. In fact, several of the items dealt with people like Dr. Hans Fiedler and made no mention of Russell or his company, INTELCON. Janet replaced the doors, padlock intact, and screwed the hinges back onto the cabinet.

That evening, ever so casually, Janet inquired of Russell, "Where would someone go to find old newspaper and magazine articles?"

"How old?"

"Thirty, forty, fifty years, maybe."

"I don't know."

"Russell?"

He looked up from his newspaper, eyeglasses half down his nose, peering at her.

"There must be someplace to go for such material," Janet persisted. "Where would it be?"

"I don't know, Janet." He waited to be sure there were no further questions to interrupt him. Finally, he shook the newspaper, straightening it, and continued reading. Several minutes later, without lowering the paper, Russell said, "The public library, possibly. If not, they should know where to seek such things."

Pamela was a regular visitor to the library, the downtown branch near Five Points! Janet held her book as though reading, but she no longer saw the words. Across from her, his feet on an ottoman, the aroma of pipe tobacco in the air, Russell continued his front-to-back study of the daily news.

"May I help you?" the clerk rested two prominent bosoms atop a Formica counter, speaking to Janet.

"Where may I find old newspapers and magazines?"

"In the basement, down those stairs, follow the red arrows on the walls."

Janet did as instructed and came face-to-face with a tall, thin, bespectacled young man whose collar circled his neck but did not touch flesh. He wore a clip-on bow tie.

"I'm looking for out-of-date newspapers and magazines," Janet said. "Can you help me?"

"What are you looking for, exactly?" he asked.

"Old newspapers and magazines."

"Yes, but is there a particular item or subject?"

"Uh—World War II, I suppose."

"Any special theater of operations?"

"Let's see—Germany, I guess."

"American involvement only, or before?"

"Both."

He ran a bony finger down a cellophane-covered index, flipping pages.

"Won't take long to find all we have, I have one other person who bugs me half to death on the same period."

"Young girl?" Janet asked.

"As a matter of fact, yes."

He led Janet down a musty smelling corridor between floor-to-ceiling racks and shelves. "We have a limited number of magazines on microfilm," the guide stated. "From 1949 to now, we have all issues of the *Atlanta Journal* and *Constitution*. However, at the newspaper offices you will find they have microfilm of back issues all the way to the twenties, I'm told. Pamela, that's the girl who's so interested in the same period—Pamela says they will help photograph articles if you ask. There's a nominal charge, she says, but I have no idea how much."

"Can you photograph articles here?" Janet asked.

"She does, all the time. She's a whiz-bang kid, that one. A walking encyclopedia of the Hitler years. Ask her who some general's aide-de-camp was and she can tell you that, his family background and dentition, I suspect."

"That's—remarkable."

"Oh, kids surprise you now and again. I have one boy in the fifth grade who comes in here interested in Greek mythology. Comes every Saturday and spends all day poring over antiquities, comparisons with Roman mythology, old articles about same—another one is an expert on herpetology—snakes. Kids get hung up on this or that and before you know it they can tell the experts a thing or two. There's a kid comes here who's hung up on photography. He's the one who taught Pamela how to take photos of the microfilm. He develops films for her and the other kids, I think. Anyway, here we are!"

Janet received a crash course in the operation of the microfilm projector, the young man speaking as if by rote, telling her how to pull a given issue, scan it for page number and project the article sought.

"No smoking, use the room as long as you wish, and call if you need assistance," he concluded.

Staggered with the immensity of the material, and not knowing even where to begin, Janet sat before the humming machine doing nothing for perhaps fifteen minutes. She was thinking about Pamela, the girl coming here week after week for all these years— since she first learned to ride a bus by herself, virtually. Obviously, too, she had been a regular visitor to the newspaper offices. "The morgue," the young librarian had called it. "Nobody dead there," he'd said, as though Janet were ignorant of such matters. "It's where they keep biographies, filmed records of newspapers, that sort of thing."

Janet flicked off the machine, the opaque screen going black. She had looked at nothing. It wasn't necessary. She now knew how Pamela gathered her information, the photographs, articles, and with what dedication the child had pursued the subject. The question now was, why?

Postcards arrived from several countries, brief neatly inscribed notes typically teen-age and more typically tourist: "Lotsafun! Wish you were here! Love, Pamela."

"I wonder why she sends them airmail?" Janet asked over dinner. "It's so expensive that way."

"If not, the traveler would be home before her postcards," Russell said. "Regular delivery might take thirty days or more."

"Oh." Janet studied a color photograph of the Eiffel Tower. "Evidently she's having fun."

"But of course," Russell said. "Imagine such an adventure at Pamela's age! I would have given a leg for it when I was so young."

It struck Janet that this was the first time in her seventeen years of marriage that she had heard Russell refer to his childhood.

"You did not travel much as a child?"

"Not at all."

"When did you first travel then?" Janet asked, choosing her question with care.

"Not until—" he looked up at her. "The war," he concluded, quietly.

The meal was completed in silence.

When the huge aircraft settled onto the runway at the Atlanta International Airport, Janet stood on tiptoe in the throng of waiting parents. As passengers emerged she sought Pamela among the smiling faces. Finally, jumping up and down, there she was! They met in one another's arms, frantic, too-tight clutching, a few happy tears and then Pamela bubbled and babbled from that point to a restaurant where Janet took her for lunch, trying to kill the day until Russell would be home. Russell had said he would leave the office early and be home by three.

"It was super fantastic, Mom!"

Super fantastic? Mom?

"I met the most out-of-sight guy you ever saw, a Nordic delight, believe me, and wow! He was my personal guide for most of the trip. Of course, I had to pay the bills, but he was a perfect Parisian gentleman!"

"Somehow I carried a concept of Parisian and *gentleman* as something other than synonymous," Janet said.

"Forget it!" Pamela said, laughing. "Not on my nickel. If he wants to get fresh he can go find the old biddies. I mean he was great—not physically—but because we had the same interests."

"Platonic, I presume."

"Mother," Pamela gazed at her with chin down, peering through blond lashes, "let's clear the air, shall we? Nothing then, or at any time, happened. Nothing that would make you unhappy with me."

Gratefully, Janet put her hand over Pamela's and smiled. "Thank you, Darling."

"No sweat," Pamela lifted the menu, ending the exchange.

Over eggs Benedict, Pamela rattled nonstop and effusively, tracing their trip from the Atlanta departure through Switzerland,

France, Italy, Greece, speaking fast and with an acquired jargon of American-teen and international-traveler.

"Most of it was look-see stuff, pretty boring after a while. It all looks just like it looks in movies, anyway."

"I see," Janet accepted a second cup of coffee.

"But some of it—really beautiful—and places to go you'd love, Mom."

"Oh, such as?"

"The Louvre, for one. The Vatican."

"Sounds pretty stuffy to me."

"Maybe it would be to you, I don't know."

"I didn't mean for me," Janet amended. "I meant it sounds pretty stuffy for you."

"Oh. I didn't go."

"You didn't?"

"No. I spent my time with a few students who are interested mostly in history. That sort of thing."

"You don't consider the Louvre and the Vatican historical?"

"Oh, sure! I meant, we were more interested in recent history."

Pamela toyed with her spoon for a moment, as though her mind had slipped away to some far place. When she looked at Janet again, the child's joy had gone.

"We went to Germany," she said, voice odd.

"Did you like it?"

"It's okay."

"Don't say okay."

"All right."

Janet waited, then probed, "Well, are you going to tell me about it?"

"Nothing to tell, really. It was the last of the tour and everybody was grumbling about side trips and wanting to sleep late, mostly."

"All the fun was gone by then?"

"They overload you on trips like this," Pamela said, testily.

"It's like being starved and cramming yourself at a banquet. It's great for a while, but after a few days you just want to eat your favorite things, not everything."

"I can see that."

"I wanted to see several things—oh, well, maybe someday I can go back. Next time I'll begin where this trip left off."

"Very wise." Janet signaled for their check.

"I took lots of pictures."

"Good!"

Pamela's voice carried a veiled tone, "I spent a lot of money."

"With careful consideration, I assume."

"I didn't consider it wasted."

"In which case," Janet said, "I'm sure it wasn't."

Unpacking Pamela's suitcase, tote bag, two additional boxes acquired along the way, Janet sorted dirty clothing from crumpled clean and put Pamela's toiletries in the bathroom. She placed unused postcards on Pamela's vanity table, the distant sounds of father-daughter laughter coming from downstairs. Credit card, passport—Janet started to pocket these, then halted, looking at the validated border-crossing stamps. One could almost chart the tour by these stamps alone—date of entry, exit, time of stay inclusive—

She carried the passport to better light at a window. What was this? Poland? The letters were difficult to decipher, the script so foreign to Janet's eyes. Trying to read it, she pushed back the curtain, adjusting the document to a certain distance from her eyes, turning it slightly to eliminate glare. A snapshot of Pamela, unsmiling, was pasted herein.

"Mother?"

Janet spun so sharply she dropped the passport. "Pamela, you startled me!"

Pamela picked it up, looked at the passport a second, then extended it.

"I—you—I see you went to Poland," Janet said, her voice anything but casual to her own ears.

"Mother, you don't have to bother with all that junk. I'll do it later."

"Pamela?"

Pamela turned at the door. "Yes, Mother?"

"Pamela, did you go to Poland?"

"Yes, I did."

"I didn't know Poland was on your tour." Pamela's expression was bland, an ability the child had inherited from her father, revealing nothing.

"Well?" Janet asked.

"Well, what, Mother?"

"Did you—enjoy it?"

Pamela's eyes wavered an instant, recovered. "It was all right. Like Germany. We were tired by then. I told you."

"Yes. So you did."

"Oh. Mother, Papa sent me to ask if you'd like to go out for dinner tonight, the three of us?"

"Yes. Tell him. That would be nice."

After Pamela left the room, Janet felt goosebumps race over her shoulders and erupt down her arms. She looked at the passport again. Entry: Zasieki. A day later, exit: Forst.

Janet put the document in her pocket and left everything else as it was.

CHAPTER SIX

JANET STOOD AT THE FRENCH DOORS, looking through toile curtains. Midday. Since Russell left for the office this morning, Pamela had been sitting on the patio overlooking the terraces and swimming pool. Today and yesterday the child had been reclusive, untalkative. All the youthful mannerisms she'd exhibited upon her arrival home had vanished. She was once more a withdrawn, brooding child.

Janet had no one to blame but herself. She had cast a pall over Pamela with one statement: "I see you got rid of your books, Pamela. Thank you."

Pamela had nodded, petulant.

"What did you do with them?"

No reply.

"Pamela, what did you do with all those books?"

"I did as you told me, Mother."

The response irritated Janet. "Pamela, I'm tired of periphrastic answers to questions. I asked what you did with the books and I want to know."

"Got rid of them," Pamela retorted, standing to leave the room.

"Pamela, sit down!"

The child's expression hinted at subterfuge.

"Let me tell you something, Pamela. There are several things happening around here which I do not appreciate."

"Such as?"

"Don't be insolent!"

"I'm not being insolent. What's the matter with you?"

"What did you do with those books?"

"Took them out of the house."

"Took them where?"

"You said get rid of them. I got rid of them!"

"Pamela," Janet advanced, trembling. "I don't think you're telling the truth."

"Then what I say won't matter, will it?"

"That many books would fill several garbage cans."

"We *have* several garbage cans, Mother. However, since the books are so important to you, why don't you ask Eleanor? She and Harold carried them out for me."

Janet fumbled with an apology, cursing herself for the accusatory outburst. Pamela accepted this with a nod but was obviously unforgiving.

Almost defensively, Janet had gone to the gardener. "Harold, did you help Pamela carry out some books several weeks back?"

"Yes, Mrs. Roth."

"Several boxes?"

"Yes, I did."

"What did you do with them?"

"I put them out in the service alley, Mrs. Roth."

"All right. Thank you, Harold."

To compound the situation, Harold then mentioned this to Pamela. In self-righteous indignation, Pamela stormed into the master bedroom where Janet was sewing.

"Mother, I have given you no reason to doubt my word!"

"Well, Pamela—"

65

"I do not appreciate your distrust."

"Now, Pamela—"

"But I particularly loathe being called a liar twice!"

"Wait just a minute, Pamela!"

"Harold questioned whether I did the proper thing taking out those books. He said you asked if he did!"

Face flushed, Pamela left Janet at the sewing machine, chastised.

Now, standing here in the library, looking at the girl, Janet was debating a move, a word, which might ameliorate the discord between them. Why must silent walls stand between members of this family? Janet tried to be a good mother. She worked at being a good wife. But damn them both, Pamela and Russell gave her the feeling she was somehow inferior to them. Intellectually, emotionally inferior! It had never been Janet's nature to camouflage her motivations or inner thoughts. But recently she had begun to guard against candor; she caught herself considering *how* to say what she wanted said. Why in God's name couldn't they communicate with a candid intercourse of ideas and emotions?

It certainly wasn't very adult to stand here like a wounded child, arguing with herself about how to patch up an infantile quarrel. Janet opened the double-glassed doors and walked into bright sunshine and summer heat.

"Pamela?"

The child turned, a physical response without words. Janet pulled a lawn chair nearer and sat, looking at those incredible eyes.

"Pamela, I want to apologize for impugning you to Harold."

Pamela nodded.

"I would like to clear the air between us."

"No sweat."

"Darling, that is a somewhat offensive term to me."

"What is?"

"That 'no sweat' comment."

Pamela drew a chest expanding inhalation of air, exhaled in a sigh. "Let's see," she mused, without humor, "no perspiration? No moisture? No bodily fluids excreted?"

"I yield!" Janet's laugh was mirthless, forced, her face warming. Easy now. Why was she so irritable?

"No sweat it is," Janet conceded. "Given the alternatives, it seems the most expressive and least offensive."

Pamela was unsmiling.

"At any rate," Janet sensed failure despite her efforts, "I do want to sweep away the cobwebs. I was wrong about the books. I was being suspicious and unjustifiably so. My only excuse is so many things have come up that have worried me lately."

"Papa says you are an inveterate worrier, Mother."

"I guess I do appear that way to Russell."

"Worry without logic is futile, you know."

"Yes it is."

"Dr. Charles Mayo, the surgeon, said, 'Worry affects the circulation, the heart, the glands, the whole nervous system.' He said he'd never known a man who died from overwork, but many who died from doubt."

Janet gazed at her own clasped hands, subduing her temper. In the ensuing silence, Pamela's eyes turned again to the expanse of terraced flowers, the far pool.

"Pamela, do you ever have an urge to—talk with me?"

"We're talking now."

"You know what I mean, don't you? Sometimes I ache for somebody to talk to. Don't you ever have moments like that? Worries and nobody in whom to confide?"

A subtle shift in Pamela's eyes, more an emotional change than physical. Janet persisted, clumsily, "Sometimes, when I have a woman kind of problem, I would give anything to have somebody I could turn to, to unburden myself."

"I'm sorry, Mother. I didn't realize."

"Realize what?"

67

"How isolated you are."

Oh for heaven's sake! Impertinent, self-centered—

"Do you have something you'd like to talk about, Mother?"

Janet shook her head.

"If I have not been available to you, Mother, I'm sorry."

"No. It's all right."

"I want you to feel free to come to me, Mother. Anytime."

"Thank you."

Janet stood, turning quickly to hide her feelings, and walked inside. That was so typical of them. Father—child, so typical! She attempted to form an emotional attachment with the girl and ended up feeling *like* a child, defeated. It must be in the blood, damn them both! She glanced out again and even Pamela's unmoving posture was infuriating. Mother dismissed. Back to more important things. Solitude again and less mundane thoughts!

Impulsively, Janet went upstairs and got Pamela's passport. She left the house without telling anyone she was going. Then she drove to Pamela's teacher's house in Buckhead.

The surprised tutor answered the front door with her head tied in a bandana. "Why, Mrs. Roth! What a pleasant surprise!" Obviously surprised, but not pleasantly.

"May I see you a few minutes, Mrs. Jones?"

"Of course, come in! Would you care for iced tea?" Mrs. Jones faced Janet with closed eyelids. "You must forgive my appearance, Mrs. Roth. I've been repotting. Are you interested in flowers?"

Janet followed the teacher through a small, neat, inexpensively furnished living room into a box-like hall connecting bedrooms and bath to the kitchen. They stopped in a glassed cubicle Mrs. Jones called her "work room."

"My husband, before he died, was a flower fanatic." Mrs. Jones washed her hands in a laundry sink. "Before Tommy died, I never put a scoop of soil in a single pot, never watered anything— couldn't have cared less! But after the funeral I came home—you won't believe this—"

Janet found herself confronting a woman who had embarked on a topic she hadn't intended to bring up.

"I never told anybody this," Mrs. Jones said, embarrassed. Seeing no way out, her eyes fluttered, closed. "I came home the day of the funeral and the house was filled with all these flowers. Tommy spent every free hour working with his flowers and oh, Lordy, he took pride in his succulents."

Mrs. Jones glanced sidelong and she added, "Succulents are cactus."

"Yes," Janet said.

"If his succulents bloomed, you'd have thought he'd given birth, honest enough you would. He pored over these plants."

Unsure how to respond, Janet said nothing.

"I'm getting too personal I guess."

"It's all right," Janet reassured.

"Like I was saying," Mrs. Jones said, eyes closed again, "I came home from the funeral to all these flowers about which I had never cared a whit. I sat down, too grieved to cry; I hadn't cried even when they told me Tommy was dead. He was a fireman, twenty-four years. They drove up to a burning building and a power line fell on the truck. The men said Tommy didn't see it and when he stepped off—"

"I'm sorry, Mrs. Jones."

The teacher's lips grew pale, twisting. "So I came home—"

A long silence, Janet motionless.

"These plants—"

The teacher threw back her head, looking at the ceiling, swallowing, trying to compose herself.

Abruptly, Mrs. Jones shifted her gaze, eyes moist, and she stared—no, *glared* at Janet. "I came into this house and sat where you are sitting this minute, Mrs. Roth, and I said out loud, 'Tommy, Tommy, I'll water your plants,' and so help me as God is my witness! I heard his voice as clear as day and Tommy said, 'Not too much on the succulents, please.'"

Mrs. Jones burst into laughter. "You'd have to know Tommy,

69

he was so droll. He had a dry wit and it was so like him to reach out at a time like that and make light of the situation. I laughed and laughed and—"

Mrs. Jones threw both hands over her face and sagged against a wooden table loaded with potted plants.

"I'm sorry, Mrs. Roth."

"Please don't be."

"I really heard him say that."

"I can imagine."

"I didn't imagine it. He talked to me. He never did it again. But he did that once."

"I know."

"I'm making a spectacle of myself."

"I'm glad I was here."

"You're so kind. You always are."

Janet found a tissue in her pocketbook and gave it to the teacher.

"Let's see," Mrs. Jones blustered, "we were going to have tea, weren't we? Do you take it with sugar?"

As the teacher prepared the beverage, she and Janet tried to maintain conversation, but the exchange was awkward, their only point in common being Pamela.

"She's brilliant, of course," Mrs. Jones said. "A joy to teach. So mannerly, inquisitive, with an absorbing mind."

"Mrs. Jones, was Pamela well behaved on the tour?"

"On the tour to Europe? Oh, goodness." Mrs. Jones blinked rapidly. "You found out, didn't you? Pamela practically made me swear I wouldn't worry you with it."

"Mrs. Jones, I need to know."

"Mrs. Roth, it was nothing as it turned out. Mrs. Lily thought Pamela was with my group and I thought she was with Mrs. Lily. By the time we got to Berlin, everybody was exhausted. Every student and every adult wanted only to sleep. Well, I wouldn't hear of it—I told Mrs. Lily and the other chaperones we must find the strength to rouse up those students and go see Berlin. We didn't miss Pamela for a day and a night, because Mrs. Lily went one way and my group another. We each had fifteen students and although that doesn't sound like many, Lordy! It's like standing in a bed of ants. I hope you aren't angry."

"I only want to know what happened," Janet said.

"Well like I say, by the time we discovered Pamela gone, we were nearly hysterical. We called the police and hospitals and I don't know who all—you can imagine the thoughts we were having! I was ready to call you, Mrs. Roth. I had my finger in the dial to turn it almost—and Pamela came in. I hope you don't fault us for it. When Pamela told us what happened, she said there was no reason to call you. You know how *logical* that child can be. She said no harm done and all was well, so let's forget it. Pamela says you worry about her. But everything seemed all right then."

"I would still like to know what happened," Janet urged.

"She got on the wrong train! You know how those Eurailpasses are, we could go anywhere during the time we were there. Pamela got on the wrong train and as I said we were all exhausted. The child ended up in Warsaw! That's a less than friendly country, I should think, being Communist. But no, Pamela said they helped her get connections the next day and she was back in Berlin by nightfall."

"What did she do in Poland?" Janet asked.

"I expect she spent most of her time trying to get back. Two days on a train and she was bone weary when she came into the hotel. Slept all that evening and late into the next morning. Pamela convinced me no harm was done and she didn't want you to worry needlessly, so we didn't call. I hope I haven't upset you."

"No," Janet said, dully.

"Except for that incident, Pamela was a perfect student, the perfect young lady, as she always is."

"I see."

"We had our teensy frictions, but—"

71

"Frictions?"

Mrs. Jones laughed, her expression suggesting a less than willing informer. "You know how Pamela is. So serious. I wish she'd laugh more and relax, but she is so serious! She wanted to see what she wanted to see and go where she wanted to go and she was very specific about it. She has a will, she does. So we tussled over that until this nice, nice young man said he'd take her to the archives and the ministry on certain days, if she'd go with the group without fussing the other days. It worked fine. He was a nice, nice young man. A teacher working part-time."

"Well, where did Pamela want to go?" Janet queried.

"You know how she is about World War II. She lives and breathes it! So, she wanted to see dusty old files and go to newspaper offices and the National Archives—she spent all day one day trying to see some man who is supposed to be a famous partisan general, according to that nice young man."

"Who was he?"

"Oh, goodness, I don't know. But the nice young man said she got in! He said nobody else could have done it, but Pamela had a private audience for over an hour. She can accomplish anything she wants, you know. Keen young mind. Inquisitive."

"Thank you for the tea, Mrs. Jones."

"I'm afraid I've rattled on."

"I've enjoyed the visit."

"I hope you aren't angry with me about not calling from Germany."

"I know how persuasive Pamela can be."

"She can be, you know that, and I didn't want to worry you over nothing."

"As a matter of fact, Mrs. Jones, I would appreciate it if we could keep this teacher-parent meeting between ourselves. I wouldn't want Pamela to suspect I was checking on her. She doesn't know I'm here to see you."

"She didn't tell you about Poland?"

"No. I found it in her passport."

"Passport?"

"Yes, I saw the border stamps." Janet withdrew the passport and opened it, showing the validation for entry and exit.

"Isn't that odd," Mrs. Jones said, softly.

"What?"

"Pamela had her passport."

"Isn't it required?"

"Yes. It is." Mrs. Jones looked at Janet strangely.

"Is something wrong, Mrs. Jones?"

"Probably not. But—"

"Yes?"

"See, I kept all passports. I'd hand them out at the border crossings and gather them up immediately after clearing customs. So nobody would lose their papers."

"Yes?"

"I don't see how Pamela got her passport without my—I really must be frank, Mrs. Roth."

"I wish you would, Mrs. Jones."

"Well see, I asked Pamela about crossing into Poland without a passport. She said there was no problem. I took that to mean she had no passport and they let her through and out again anyway. But apparently she had the passport. Which is required. Like—"

"Like she planned it," Janet completed the thought.

"Must be a misunderstanding."

"Yes," Janet said, disguising her feelings. "I wouldn't worry about it, Mrs. Jones. Pamela is home now, safe and sound."

CHAPTER SEVEN

"IT'S ONLY FOR THE WEEKEND, MOTHER," Pamela pleaded.

"But I don't know these people, Pamela."

"She's a classmate, Mother. A friend."

"What do you think, Russell?" Janet asked.

"I have no objections," Russell said.

"Thank you, Papa!"

"All right," Janet agreed with some misgivings, "I'll call your friend's mother."

"Oh, Mother, please! That is so maternal and I know Mrs. Timmons doesn't mind, she said so."

"Pamela, I'm going to have to check first. It's only good manners. I can't let you go spend Friday and Saturday nights there without acknowledging that I know."

"Mother, really — please don't make me look so childish."

"Russell?" Janet sought support.

"The mother has spoken to you, Pamela?" Russell questioned. "You are positive she approves of a guest for two days?"

"Yes, Papa! It's a going-away party for Sue, she's moving to Baltimore and there'll be several girls there."

"Then this once, Janet," Russell advised, "perhaps it isn't necessary to confirm it. But Pamela, you will call when you are there. Agreed?"

"Agreed, Papa. Thank you."

Pamela spent Friday morning struggling with a decision as to what to pack, what to wear, how to coordinate her selections so that blouses matched slacks, shoes and accessories. She took one pair of shorty pajamas. She put it all in a small overnight bag; insisted that she be allowed to catch a bus rather than be delivered to the house.

That evening, Janet got the telephone call around nine.

"I'm here, Mother."

"Everything is fine?"

"Oh, yes!"

A crowd sound behind Pamela made Janet ask, "Where are you?"

"We're at a recreation center near Sue's house. But Mr. and Mrs. Timmons are with us."

"All right, Darling. Have fun."

Janet hung up. Russell made sucking sounds on his unlit pipe.

"Worry, worry," he chided softly.

"I should've called the parents," Janet said.

"Nonsense! Pamela is fine. Why always do you fret so?"

Later, Janet concocted an excuse to leave the house, ostensibly going after fresh-baked bread from a 24-hour delicatessen. She drove the freeway through Atlanta to a Decatur address, wound through a lovely old neighborhood just off Ponce de Leon Avenue, and found the house, a Victorian two-story stucco building. The house was brilliantly lighted, several automobiles were in the yard. Janet parked half a block distant and walked through the warm July night air to the driveway. As she approached the house, the shrieks of laughter came to her ears, and the loud cacophony of contemporary music pounded the evening calm. A party. No doubt of it. Janet returned to her car, slightly shamed, and hurried home.

Russell was going up the stairs to bed when Janet let herself in. As he turned to look at her, Janet realized she was empty-handed.

"You did not get the bread?" Russell asked.

"I — no. They didn't have what I wanted."

"Hmm." Russell studied her face in the dim hall light. "Too bad. Good night."

"I'll be up shortly," Janet said, with the distinct impression Russell had seen through her.

"Yes. Well. Good night."

Russell had a golfing date Saturday morning. Janet was there alone when the mail came. She sorted through the usual mixture of magazines, junk and bills. She always put any bill on Russell's desk, unopened. But this morning a credit card statement addressed to Pamela, in care of her father, aroused Janet's curiosity. She ripped open the envelope.

"Fifteen hundred dollars!" Janet said aloud. In 21 days that child spent fifteen hundred dollars? For what?

Janet leafed through the attached duplicates, Pamela's name neatly penned by carbon to each. Cash, cash, cash, all cash! The child had come home without a single gift, no new clothing, nothing whatsoever had she bought! But here, voucher after voucher showed cash requests. This in addition to the five hundred dollars in traveler's checks.

Angered, Janet went to the telephone and called the Timmons residence. But as the phone rang, before anyone answered, she hung up. The explanation would be sure to elicit resentment. Over the telephone was no way to question Pamela. It could wait until the girl arrived home Sunday evening. Burning with suspicion and resentment of her own, Janet sat by the telephone reexamining the American Express billing.

The telephone rang and Janet lifted the receiver. She heard Eleanor on an extension, "Roth residence."

"Mrs. Roth?" a drawling male voice.

"No. May I ask who's calling?"

"Fotomat. Calling Mrs. Pamela Roth."

"Miss Pamela isn't in at the moment, may I take a number?" Eleanor said.

Janet interrupted, "I'll take it, Eleanor, thank you."

"Hello," the southern voice said. "Mrs. Roth?"

"Yes?"

"We have your film here."

"All right."

"Mrs. Roth, due to the size of the order, my supervisor requested that you pick it up as quickly as possible."

"How much is the charge?"

"The balance is one twenty-two plus tax."

"A dollar twenty-two?"

"No ma'am. One hundred and twenty-two dollars."

A hundred and twenty-two dollars! Janet's palm was perspiring against the plastic receiver, anger making her voice tremble. "Will you accept my check?"

"If you have identification and a couple of credit cards."

"Very well. I'll be down to pick it up shortly. Where are you?"

"Sandy Springs Shopping Center."

Janet drove there, proffered her credit cards and was staggered at the size of the packages—two large sacks filled with manila envelopes.

"We don't often get an individual order in this amount," the clerk explained. "Must've been some vacation."

"Must've been," Janet said, acidly. "Over a hundred dollars worth of developing."

"You mean six hundred," the clerk stated. He handed Janet a clipped sheaf of billing — the total was $622.38.

"Do I owe you more?" she asked sharply.

"No ma'am. Miss Pamela Roth paid in advance, except for the $122 you're paying."

Five hundred cash in advance! Janet accepted the billing, took back her credit cards and put the two bulky packages into the front seat of her automobile. Pamela was going to have to answer for a lot and her explanation had better be good!

Alone at the house, Janet went into a bedroom suite reserved for guests. Here, she spread the packages, opening them, and spilling out photographs. Some were color photos. Others black and white, also 35mm transparencies. But included in the order were blow-ups, all black and white, and these mystified Janet.

Documents. Like the ones in the locked cabinet of the attic. Letters, certificates, newspaper stories. Nothing whatsoever in English, but she could guess the subject easily enough. Janet sorted through regular snapshots of the usual sights recorded on film by tourists: towers, rivers, companions, mountains. In one package were 36 different photos of the same thing — a white windowless building. There was nothing to suggest an architectural interest. The concrete structure might have been a storage building. Janet scrutinized the background. More buildings, a corner, the edge of a roof, in the distance a couple walking arm in arm. But obviously it was the nondescript building itself which had interested Pamela.

Janet went from folder to folder, envelopes containing a total of, she estimated, nearly a thousand exposures. In a series of photographs, Janet saw what appeared to be a deserted factory of some kind with neat walkways and tended lawns. The significance escaped her, but then, in one of the views she peered hard at a background area and she saw the white building so carefully filmed in the other package. Examining this series more closely, Janet noticed a distant sign, too far from the camera to be of help, but the type and placement of it suggested this might be a park or sanctuary of some kind.

So, Pamela had continued her stupid quest, and these photographs were an extension of what the books and the attic evidence had been all about. More sources of possible embarrassment for Russell. More cruel and thoughtless indications of Pamela's preoccupation with this terrible subject! Enough was enough. Pamela wasn't about to receive these photographs and that was that. Janet pushed it all back into the two paper sacks the Fotomat had provided and put them into a walk-in closet.

There was no way to know what the documents might be. Janet neither spoke the language nor knew anyone she could trust to translate it. She considered the ramifications of taking the entire matter to Russell for his advice and assistance.

Pamela's secretiveness, her tenacity, doubled the importance of what she did, magnified the subject completely out of proportion. Of one thing Janet could be sure, if Russell discovered this, he would be deeply hurt. It would seem to him that his child had distrusted and suspected him. Russell simply did not deserve that!

The servants all had Sunday off. When the phone rang, Janet answered.

"Hey, baby!" A youthful voice.

"No, I don't think so," Janet warned.

"Oh, 'scuse," the male tone altered. "This is Arty, is Pamela in?"

"No."

"Ouch. Okay. You her mom?"

"Yes I am."

"Yeah, okay, well I got to unload this on somebody. Mrs. Roth, I've been keeping these boxes for Pamela and I joined the Navy Friday so she's got to take them back. I'm probably going to regret it. I mean Uncle ain't above laying it on you to shanghai a strong back, know what I mean?"

"No."

"Oh. Yeah, well. Listen, I got to drop these books back by or junk them or something. See, I'm leaving unexpected like."

"Books?" Janet said, numbly.

"Yeah. Least I think that's what she said they were. Seven, eight boxes of books. So what can I do with them?"

"Would it be convenient to throw them away?"

"Throw them — say, are you sure this is the Roth residence?"

"I'm positive."

"You're Pamela's mother, right?"

"That's correct."

"Believe me, Pamela does not want these thrown away. Where can I call her, maybe?"

"Never mind," Janet said, abruptly. "I'll come get them."

"Yeah?" a tinge of suspicion in his tone now.

"It's either that, or you bring them back here," Janet said. "Which would you prefer?"

A long pause. "Okay. Yeah, well, okay. Can you come today? I've sold my soul and I want to spread out my laundry so to speak, before I leave tomorrow."

"All right," Janet said, "what's your address?"

She wrote it on a pad, a downtown number on Tenth Street. "Near the Fisk Tire place," Arty said. "When can you come?"

"If right now is all right, right now."

"Super. I'll watch for you."

The address was a four-story apartment building overlooking the expressway, across the street from a small theater upon which the marquee advertised an X-rated film. Lounging on the steps of the building were several long-haired young men, one of whom wore a sleeveless "tank" shirt. A pregnant girl sat with her back against a brick wall, knees spread to make room for her swollen belly, smoking a cigarette between pinched fingers.

"Mrs. Roth?" One of the boys stood as Janet approached.

"Yes."

"Arty here." He grinned through a beard. "Look, I hate to lay this on you, but this trip was unexpected. I mean, I didn't *mean* to join the Navy, but I did."

80

"How can one join without meaning to?" Janet questioned, following him down a hall redolent with cooking odors.

"Yeah, well, see, I was watching TV and they got these ads and there's this one of a guy sitting outside a service station wasting himself. He looks up and a jet goes over and you get these shots of exotic places and aircraft carriers and a toll-free number. Tell the truth, I'm not sure what came over me, but up I did and tomorrow I go. So I can't keep the books. Tell Pamela, will you?"

"Yes I will."

"Hey Louis!" Arty yelled, in no particular direction, "gimme a hand, will you?"

"How many?" a distant reply.

"More the merrier!"

Several young men appeared, mumbled through introductions to Janet, then under Arty's direction carried out all the boxes in a single trip.

"Pamela's one more girl," Arty said.

"I beg your pardon?"

"You know — nice looking. Brains too. I used to see her at the library all the time. We were both interested in photography. That's what I'm upping for, photography."

"I see."

Arty closed the car door after Janet as she slid behind the wheel.

"She's out of my class, you know."

"You attend an Experimental High School?"

"What?" Arty frowned, then laughed. "No. I mean, she's straight. Above me."

"Oh."

"I see how come she's so pretty, though."

Janet felt her face warming. "Thank you, Arty."

"No sweat. Swing easy. Tell Pamela I'll see her in about four years, maybe."

"I shall. Again, thank you."

As Janet pulled away, she heard one of the other boys ask, "That's Pam's old lady?"

With the boxes in the trunk, and convinced they held all the books, Janet nonetheless stopped to open one to be absolutely sure. The carton contained exactly what she'd expected. Very well, this was proof indeed that the child had lied about throwing away the publications. This and the credit card charges and the photographs — Janet had reached her limit.

She turned toward Decatur, determined to pull Pamela from the party and take her home. She reached the stucco Victorian home, pulled into the empty drive and set the hand brake. She walked up the steps to a wide, open patio front porch and knocked. After a few moments, she knocked again. Then she noticed the windows were without curtains. Janet cupped her eyes, face close to the screens, to peer inside. Vacant! She circled the house, looking in where possible. It was obvious the furniture had been moved. In back, she found trash and cardboard boxes discarded, mute testimony to the recent departure of the tenants.

Pamela was probably home, or on her way, right now. Janet drove home, put the Continental in the four-car garage, leaving the books in the trunk. Inside, she located Russell.

"Is Pamela here?"

"I haven't seen her."

"I want to see her when she comes in," Janet stated.

"Something wrong?"

"Yes. She spent fifteen hundred dollars in Europe which she got from cash vouchers on her credit card. That, in addition to the five hundred in traveler's checks!"

"I know," Russell said, calmly.

"You know? What did she spend it on?"

"She bought gifts, she said."

"Russell, that child didn't come home with anything but a few extra postcards!"

"That's true. But she told me what she bought for you — it's for Christmas. I'm sure it will arrive later. It's rather a large gift."

"That's a lot of money, Russell."

"Did you place a limit on her spending?"

"No, but — "

"Nor did I, Janet. I assumed you might have done so. However, since you did not, is it truly fair to now criticize her for spending the money?"

"Russell, that is far too much money!"

He shrugged his shoulders, "Then I might suggest, next time place a ceiling on her expenditures. But the moment for such restrictions is before the money is spent, not after."

"All right," Janet halted at the door. "I want to see her anyway."

"If I see her first," Russell intoned, "I shall tell her."

"Russell, Pamela spent another six hundred dollars on film."

"She told me."

Defeated, Janet left him reading, tobacco smoke curling up from the high-back chair where he sat. The minutes passed with lethargic tedium, Janet waiting, distressed, and covertly disguising her mounting anger from Russell. She hadn't noted the time when she'd gone to the empty house, but it had been early afternoon. Now, the sun was setting and Pamela still had not arrived home.

"She's not here yet, Russell."

"Obviously."

"It's nearly sundown."

Russell lowered his newspaper and peered at a window. "Yes, Janet, it is." He studied her with thinly veiled irritation. "You are worrying about what, this time?"

"Pamela left the party and hasn't come home."

"It is, as you say, only sundown, Janet."

Janet looked at the mantel clock. "It's nearly nine-thirty, Russell."

"So late?" he turned to see the clock for himself.

"Daylight Saving Time," Janet commented. "She should have been home by now."

"I wouldn't worry, Janet."

"No," Janet said, testily, "you wouldn't. But I would and am worried, Russell! She should have called before going from the party to any other place."

Russell considered this, nodded, "I agree."

When Pamela arrived, Janet's anger had dissolved into gut-knotting worry. It was eleven thirty.

"Where have you been?" Janet heard Russell's voice downstairs, cold, angry.

"To a movie, Papa."

"When did you leave the party?" he was talking loudly.

"This morning. They moved this morning."

"For all of a day and this late at night you have been elsewhere than the place you said you would be, Pamela."

"Yes Papa."

"Do you know your mother and I have been worried all afternoon?"

Surprised, Janet moved to the balcony, listening.

"I'm sorry, Papa."

"Pamela," Russell said, "you are restricted to the grounds for two weeks. Never again, never, understand?"

"Yes Papa."

"I am very angry."

"I see you are. I'm sorry, Papa."

"Go to bed." Janet hurried away from the stairs. Surprised at her own elation at this fatherly rebuke, she stepped inside her bedroom door and heard Pamela run past to her own room. A few minutes later, Russell entered.

"Pamela is home," Russell noted softly. "She is restricted to the grounds for two weeks."

"That's justified, Russell."

His expression was chilling, eyes darting, muscles in his jaw corded, teeth clamped to his pipe stem. "If she were younger —"

After a moment, Janet questioned, "What?"

"If she were younger," Russell said, harshly, "I would blister her legs for this."

"I think the restriction will serve," Janet observed.

"It'd better," Russell said. "I won't tolerate this again."

"I agree, Russell."

Well, well, well. Old stone face had been worried himself beneath that expressionless mask. For now, his reprimand would suffice. But tomorrow, Janet vowed, there was still the issue of the books and the lies.

In the dark, wide awake, Russell slumbering beside her, Janet experienced an emotion which disturbed her. Not anger or maternal indignation so much as — fear? Was she afraid? Of what? Of the books, Pamela's duplicity? Hurting Russell? For a reason she could not pinpoint, Janet was filled with a sense of dread; as though somehow her whole existence were being threatened.

CHAPTER EIGHT

"You lied to me, Pamela."

"About what?"

"About the books."

"I did not lie."

"Don't compound it with an insult to my intelligence, Pamela! You told me you had gotten rid of the books. Threw them in the garbage, you said."

"I did not say I threw them in the garbage, Mother. *You* said they would fill several garbage cans and I said we had several cans."

"You intended for me to think you threw them in the garbage, Pamela. It was deceptive and your lie is no less a lie because of the semantics employed."

"You wanted the books out of the house. I got them out. You have no right to ask me to destroy them!"

"If I have no right, who does?"

"Nobody does."

"Little girl," Janet advanced, fists clenched, "you are very near to physical punishment. I will not tolerate this, do you understand? I've had all the nonsense I intend to suffer about this subject! The books will be destroyed. Those photographs you took in Europe will be destroyed."

"Photographs? You got my photographs?"

"Six hundred dollars' worth!"

"Those are mine, Mother. I paid for them and they are mine!"

"Yes, you paid for them. Where did you get the money?"

"From my traveler's checks."

"What about the fifteen hundred in cash you got with your credit card? Fifteen hundred in twenty-one days!"

"I bought — things."

"What?"

"Gifts."

"What gifts?"

"A grandfather's clock for Papa. Something for you."

"Fifteen hundred dollars' worth?"

"I didn't go to a bargain basement, Mother!"

"I want a satisfactory accounting of the money, Pamela. That is entirely too much to spend. Your hotel, travel and meals were paid in the tour costs."

"If you didn't want me to spend the money, why didn't you tell me?" Pamela shouted.

"I expected you to exercise mature judgment, that's why."

"This is so typical of you, Mother. You badger, harangue, nitpick and wheedle. You keep everybody tense! Things run quite smoothly until you enter the picture."

"Pamela!"

"Well I'm fed up with it, Mother."

"Child, you are asking for — "

"For what?" Pamela screamed. "Are you going to beat me? I'd advise you not to do that, Mother."

Janet's hand came up too fast for Pamela to dodge. She slapped the girl hard, knocking her backward. Janet swung again. Pamela blocked it, the impact of arm against arm shooting pains into Janet's shoulder.

"All right, Mother — I've had all of your paranoia I can stand. You go your way and I'll go mine. But fair warning — don't ever hit me again."

"Pamela! I am going to discuss this with your father!"

"Do that," Pamela said. "Tell him, Mother. I dare you."

They glared at one another, faces flaming. "Sure," Pamela taunted, "you'll discuss it. Like hell you will. You're scared to — and with good cause."

"What does that mean?" Janet demanded.

"It means precisely what I said! You don't have the guts to face your own husband. Do you know why, Mother? I doubt it."

"Pamela," Janet cried, "I can't believe this is happening!"

"You think in half circles, Mother. You think from here to half-way around and instead of completing the logical progression to a solution, you go back and reworry the same thoughts — never to a conclusion."

"Pamela, you can't speak to me like this."

"It's about time somebody did!"

"Pamela, sit down and let's discuss this rationally."

"That is one thing you seem incapable of doing, Mother, discussing something rationally."

"Pamela, I apologize for striking you. Now please sit down."

"I want to ask you a few questions, Mother. Let's see if you are emotionally able to handle them."

"Pamela, sit down."

"Tell me about your husband, my father," Pamela challenged. "Tell me everything you know. It won't take long, I'll shut up and listen."

"Your father is a successful — a good man."

"Very nebulous, Mother. Be specific. Tell me, where was he

born? Where did he attend school — how much education does he have? Are you his first wife?"

"Pamela!"

"You don't know, you know. You don't *know* him at all!"

"Pamela, darling, please — "

"No, let's not back down on this — we've backed down a hundred times. I ask questions and I get no replies. Not from Papa, not from you. Are you his first wife?"

"I — Pamela — "

"Something to think about, Mother: am I his only child? Have you ever met his parents? Do you even know about them? Has Papa ever said so much as a single word about his childhood to you? How about the war years, Mother? Was he a Nazi? A murderer?"

"Pamela! I will not allow you to speak this way!"

"No, of course you won't! You'd go to your grave without a single deduction — just worry, worry, worry. No conclusion. Worry! Fine for you, Mother. My head doesn't work that way. I want to know what blood courses my veins, what genetic factors form my body. Enviroment is not everything, Mother. But if it is, there's something lacking there, too. A secretive father and a mother who is afraid to face reality!"

"Pamela — " Chest aching, Janet reached for the furious child.

"Forget the kiss and make up, Mother! Let's talk for once in our lives. Open up and talk!"

"Pamela, darling — "

"No, Mother, you won't tell Papa. Because you are deep down gut-scared. I'm asking questions that must have come to your mind many times. I'm going to find answers to questions you would rather never think. I'm doing what you don't have the courage to do, Mother. I expect I know more about Russell Roth than you do!"

Pamela glared at Janet, a fire in her chameleon eyes that drove out all but the darkest hues. The child's features flowed from anger to contempt.

"No, Mother, I'm not going to quit. There's nothing you can do to stop me. If you have no strength for it, at least do not try and deny me the right to know. I'm soon to be fifteen, Mother. Eighteen is around the corner. If you choose to keep your head buried in marital sand, so be it. But don't try to block me. I could tell you things that would — "

"Pamela! Stop it! Stop it!"

After a long contemplative moment, Pamela walked from the library, leaving Janet gasping, stunned.

That child — that — damn that child! Janet ran to the backyard and called Harold. "I want a screwdriver," she commanded. With the tool, she went upstairs to the attic.

"What are you doing, Mother?" Pamela shrilled from the stairs below. Janet slammed the attic door, locked it. Pamela's fists pummeled the portal. "Mother! What are you going to do? Mother!"

Janet disassembled the cabinet doors, threw them aside, lock intact, and began removing the clippings, photographs, everything! She found a large cardboard box Pamela used to store radio-call notes and dumped it out. In this she placed the assimilated materials. This done, she started down the narrow stairs — halted — suddenly afraid with Pamela out there waiting. Trembling, Janet eased down the steps, listening. She held her breath. A scraping sound. A rending of wood. Not here, but — behind her! Pamela had climbed the roof outside a bedroom suite and was ripping at a closed attic window!

Janet unlocked the door, a gust of cooler, fresh air coming to burning lungs as she ran along the hall, down the spiral staircase. A scream, distant, furious, almost demented, Pamela in the attic. Cursing!

"Is something wrong, Mrs. Roth?" Eleanor stood in the main-floor hallway, wiping her hands on an apron. Behind her, Harold hung back, worried.

She gave the box to Harold. "Put these in the trunk of my car, Harold. In the blue room suite upstairs, there are two sacks of photographs in a closet. Get those and put them in the trunk of my car also. Eleanor, when Pamela comes down, tell her I am at the pool."

"Yes, Mrs. Roth."

To the pool — away from curious ears, this the first family argument the servants had ever witnessed. Pamela was acting disgracefully! Well Janet had had enough! Adrenaline flowed, heightening anger, urging her to physical combat if necessary. She hurried out the French doors of the den, across the patio and down terraces to the swimming area.

Behind her, screaming, Pamela burst outside. Something gleamed in her hand. The screwdriver! Heart pounding, mind numbed, Janet sought a vantage point for passive defense. Think, think! This had gotten out of hand. But she wouldn't yield, this she swore.

"Damn you!" Pamela yelled, running down the terraces. "Damn you!"

The child reached the fieldstone parapet surrounding the pool and halted. She held the screwdriver with knuckles white from the strength of her grip. More cautiously, with feline steps, she circled the pool, face livid, teeth bared.

"Pamela, get hold of yourself," Janet said, evenly. She circled, keeping blue-green water between them.

"How dare you take what is mine?" Pamela seethed. "How dare you? You knew what was in there because you have been sneaking around spying all along, haven't you?"

"Pamela, you are saying things that will be hard to erase."

"You are no better than Papa!"

"That is an insulting and juvenile remark," Janet said, voice lifting. "Your father is a good man!"

"How would you know? Good for what? For whom? For you, Mother? Hitler loved his dog Blondi, too!"

"Pamela!" Janet halted now, fury ascending.

"I want my materials back, Mother. I've spent too long, worked too hard getting them together. They do not belong to you. They are mine and you are not going to take them."

"Pamela, I have had all the insolence I'm going to take, child. You are about to get the whipping of your life from me. Drop that screwdriver."

Pamela seemed to become conscious of the implement for the first time. She looked at it, then Janet, and continued to close the gap between them.

"Pamela," Janet said, "drop the screwdriver. Don't make this any worse than it already is."

Pamela shoved aside a redwood lounge chair, her steps deliberate.

"Child, I don't wish to hurt you. Understand? Drop the screwdriver."

Fifteen feet, then ten, Pamela's face twisted. From the corner of her eye, Janet saw the maid and gardener on the patio up at the house.

"Pamela," Janet spoke softly, "Harold and Eleanor are watching. Let's stop this here and now. If you wish to talk, then talk. But in any case, you must drop the screwdriver."

"I want my materials, Mother."

"You cannot have them. Those things are going out of this house. I have given you ample opportunity to be responsible about it, and you haven't done it. Therefore, it becomes my responsibility. You are fourteen years old. Whatever you may imagine yourself to be, you are still a child, a ward of your parents. So long as that is the case, you will do as you are told. Is that clear?"

"Either give them back to me, Mother, or —"

"I am going to tell you one more time, Pamela," Janet took a step forward and Pamela stopped. "Drop the screwdriver. Do it now. Or I'm going to take it from you. If that happens, if you make me do that, it will alter our relationship perhaps forever. You might maintain your fantasies with my assistance, or even if I ignore them. But without me, you face a form of punitive submission you've never known before. If you think your father and I are divided, you are in for a rude awakening. If I tell him about this scene, you will be in for the shock of your life — at your father's hands. Now, drop that screwdriver this instant."

A breathless pause, then Pamela's fingers uncurled and the tool clattered and rolled away.

"If you are smart, child," Janet said, voice controlled, "you will come and hug me, dispelling the thoughts now going through the heads of Harold and Eleanor."

Logic. Rational logic. Pamela came forward stiffly, put her arms around Janet's neck. Over the child's shoulder, Janet saw the servants glance at one another and return to the house. "They're gone," Janet said, finally. Pamela stepped back, eyes shimmering.

"I think we owe one another an apology," Janet suggested.

"Yes."

"Very well, I shall go first. I apologize, Pamela."

"I'm sorry, Mother."

"Fine. Let's forget it."

"Mother?"

Janet picked up the screwdriver and turned.

"Mother, please let me have back my materials. I've spent years getting it together. It's very important. Please."

This was the reasonable point for compromise. This was the give before the take and without it, the rift between them could only deepen, becoming a chasm it might take years to span.

"Pamela," Janet said, "I will agree to this: First, you have made several accusations by innuendo and directly. Therefore, since it affects me as well as you, I think I have a right to examine all of this. Do you agree?"

"If you don't destroy it."

"Given that, after looking it over so I can draw my own conclusions, I will consider — note now, I said *consider* the advisability of returning part, if not all, of it to you."

"You won't understand it," Pamela accused.

"Perhaps."

"What you think you understand will probably be wrong."

"You belittle my intelligence, girl."

"No," Pamela said, flatly, "it's just that things are not what they seem."

"That's the hazard I must take, Pamela."

"Let me explain it to you."

"For what purpose?"

"To make you understand, Mother. So you won't throw away anything important!"

"Make me understand what, Pamela?"

"It's very complex."

"Believe it or not, Pamela, I am not stupid. I may not measure up to your criteria, but I have more than a passable IQ."

"It isn't a matter of intelligence," Pamela argued, gently. "It's a matter of — deduction."

Clearly, more compromise was required. Janet considered what, if anything, she might do to cure this wound, or at least to cauterize it temporarily.

"I'll yield to this degree, Pamela — before I discard even one photo or paper, I will allow you to sit down with me and tell me *why* it's important. If necessary, we can take each item separately."

"That might take years!"

"All right," Janet smiled tightly, "if on your eighteenth birthday it is still in progress, I will return it *in toto*."

A disturbing, almost imperceptible change in Pamela's expression; as though the child saw ultimate victory for herself.

"That is acceptable, Mother."

Pamela held out her hand, "Would you like me to return the screwdriver to Harold?"

Janet relinquished the tool. She stood at poolside, mouth dry, feeling oddly defeated when in fact she had accomplished all she set out to do, hadn't she? She possessed the books, documents, letters, all physical evidence of Pamela's fixation. She had weathered a serious breach, averted a potentially dangerous confrontation, with the child so angry she had momentarily lost her senses! How could Janet be the loser? Even her points of compromise gave Janet final control. She had not said she *would* return anything. She had said they would discuss anything Janet was about to discard — and that was virtually everything!

She saw Pamela pause, give a brief glance back, then go into the house. Trembling in the aftermath of combat, Janet sank to a lounge chair, swallowing, struggling for composure. What was going wrong here? What was happening to them?

She must talk to Russell. She must.

Janet purposely chose the dinner table to broach the subject, so Pamela would see communication between husband and wife. That was what the situation called for, open conversation between them all, to banish the childish doubts which Pamela seemed incapable of forgetting. If Russell answered questions, were more open, this would all soon be forgotten.

"Russell," Janet said, "Pamela and I were talking about her grandparents today. I was telling her about Grandfather Miller and my mother. It occurred to me, Pamela doesn't really know my parents at all and they're only a hundred miles away. What would you think of Pamela going to visit them?"

"Sure." Russell placed his glass so Eleanor could pour wine.

"It occurred to us too," Janet said, her heart inexplicably hammering now, "Pamela knows nothing about your parents, either."

"They're dead."

"But they haven't always been," Janet laughed. "To keep their memories alive, you should tell us—Pamela—about them."

"There is nothing to tell," Russell's voice lilted a bit, an exercise minimizing it all. "I left home for school younger than Pamela now. I traveled. I did not know my parents well."

"I thought you told me you never traveled, until the war," Janet commented.

Russell's eyes lifted from the ocher wine, gazing at Janet without expression. "I meant, in the context of the moment, I had never traveled in a recreational sense."

"Where all did you go?" Janet pressed.

"Where required," Russell said, his words more clipped.

"Did you have — friends?"

"Is this now third-degree time, Janet?"

"Oh, no. We were just wondering."

"Wondering what?"

"About you. About your — childhood. When Pamela asks, I realize I know so little about that part of your life."

Russell put down the wine, standing, "It is past and good riddance. The present is all that counts. Right, Pamela?"

"I guess so, Papa."

Russell's eyes darted to Janet. "You two are collaborating on something!"

"No," Janet said. "We love you. We only want to know more about you. Weren't you ever interested in your father's father and mother?"

"No."

"Well I was," Janet said. "Pamela is too. It's natural."

"Any more questions?" Russell stood with fingertips of both hands on the table as though resting on them.

"I don't think we've gotten an answer to the first one," Janet said, trying to smile.

"Oh?" Russell straightened. "What was the question? I have forgotten."

"The question was — about your parents."

Russell took a deep breath, irritated. "Very well," he said. "My mother was Anna Stehlman, married to my father, Rudolph. Neither had formal education. I was born on a small farm near Bremen, grew up there and attended school as seasons and crops allowed. My mother died with a ruptured womb giving birth to a second child when I was at the time nine or ten. My father was killed when a returning fighter plane jettisoned a fouled bomb from the undercarriage on return from a mission. I was a ward of the state, strictly regimented, I showed aptitude and was therefore given formal schooling. I did not know my parents well. They did not indulge me. I was a hand on a farm needing labor. I am sorry I cannot be more expansive, but for me childhood was cold, hunger, a deprivation. It culminated with my mother's death and the bomb. We could never find any part of my father's body, except one finger which they would not allow me to keep. Is there anything else you wish to know?"

Eyes wide, Pamela sat with arms at her sides. Russell waited for a response, then turned on his heel and walked from the dining room, spine straight, shoulders back.

"Pamela," Janet whispered, "don't you see how it hurts to remember?"

Pamela stared at Janet.

"Bad memories which cause pain and suffering, Pamela. Don't you see?"

Like concrete setting, Pamela's expression set. "Read the materials, Mother."

"Pamela!"

The child stabbed English peas with the tines of her fork. "Hush, Mother. He may be listening. Read the materials. Remember our agreement."

"Pamela, shame on you!"

"Then forget it, Mother. Return my things and forget it. I'm not asking you to suffer anything."

Russell appeared in the doorway. "Something wrong?"

"No, Papa."

"I thought I heard angry words."

"No, Papa. Everything is fine."

CHAPTER NINE

JANET FOLLOWED RUSSELL UPSTAIRS, closed the bedroom door, and stood watching him undress.

"Russell, I need to talk with you."

He continued removing his clothing, "Very well."

"You know what an inquisitive child Pamela is. She won't accept no for an answer, nor will she drop a subject until she is satisfied she has learned all she wants to know."

"Yes?"

"Russell, you are making a mistake not discussing your background with her. She wants to know."

"Strange she does not ask me herself, these questions."

"You do nothing to encourage her, Russell."

"How might I do that?"

"Talk to her."

He put on his pajamas, got a book he'd been reading, went to the king-size bed, and got in.

"Russell?"

"Yes, Janet," an edge to his tone now.

"I said, you could talk to her."

"I was not aware we had a communications problem, Pamela and I. We talk about many things. We always have. More between us than between you and Pamela, I think."

"Russell, you evade every question concerning yourself," Janet said, voice rising. "I married you when you were forty. Forty years of your life is a complete mystery. I know nothing about it. Nothing!"

"I think I see now," Russell said, his eyes never leaving her face.

"See what, damn it!"

"The curiosity is not altogether Pamela's."

"So what? For God's sake, we are husband and wife!"

"Then I must address myself to you, and to Pamela?"

"Do you object to that?"

"I do."

"Why?"

"Do I question you concerning your past?" Russell asked.

"You may if you wish."

"Yes. That is the difference, I suppose. I do not wish."

"You mean you do not care!"

"As you wish."

"Russell, where did you go to school?"

"Germany."

"Where in Germany?"

"Janet you are beginning to irritate me."

"How much schooling have you had? High school? College?"

Russell lifted his book to read. Janet snatched the book from his hands. Instantly she regretted it. Russell's face darkened and he threw back the covers, legs coming over the side of the bed, sitting up. He stared at her with an expression so hard, so cold, Janet was moved to extend the book without a word. Russell took it, put it aside, still holding her with a glare.

"Janet, this you should know about me," Russell said very softly. "A physical act evokes a physical response. If, say, you should strike me, I would, before I thought, probably strike back twice as hard. It is my nature."

"I'm sorry, Russell."

"You want I should discuss my past," Russell said, anger giving his words a more distinctly noticeable accent. "You want I should tell my daughter about me."

"She wants to know, Russell."

"When I was born the edges of my ears turned black and peeled off. It was frostbite. There was no heat. When I am six years old I was beaten with a mule's harness because I was playfully throwing hay over the wagon. I bear scars to this day. When I was nine, in one year, I watched my mother die, screaming, which I mentioned at the table; and the bomb which killed my father blew off all my hair on the back of my head. For months I could not remember anything except I had found his finger and the rescue workers took it from me. When I was twelve, I was a youth leader and was shot in a student riot, left for dead in the street overnight. It was snowing. When I was twelve also, my ears froze again and the skin peeled from my ears as before."

"Russell—"

"When I was fourteen, Pamela's age, I went to war for the first time. It was not the American youth's glamorous view of war which drew me to fight. I fought because if I did not, I would be shot. In three months time, every companion I had was killed. I held my best friend's head in my lap as we tried to put back his intestines from where they fell out from shrapnel."

"Oh, Russell, I—"

"When I was fifteen I became a sergeant, the only survivor of my platoon. When I was sixteen I was drafted into the drive to organize youth for the government. Two of my friends were hung before my eyes with piano-wire nooses."

"Russell, stop!"

"But I have not yet come to the school I attended."

Janet knelt before him, her hands on his legs. "I'm sorry, Darling." She felt him trembling.

"Which of these things would you think I should tell Pamela?"

"None of them."

"The horror, the cold, the hunger and death, I fight them from my mind each hour of my waking day. A smell, a pall of smoke hanging over the city, a certain taste of food — all bring back pictures. Not nice pictures. Ugly, cruel, terrible — "

"Russell, I'm sorry," she kneaded away the tremor in his legs.

"I do not wish for my daughter to think such things. I will not put such thoughts in her head. Even should I try to speak of happy times, there were a few of these, tears come to my eyes and I cry. Alone I have done this."

"Yes, Darling."

He allowed her to gently push him back, down on the bed, lifting his feet. He lay staring at the ceiling, hands clasped over his abdomen.

"The dreams have almost stopped now," Russell whispered. "This I do by will, by never allowing myself to sleep so soundly that I cannot see the dream forming. When this happens, I wake myself immediately. I could not live with the dreams. The terrible — the terrible — "

"Hush, Russell. Hush, Darling."

He was breathing in short gasps, eyes unblinking, staring without seeing, his body shivering as though chilled.

"Never," he choked. "Never will I tell Pamela such things."

"Of course not." She stroked his brow, pushing back hair.

"The suffering. She must never know such suffering."

"Please, Russell, that's enough. I understand."

"I live my life for one thing — Pamela and you. To make for my family a happy home. No troubles, no danger, no terrible things like — "

Janet put her fingers over his lips, stanching the flow of words.

102

The act also made his eyes close. His Adam's apple bobbed, swallowing, bobbed, a crescent rim of tears in his lashes. He shook his head, a short, quick movement like a mongrel emerging from a pond, throwing off water.

"Sleep," Janet intoned. "Sleep now."

Until his breathing came in smoothly drawn and exhaled movements, she sat beside him, stroking, soothing, easing; she felt his body jerk suddenly, the spastic final step before complete slumber. Janet cut out the lights. She went to the bay window of the bedroom, sat in a stuffed chair looking out into the dark moonless night. It would be easy at this moment to dislike Pamela. She almost wished the girl had heard her father a moment ago.

Janet, not Russell, would have to alter the child's thinking, to redirect her suspicions and the condemnation she had cultured. Watching the winking of distant street lights between swaying limbs of trees, Janet swore a silent vow — never again would she subject Russell to the torrent of images she had just seen mirrored in his face.

In seventeen years of marriage, not once had Russell burdened her with a single negative thought. No hint of the torture in his soul. She understood now, she thought, the frigid exterior he exhibited to the world. Like the calcified shell of a crustacean, Russell's emotionless facade was a dam for hurts from without, but more importantly, a cage for the tormented throughts within. At this instant, truly for the first time in her married life, Janet had an overwhelming urge to take Russell in her arms and rock him, kissing away the past, making him secure in her love, building a cocoon of her compassion.

If ever he discovered what Pamela had dared to voice — God forbid! More sharp than a serpent's tongue — oh, God forbid! Janet must not, would not allow that to happen. Those wretched photographs and books would have to be destroyed! Russell must never ever know.

But then? Then there was Pamela, the logical, dogmatic researcher, the child of her father's mold. If Janet could not dissuade Pamela by one method, she must by another. She must be wiser than her daughter, even more adept and more logical than the calculating child. There was only one way to win this deadly psychological game Pamela had begun.

Logic. Rational cold, undeniable and irrefutable logic. Pamela would accept nothing less. Janet must, she realized, use the very tools Pamela employed to conjure her misgivings and accusations. The books. Photographs. Documents. To refute Pamela was one thing. To truly convince the child of her error was quite another. Janet felt a cloak of depression settling on her now, sitting here with Russell's resonant, soft snoring coming from the dark.

To enlist Pamela's aid was out of the question. That would most assuredly be interpreted as collusion, abetting, tacit encouragement. If Russell ever discovered Janet had been a party to Pamela's delusions, his pain would be twofold, the damage perhaps beyond repair.

Yet, Janet was stymied by the language — she spoke not a word of German — or whatever language those copies of documents were. She needed someone who could translate, someone with a mind as calculating as the child. Janet must find a person who understood human nature, psychology, history *and* German. Furthermore, she needed a person in whom she could confide completely. She must be able to spread all of this — her feelings, Russell's, Pamela's life story — before an impartial judge of character. To gamble with potential success by being less than frank would be utter stupidity. When Janet finished her story, telling the deepest darkest secrets in her mind, this one person would know her and her family better perhaps than they now knew themselves.

A name sprang to mind immediately. But to be sure she had "thought things through in full circle," Janet mentally compiled a list of every person she had ever known who might be qualified to assist her. The first name kept surfacing in her mind: psychologist, German, a man who had lived history in the making during the Hitler years.

The sky was beginning to pale and still she sat, thinking, remembering:

"One day one of you may be President," the thickly accented voice came from Janet's past. She could still smell the chalky aroma of the classroom at Mercer.

"Or, perhaps, one of you will murder the President," the tutor concluded.

He would lace his thick, stubby fingers together, locking his hands atop a protruding belly, gazing down at the fourth-year psychology students with speculative, boring eyes.

"I wonder," he once said, "how many of his classmates would have thought Adolf Schicklgruber was destined to be the man he became? A sickly looking, short, albeit occasionally bombastic man — the incarnation of Lucifer himself! I knew his physician, Dr. Theo Morell. Many the times we sat in *die Bierhallen* sipping the fruits of barley, foam in our moustaches, neither of us ever dreaming what destiny held in store for us. *Gute* friends, *gute* days those —"

He often lapsed into mumbled moments of gutteral German, as though his students had vanished, or as if his English was inadequate to express his point.

But he was a brilliant professor, a colorful, intelligent and kindly man. A refugee from Nazi atrocities, a consultant at Nuremberg who spoke to counsel for two days concerning the fascist "mentality." He had come to Mercer over offers from two dozen larger universities, resisting the enticement of huge sums for his services.

Janet had developed an immediate rapport with the man. Had he been younger, or she older — well. It was Otto Ebenstein who lured her into graduate classes. He had come within an inch and a whisper of convincing her to take up medicine and psychiatry as a profession. But of course, Janet had gone to Washington, met Russell.

For all these years they had corresponded with printed Yuletide messages and abbreviated notes therein. Janet left the bedroom and went downstairs to a large closet beneath the staircase where all things Christmas were stored each year. In one of the boxes she found last year's cards received — it was from these that she prepared her own Christmas card mailing list, thereby weeding out any who had not sent cards the year before, adding new acquaintances (always Russell's business associates) who must be recognized this season. She pawed in the box until she found a particular envelope. She tore off the vague address: Mr. Otto Ebenstein, c/o General Delivery, Eastpoint, Florida 32328.

Janet stepped out of the closet and a squeal made her spin, startled. Eleanor, hair in curlers, stood with both hands clapped to her breast.

"Mrs. Roth, I nearly had a failure."

"I'm sorry, Eleanor."

"I heard a noise."

"I was looking for an old address, Eleanor."

The maid wore slippers which ran over to the outsides. "Would you like coffee, Mrs. Roth?"

"That would be nice, Eleanor. Thank you."

"Where would you wish to be served?"

"The kitchen is fine, Eleanor."

The tantalizing aroma of eggs and bacon rose in the warm, brick and stainless-steel kitchen as Janet penciled notes to herself: things to take, actions required with the single-minded purpose of leaving today. Eleanor shuffled from Dutch oven to cutting board preparing Russell's omelet, with an eye on the clock. Russell would not deviate fifteen seconds, arriving precisely the same time Monday through Friday for sustenance before departing for a day at the office. The weather dictated whether he ate on the patio or here in the kitchen, but nearly always he dined alone.

When the bedroom signal light flashed on the kitchen wall, Eleanor began putting things on the table. On the dot, 6:15, Russell entered the kitchen and paused long enough to give Eleanor instructions on several yard duties he wanted performed by Harold.

"I will be driving myself in this morning," Russell said. He then sat opposite Janet, with a nod.

"Up all night," he noted her clothing.

"Yes. Russell, I would like to get away for a few days."

"All right." He poured cream in his coffee.

"I want to go to the Gulf Coast, a place called Eastpoint. There's an island there, St. George."

Russell sipped coffee, eyes squinted through the vapors.

"Do you mind?" Janet asked.

"No."

"I would like to drive down today."

Russell nodded, sitting back as Eleanor placed his plate on the table.

"Alone you mean," he stated.

"Yes, of course."

"Of course?" Russell looked up. "Why of course?"

"Well, Russell, who would I be going with?"

"Pamela — of *course*."

"Oh! No. No, I'd like to get away by myself a while. Is that all right?"

"Of course," Russell said, his tone a hint of mockery.

This was so characteristic of their relationship. Russell exhibited not the least curiosity as to why, precisely where, no questions about when she would return! Respect for her privacy? Or, because he didn't care? Janet sat with him as he finished eating, reading an early edition of the newspaper, no further conversation between them. He left with a curt good-bye and through the window Janet watched him back out his Continental and drive away.

C. TERRY CLINE, JR.

"Will you be needing assistance in packing, Mrs. Roth?" Eleanor inquired.

"No. I know exactly what I want, Eleanor. Thank you."

When Pamela arose, then Janet would go. She could be ready in a few minutes. She felt an ascending sense of excitement, of freedom! She sipped coffee, face stoic.

Janet turned south, the air conditioner displacing the warmth and leatherette smell of the automobile interior. She was experiencing the strangest elation, as though she were somehow escaping something. She drove effortlessly through Atlanta, on Interstate 75, and set the speed warning indicator precisely at 55 mph.

How many years had it been? Eighteen? Nineteen? Somehow she couldn't imagine Otto Ebenstein two decades older. She was positive he would not have changed all that much. He had seemed ancient to her as a student. A bushy head of gray hair, always wind-blown, his thick lips giving him the ludicrous appearance of a toad in human form.

The ties that bind — many times she had thought of him. Not once had she telephoned. A letter she'd received from Otto when she married suggested that the professor had somehow managed to keep up with Janet. She remembered another note too, upon the birth of Pamela, and flowers at the hospital.

Theirs was one of those delicious alliances which only the very young can create with the old. Janet the embodiment of youth with life still out before her, and Otto the antiquarian and sage, vesting his knowledge in her. True to his German heritage, Otto was a drinker of beer, quoting A.E. Housman as his justification, "Malt does more than Milton can to justify God's ways to man . . ."

Janet remembered herself as a quiet, withdrawn student. Deprived of the joy of living on campus, required by a too strict father to go to the nearby university where he sat as a regent, she

108

had walked to classes daily. Like all things in her youth, college was a lackluster experience through which she moved without conscious thought of yesterday or tomorrow. Until she met Otto. If anyone could influence her, he could. Perhaps not drastically, but radical alterations were not his style. Subtle variances emerged when Janet was with the teacher.

Otto would recount humorous events from a tragic past, finding laughter even in the horrors of war-torn Europe where he narrowly avoided execution at the hands of the Nazis. Spellbound, Janet the coed became his willing audience, quasi-confidante and friend.

"Joy comes in when you arrive," Otto once said. "I bask in your beauty, bathe in your understanding and revel in the attention you so generously provide."

If he had been younger, she had been older —

But there was never anything untoward. In years hence, Janet had come to think of Otto as a father figure. That's what a psychologist would say, would he not? The poor little rich girl with an attentive father figure? Otto was a fascinating mind, in a bloated and abused body. That he had lived to sneer at his critics, liver intact despite the quantity of alcohol he drank, that he outlasted his detractors and enemies and survived a holocaust — this was tangible evidence of God's good grace.

"I wish only," Otto once said, "that I could track them all to tree. But one can live on hatred and revenge only so long. It is detrimental to the bodily functions, is hate. So now I teach in a small Georgia town. Beer is weak but cheap. Life is pleasant and without event. Someday I will retire to a fishing village where the weather does not too often change. God's will be done."

Still, it had shocked Janet to learn, years later in a university announcement, that Otto was retiring: the publication listed his accomplishments, kudos, and reported that Otto had once been a rabbi. It was something he had never mentioned. But then, neither had he discussed his postwar years working with a Jewish league to track down Nazi war criminals, and the three books he had written concerning international law as it related to the morality of political crimes. He was an odd mixture of braggart and modesty. What fell into which category in his mind eluded Janet. He could be uncouth, vulgar, and moments later a gentle, tender, compassionate man.

Whatever he was, in the final analysis, Janet had once adored him. An emotion which time had not mellowed. Otto was the perfect person to help her with this problem.

Assuming, of course, that he would.

CHAPTER TEN

IN TALLAHASSEE, eighty-one miles from her destination, Janet stopped at a liquor store to purchase four bottles of Moselblümchen, this from the depths of her memory, Otto Ebenstein's favorite wine. By 7:30 P.M. with the sun still high, the air had turned salty as she drove with the windows opened and the air conditioner off. To her left lay open waters and she followed a winding narrow highway. Eastpoint was a cluster of sheet-metal wholesale seafood houses and a convenience store. The young clerk in the grocery store knew no Otto Ebenstein, nor did the workers in the seafood places.

A rank scent of fish, fetid and lung-locking, permeated the "town" part of Eastpoint as Janet pulled into a service station.

"He's about sixty-five, German, short," she described Otto. The proprietor chewed a broom straw, leaning lazily on the car door, his underarm the most expansive view Janet had.

"We got so many tourists you know," the man drawled.

"Oh?" Janet questioned, "Where do the tourists go?"

"St. George Island, mostly. Not come-and-goers, these folks usually stay a few weeks. Mostly from south Georgia, Alabama."

"No. Mr. Ebenstein has been living here awhile, year-round."

"Might ask up to Maude's restaurant." It was there she was told where to find the former teacher. "Perzactly two-tenths mile right down that blacktop," a coveralled gentleman noted. "Second house to the right, kindly nestled back in the trees, but look close and you'll see it. I done some plumbing for him a time or two."

As described, the concrete block building was almost unnoticeable, close to the water, down a sandy drive and painted a faded yellow which gave it a nondescript appearance. From the highway, it might have been a storage building, rather than the two-story home it was in fact. Parking beside a rusting ancient Ford sedan, Janet rounded the house. On the waterfront side, large twin windows exposed a desk, casual den, and through yet another large picture window, a more formal living room. It was still well before sundown. Janet knocked on the door, despite sudden second thoughts about appearing without advance notice. From within she heard muted musical refrains. She knocked again.

A thick necked, round shouldered, short silhouette appeared in the formal living room, stopped, stared, then hurried to the door.

"Otto?"

"Ja?"

"Otto, it's Janet Miller—Roth."

"Janet?" He pulled open the door, folds forming in his face, crow's feet wrinkles at the corners of his eyes. His thick lips parted, stretched, almost as if to touch his ears. "Janet?" Otto said again, questioning. Then gruffly, he threw his arms around her and held her tightly. Immediately, Janet began to cry. He patted her back, holding her, and only when she stepped back a few minutes later did she realize he too was weeping.

"Always," he snuffled, "so sentimental I am! With a nose so big as this one, sniffles are a major calamity. Well, well, come in, child!"

The interior was surprisingly large. Bookshelves along a pan-eled wall were overflowing with titles spanning the classics to psychology, a medical encyclopedia, *Young's Concordance to the Bible* and a complete set of *Britannica* with Yearbooks going back to 1941.

"Lovely as always," he said, taking her purse and putting it on a four-drawer filing cabinet incongruously out of place in the living room. He cut off the record player.

"I am older," she said.

"Ah, but with grace," Otto beamed. His eyes seemed not to belong to the florid, ruddy face; youthful, sparkling alert eyes.

"And you, Otto. You actually look younger!"

"I am! Sixty-seven and never felt better, Janet! I fish, I swim, I smoke too much and drink too much as always and still I worry about the surgeon general's warning on my cigarettes! It would seem a man my age could enjoy his sins without the government nagging, eh? Sit! Please. May I get you something?"

"Have I interrupted your supper?"

"*Nein und abermals!* My hobby is the baking of bread, this is all. Please, sit! Ah, you make me so happy, Janet. Wonderful that you are here. If this is dreaming I wish not to awaken soon. Again I ask, may I get you something?"

"What have you?"

"Anything! Coffee, tea, milk, orange juice like any self-respect-ing Florida resident, wine, liquor, what is your pleasure?"

"Hot tea would be nice."

"*Ja*, and for me."

She followed him into the kitchen, watched him draw water. "Brown with iron, but makes good coffee and tea," he said. He checked the electric stove, pursed his lips and nodded, sending ripples into a double chin. "Soon enough we have fresh hot bread and butter."

"Great."

He turned, grinning, "How long can you stay?"

"A day or two."

"Oh," he whispered, "wonderful."

"Is there a motel nearby, Otto? I didn't see one."

"Do not be foolish! You will stay here with me; I have a half bath here off the kitchen, two daybeds in the living room, your choice, or another daybed in the office overlooking the water. Or, you may have the bedroom upstairs and I will take these."

"Downstairs is fine."

He wiggled, almost as a puppy might, taking her hand between his, short stubby fingers cool to the touch. Had he shrunk? Or had she grown since college? She was a head taller.

The tea and loaf of bread reached perfection in the same instant. Otto served both at a small table for two in his "office-den" looking out at wispy fingers of Spanish moss draped over limbs of hickory trees. They sat sipping tea, eating creamery butter on hot bread. As though twenty years had not passed, Otto chatted loquaciously about his retirement "fishing" and other pursuits, "music, except for Wagner which Adolf ruined from overexposure," and the local people: "they look to the elements for their living; fishing, oystering, shrimping. Those boats you see out there are casting now for mullet. These people live a simple hardworking life. They look not to government or charity, but to themselves and their God. The kinds of people who settled America and made it great."

"You're happy here are you?" Janet asked.

"So happy. Each day I expect God to drop his other shoe and end it. Of course, one must sacrifice certain societal conveniences by living here. I have not discussed philosophy with a single soul, nor have I been to a concert in three years. The TV reception is uncertain at best, and only the hillbilly do you hear on radio. But life is uncomplicated, the people are honest and friendly. What more could an old man ask? I could not see myself shuffling boards."

"Shuffling boards?"

114

"With the push sticks—shuffling boards." Otto shifted a bite of bread and butter to one cheek. "Like old men play in Fort Myers and such retirement cities."

Over a second cup of tea, Otto rambled along on a variety of subjects, always with wit, lapsing into his native tongue just as he had done in the college classes where he'd taught Janet psychology.

"For dinner I give you a choice of flounder caught with my own hands, or shrimp big as small lobsters which a friend brought from the Gulf."

"Either is fine."

"Then we have steak. I am sick of seafood."

They broiled the meat over a grill in the backyard, Otto talking about his "boat" which was 21 feet long with a small outboard engine, kept "around the bend at a seafood house." He invited Janet fishing—was soundly rejected—and as the steaks were sizzling, Janet got the wine from her automobile.

"Ahhhhh," Otto fondled the bottles one at a time, saying over and over, "Ahhhh—"

With the chirp of crickets, staccato cries of "tree frogs" and the answering chorus of cicadas in the night air, Otto puffed his cigarette, inhaling deeply, savoring the smoke before exhaling slowly. As always with all things, he enjoyed it to the fullest. When time came for Janet to explain her abrupt appearance after all these years, it was as a natural sequence to a long evening—and as though Otto had asked, which he had not.

Without interruption, Janet told the squat psychologist of her marriage, pregnancy, sense of fear and birthing of Pamela. She described Russell as "reserved, almost cold," and her life with him. She told Otto as much as she knew about Russell, acutely conscious of the fact that, as Pamela claimed, she didn't know much and it "wouldn't take long" to cover it.

"Pamela *is* her father," Janet said. "The same logical, calculating mind, very intelligent, inventive; she's a child difficult to get close to, Otto. Russell is a hard man to know. After seventeen years of marriage, I realize I know almost nothing!"

"Sometimes we think we know and don't. This is not so unusual, Janet."

"It goes deeper than that, Otto. Russell doesn't thaw, ever. I mean, sexually, for example. I don't miss it and maybe that disturbs me as much as anything. But we coexist—we don't commingle."

The glow of Otto's cigarette brightened as he puffed, the odor of burnt tobacco wafting to Janet's nose. When he said nothing for a very long time, Janet continued.

"My real problem is Pamela."

She left out nothing: the shortwave radio, books, photographs, documents, all the damning material and how it would hurt Russell if he ever knew. Then, she told of Pamela's assertions and accusations.

"Have you discussed this with Russell?"

"He refuses to discuss such problems, Otto. He freezes when it's brought up, draws away and actually punishes me for broaching the subject, by avoiding all conversation for long periods."

"What significance do you attach to this?" Otto asked.

"Only that it is a painful period which he'd rather forget. But I see that Pamela interprets her father's actions as 'secretive' and sinister. I swear, Otto, when she tells me to 'read the materials, Mother,' it sends chills to the marrow of my bones. As though she knew something, as though the books and all could *prove* her father guilty of some heinous act.

"I know this is ridiculous. But my problem is convincing the child, using a logical approach to change her thinking. She's become obsessed with this thing. I'm not talking about a recent manifestation. This has been going on for years."

"Very interesting."

"It could destroy us all. I'm the only one who knows that yet. When Russell—if Russell—if he finds out he may never forgive Pamela. He's that kind of man."

116

"Unforgiving?"

"In this case, yes. He would feel that his daughter had betrayed a trust. From his own child, this is much worse than if the accusations came from someone else. Do you see that?"

"Yes I do."

"I need help, Otto."

The cigarette embers wobbled away in the night as Otto flipped the butt aside. She could feel his eyes on her in the dark.

"How do you wish for me to help you, Janet?"

"I'm not sure, actually."

"You need someone to talk to, this is it?"

"I need more than that."

"You must tell me then. Because I do not see how I can do much but listen to you, at this time."

"I brought the stuff with me."

"What stuff?"

"The books. Pamela's photographs and everything."

"What am I trying to discover?"

"I don't know."

"You wish for me to prove something from this?"

"If you can."

A flare of a match, the acrid fumes of phosphorus, another cigarette arcing the black of night as Otto smoked. Each puff briefly bathed his eyes with red. Minutes passed.

"The child is obsessed, you say," Otto finally remarked.

"Yes."

"You remember your psychology well enough to know the literal meaning of the word?"

"I think so."

"To the point of—psychotic reaction, you think?"

"I think so, Otto."

He grunted, puffed. More minutes passed.

"You do not wish truly that I be a detective, you know. You wish that I be only an attorney for the defense."

"I don't understand."

"You hope to secure my help to uncover the truth, only if the truth serves your purpose," Otto said. His disembodied voice had grown ominous.

"I still don't understand."

"I think you do. But I shall explain. What would you have me do if, let us imagine, I discover Pamela is correct? Would you want to know this?"

Janet's chest contracted, a muscular seizure like a cracked rib responding to a sudden awkward movement. She could neither inhale nor exhale, her voice choked and halted. Well? The query was a legitimate one—answer him! She tried to bring sound from her throat. Nothing.

"You must consider the possibility, remote as it may be, Janet. To overcome this 'obsession' I would have to play her game, wouldn't I? I would have to see if she has a case, what her proof might be, and only by using her own evidence to refute her case could I win her over. Like a patient under psychiatric care, the doctor does not prove the patient is having delusions, this is impossible! To the patient, the delusion is very real. The doctor must make the patient himself realize what he thinks *is* a delusion. Thereby cure is effected. Do you understand?"

She nodded, shaking, regaining her breathing.

"The hazard is obvious," Otto said, voice low. "There is, remote though it may be, the distant possibility that your daughter might be correct. Before I can accept the onerous responsibility of entering into such a thing as this, I must know what you want. If you want the truth, regardless, this we might learn for better or worse. If you want a whitewash of Russell—I would be disarmed at the outset."

"It isn't true, Otto."

"Of course it isn't. That is not the point, Janet! The point is, to change—to *cure* your daughter of the delusion, I must become her ally, not an enemy! I must enter her delusion with her and examine her so-called evidence and use that to break her delusion."

118

"Yes, yes, I see that."

"I am a practical man, not a dreamer. If Pamela is the child you have described, she is going to have something more than idle fantasies. I am willing to wager she can prove to her satisfaction anyway, that Russell is guilty—of God knows what, but something."

"Otto, this is hurting me so much."

"I see this."

"I can't stand it."

"Now we come to phase two of our problem. You see, from what you say, Pamela is right on one point—you *are* afraid. Afraid she is right, is that it?"

"No!"

"Umm. Well we can do one thing, but it will be costly."

"You mean money?"

"Yes, money."

"How much money?"

"I don't know that."

"For what?"

"You could hire detectives to trace this man's life from the present into the past."

"Otto—I can't—"

"To find this man Russell, the true Russell, and compile his history would, I think, solve two problems with a single thrust. It will offset and disprove any evidence Pamela thinks she has; it will dissolve the fears you are now suffering for the same reasons Pamela is suffering them—a lack of knowledge. Fear of the unknown. This man is, despite your years of living with him, a mystery to you yet."

"I could not be a party to an investigation, Otto. The idea is built on the premise that he's hiding something. It is a form of being unfaithful—I simply can't do it."

"If Russell will help, it can be simple, quick, easy."

"He mustn't know, Otto!"

119

"Very well. It is no longer easy or simple."

"Despite my restrictions, will you help, Otto?"

"Janet, I am old, tired, long past my days of global trotting. I tell you this: first let me examine what you have. Leave everything with me for a few weeks. Perhaps I can find a clue to the little girl's thinking. Perhaps you are wrong in what she thinks. She may have discovered some indiscretion in his past which to her young eyes seems more dastardly than it would seem to you or me. Perhaps, as Pamela suggested, Russell has had another wife. Or child. Or he is older, or younger than he has led you to believe. Minor infractions which, to a progeny, seem momentous."

"You think so?"

"No, I don't. The child sounds too capable and mature for that. But it's a possibility, isn't it?"

"Otto, I have no one else to turn to."

"Then I am happy you turned to me."

"Thank you, Otto."

"I need an answer to my question, Janet."

"Question?"

"Yes."

"I'm sorry, Otto. What was your question?"

"If Pamela is right—what then?"

"She's not right, Otto."

"Very well. This is a silly game. *If* she were right—what would you have me do then?"

"Otto—I can't—she is not right. I can't answer that question. It's too absurd."

Otto pushed himself to his feet, put a foot on the remnant of his cigarette and began gathering dishes to carry into the house. Without conversation they did this together.

In the living room, testily, Otto grumbled that he had missed the news, then poured drinks for the two of them. Sipping hers, Janet came to grips with his question.

"I would want to know, Otto."

"You understand the possibilities of such a thing? The ruination of your lives as you know them this moment? Let us imagine the worst. Let us say your husband is a war criminal, wanted by the Israelis or Germany. A murderer perhaps."

Janet began to cry.

"There would be newspaper stories and defamation of character. Nothing would ever again be the same for any of you. Russell might be faced with trial. The United States has never deported an accused Nazi criminal, but this time they might. His business would be destroyed—"

"Oh, my God!"

"Neighbors would spit at you in passing, the press would never allow you or Pamela to live in peace. There would be no place in the United States, or much of the world, where you could go to regain your privacy and restart your lives. When Pamela approached marriage, as someday she will, this would become an issue like religion, race or—"

Janet cried out, almost a scream, sobbing. Otto sipped wine between puffed lips, a patina of the beverage still there after he swallowed heavily. He stared into space, a hard unyielding figure in the soft lamplight. Because he did not speak to comfort her, Janet had an alien emotion rising—she put it down with force.

Otto Ebenstein's wine glass was poised as though to sip, his other hand at rest on the arm of his chair, the tobacco-stained short fingers curled—his eyes were anthracite pinpoints between folds of facial flesh. No twinkle in those black pupils now, no hint of laughter a breath away. He was letting her suffer "the very worst" of her imagination.

Crying, dabbing her eyes, she almost *hated* this cold, foreign man. So cruelly frozen with his mind gone to distant thoughts. How could he bring her to tears like this, frighten her as he had, and then not reach out to reassure her? A dream, Janet, only a thought, Janet, a nightmare which is not true, Janet! There, there, my child, dry your eyes—why did he not cast out these dark terrifying visions?

Then she realized what was happening here. She saw what he

was thinking! To Otto, victim of the pogroms and fodder for ovens of the holocaust, the possibility that Pamela was right was not so remote! It was no less possible than the impossible past! He must consider this; his friendship with and love for this student from long ago would be gone. Her child. Her life. Yes, Janet saw that now. Otto had sniffed the stench of war and survived the most inhumane of all man's inhumanities! He had seen, known, talked to such criminals.

It might be true. Let us hope. That was what he was thinking! But if it *were* true. Dear God. This was not happening! This could not be happening! Janet stared at him, Otto the "bit of straw" he once called himself, "which somehow the flames did not consume."

It was not true! Have faith.

But if it were—

Dear God.

If it were—

Otto spoke without a change in his face, his voice almost that of an afterthought.

" . . . what would you have me do, Janet?"

CHAPTER ELEVEN

OTTO USED THE TIPS OF HIS FINGERS to spread photographs on his desk. "It will take some time to read all this," he said. "Three weeks. Four maybe."

As Janet prepared to leave, Otto walked her around the outside of his house, lamenting the porous sandy soil in which he tried to garden. The septic field was his most fertile plot, he admitted, requesting that Janet bring him "a bucket of good rich Georgia soil" when she returned. Finally, midmorning, Janet got into her automobile.

"Thank you, Otto. For everything."

He looked like a lonely gnome, stomach rounded, shoulders slumped, legs spread, hands in his pockets. He gazed at her, chin down, his long eyebrows wild, hair askew, blown by a fresh westerly breeze coming off Apalachicola Bay.

"Do not worry needlessly, Janet."

"That's what Russell is always telling me. And Pamela."

"I shall expect your call in about a week."

"Talk to you then," Janet said.

Otto still stood in the drive as she turned onto the paved road, a sinking feeling in her chest. For the first time ever, she did not want to go home. But she'd been here three nights, had not so much as telephoned to touch base, and to stay here longer would serve no purpose, so far as Otto was concerned. He had peremptorily stated that he would not waste precious time while Janet was here, reading any of Pamela's material. Therefore, to remain longer was to delay his attention to the matter at hand.

Despite what Otto had said, though, Janet had risen during the night to find the upstairs bedroom light still burning. Then, in passing through his bedroom to the only full bath the next day, she found the floor littered with books, papers, photos.

She accomplished the drive back to Atlanta in one long day, arriving home after dark. She turned into the opened wrought-iron gates, drove the long paved drive to the garage and pulled in. Russell's car was gone. As Janet fumbled with her seat belt, the outside lights blinked on, flooding the backyard with illumination.

"Need any help, Mrs. Roth?" Harold's voice.

"No, thank you!"

She found Pamela reading in the den, TV on but with volume off, her legs curled beneath her. The child glanced up as Janet came toward her, smiling.

"Hello, Darling!" Janet kissed her.

"Did you have a nice trip, Mother?"

"It was wonderful."

"Good weather?"

"Beautiful." Janet turned full circle. "Where's your father?"

"At the office. He's been getting a lot of long-distance calls since—Monday."

"Are you watching this?" Janet indicated the silent TV.

"More or less. Turn it off if it's bothering you."

"No. No bother." An awkward silence. Janet smiled broadly,

trying to accumulate what the teen-agers would call "good vibes."

"I saw an old college friend, a man who taught me in school," she said. "I spent a very pleasant three evenings with him. He has a great place on the bay. We ought to consider buying such a place, Pamela. It would be a grand way to get away for a few weeks each year."

Pamela's liquid, large eyes followed Janet's movements. The child was being politely attentive, not truly interested. For some reason, Janet persisted, "We could maybe buy a small boat and go fishing."

"Fishing?" Pamela laughed.

"Wouldn't you enjoy that?" Janet questioned.

"I doubt it. Nor would you, Mother. Nor Papa. I don't think this is a fishing family."

"We could be. We could be anything we want to be! We could climb mountains, go deer hunting, swim, water ski—anything!"

Pamela nodded. Somewhat deflated, Janet sank into a chair and dragged a current issue of a woman's magazine into her lap. Could and would were worlds apart. After several minutes of turning pages, without reading what she saw, Janet realized Pamela was staring at her.

"What is it?" Janet asked.

"Why do you read a magazine from back to front?" Pamela questioned.

"I hadn't realized I did it."

"You always do. It's a unique habit, I've never seen anyone else do it. You have a good many unique mannerisms."

"Oh?" Janet said. "Such as what?"

"The way you prepare your breakfast cereal, for example."

Vaguely discomforted, Janet said, "How's that?"

"You pour in cereal, then sugar it, then pour in milk."

"All right," Janet said. "How do you do it?"

"I pour in cereal, *then* milk and finally the sugar. That way the sugar doesn't sift straight to the bottom of the bowl where it's hard to dissolve."

Janet tossed the magazine aside. "Just my curiosity," she said, "do you give careful thought to everything in your life, Pamela?"

"I guess so."

"No little detail escapes you, does it?"

"I expect I miss a good many things."

Janet excused herself, went upstairs, took a long hot shower and went to bed. She tried to read and couldn't concentrate.

As a child, Janet had once taken a woodland stroll with her paternal grandfather. He was, at that time, an old man afflicted with stiff joints and inflexible muscles. But he nonetheless insisted on "walking the homestead" every spring. That particular year, perhaps to look after the venerable patriarch, the family had sent Janet along. She hadn't wanted to go, but as it turned out, it was one of the few truly memorable days of her youth. Pawpaw, as they called granddaddy, was a keen observer of life. His eyesight dimmed by eighty-odd years, his steps slowed to a shuffle, he saw more even at a glance than Janet's youthful, perfect vision.

In that mile-and-a-half stroll, Pawpaw pointed out the chitin remnants of an insect which had molted and gone. He paused to wonder at the majesty of a symmetrical spider's web, the cocoon of a dormant moth, the unfurling of fresh green leaves budding upon hardwood trees. To speak to him, his ears dulled to certain pitches of sound, almost all women had to shout. But somehow Pawpaw heard the rasp of a katydid, the claws of a scrambling squirrel, and the whirr of a startled covey of quail.

"Spring is the surest proof of existence after death," Pawpaw commented.

The memory was rekindled at this moment, reflecting on Pamela. The child had accepted Janet's appearance without joy. The kiss of greeting was perfunctory and she interrupted her book long enough to inquire about her mother's trip, but in truth, Pamela didn't care. Like reptiles, were they in this family, Janet thought. It had triggered the mental recollection of that long-ago walk with Pawpaw.

"See here, child," Pawpaw had said, pointing at the pine-needle carpet of the woods. Janet had looked and at first saw nothing. Then, on closer examination, she followed Pawpaw's pointing, gnarled finger and saw a snake.

The serpent was giving birth. Each wiggling baby the garter snake produced was a replica in miniature of the mother. And, upon the emergence of the infant, each baby immediately slithered away.

"She's losing them!" Janet had cried.

"It's the way with snakes," Pawpaw had said. "There beats no mother's love in a reptile's heart, child."

Janet had never forgotten that succinct, cold-blooded summation of the mother snake. It had shocked and worried her at the time, the prospect of babies instantly abandoned, going through life uncaring and uncared for.

Yet now, with a husband who didn't question where Janet was going when she left and a daughter who didn't ask "where" Janet had been—how different were they from the unloving snakes?

The bedroom door opened and Russell entered. He was unshaven, a rarely seen neglect of personal appearance for him.

"Hello, Darling!" Janet put her unread book on the commode at bedside.

Russell spoke in passing, going to the bathroom. Janet heard a rush of toilet water, then the sounds of a shower. She went in and sat at the dressing table, watching steam rise above the sliding shower door. Russell's opaquely visible image moved in shadow patterns behind the screen.

"I had a good time," Janet volunteered.

"Good."

"I visited with an old college professor," Janet said. "I haven't seen him in nearly twenty years."

"There's no soap in here," Russell stated. His tone suggested incompetence.

"Eleanor probably cleaned the tub and forgot to replace it." She gave him a bar from the lavatory.

"He's an interesting old man," Janet commented.

"Who?"

"Otto Ebenstein. My old professor."

The water sounds ceased abruptly and Russell threw open the shower door, drying his head.

"He's an old friend," Janet said.

Russell looked at her, now daubing his arms and chest. "You have said the word 'old' four times," Russell remarked. "Is this to impress me that he is old? Or to make me doubt it is so?"

"I—well, he *is* old; I didn't—it was unintentional, Russell."

He grunted, toweling his legs. He stepped from the tub and gazed at his image in the mirror. After a brief hesitation he pulled out his shaving paraphernalia.

"I don't suppose you'd ever be jealous of me, would you, Russell?"

He squirted lather into one palm from an aerosol can and applied it, speaking, "You have never given me reason to be."

"If I did? Would you be jealous?"

"Would you wish that I were—jealous?"

"A little can be very flattering."

"Hmm." He shot a glance at her, rinsing his razor.

"Would you be?"

"Not for long."

Janet stood, to better see his face in the mirror. "What does that mean?"

"I would be jealous for only a short time, that is what it means."

"Do you mind explaining that?"

Russell pulled taut the flesh of his neck, the blade scraping stubble. "I would send you away. Or leave myself. Or kill the man."

"You would?"

"Yes."

"Guess I'd better not make you jealous then," Janet joked.

"Better not," Russell said, his voice the same monotone. "There are times when a man is justified in protecting what is his."

"My God, Russell, you make me sound like chattel!"

He stared at her, their eyes locked in the mirror. "If this is to suggest you are my property, this is true."

"Russell!"

"The society is so civilized here, do you know this?" Russell said, evenly. "But now and again something happens to remove the veneer of this civilization. Something to remind a man that the world is no less feral merely because our jungles consist of tall buildings and mass-transit systems."

"I don't understand."

"Perhaps you don't try!" Russell snapped.

"Then explain it!"

"A man's best friend today may be his worst enemy tomorrow. A neighbor in time of hunger may steal from neighbor. Brother kills brother. Man is always the animal, always hunter and hunted, but he forgets this. You are my wife. Given the jealousy of which you speak, it would depend on the state of my civilization, wouldn't it? As to whether I killed him, drove you away, or chose to withdraw myself."

He returned to shaving, smooth even strokes of stainless steel over skin. Janet blinked her eyes fast, watching, throat constricted. Russell said nothing more, did not glance up to see her leave the room. He completed shaving, brushed his teeth. When he came into the bedroom, Janet had turned off her lamp and was feigning sleep. Russell made no effort to rouse her.

129

* * *

Pamela was swimming in the pool, her head capped in rubberized apparel which gave her the sleek contours of a human bullet cutting through the water in powerful strokes. Janet, in a bikini, lay on a lounge chair trying to deepen a poorly accumulating tan. After two days of sunbathing, she was blotchy at best, with rumpled flesh at the thighs and a network of broken blood vessels in her ankles and behind the knees. She had never been a vain person, although she had never neglected her appearance, either. However she hoped the tan would have a cosmetic effect on these recent blemishes.

To while away the hours, she fanned a new copy of *Time,* careful to read the damned thing from *front* to *back.* It had been a poor selection—Janet was not the least interested in the debates between Jimmy Carter and Gerald Ford. Politics confused her and she was distrustful of any man who would willingly subject himself to such a life for the sole purpose of power. There certainly wasn't enough money in it to make the job attractive. Or at least, there hadn't been until congress voted themselves a largess with steady increases to keep them ahead of the inflation they were bringing upon their constituents.

Janet scanned each page and turned it. Her eyes fell on "Milestones ": births, divorces, deaths—

"Dear God!"

"What is it, Mother?"

"That doctor—Hans Fiedler—he's dead!"

Pamela sputtered water from her upper lip, clinging to pool side.

"Murdered, it says. A brutal slaying in Houston at the doctor's home. I must go call Russell and tell him."

"He knows about it, Mother."

"He does?" Janet halted, half out of her chair.

"It happened while you were in Florida. It was in all the newspapers and on television."

"I didn't see it." Janet recalled Otto's complaining that he was giving up his news programs for her company.

"It was big news for about a day," Pamela said. The child didn't seem the least perturbed by it. A man she had so ardently admired at the seminar, she now laconically commented on his tragic death!

"Was Russell upset?" Janet queried.

"If he was he didn't show it," Pamela said. "You know how unemotional Papa is."

"But they were such good friends, weren't they?"

Pamela heaved herself up, the slap of a buttock on the tile. She pulled off her cap and shook her hair loose.

"Friends?" the child said, her voice strange, "Papa said he and Dr. Fiedler were 'acquaintances' only."

"You talked with Russell about it?" Janet inquired.

"I specifically asked if Papa was going to go to the funeral, or at least send flowers. He didn't do either."

Thinking the girl was hurt by this, Janet said, "If I had known, I would done that, Pamela."

The child shrugged. Her eyes were watery—from the chemicals in the pool? Emotion?

"When I asked Papa if he and Dr. Fiedler were friends, Papa said, 'We have known one another for a number of years, yes. But friendships do not come easily in business, Pamela.' I think I made him angry asking so many questions. He resents questions."

Janet felt an urge to hold the child closely. "Maybe we could still send a floral arrangement by wire, Pamela."

"I wouldn't do that, Mother."

"Why not?"

Pamela shook her head.

"It would be a nice tribute to a man you admired, a thoughtful remembrance."

"No, Mother."

"Baby, you perplex me so—first you sound as if you are finding fault with your father for not making a move concerning the funeral, and now you don't want to do it yourself. Why?"

Pamela sat at the foot of the lounge chair, eyes downcast. "While you were gone, I did a lot of thinking, Mother."

"About what?"

"About how childish I've been acting. About all those books and photographs and things."

Heart lifting, Janet took Pamela's hand.

"It's been a stupid and juvenile thing. Not logical at all. I tried to examine my motives and I must have been rebelling against parental dominance, that's all I can figure."

"Oh, Sweetheart—"

"I have a fine father, a good man just as you said. You are the best mom in the world. Here I am surrounded by all this," she indicated the house and pool with a sweep of her hand. "I was indulging in a—sick line of thought. Stupid."

"Baby, bless your heart."

"Anyway, I never want to see the books and all that stuff again, Mother. Just throw it away, burn it—whatever."

"Pamela, I'm so proud of you. Sometimes, we all get caught up in something and it has a way of carrying us along, gaining momentum until sure enough everything is distorted . To come to this realization by yourself, all alone, that is a remarkable and very mature move. I'm so proud! I—I could cry—"

"Don't do that!" Pamela laughed, huskily. "I'm just ashamed that I put you through all the nonsense, Mother. If Papa ever found out—he'd never forgive me!"

"He never will, Pamela," Janet grabbed the girl's shoulders. "It's a secret between us, a woman's secret, and you'll learn that women do have certain secrets from their men."

Pamela brushed away the threat of a tear with the forefinger of one hand. She laughed, abruptly. "I'm such a ninny!"

"If you are," Janet said, "you're a beautiful ninny."

"Want to take a quick dip?" Pamela dared, donning her swim cap.

"Oh, Pamela, I glooped myself with suntan lotion."

"Come on," Pamela pulled her arm, "you can put on more later. Swim with me."

Protesting, Janet allowed herself to be pulled into the cool water, bubbles roaring in her ears. She surfaced to Pamela's shrieking laughter.

"That's not a dive, Mom! That's a belly whopper!"

"And I have the belly to whop with," Janet sputtered.

"Race you two laps," Pamela declared.

Instantly, Janet reached out and brought back cupped hands—she had always been a powerful swimmer. She intended to allow Pamela a win, but just barely. Instead, she found herself swimming for all her worth and still losing.

"I didn't know you swam that well," Janet gasped.

"Sure!" Pamela's teeth flashed in a smile. "Swim, gymnastics, all that good stuff. You ought to come to the school meets more often."

"You compete?"

"Sure! Didn't you know that?"

"No," Janet confessed, "I didn't. You never told me."

Pamela pushed away executing a beautiful backstroke, lazing to the other side. Janet pulled herself out of the water, toweling her face, wrapping her head turban-style.

"Hey, Mom!"

Mom. It had a warm, intimate closeness—"Yes, Darling?"

"Did you throw all that stuff away yet?"

"No."

Pamela gave gentle kicks of her shapely legs, only enough to keep her moving on her back.

"What'd you do with it, then?"

133

"I—uh—I stored it. Why?"

"Oh, nothing. Just wondering. You will get rid of it won't you?"

"I will with your permission."

"Do it Mom. Do it right away will you? I wouldn't want Papa to ever find out."

"All right."

"It's very important to me. Will you get rid of it?"

"Yes I will."

"How?"

"I don't know." Janet noted an intensity in Pamela's tone, almost—almost as if she now feared her father's detection.

"Why don't you burn it?" Pamela asked.

"If you wish, Pamela. Darling, don't worry about it. I promise, he'll never know. Okay?"

"Hey, Mom?"

"What?"

"Don't say 'okay.'"

CHAPTER TWELVE

THE LONG-DISTANCE LINE HUMMED in Janet's ear. Now and then, a rush of wind as Otto inadvertently blew into the receiver.

"It's as though she snapped to her senses, Otto. Pamela said she'd been acting juvenile, bucking parental dominance!"

"She must be a remarkable child," Otto said.

"She is, Otto. An amazing child. She has done a 180-degree turn, mentally. Now she's mostly worried that her father will somehow discover the books and all."

"What did you tell her?" Otto questioned, voice distant.

"That I would destroy the materials."

"I see."

"That's what I'm calling about, Otto."

"You wish for me to do this?"

"Yes, I do."

"Umm." Otto's exhalation into the mouthpiece of the telephone made Janet withdraw slightly. A long silence passed between them.

"Will you do that for me, Otto?"

"It seems a shame to destroy the books," Otto said. "I have a psychological aversion to that. A carry-over from the thirties."

"I understand, Otto. But I did tell her I would burn it all."

"I will of course abide by your wishes. Let me ask you, what brought about this miraculous turn of mind?"

"I think she'd been thinking about it. I think she saw how foolish and potentially harmful all this would be to her father. She's a very mature young lady."

"Apparently."

"Otto, it's like going from dark to light around here since Pamela reached this decision. Little things. Like her calling me 'Mom' instead of 'Mother.' She's warmed again to her father and there's been laughter between them—and me—for the first time in months! Russell and Pamela are closer than ever before."

"I am glad."

"So I think I should be true to my word. I think I should be sure Russell never sees that conglomeration of stuff."

"I agree."

"Then you will destroy it?"

"May I have the books?"

Janet's heart was slamming. For God's sake! He could get such books from libraries, publishers—

"As a personal gift, consider it."

"Sure," Janet said. After all, it *was* foolish to actually destroy the books. They had a value. Particularly to a man as erudite as Otto Ebenstein.

"Why not?" Otto said, as though she'd refused.

"Sure, Otto. Consider them yours."

"For that I thank you."

"You—you didn't find anything in them, did you?" Janet questioned.

"The books?" Otto snorted into the phone again. "Well, with over two hundred books on the subject, it is hard not to find most anything I wish relating to the Hitler war years. It is a complete history. The child obviously knew what she wanted in subject matter. There's little duplication. As I said, she must be a remarkable child."

"Yes she is." Janet cleared her throat. "About the photographs and all—"

"Oh do not worry about that. I shall stir the ashes."

"Thank you, Otto."

"Now to important things," Otto's voice rose. "When will I next see you? Or must there be always a problem to force you down here?"

"Don't be silly! I'll come again."

"When?" Otto pressured gently.

"Soon. I promise."

"I consider it that: a promise."

"Otto?"

"Yes?"

"Thank you."

"For nothing, dear friend. Come to see me."

Otto fumbled the receiver into place. He sat, hand on the phone, thinking.

If Janet had called three days ago, he would have complied with relief. He would have bundled the photos, documents and books and doused them with gasoline, happy that he was no longer obligated to examine them. He had spent the better part of six days doing nothing but sorting through the bulk of the material, smothered with the immensity of his task—and seeking what?

Then he began to think as surely this child must have thought. He began where most assuredly she had begun, with the books. Many of these he had read previously. All of them were distasteful to him. Page after page of photographs, the infamous swastika spread before his eyes, crooked-L symbols of black, white and red. German armies, youthful Aryan faces, shiny *objets de la mort,* instruments of destruction. He fanned the leaves of each

137

book, his mind numbed to prevent the escalation of memories they evoked. Some of the pictures seized him violently, bringing tears to his eyes, his hands trembling as he stared at each. He had witnessed real-life scenes to rival any these books might depict— but with a macabre masochism, he went from page to page, seldom reading the text, but gazing with aqueous eyes at things which pained him anew.

He was alert for any clue, a tattered edge dog-eared from handling that spot, a pencil or pen scribble, anything! And he found them. A tiny penciled mark as though made with a hard lead, a check, a faint notation referring to another page or book. A total of 297 books in all. Page after page he scanned, pausing to study any note he discovered.

It hadn't taken long to learn where the child's interest fell. Broadly, the Hitler years. She had every book Otto had ever seen on the man himself, his youth, questionable lineage, years in the service and imprisonment where he wrote *Mein Kampf,* a paperback copy of which was here also. But Hitler the man was a periphery subject, like the book or two he found on armaments, one on World War II tank warfare, another dealing with airplanes. These he set aside because within them he found photographs, faded but journalistically acceptable. In one, standing in a command car, an artillery officer was using binoculars to gaze into the distance. But it was not the scene, nor the officer that Pamela had noted. It was a man in the rear seat, a two-thirds view of his face: this she had circled. The blurb did not identify anybody. But Pamela had circled this one face. Otto was still pondering this when he chanced upon a similar marking of another photograph. In this, Adolf Hitler was speaking to a child and beyond Hitler was the ubiquitous Bormann. Again, the obvious was not Pamela's concern. She had drawn a dart pointing to a German officer, only part of his face visible. The same man? Otto had compared them. He couldn't be positive. But it was intriguing, enough to

138

keep him working, ever more careful in his examination of each photograph.

The child's interest was not so broad as it had first appeared. Sipping a chilled glass of the Moselblümchen Janet had brought him, Otto examined the piles of books. The smallest stack concerned *der Führer*. The next, slightly larger pile covered such diverse subjects as implements of war. But he was convinced now it was not the war machine but the men in the photographs which had caused Pamela to acquire these—a random search that had evidently paid off with at least two photographs of that indistinguishable officer. The third stack of books was restricted to Nazi atrocities, specifically the pogroms against political and ethnic groups the fascists had determined to liquidate. The last of the books, by far the greater quantity, was very specific: The Jews. Even more specific—the Jews of Poland. The death camps. Surprisingly, there were few notations herein. Had the child found nothing in these? Not one photo marked.

He returned to the officer in the command car, and in the photo of Hitler and Bormann. Had Pamela seen a resemblance here between this young officer and and her father, perhaps? Otto had never seen Russell. A child's keen eye and familiarity might note such things as a dimple, a cleft chin or—he got a magnifying glass and studied the head. Beneath the glass, the dotted ink spots became only dots. He backed off slightly, looking again.

"Ah, so—" Otto said aloud. He adjusted the magnifying glass to his own imperfect vision. The left ear of this man was slightly misshapen. The lobe was partially gone. Janet had told him Russell's story of the frostbitten ears and how frozen flesh had peeled away. Had Pamela taken this as her cue?

He had neglected his garden. Otto went out now, the afternoon sun casting a fiery path across placid Apalachicola Bay, dappled water turning the orb's reflection into liquid tongues of flame. He had two bathrooms, but he relieved himself along the perimeter of his tomato plants which grew from the moist septic field. He had learned that urinating around the garden plot kept away most predators, animal or insect. Something to do with "marking" perhaps, much as a dog posts territory, or a white-tailed buck does the same.

He stood here now, exposing himself, forgetting where he was as he thought back. Before Janet left for home, he had known something he hadn't told her. He realized instantly when he saw the photos of documents what Pamela was trying to establish. The report related to several men. Birth certificates, marriage licenses, obituaries, the arrest record of one, school records of another. He had counted nine in all with a perfunctory examination. Not all German. One was French, three Latvians, two Poles, three German-born. Signifying what? At that moment, nothing.

Suppose the child had recognized her fantasy as a fantasy when she realized an inquiring adult was about to see her storehouse of materials? Like telling someone your favorite recurring dream— this might have burst Pamela's illusion, forced her to see the matter realistically. Then when her mother came home, Pamela might have been transformed from a detective to the embarrassed meddler. Now she'd as soon forget the whole thing. That made sense. Very human. Very childlike. Except Otto did not believe that. To the contrary, Janet's call had only deepened his resolve to uncover whatever Pamela thought she saw. The mass of material, the assimilation and reading of it, this built a respect in him for this child he had never seen. Thousands of minute details captured in libraries, from public documents. She must have devoted her entire time in Europe to expanding her materials.

Otto came to his senses, zipped his trousers and picked several tomatoes. These he took to the kitchen and rinsed. They were still firm, but too ripe to leave on the vine another night. He dried his hands and wandered to the office-den where he sat at his large desk which was covered with Pamela's photographs.

He was a meticulous man and prided himself accordingly. He

was unhurried, careful to check every shot, foreground, background and areas between. No matter how inconsequential a photo seemed, he examined it thoroughly. Here, a photo of a death certificate and he had not only noted the obvious name, age and address of the decedent, he had tried to guess the texture of the document itself.

Some of the pictures flatly mystified him. This series, repeated exposures of a small concrete storage building. Something here niggled at Otto's subconscious. A total of thirty-six color shots of this building with no windows, a double-width door, a slate roof. These he stacked together and put to one side.

In all of this, there was something more than his old eyes were seeing, he was sure of that. He brought to bear nearly fifteen years of training and discipline from the postwar days when he had helped track down Nazi criminals around the globe. There were a few tricks he might have missed, but attention to the tiniest detail had always paid. It had been Otto's work, sifting through hundreds of thousands of Argentine documents which had told the world where many of the murderers had gone for safety. Month after month, he had run down visas, passports, all the time checking political bank accounts through paid informers, seeking the tie between the criminal and his bribed protector. Oh yes, Otto knew the value of every grain of sand which comprised a beach. If necessary, he would go over all the books, all the photos and documents a hundred times, if there were so much as a million-to-one chance he might find one of the bastards who had escaped.

For dinner that evening, he baked a flounder which was freezer burnt. The malodorous dish ended up in his compost heap and he settled for a liverwurst sandwich instead, with a Polski-Wyrob kosher dill on the side. As he ate, he studied another photo. His eyes did the searching, his mind was elsewhere.

He had quit the chase, taken a job teaching at Mercer, when the last three he'd uncovered could not be prosecuted, or even exposed without fear of libel suits. Americans. Such an idealistic, forgiving people. Any crime, or criminal who could escape long enough, would find mercy in the American heart. The American psyche was a phenomenon in itself. A nation spawned by misfits and thieves, after two hundred years it was still a nation which instantly identified with an underdog. Oddly, the hardworking, honest, open, generous American *per se* enjoyed a delicious crime. Scum like Dillinger, Floyd, even massive wealth accumulated over the bodies of downtrodden workers, generated a certain respect from the very children of the victims. A colorful criminal in Americana was destined to become the same folk hero which Europeans accorded to royalty and rogues in their fairytales.

So determined were the American courts to protect the criminal, Otto had been warned not to expose a New Jersey janitor as a man who willfully executed a Yugoslavian village of sixty partisans. Nor, he was cautioned, should he bring such comments to the press unless he wanted to spend years in court fighting a countersuit for defamation of character. Three times that had happened. So Otto retired. Still, back there in his mind, deep down, he had toyed with the idea of finding those sonsofbitches and murdering them himself.

Why didn't he do it? He'd thought about it. Many times he'd thought about it. First, due to his intensive investigation, he would surely be a prime suspect. The injustice of seeing the tables turned, with himself portrayed as a gruesome murderer—this in itself was appalling. He would surely have been caught. Killing one criminal accomplished almost nothing. Killing all of the three he knew about would turn his vendetta into a gory bloodbath which might actually diminish the atrocities his victims had committed! God forbid that Otto give them an iota of glory or glamour even in death! However, the true reason he had not killed them was a very simple and basic conviction that dead men suffer nothing. Alive, in this life, on this planet, the swine at least stood a chance to suffer, even if no more than the slings and arrows of their daily existence. So he prayed for hemorrhoids, bedbugs, psoriasis, renal failures, or any pestilence God in His infinite wisdom might wish to cast upon the scum.

He knew before he started he wasn't going out Nazi hunting again. He knew by the ache in his knees and knuckles, the throb of arthritis on cool damp evenings. He knew by the head waggling on a stout neck as he shaved his face in the mornings. He was old. Say it, Otto, admit it! "I am old." Tell your ugly face. "I am old." Out loud! "I am old!" Too old to chase Nazis. Too tired. Spent. It was in God's hands now. May they be blest with intestinal parasites, that was his prayer.

He didn't believe in hell anymore. He'd seen hell. He'd felt the flames of perdition, the scald of urine, the scent of retching humanity, each a bald-headed likeness of all the other cargo in the swaying cattle car. Oh yes, that was hell.

He'd lost his faith. He'd lost his family. He'd lost, as did mankind as a whole, six million particles of himself. He'd been drafted into the Nuremberg spectacle, investigated the death camps, walked ground so blood-soaked it would smell for a decade.

"We didn't know!" the villagers declared. They knew. Children would run through the streets yelling, "Here come the death trucks, here come the death trucks!" They knew. The stench from the ovens permeated the land for 40 kilometers. Nothing smelled like burning flesh—they knew. They cried to the world, perhaps to their newborn in later years—"We didn't know!"

But they knew.

Otto rose heavily, a taste of bile on the back of his tongue. "Destroy it," Janet had said. Otto ran a finger over the covers of the books, stood looking at his desk covered with documents and photographs. He'd said he would. He didn't say when.

Yes, three or four days ago even, he would have been happy to give it up, forget it, return to his daily fishing and digging in this nonarable soil. It tortured his mind to remember, to see these visual reminders, bringing back the fear and dread he'd once known.

Otto rolled up his sleeves, dashed his face with cold brown water, a taste of iron in the liquid as he washed his mouth. He leaned against the vanity table, over the lavatory, water dripping from his face.

"You are an old man," he said to his image. "You fall to sleep before the television most nights, miss your news, can't see the newspaper too clearly anymore. Old, Otto, that is you. Older even than the 67 years you have lived."

He saw the bloated reflection, broken blood vessels on either side of his large nose. "Not a nose," he was fond of saying, "a proboscis, more aptly." He needed a haircut. Poor Jew bastard. His eyes dropped to the tattoo on his arm. That was his alone. Nobody else in the world had that number.

"Go to bed. And don't talk to yourself. It's a sign the wheels are creaking. Go to bed!"

He dropped his clothing on a platform rocker he'd been intending to repair—the arms were broken off. He turned on the air conditioner, closed the windows and bedroom door. Between the clean sheets he lay on his back in the dark, eyes open.

The pictures would not stop coming. He struggled with them, to contain them, but they would not stop. Flickering mental images projected upon a horrified mind, his stomach curling around a hot iron of agony, pictures he'd seen a thousand times and then a thousand more.

" . . . psychiatrist?"

"*Ja.*"

"Do you think you'd have time to talk to him?" the uniformed guard jabbed a finger at another guard. "I think sometimes he is crazy!"

Innocuous, nonsensical, unrelated dialogue neither witty nor tragic—why did it come to his mind now? A scent. Oh, God. Not that. Otto gasped air, quelling the twisting of his belly. His ears

144

roared with the air conditioner motor. Not the stink. Not the stink—

He vaulted from the bed, clawing for the wall, fingernails scratching paneled wood.

Screams . . . nails scratching concrete . . . the odor of . . . almost floral odor of—

He found the light switch, threw it, and his cheeks puffed as he rounded a corner and fell to his knees before the commode. Mouth agape, eyes bulging, his reflection in the toilet water. A deep retching sound, heaving, nothing there to give. Eyes watering, mouth open wide, tongue protruding. Oh, God!

"Don't call God. There is no God."

Purpled flesh, sunken eyes, furred tongues, their breath fetid from lack of food, bones cutting through flesh, the stench of feces and menstrual discharge, the whack of sticks and shuffle of feet— oh, God—

" . . . no God . . . "

Give it up, Otto. Do as Janet said. Destroy it! Put it out of mind, far away, think not—

He flushed the commode and slumped, watching spittle swirl and disappear going to water the tomatoes. His garden needed tending, almost daily care. If he should be away, even a week or two, who would pee around the perimeter? Who would drive off the predators?

His rib cage aching from the exertion, Otto rinsed his mouth at the lavatory. He refused to consider his nude body in the mirror. He turned off the light and returned to bed, chilled now as the air conditioner did its duty.

Four days ago—even three! He would have done it. Gladly.

Otto put a pillow between his bony legs, appendages which had always been too thin for the mass of the body they supported. He turned on his side, the cool air currents driving out heat, making his bed his nest, a haven.

If she had only called three days ago. Not now; now as though the cosmic forces of the galaxies clicked into place, as though extraterrestrial influences were sucking him into a vortex, a maelstrom, Otto could not comply. Pamela was, surely a remarkable child. She had done what the Jewish League and a horde of hunters much her senior had failed to do. In the books, documents, the mountain of material strewn throughout four rooms, Otto had caught a glimpse of a phantom.

The child had done it. An unbelievable, tedious and unrelenting pursuit. An assimilation of data predating her own birth nearly twenty years! Yet she had resurrected a ghost and his ephemeral shape took form in the body of a living, successful, respected American. His was not yet hell. But it would be. He would know hell, this man. This man was not a janitor grubbing for his daily bread. This man was rich, powerful, *happy!*

Otto drew a long, aching breath, exhaled slowly. Come, come, sleep. Tomorrow would dawn soon enough. Come, come to an old man and rest these brittle bones and tired sinews.

The air conditioner hummed away his thoughts, drowned the cries from long ago. His heart slowed, breathing easy, a muscle twitching here or there as he slipped ever deeper into the lower levels of slumber.

His last conscious thought: *brilliant. Remarkable child.*

CHAPTER THIRTEEN

"I WAS SURE WE HAD THIS ONE," Otto had said, in Hebrew.

"Too bad, my friend," Jules Lutze had replied. "Somebody else got him first."

"Dead," Otto had said, dully. Then, in German, he'd sworn softly. "All right. Jules, will you make it possible for me to get information from the Houston police?"

"I will call back momentarily."

Jules had done that. "See Lieutenant Doyle McElroy," he had instructed. "The name's Irish, but the lieutenant isn't. He changed his name when he moved south."

With thanks, Otto had then called for airline reservations and drove his halting, oil-burning automobile to Tallahassee. Now, with the Astrodome in the distance, he was here in Houston doing what he'd said he wasn't going to do anymore—chasing phantoms.

If Otto had been blindfolded and carried into the modern, air-conditioned building, he would have known immediately it was a

147

police station. Such places were alike the world over. Of course, there were the uniformed officers. But more, there was a sense of worry, melodrama, a faint scent of poverty from the people who sat on hard benches against the walls, waiting, waiting. At first, to a neophyte, it appeared there was a certain tension, an air of expectancy. But Otto now knew this was an error in judgment. The only emotion here was in the faces of the poor souls who had somehow run afoul of the law. A policeman's job entailed mountains of paperwork, ennui, boredom born of a calloused life. Styrofoam cups with coffee residue and smelly cigarette butts littered desks. Electric typewriters chattered, teletype machines rang insistently for attention and over it all the murmur of voices. America was one of the few nations which erected such modern facilities for its public servants.

Otto stopped outside an open, glassed door. Behind a cluttered desk stood a tall, broad-shouldered man, an empty holster on his belt. He was reading something on his desk, a large finger tracing the line, his lips moving silently. He sensed Otto's presence and looked up.

"I am Otto Ebenstein."

"Come in, Doctor. Close the door." This done, the detective nodded at a chair. "Dump that junk on the floor and sit down, won't you?"

They studied one another unabashedly. Then the detective lifted a thick file folder and dropped it on a far corner of his desk.

"I think this is what you want."

Otto opened the folder, nodded. "Am I in the way here?" he asked, without lifting his gaze.

"Take your time."

He read the forms, typographically inaccurate, abbreviated terms. Name: Fiedler, Hans L.; age (appx) 64; address: on down the page, "homicide."

"You are certain it was homicide," Otto remarked.

"Nobody dies like that on purpose."

148

"Torture?"

"The photos are there."

The coroner's report gave a slightly more scientific feel to a gruesome description of the agonies the man had endured before death.

"Very professional," Lt. McElroy noted. "Systematic. He probably didn't die until his assailant permitted it."

Otto examined an enlarged photo of a body, backside down on a table, wrists and ankles tied to the legs of the furniture. Shattered glass, a kitchen knife, and a garden hose lay on the floor.

"Any clues?" Otto asked.

"Nobody heard anything. Nobody saw anything. The old man lived on a very large plot of land; he had extraordinary security precautions. We surmise it was somebody he knew. He obviously let them in."

"Them?"

"A term of speech. One man could have done it. In fact we think one man did."

"Strong, large man?" Otto asked.

"Not necessarily. The few fingerprint smudges we found suggest a small delicate hand—one of the reasons I think it was a sexually motivated crime."

"Anything else make you think that?" Otto pressed.

"The nature of the torture employed. That garden hose isn't there to clean up the place. That, and the burns on the lower parts of the body. Look, see this wire? It's a stripped down lamp cord divided into two strands, twisted at the ends. The murderer plugged it in, touched the body here with one wire, then here with the other, completing an arc. He did it so many times it blew a fuse and he had to insert a penny in the electrical box."

Otto shuffled the photos slowly, examining each in detail. Hans Fiedler had met a fitting death, that was certain.

"Know what it reminds me of?" the detective said.

"Yes."

"That why you're here? Why Jules called in your behalf?"

"I don't know yet."

The policeman lit a cigarette, inhaled deeply, held it, exhaled. The smoke had disappeared, only a faintly bluish aura of fumes suggested the man had drawn on the cigarette.

"You know something I don't know, Dr. Ebenstein?"

"Nothing that will help you."

"Tell me one thing, am I wasting my time trying to solve the damned thing?"

"I really don't know." Otto handed back the folder. "If you are asking whether I suggest you suspend the investigation, I would say no. If you are asking whether I think you can solve it with any local perpetrator, I don't know that."

"I'm asking if this is a political crime."

"I'm not being evasive. I truly don't know."

"Would you tell me? Off the record?"

"No."

"Fair enough."

Otto stood, extended his hand. "But it does appear that way, doesn't it?"

The detective nodded, stubbed out his cigarette. "Last time I saw anything that methodical and cold-blooded was a series of homosexual murders here in Houston a while back. You may have read about it. Tortured young boys and killed them."

"Yes, I recall."

"But this one goes a step further," McElroy stated. "Things in this one are more like the Gestapo treatment. Do you agree?"

"I agree."

"Now, since your people contacted me after all these years—I am moved to assume it *is* a Nazi thing."

"Could be. I don't know yet."

"You'll let me know?" McElroy asked. "Curiosity."

"Jules will," Otto said. "When we know, and if."

"Take care, Doctor."

Otto had thought he might rent a car and drive to the scene of the crime, but that wasn't necessary now. The coroner's report, police description of the property, the photographs of the murder itself—he knew what he needed to know.

He had no idea who had committed the torture-murder. But he was relatively sure Lt. McElroy wasn't going to solve it locally. The Jew-turned-Irishman knew that. As a long-ago albeit brief associate of the League, the detective was given an inkling of what had happened by the physical evidence of the body. But then when Jules called, and Otto came, any suspicion the police officer had nurtured was confirmed.

The only thing Otto and McElroy did know was perhaps *why* the man was so killed. Neither of them had the vaguest notion who had done it. Even the why was purely speculation.

Otto confirmed his reservations on the next flight out, sought a remote booth in the airport coffee shop and sat brooding over the facts he had at hand. The only thing he had, concretely, was a slim connection between a fourteen-year-old child and the victim. And the child's father became the unknown in this equation. But the link between them, flimsy as it was, would warrant an investigation if the authorities learned what Otto knew at this moment. The evidence of the books, the European documents— damning all.

Pamela had an advantage in her search, obviously. She had not begun with a criminal who had disappeared, and hence where he had gone and under what identity was not her problem. She had begun with the suspicion that this new identity *was* a criminal. Armed with this, she had traced him back to his origins—and uncovered his secret.

Hans Luther Fiedler died in Chelmno in 1942. A native of Austria, born in Vienna, with one maternal grandparent and one paternal grandparent who were Jews, the good doctor had been seized by the Nazis. He was, truly, a doctor. In fact, a little-known physicist with a mathematical and inventive genius, the Jew had published several lengthy reports on his theories. If a like German Nazi assumed the doctor's identity, who would there be to betray him? Of the 240,000 Jews in Germany and Austria in the prefinal "solution" population, 210,000 were annihilated! Entire families, whole townships, every friend or acquaintance of the real physicist had been put to death.

Pamela's perseverance had paid off. Her mother had told Otto about the child's ability to listen to speech and determine a man's background influences. Undoubtably, this had led her to Cologne, Munich, the places where she had photographed birth certificates, school records, deeds, titles, up to December, 1944 when one Josef Braun Haas disappeared from the world, and Hans Luther Fiedler miraculously emerged in Canada, an escapee from the concentration camps. It was a beautiful coupling of like abilities, that of the exterminated Jewish inventor and the fleeing Nazi who had assumed his identity. Both were mathematicians, both were "doctors," but they were different in several ways, which Pamela's documents proved: Fiedler, the true Jewish physicist, would now be eighty-six years old. The man lying dead in Houston was "appx 64." A difference of 22 years! Further, from Pamela's meager account of this dead Jew, he was shy, retiring, hardly the kind of man to seek high government positions in the new country, or to be an articulate and willing speaker.

All right, true enough, Pamela did not have the kind of "hard" evidence that would hold up in court. But her case was clear and her suspicions strong. It certainly warranted an investigation. This Otto had begun, through normal channels in conjunction with his old ally and fellow detective, Jules Lutze. But, of course, Dr. Hans Fiedler was dead. Both of them.

Otto sipped acrid, too-strong coffee, then abandoned it as his flight was called. He nearly forgot his small bag and had to rush back for it. He paid his tab and with quick short steps made his way to the proper gate.

"Dep Houston 5:25 Arr Atlanta 8:10 EDT."

"Smoking or nonsmoking?" the ticket-taker inquired.

"Smoke." Otto's ticket was marked accordingly.

If Janet could drop in on Otto unannounced after two decades, Otto now mused, surely the same privilege was his. He stowed his bag beneath the seat, adjusted and hooked his seatbelt and sat staring out the window. Of one thing he was positive. He must meet this Pamela. In that young mind were locked the pieces of a puzzle which she had already constructed. Otto had an idea of the personality he faced based on Janet's descriptions.

What kind of child would assimilate all of this, put it all together, draw the conclusion that she was correct and had truly found a Nazi criminal — then casually abandon the entire project?

"She's been more like a child than ever in her life," Janet had commented on the telephone to Otto.

An actress? A child with such cool nerves, with her wits so controlled that she could fool her mother and father? And the father — how did the child see him in connection with all of this?

The airplane banked sharply, jets dropping to a whisper as Houston fell away below. Otto gazed without seeing at the patchwork quilt of farms, oil fields, and city, a hazy pall overhanging it all.

Whatever the girl was, Otto had to know. Whether she became a coconspirator or not, whether the child wished to discuss her findings or not, Otto wanted to learn what made that amazing young mind tick.

He was filled with anticipation. Like the electric moment before a curtain rises on a long awaited film spectacle, or opening night at the Met, with one's favorite tenor, baritone and coloratura in the wings. Otto respected intelligence, cunning, wile. He, above anyone else, could appreciate the calculating, deducting mental exercise in running a prey to ground.

He admired this child even before meeting her. Composed, aloof, her emotions and thoughts reined, playing her game with

153

deadly seriousness. Wiser than her mother, more sly and devious than her father; Pamela had slipped only here and there — by letting Janet uncover her search.

Otto recalled a penned note in a certain book. In German, but written almost like shorthand, the child had jotted a word which Otto could only translate as "Gotcha!"

Oh, indeed, this was something to be appreciated, to be anticipated! Otto accepted his order from the stewardess: two whiskeys, each double. He lit an unfiltered cigarette and inhaled with satisfaction. He so enjoyed his pleasures. At his age few were left to him. But good God, he trembled this instant with a feeling akin to lust as he savored the moment when he could meet this uncanny child!

"He's coming here?" Russell questioned.

"He's on his way, Russell!" Janet lamented. "I'm sorry."

"For what are you sorry?"

"That he's coming like this. Without warning. Pamela, please tell Eleanor we're having an overnight guest."

Russell looked slightly amused. "Why are you so upset by this, Janet? Did you not tell me he is an old college friend?"

"A professor, Russell."

"A friend you said."

"Yes, a friend, too."

"Then are you not happy he is coming to visit?"

"Russell, he didn't give me any warning!"

"How long ahead did you call before going to see him?"

"I admit that," Janet said. "But, well, thank you for being so understanding about it."

Pamela reappeared in the den, "I told Eleanor."

"Thank you, Pamela." The child and Russell were both staring at Janet with identically amused expressions.

"What's so funny to you two?" Janet asked.

"You're shook, Mother. Flustered. Is this an old beau?"

154

"Of course not."

"Hmmm," Russell looked at Pamela. "That thought had not been mentioned."

"But you thought it, I'll bet," Pamela said, grinning at her father.

"You two are talking nonsense," Janet said, peevishly. She was trying to collect her thoughts. "Perhaps I'd better instruct Eleanor about which bedroom to prepare."

"Say, this might be fun," Pamela stated.

Janet walked the hall hurriedly, the sound of Russell's laughter behind her. Pamela made another remark and Russell laughed harder, longer.

This was so unlike Otto! Almost flaunting himself! "Janet, I am on my way to your house for a long weekend stay. Should I eat before I arrive?"

"Otto, where are you?"

"At the airport here in Atlanta."

"Otto!" Janet had wailed. "Why didn't you call ahead and I would have met you?"

"No, no. I didn't wish to put you to any trouble. You and I can drop in on one another without fuss, can we not?"

"Yes of course, Otto."

"I'll be there, the taxi man says, in about an hour."

"Are you sure you don't want me to send a driver?"

"No, Janet. I look forward to seeing you."

"Otto?" Janet felt her throat tightening. "There's nothing wrong, is there?"

"Nothing whatever. I only wish to visit. No inconvenience is there?"

"You know there isn't! Come on," Janet declared.

Why was he coming here like this? Otto had never been to any place Janet had called "home."

"Don't be stupid!" Janet said aloud, to herself.

"What's that, Mrs. Roth?" Eleanor questioned.

"Nothing, Eleanor. Talking to myself I guess."

The maid dusted furniture, already dustless, and put fresh towels into the adjoining bath.

"Everything look all right to you, Mrs. Roth?" Eleanor asked, noting Janet's prolonged, frowning scrutiny.

"Looks fine, Eleanor. Thank you."

Together, Eleanor and Janet descended the spiral staircase. "I'll get some flowers for the vase upstairs," Eleanor volunteered.

Seized with a sudden embarrassed hesitation, Janet paused before entering the den. When she did, Russell glanced up from a magazine, eyes sparkling, and Pamela soberly studied Janet's face.

"Everything's ready," Janet said.

"Should we dress more formally?" Russell chided.

"I don't think that will be necessary."

Pamela giggled. "Mother, your face is scarlet. Are you worried?"

"Don't be silly."

"We'll mind our manners," Pamela said.

"You are both getting a big laugh out of this, I suppose," Janet observed.

"I don't ever recall you having a guest before," Russell said. "A personal friend of your own, I mean."

"No," Janet replied lightly, "I don't guess I ever have. I never had thought about it."

"Ah then, a first," Pamela said.

"Was that the doorbell?" Janet asked suddenly.

"No," Russell half smiled. "That was the hall clock."

"Maybe we ought to go stand in the driveway and watch for him," Pamela suggested.

"Sit down, Pamela," Janet said, without humor.

"I could go," Pamela offered. "I could wait until I saw him and begin screaming, 'Here he is, here he is!'"

"Just be your normal selves," Janet urged.

"I think we should pick our noses and scratch," Pamela said to Russell.

"I can think of worse," Russell added.

"Yes, well, part of the problem is, this man may exhibit the 'worse' you mentioned," Janet defended. "He is not always genteel, I'm afraid."

"Oh, phooey!" Pamela huffed. "I thought you were afraid *we* would embarrass *him!*"

"Certainly not!"

"There goes the fun, Pop."

"Pop!" Janet snapped. "I don't remember you ever addressing your father as Pop!"

"Sorry about that — Pappy."

Russell winked at the child.

"How about 'Father'?"

Russell considered this, shook his head.

"Padre?" Pamela said.

"Too religious," Russell protested. He began stuffing his pipe with aromatic leaves.

"That was the doorbell," Pamela said, eyes widening, looking at Janet. Only Russell did not look toward the hall. Eleanor passed — bless her, she had changed clothes! A murmur of voices and Eleanor appeared in the door of the den.

"Mr. Otto Ebenstein to see you," Eleanor announced.

"Show him in, please," Russell said, standing.

"Russell Roth," Otto came through the door, the slash of his mouth wide in a grin, "Russell Roth of the recent bent light laser transmission experiments!"

Russell shook Otto's hand and the two men stood looking at one another. Russell's face warmed and Janet was surprised to see him put a hand on Otto's shoulder.

"We have heard a good deal about you, Otto," Russell said. "How are you?"

"Never better. Ah," Otto turned, beaming, looking at Pamela.

The child smiled in a decidedly infantile manner, almost a wiggle in her posture. "This is Pamela," Otto whispered. He held out a hand which Pamela took. "You may call me Uncle Otto, if you wish," Otto said.

"Thank you," Pamela agreed. "I never had an uncle before."

"You have one now," Otto stated. "And soon a favorite, I hope."

"When you are the only, there's no problem," Pamela said.

"Janet." Otto put his hands on her shoulders, looking into her eyes. She hoped they did not mirror her distress.

"Janet, Janet, Janet," Otto said.

"Won't you sit down, Otto?"

Russell asked, "Would you like a drink?"

"With pleasure."

As Russell was working at the bar, Otto sat, his stomach nestled between spread legs, hands on his knees, gazing at Pamela. Child and man appraised one another, then both smiled. Otto patted his knee and to Janet's utter amazement, Pamela arose, walked over and sat on Otto's lap!

"Four times strong and with a spare bottle in the bin," Russell commented, delivering Otto's drink.

"A toast, Russell," Otto lifted his glass, one hand slipping around Pamela's waist. "To you, a genius, to your beautiful daughter so obviously a part of you—and to Janet who has brought us all together."

"Well put," Russell touched glasses, took a long sip. Stunned, Janet sat watching. "Janet," Russell said, "would you like to join us in a drink?"

"No," Janet stammered. "No, thank you."

CHAPTER FOURTEEN

THE EFFECT OTTO HAD on the Roth household was astounding and distressing to Janet. Since his first unannounced arrival nearly five weeks ago, Otto had been back to visit four times for a total of fourteen days! Any fear Janet might have had that Russell would resent this had been dispelled with the first visit. Never had she seen her husband warm so quickly to another man. Indeed, Russell *anticipated* Otto's arrival and even argued that Otto should stay longer each time.

"An amazing gentleman," Russell had commented. "He has an unusually perceptive and ingenious mind."

Russell was referring to Otto's grasp of electronics, lasers, communications systems and the computer sciences. One evening the two men sat in the den debating problems concerning recent experiments in the field of radio and TV transmission via "bent light" beams. Janet was astonished to hear Russell actually offer Otto a position with the company.

But if Russell was taken with Otto, it was as nothing compared

159

to Pamela. Janet witnessed an incident at the dinner table which she would have predicted would make Russell very angry. In passing a dish to Pamela, Otto suddenly began speaking German. Pamela replied in kind as Janet darted a glance at Russell for his reaction. Instead of the displeasure she anticipated, he joined in the exchange. It was as though a dam had burst — a rapid and animated intercourse ensued with all three of them speaking in turn. Then they howled with laughter.

"I am afraid we're being rude," Otto said, "Janet does not speak the language."

"No," Janet said, "but please don't let that stop you. I — I rather enjoy hearing it, actually."

"You do?" Russell questioned.

"Yes, certainly. German has a strength to it."

"Janet doesn't speak the language but she reads the mind," Otto said. "That was the point just made."

In German then, Pamela asked Otto something and the professor went into a long discourse, his voice rising and falling as both father and daughter hung on every word.

"Beautiful," Pamela said, when Otto halted.

"Ja," Russell nodded. He was beaming.

Later, Pamela told Janet, Otto had extolled the virtues of the Teutonic peoples, giving a moving history of their language and accomplishments, illustrating his points with lengthy quotations from the poets, philosophers and scientists "who made the German peoples the masterful race they were."

"He said that?" Janet questioned.

"His love for Germany and all things German is a powerful influence on Papa, I think," Pamela had said. "Papa said, in German, Otto rekindled his pride."

"Your father said that?"

"I always knew Papa was proud of being German," Pamela noted. "Even though he shunned the subject. It was written all over him, you could tell it. I think he missed the speaking of German, too. You know how he loves German music."

"He does?" Janet could think of nothing that would lead to this conclusion.

"Sure he does, Mother! Haven't you ever noticed how misty-eyed he becomes when the old German songs are sung?"

"Darling I don't ever recall hearing 'old German songs' sung. Where did you?"

Pamela went to the record library and the built-in Garrard turntable. There were speakers, but these were seldom activated. Usually, Russell listened with earphones, and for that matter, so did Pamela.

"Papa must have a couple hundred albums," Pamela said, selecting one. "From the classics to beer-hall group sings. Don't you ever listen to any of these?"

"No," Janet confessed. "I never have."

In another conversation, after Otto's third visit, Pamela said, "I'll tell you why Papa is so fond of Uncle Otto."

"I wish you would," Janet had said, testily.

"Because Uncle Otto talks about the good things. He's always telling me the great things about Germany. Papa appreciates that, I think. If Papa told me, it might seem that he was offering a defense. But Unclo Otto, a victim of Nazi hatred, when he tells me about these things, it carries more weight!"

"Otto told you of his experiences?" Janet asked.

"Not in so many words. I mean, he didn't dwell on it. He made a casual mention in passing. You know, he is a fantastic man. So—forgiving. He doesn't blame the German people at all."

"Who does he blame?" Janet questioned, brusquely.

"He didn't say. The Nazis. More precisely, the Gestapo segment of the Nazis."

Behind it all, beneath the jovial exterior and Germanic pride, the "perfect" things said to win over both Russell and Pamela, Janet felt an ulterior motive in the retired psychiatrist.

"Otto," Janet had asked when they were alone, "what are you up to?"

"Up to?" Otto's tangled eyebrows rose, eyes twinkling. "I'm up

161

to about your nose, perhaps. I don't think I shall grow any more. Possibly even, I am shrinking with age."

"Otto," Janet was less than gentle, "you are here for a reason. What is it?"

He had put a hand on her cheek, mirth gone. "Nothing, Janet. Be reassured. I will not hurt you or yours. I promise this. If you wish me to go—"

"Of course not." And if she did, how would Janet explain that now, to Russell and Pamela?

"I am after nothing, child," Otto said to Janet. "I have come to adore your family. But if too much bother this is—"

"Otto, please don't be silly! I am just worried."

How many times had Janet said it? How many times? To Russell and Pamela, now add Otto. He replied, "You worry much about little and like a wee terrier shaking a dead hare, you worry, worry, Janet. Relax. Enjoy. There is nothing sinister here. But I tell you, if my presence is a concern, no matter how slight, I will go. I know I have overworked my welcome. But such a delight, this family."

What could she say? Everybody was happy with everybody, except Janet! Moan and bitch, wasn't that what Pamela once accused? Janet had worked very hard to put aside the wiggling in her belly, the knot of tension she experienced when Otto and Russell sat chatting, smoking, drinking, enjoying one another. What could there possibly be in such a scene that strummed the chord of fear in Janet's mind? Like all the other foolish and unfounded fears—despite her own mental assurances, despite the *facts*—she still worried, dread a lump in her stomach.

"Otto," Janet had warned him, at pool side one afternoon while Russell and Pamela were away, "I could never forgive you if you hurt my family."

Otto studied her, somberly. He nodded.

"You aren't going to do that, are you?"

"No."

"What did you do with the books and photos I took to your place in Eastpoint?"

"As you ordered."

Why didn't she believe that? He met her eyes evenly, his tone and expression indicated nothing but sincerity. She had no reason not to trust this man! Yet, Janet worried.

She reasoned with herself that she was a bit jealous. This was true. Otto had come into their lives and in a few short weeks seemed to have captivated Janet's husband and daughter. Otto could do no wrong. He rambled endlessly, voice a monotone from too much drink, and still Russell and Pamela listened as though enchanted. Otto could be crude—breaking wind over cocktails—and it was as though no one heard the blubbery flatulence, or his burps at the dinner table. When Otto allowed his cigarette to touch fabric and burn a hole in the divan, Russell dismissed it with a shrug and had the furniture sent out for repair. Otto told a ribald story and Russell and Pamela collapsed with laughter.

"I think I have offended the lady of the house," Otto had commented. Thereafter, he told his off-color tales in German.

Janet was being excluded, invited to sit with them almost as though she were a new member of an old fraternity and the chummy older members had agreed to include her, but would rather not.

"We need clean towels for Mr. Ebenstein," Janet snapped in passing to Eleanor. "He's dropped them all on the floor again."

Overhearing this, Pamela had followed Janet to the linen closet. When Janet turned, Pamela reached out and took the bundle.

"Eleanor will do this for you," Pamela said.

"Eleanor has other things to do."

Pamela followed Janet up the stairs to Otto's guest suite.

"You don't like Uncle Otto anymore, do you?" Pamela queried.

"I like him fine," Janet retorted. "But I don't want him to live with us."

"I like him a lot, Mom."

"I see that."

"Papa, too."

"I see that, also."

"Are you jealous?" Pamela asked. "There's no need to be, you know. Uncle Otto adores you."

"I'm not jealous."

"Uncle Otto isn't taking anything away from you, or us. He's actually performing a function which is long overdue around here," Pamela said, hanging towels.

"Pamela, I am not in the mood for a psychological treatise on my reasons—but suffice to say, I am a bit tired of company right now."

The child fixed Janet with a contemplative gaze. "Haven't you noticed, Mother?"

"Noticed what?"

"We're a happier house! Papa has a friend. He needed a friend. I have an uncle. But first and foremost, Uncle Otto is your friend. It would be a shame to lose that."

The child was correct, wasn't she? Janet was being stupid, suspicious, doing what she had always done, wasn't she? Worrying. Fretting. Bitching! Damn it!

When Pamela went away on an annual back-packing hike sponsored by a school club, Otto had helped the child sew labels in all her clothing. He drove Pamela around town looking for this item or that which she felt the trek required. He counseled her on liquid "bug-chasers" and "Alpine packs" and the new "Space Age sleeping gear."

Janet was jealous, she admitted that to herself. Otto was providing Pamela something the child didn't, couldn't get from her father or mother—Otto knew about such things; had the time and inclination to accompany Pamela on shopping forays of this nature. Janet should be thankful, not resentful!

"While Pamela is away this week," Russell had unexpectedly

offered, "why don't you spend some time with me at the office, Otto? I want to show you some new projects we have underway."

For God's sake! Now the weekend visits had been extended to a week! Otto accepted. It was a hot, late August week of interminable length for Janet. With Pamela hiking in the north Georgia and south Tennessee mountains for seven days, and Russell staying late at the office with Otto—she bumped from room to room, irritated, sulking, being absolutely childish.

When Pamela came home, she had hugged and kissed "Uncle" Otto and Russell even before Janet. Now, ridiculous or not, Janet felt as though she had been displaced to third, and she bitterly resented it. Although later, Pamela had retreated to her bedroom with Janet alone to pore over three arrowheads and a sock filled with smooth shiny stones found in several mountain streams. The child rendered a two hour, step-by-step report with enthusiasm and sprinkled with an occasional new slang term she'd picked up in transit.

"Doesn't that blow you away?" Pamela said, bringing Janet's mind back to the present.

"I'm afraid I don't know that term," Janet said. Instantly she bit her tongue. Superimposing her parental big mouth on the moment burst the illusion between mother and child. Pamela's smile waned and she fingered the stones she had spread across her bed. She talked a while longer, but the momentum was gone. Janet cursed herself all the way into her own bedroom. Dumb, neurotic, paranoid—couldn't she keep her silence just one time and allow that child to be a child?

"Pamela didn't get as much tan this year," Russell said, glancing up from a book he was reading in bed.

"I'm going to take a bath, Russell."

The bathroom connected to Pamela's, and as Janet sank into a tepid tub, she heard voices, muted, conspiratorial, then laughter. The sounds came through a vent near the ceiling. Too muffled to distinguish individual words, but the tone was obvious enough—Otto and Pamela recounting her hiking trip, enjoying it anew, in a way Janet never could.

Janet closed her eyes. Who was she going to blame? Otto? Otto was responsible for bringing levity to this family which Janet had wanted and never accomplished. Blame whom then? Russell and Pamela had always gyrated toward one another, more now than ever. Be practical, be honest, Janet. You are your problem. Nobody and nothing else. You alone. Worry, worry, moan and bitch, that's you.

The tinkle of Pamela's laughter, Otto's mellifluous voice ooh-ing over some relic, happy sounds in Janet's ears. Her eyes closed, the bathroom door shut, Janet allowed her body to float in the tub, arms limp at her sides.

Then for a reason she could not identify, Janet wept, her tears dropping to the water, making tiny ripples crisscross over her submerged breasts.

Otto sat at his desk, a mug of hot coffee to one side. He tapped a photo with a nicotine-stained forefinger as he held the telephone to his ear.

"Hello?" a low voice as though not speaking into the receiver.

"Jules, this is Otto."

"Yes."

"Did you get the information?"

"Yes. It was who you said; Dr. Hans Luther Fiedler was in truth Josef Braun Haas."

"The Irishman in Houston asked for confirmation that this was something he couldn't solve. For his curiosity, he said."

Jules grunted into the phone. "I'll have to think about that, Otto."

"Up to you," Otto said.

"Do you have something else?" Jules questioned. Otto could barely hear him.

"Not yet."

"If you are onto something, you should enlist our full assistance, Otto."

"Never fear, Jules. I know."

The distant voice now spoke in Hebrew, "When will you come and see me, my friend?"

Otto replied in the same language, "I don't know."

"You don't fool me, you know."

"How is that, Jules?"

"The vibrancy of your voice tells me you are onto a chase, and you are holding back information."

"It may all be a waste of time."

"We could help determine that. We need a shot in the arm after all these years of nothing."

"When I know more," Otto still spoke Hebrew, "then I will contact you."

"I have your vow?"

"You have it."

"Good."

They hung up and Otto stared at the collage of photos, pieces of a past captured in stills. He pushed the button of a tape recorder and listened to the baritone male voice. It was not the words Otto wanted to hear, but rather the vocal inflections—Russell Roth's voice captured in secret during one of their lengthy conversations in German while alone in the den.

Once more, Otto read the report he'd gotten on the tape. He'd sent a copy to an Israeli linguist, a professor now retired, who had spent a lifetime analyzing dialects and languages. A man who did what Pamela could do, but infinitely better. "The subject is an educated man," the report stated. "From a cultured background, with formal education. If forced to submit a subjective report based on the manner of speech alone, I would conjecture the following:

"Born Berlin. Extensive and prolonged cultural advantages,

167

possibly involving travel to various countries but which influence was neither significant or lasting. In the mastery of English, American influence is most dominant, most recent, most pronounced. Vocal manipulation of the Germanic diphthong and consonant 'W' show concentrated speech alteration by the English-American influence. However, this influence was late in adult life, well after the subject was fully mature and speech patterns had been set.

"From early childhood the subject apparently knew educated companions; syntax and enunciation suggest good education at an advanced age. Speaks 'high' German. Societal influence in the formative years of preadolescence suggests the parents were probably affluent and themselves educated. Possibly nobility, the influence of which is suggested in the subject's persistence in 'formal' speech which, when carried into English, becomes stilted and 'old worldish.'

"To hazard a guess, and with only speech patterns from which to draw these conclusions, I would state that the subject is never truly relaxed, his subconscious now consciously altering his speech to conform to his present living conditions and the society in which he works and lives. Subtle variances of inflection are nonetheless quite like the fingerprints of one's hand—virtually unalterable despite conscious efforts to erase them. Hence, and again with caution, I would state that the subject spent most of his youth in Berlin, Germany. However, possibly during the formative years of early education, the subject attended school in Danzig; the Polish influence is evident in key words, primarily the pronunciation of certain names of cities, and names of composers he mentions on this tape. If I could hear him speak Polish, it would help confirm this summation. That he speaks it fluently I have little doubt.

"Subject probably received higher education in the Munich area. Conversely, however, the predominant influences of this period were less cultured than the subject himself. Similar here, I would surmise, to an educated man who deliberately adopts the argot of his companions to attain camaradarie which he might lose speaking in his usual manner.

"Following this young-adult period of his life, speech patterns suggest more extensive travel, with British, Canadian and American-English influences most dominant."

Otto lit a cigarette from the butt of one he was smoking. He sipped his coffee, the vapors bringing a pungent odor of whiskey to his nose. He gazed across Apalachicola Bay at the winking lights of a town six miles distant and the John Gorrie Bridge as it opened for barge and shrimpboat traffic.

So Russell lied. About the hardships and privations of his youth. But that did not make him a criminal. Besides, he had lied only to Janet—he told Otto none of these tales of childhood hunger, cold and parental influences. He may have concocted such stories to put off his wife's probing inquiries. For whatever the reason, however, Russell Roth had lied.

Otto sipped the laced coffee, his elbows on the desk. He had gone to Atlanta with the intentions of meeting the child. Not altogether for that, although that's what he'd told Janet. Otto had presented himself with an outward nonchalance and joviality which masked his covert intentions. He had gone to the Roth home specifically to see Russell. More specifically, to see Russell's left ear! To see if the two marked photos in Pamela's books were youthful portraits of the man now residing in Atlanta. He had not been disappointed. He was relatively sure, the two obscured faces Pamela had marked were identical. Of course, it was possible that two men could both have a small piece of the ear missing. As with the officers in the photos, Russell had a part of the lobe gone.

Otto had seen many men with ears like that. Frostbite in frozen cattle cars, in barren prison camps, working as ill-clothed forced labor in unheated factories—the exposed ears blackened and

169

peeled away. So he had no doubt that the tale Russell told about frostbite was true enough. But as to whether this occurred in Russell's youth—this Otto had no way of knowing.

Another lie: Russell stated he had first "gone to war" in his early teens. Yet, judging from his appearance, Russell was an infant in World War I. By the time Germany engaged in the first battle of World War II, Russell would have been in his twenties.

Otto had stolen a wine glass from which Russell drank. He had recorded the fingerprints and sent them to Jules. It was an exercise in futility. It would prove nothing. Unless, by sheer luck, the League had a known criminal's fingerprints in their files.

Jules, with contacts around the globe, had done a complete check. The only results had come from the American FBI—the report stated that the fingerprints belonged to Russell Roth! That was true. The question *was*, did they belong to anyone else? Jules could not answer this.

Otto sat, chain-smoking, sipping coffee gone cold, the house dark now that the sun had set. Coming across the causeway over the long bridge, automobile lights flicked like strobe units, brief flashes between concrete supports.

"Are you onto something?" Jules had asked. Otto had said he didn't know. But he was. He could feel it in his old bones. He was. One final chase, before it was all over. And if he was wrong? Otto doused his cigarette in an overflowing ashtray. If he was wrong? Well. Then. He'd gained a remarkable "niece" hadn't he?

CHAPTER FIFTEEN

SATURDAY FOLLOWING THANKSGIVING, Otto still remained as a guest from the previous weekend. This at Russell's insistence and with Pamela's concurrence. For six days the three of them had been locked in fiercely competitive games of Scrabble. To offset Pamela's disadvantage against her father and Otto, the child had been given unlimited advance use of an unabridged dictionary. The hours of silence, while the trio stared at the criss-cross of words, drove Janet to distraction. She had paced the house, gone shopping, then returned to find the games still in progress.

She sat now on an open side porch, facing the drive, bundled in a sweater against the rainy chill of a sunless day. An automobile with Tennessee license plates pulled into the rear entry, wind-shield wipers lazily swiping. It was several minutes before the driver stepped out. He started to round the house toward the front door when Janet called to him.

"May I help you?"

"Yes ma'am. Looking for Pamela Roth."

"I'm Mrs. Roth."

He came across a carpet of lawn to the shrubs bordering the covered porch. He held out something at arm's length. Janet saw a small photo, identification, and a badge.

"Mrs. Roth, I'm Detective Bonifay, from Chattanooga. Could I speak with you for a few minutes?"

"Certainly. Go around back and I'll let you in the kitchen."

Janet paused at the den, in passing, and considered calling Russell, but decided against interrupting their game. She entered the empty kitchen; Eleanor was off for the day. Opening the Dutch door portal, she invited the plainclothed policeman inside. He removed a lightweight coat which Janet hung on a peg by the back door.

"Would you care for coffee?" she inquired.

"That'd be appreciated. Beautiful kitchen."

"Yes, it is. Thank you." Janet poured two cups, placed cream and sugar on the table, then joined the officer.

"Mrs. Roth, have you or any members of your family been in Chattanooga recently?"

"Not to my knowledge."

He stirred his coffee despite the fact he had put nothing in it. He tapped the rim of his cup with the spoon and laid it in the saucer. This done, he took a sip, looking over his cup with dark brown eyes.

"I didn't get your name, I'm sorry," Janet said.

"Bonifay. Charles Bonifay."

"Why do you ask, Mr. Bonifay?"

"To tell the truth, I'm down here on my day off, Mrs. Roth. I've been assigned to a case—an unusual case, and we're investigating every conceivable angle, every clue."

"All right."

The policeman got up, went to his coat and pulled a small paper sack from the pocket. Returning to the table, he opened the sack, which had been rolled, and pulled out a red and blue knit cap.

"Have you ever seen this before, Mrs. Roth?"

"May I see it?" Janet turned it inside out, heart beat lifting. Pamela's name and address were on a label sewn inside.

"It belongs to my daughter."

"Your daughter?"

"Yes. Pamela."

"Has she had occasion to go to Chattanooga, for any reason?"

"No. She's a student. Fourteen."

"Oh." The officer began stirring his coffee again. "Fourteen."

"Yes."

"That takes care of that. Mrs. Roth, we found this cap near the scene of a crime. Like I say, we're investigating every little thing, no matter how far-fetched. You understand?"

"I think so."

"Could your daughter have loaned this cap to somebody?"

"I really don't know."

"Would it be possible for me to speak with her?"

"Mr. Bonifay, let me introduce you to my husband. If you will come with me—"

They entered the den, the police officer looking it over with open admiration. He commented on one of the oils hanging over the fireplace. Then with introductions completed, the detective still standing, he exposed the cap which Janet now realized he'd been holding slightly behind his back.

"My cap!" Pamela said, instantly. "Hey, thanks! That's my favorite cap. Where'd you find it?"

"You lost it?" Bonifay questioned.

"Yes I did."

"Do you recall where?"

"Sure! Chattanooga."

"Chattanooga," Janet said. "Pamela, what were you doing in Chattanooga?"

"Oh, yeah," Pamela said, softly. "Well, I went there to catch a bus home after the hiking trip, Mother."

"Catch a bus?" Russell asked. "You have not mentioned this before, have you?"

"No, Papa, I didn't. I didn't want to worry anybody, but I got sort of queasy up in the mountains. They offered to drive me home, but I told them I'd take a bus from Chattanooga so it wouldn't break up the hike, you know. Anyway, that's where I lost the cap. In the bus station."

The officer relinquished the cap. "Well, here it is," he said, "no worse for the wear."

"Except dirty," Pamela stated. "Hey, really, thanks for bringing this back."

"A bit far for a policeman to come only for returning lost items," Otto commented.

"Guess that covers it," Bonifay smiled. "Sorry to bother you folks."

"Thanks again," Pamela said. She was back at the Scrabble board, studying the words.

"My pleasure. Good day."

When Janet returned from seeing the policeman out, she found Russell hotly questioning Pamela.

"Pamela, I told you before, if your plans change you are required to telephone. We would have come for you if you were ill."

"Papa, there's no problem!"

"There is a problem, Pamela! You do not have permission to catch a bus from Tennessee to Atlanta. I think too, you know this was wrong. Otherwise, why did you not mention it to us?"

"I told you, Papa. I didn't want to worry anybody. I caught the bus, no harm done, and by the time I got home I felt fine!"

"Pamela, I am angry about this."

"I'm sorry I have made you angry, Papa. It's a short ride, a safe ride, and I did what I thought was best for everybody. I didn't want to cause an inconvenience to the hiking club or to you."

"I don't understand why somebody from the hiking club didn't call us," Janet interjected.

"They didn't," Pamela said, "because I told them a teeny lie."

"What?" Russell demanded.

"I told them I had already called to tell you I was catching a bus home."

"That changes nothing," Janet snapped. "They still should have confirmed it. At least when the club arrived home. If anything should have happened, we wouldn't have known a thing about it!"

"They did call, Mother. Well, actually, I called the hike master, Mr. Latham, and told him I had gotten home all right."

"Pamela, this is the same situation as the house party," Russell said, sharply. "You altered your plans, went your way, and we discovered it through no admission of your own."

"I'm sorry, Papa."

Russell's eyes darted hither and yon, angry flits accompanied by corded muscles in his jaw and neck. "Again I restrict you to the grounds, Pamela. This time for a month."

"Oh, Papa! Really! That's too long."

"Three weeks then."

"Papa!"

"A month would have been right," Janet said.

"Three weeks," Russell stated. "That is final."

Pamela jumped up, bumping the Scrabble board, scattering the words into a jumble of letters. She ran into the hall and upstairs.

"I am sorry you were a witness to this, Otto," Russell apologized. Otto lifted a hand, waving away concern, gathering the game to put it away.

"She has never given us trouble before," Russell said to Janet. "Now twice she has done this!"

"Actually, Russell," Janet defended, "except for being thoughtless, there was no harm done."

"I think you—possibly Pamela—miss the point," Russell said, ominously. "I do not worry that Pamela will scrape her knee or get lost. But in these times, so many things can happen to a person, especially a child. Do you agree, Otto?"

"I do."

"Routine followed," Russell stated, "deviations noted, and communication—these are a form of security, Janet."

"This is so," Otto remarked.

"We must be able to depend on Pamela for this. Then if she does not appear where she is supposed to be, or if she does not return on time, we can be quickly and properly alarmed. But if she developed a history of such things as these two times, we might sit and worry for hours, or days!"

"Perhaps you should explain to Pamela just that way," Otto said.

Russell nodded, thinking. "Yes, the fault may be mine, Otto. I have not impressed her with the reason why."

"She is, after all, a young lady," Otto smiled. "Knowing what you have just said, she will feel less like a reprimanded child."

"I agree with Otto," Janet concluded.

"Then I shall explain," Russell walked out and Janet heard his footsteps ascending the stairs.

After a moment, Otto said, "As for me, I think it is time to go home."

"Not because of this dispute," Janet said, but she wished he would go.

"It has been one of the most enjoyable holidays of my life, Janet." He cupped her face with two hands.

"We enjoyed having you, Otto."

He nodded, the flesh under his chin rippling.

"Do you want me to drive you to the airport?" Janet asked.

"No. I shall get a cab."

"Russell won't hear of that."

"Then we shan't tell him." Otto walked from the room throwing his weight heavily from side to side with each step. Janet picked up Pamela's cap. It was the one they'd bought for the trip to Europe. The name tag had been sewn in by Pamela and Otto. The cap was dirty, stained with a reddish clay. Janet took the cap to the utility room and threw it into a hamper.

It occurred to her, the policeman hadn't said precisely where he'd found the cap. Nor, she now realized, had he mentioned the nature of the crime. At any rate, Pamela's explanation seemed to satisfy him. More, he seemed almost disappointed! Janet closed the laundry room door, reentering the kitchen. Being a policeman must be a depressing sort of occupation. Thank God she wasn't married to a man who made a living carrying a pistol!

Otto rented an automobile at a downtown hotel. It was a cold, rainy night and the interstate glistened with reflected headlights as he drove north. Chattanooga was, as Pamela noted, not a long trip. Otto extended an arm, the sleeve of his cardigan riding up over the luminous dial of his watch. He should be there by midnight. Both hands on the steering wheel again, cigarette between his lips, he maneuvered the vehicle without conscious thought. Tires whirring, sucking at the rain-slick highway, the wipers keeping cadence, rain falling harder now, he felt his stomach knotting with tension.

Before leaving Atlanta, he had pieced together the "time before" when Pamela "went her way" without telling her parents. No specific date was mentioned. Otto had approximated that by something Pamela said when he stopped in her room to say goodbye.

"I was restricted the last two weeks of July," she sulked. "I missed going to Theater Under the Stars to see *Barefoot in the Park.*" The child went on to complain, "Now I'll be restricted up to Christmas holidays!"

"You know why," Otto had said.

"Sure I know why! You heard it."

"The why is because you scared your father and mother who love you dearly."

In a most childish gesture, she tossed her head, blond hair lifting, eyes moist and near tears. He had kissed her on the forehead and she'd clung to him, suddenly sobbing.

"Three weeks is not forever," Otto soothed.

"I know. I asked for this."

"Soon enough, the time will pass."

"I'm so stupid," Pamela said, now angry. "I could have covered this better if I'd simply told them what I did!"

"Ahhh," Otto waggled a finger at her, "that is a wise deduction, my dear."

The rain was coming in wind-driven sheets, forcing Otto to drive slowly. He had a bad taste in his mouth. He was going to Chattanooga to learn something he didn't want to learn. He hoped—no, *prayed* he was wrong.

While in the hotel, arranging for this rental car, Otto had called the airline to check on flights to Houston. It was possible to leave Atlanta, go to Houston and fly back at several times of the day or night.

It was ridiculous of course. That Pamela should in any way be connected with a crime as horrible as Fiedler's torture and murder. The child was, after all, only a child!

That thought brought back a vivid recollection of a day in 1941. He'd been a visitor to Zagreb, seeking a position with a hospital there after having been refused residency in his own anti-Semitic country. He'd gone to Yugoslavia because he'd heard they needed a psychiatrist at the institution. The trip had been wasted. But motoring back again, under false travel permits, he had come upon a group of Communist youths. Children aged ten or twelve, possibly thirteen, wearing armbands of the Red partisans. A boy halted Otto's car, a rifle slung on the lad's back, the weapon almost as long as the bearer.

"Identification, please."

Otto remembered the cold fingers of fear as he produced the necessary papers to pass. For the moment, these "children" were soldiers. If caught, they would be executed by the proper authorities. If they should decide to do it, the same children could and would execute any official they caught in this illegal roadblock.

Otto had no illusions about "children." But America was not Zagreb. Pamela was no rabid partisan youth imbued with the fanatic doctrines of her adult leaders. She was an American girl from an affluent and respectable home. Violence would be as alien to her as the moons of Jupiter. Yet, here, now, a policeman had made an unexpected appearance at the Roth home—it merited the time and expense of going to the Tennessee town.

Otto arrived at 3:00 A.M. Checking into a motel at the foot of Lookout Mountain, he realized it was Sunday. He was exhausted from the tensions of bad driving conditions and long hours with no sleep. He took a hot bath, smoked a final cigarette and sipped two fingers of bourbon. It was daylight by the time he finally went to sleep.

"You were at the Roth house, weren't you?" Detective Bonifay questioned.

"Yes I was."

"What's your interest in this?"

Otto shrugged his shoulders, unsmiling. "It must be obvious, the parents are affluent. They want details. You brought the matter to them originally. Now they are concerned and want their fears put to rest."

"They don't have anything to worry about," Bonifay said, his chair creaking as he leaned back.

"You object to telling me more?" Otto asked.

"Nothing much to tell. We found the kid's cap in a field near the scene of a crime, that's all."

"What was the nature of the crime?" Otto pressed.

"Murder."

"I see."

"Pretty bloody mess. That kid couldn't have done it. So, reassure her family and tell them to forget it."

"Where did this take place?"

"About six miles south of town, just off the interstate going into Alabama. Farm house."

"Any motive?"

"Kook," Bonifay said, his patience wearing thin. "Torture murder. Sex kook most likely."

"I see."

"The kid's clear," Bonifay stood. "The hat was a grab at a straw. We didn't have the first clue and I had nothing better to do with my day, so I drove down to check her out myself."

"Thank you, Mr. Bonifay."

The detective nodded, hands hung from his pockets by the thumbs. Otto exited and drove to the newspaper office. There, in a recent issue, he got details the police officer had not provided. He spoke to the reporter who had covered the crime, an effeminate youth in his early twenties. Otto told the reporter that he was considering a magazine article on the matter.

"Yeah?" the lad said. "It's a juicy one. Think maybe I could squeeze in on that?"

"Could be," Otto said. "It's still speculation, you understand, I don't have a go-ahead on the piece yet."

"I understand that," the reporter said, quickly. "But being right here and all, I could do legwork for you. Cheap I mean."

"How about photos?" Otto asked. "Did you get any?"

"Yeah, but unless you're writing a pulp piece, these won't be any good. Too gory."

The young man pulled out a series of "contacts," a sheet of paper with tiny 35mm exposures the size of the negatives. It was from the "contact" that an experienced photographer selected the exposures he wished to have enlarged.

"Suppose you could blow up a few of these?" Otto asked.

"I don't know. They're pretty tight in developing. Holidays coming up and all."

"I would pay, of course."

"Costs five bucks each, commercial."

"When could you have them?" Otto asked.

"This afternoon maybe. Tomorrow sure."

"Make it this afternoon," Otto suggested, "and blow up one of each." He peeled off a hundred forty dollars and gave it to the reporter.

"I share the by-line, how about it?"

"If there is one," Otto said, "you share it."

"A deal!" The reporter brought his hand around in a swinging arc, culminating in an enthusiastic shake.

Following the newspaperman's instructions, Otto drove a winding country road. Even if Pamela had known this man's address, how could she have gotten here without transportation?

He found the remote frame farmhouse amid a weed-choked yard. It seemed abandoned. He circled the structure, climbed rickety back steps and cupped his hands to see through wavy panes of glass. The kitchen. Filthy. Cluttered, He tried the door. It was locked, bolted and chained with a notice that the grounds were closed except to sheriff's office personnel.

Otto looked across the trash-strewn rear yard, encircled by a barbed wire fence at the very back. He became aware of a buzzing sound, like bees in the distance. He pushed through waist-high grasses, tracing the noise.

He topped a rise and halted. From here to the house was maybe a hundred yards. Below and before Otto, twin ribbons of concrete cut through gently rolling hills and stretched away north. Despite all his driving, he was very near to Chattanooga, the skyline vis-

181

ible just beyond Lookout Mountain. The buzzing sound was tires on the highway, traffic moving at high speed. A person could walk from here to the city. Getting back would be simple, then. A stolen bicycle, perhaps. Hitch a ride to the bus station. Most people would give a lift to a young girl walking the highway.

He retraced his steps, drove the long winding route back to the city and arrived in time to catch the newspaper reporter before the office closed.

The reporter watched Otto go through the photographs. "Ain't that something?" the young man commented. "They tied the poor bastard to the table by his arms and legs. Took off his clothes. Somebody was mad with him."

Otto studied the scene, broken glass strewn around the floor, a butcher knife lying to one side.

"The killer scalded him. They found the tea kettle melted on the stove. I blew up a shot of that, too."

Otto put the 8-x-10 photos into a manila folder.

"I think you're right," he said, "these are too much for my periodical. But since I've paid for them, I suppose I'll keep them."

"You won't forget me, if you need legwork hereabouts?"

"No," Otto said. "I won't forget."

There were four major taxicab companies. For a small fee, Otto was allowed to check the call sheet on the day in question. From this he located the driver and described Pamela.

"Oh, yeah, I remember that girl." The driver removed loose tobacco from chapped lips with two oil-stained fingers. "She wanted to drive out the interstate south and right out of the blue she says 'stop' she wants out. My fare stopped there too, lemme tell you. I had to drive twenty miles before I could turn around! Swift chick. Outsmarted me. I'll know next time, believe me."

Otto offered the driver five dollars, thanked him, turning to leave.

"What's the problem with this kid?" the cabbie asked.

"We're hunting a runaway."

"American girl?"

"Yes," Otto said, "she's American."

"This ain't her then. This was a foreign kid, I can tell you. Had an accent."

"Accent?" Otto paused. "What kind of accent?"

"Russian or something."

"German, possibly?"

"Naw. I spent some cold days and warm nights in Germany. I know German. *You're* German. Naw, this was sort of like Polack, maybe."

"Polish?" Otto said.

"Yeah. Polish!"

CHAPTER SIXTEEN

COLD DECEMBER WINDS GUSTED through the canyons of Manhattan, sweeping from north to south into the garment district. Otto carried two heavy boxes into a narrow, dark building constructed between two taller structures. He rode a noisy, drafty elevator to the fourth and top floor. The only illumination here came from skylights of smoked glass. He walked the short hall to a solid door offering no number or name. He knocked.

"Yes, who?" a voice from within.

"Otto."

He heard a bolt, the turn of tumblers. A short, heavy woman with iodine-red hair peered at him through thick spectacles, unsmiling. "Come in," she commanded.

Otto placed both boxes inside the door and she locked it behind them.

"Otto!" A whispery voice, Jules approaching with arms outstretched. They hugged one another, solid pats to the back, and

Jules stepped away, his perpetually flushed face giving him the semblance of a windburnt outdoorsman—precisely what he was not.

"Come in, come in," Jules said, waving a pale hand toward the rear office. Each board of the bare floor met tongue-in-groove, with a rippled effect, the planks worn by years of scuffling feet.

"Your trip?" Jules abbreviated.

"Fine." Otto removed his coat, dropping it on a chair stacked with folders, boxes, newspapers. "Cold. It is still warm in Florida."

"I must go there sometime," Jules whispered. He shut the door, emptied a straight-back chair by tilting it to dump the contents.

"Well," Jules sat behind a desk overflowing with a mass of clutter. "Well. How have you been, Otto?"

"Older, quieter, at peace with myself, until this," Otto said, indicating the boxes he'd brought.

"Interesting, isn't it?" Jules said softly. He wiped his watery eyes, rubbed rimless glasses on his shirt and donned them again.

"Did you make inquiries in Chattanooga, Jules?"

"I did. For nothing. Except the obvious similarity between that one and the Houston case, nothing. That much you knew already."

"Still don't know who the Chattanooga man was?"

"No. We aren't likely to know ever, of course. He was known as a retired, seventy-year-old handyman, so far as the Tennessee authorities are concerned. No motives, no enemies. It's being treated as a sex crime, which we are sure it is not. And you, Otto? What have you on all of this?"

"May I smoke?"

"Certainly."

Otto lit a cigarette, looked about for an ashtray and seeing none, dropped the match on the floor. Jules watched without comment.

"Since the Tennessee police officer saw me at the Roth home," Otto said, "I cannot personally pursue the matter any further with him. It may cast suspicion on the Roths."

Jules nodded. He leaned back in his chair, one foot on an open drawer, pink hands clasped atop a rounded belly.

"It is my opinion the two deaths are related," Otto said. "Both men bound to a table, tortured, too many similarities to ignore."

His voice susurrant, Jules questioned, "The girl had something to do with them?"

"I think so."

"All right," Jules said. "You brought the photos you mentioned on the telephone?"

"They're in these boxes." Otto reached into an inside pocket of his coat and withdrew one of the color photographs. He gave this to Jules. "That mean anything to you?"

Jules studied the windowless, white concrete building. He shook his head.

"What is it?" Jules asked.

"I don't know. If you look closely, it appears to be part of a park. You can see people strolling in the background. In the distance is a marker of some sort."

Jules took a magnifying glass from his center desk drawer, adjusted a gooseneck lamp and studied the photo.

"Notice that double door, Jules."

"Steel. Heavy." Jules spoke, head down, "What does this suggest to you, Otto?"

"I don't know. But there are photos in the boxes which cover that building from front to back. I don't believe this girl would take the photos for no reason. She does everything with a purpose, I am convinced of that."

"From what you have said," Jules agreed, "she is very intelligent."

Otto tore open one of the boxes, removed the two books with

186

marked photos. They studied them together. "The one with the binoculars is artillery," Jules observed. "The man circled is SS." He studied the other marked photo. "SS again," Jules said. "Signal, motor transport, I can't see the insignia clearly."

"I don't recognize the uniform," Otto said.

"The uniform is SS," Jules explained. "But which branch I can not be sure without a better view of the insignia."

They spent the morning going over the contents of how Pamela had traced the man called Fiedler back to a point where she discovered it was not *the* Hans Fiedler.

"Very impressive, Otto."

"We don't know who the man in Chattanooga is," Otto said, "but I'm willing to bet Pamela Roth knew."

"And she killed him?"

"I don't know."

"Could she perpetrate such a crime?" Jules whispered.

"I don't know."

"As a psychiatrist, have you noted a change in her personality since the murders?"

"According to all I can judge from the unwitting parents, apparently not."

"Your professional judgment, Otto? Is she psychologically sound?"

"She isn't insane, if that's what you mean."

"A good, clean, wholesome, teen-age American girl from an upper-class environment, but you suspect she indulges in the psychotic murders of elderly men—this is sane?"

"I did not say she does these things. I said I don't know."

"But you suspect."

"That she has some connection with it, yes."

"What do you want of the League, Otto?"

"I need help."

"Ummm-hmmmm. What type of help?"

"Somebody to look over all this material, a fresh eye."

"That will be done," Jules stated.

"Somebody in Europe who can verify some of these documents. Follow them up."

"Very well."

"Also," Otto said, "I would like to have this child put under surveillance."

"When?"

"Now."

"For how long?"

"Until she makes another contact. Such as this trip to Chattanooga."

"You speak of twenty-four-hour days, seven days a week perhaps for months!"

"This is true."

"Otto, this will cost a fortune!"

"I need the best men possible," Otto continued. "With proper equipment. We must not lose her when she goes after the next one."

"You mean *if* she goes, Otto. We don't know that she goes at all, or ever will again."

"I think she will."

"Can you prove that?"

"Not conclusively."

"You are speaking of three men minimum, Otto."

"Someone has scored twice, Jules."

"Once, Otto. Hans Fiedler. Once! We do not have confirmation on this man in Tennessee."

"But you know he is one of them."

"I don't know a damned thing. I see many interesting and bizarre things here, Otto. But I know nothing!"

"You feel I am correct, don't you, Jules?"

"I feel nothing."

Otto smiled. "I want surveillance to commence at once, Jules.

The best men. What they see and learn they must forget. It is not my purpose to expose this child. I wish only to learn how she knows who these men are—and how many more there are. Call upon only your very best and most trusted men, Jules."

"Otto, we do not have the funds we once had."

"You can get the money, Jules. With a couple of telephone calls. You can do it."

"You come asking for this kind of equipment and manpower—not to track a suspected Nazi, Otto. To track a suspected child! How do I justify this?"

"You can do it, Jules."

"Otto," Jules reverted to Hebrew, "how do I explain this expenditure with a reasonable expectation of success? It has been more than thirty years since 1945! All the remaining criminals are old men now! We do not have the interest of the world any longer. Money is difficult to secure, more and more with the passage of time. I must have assurance of results! We have not apprehended anyone of value in ten years! Do you see this? Have you been listening to television? Israeli detectives uncovered three men recently. Nazi criminals from Latvia. They will be months bringing them to trial. A woman not long ago voluntarily allowed herself to be deported and will soon go on trial in Germany. She was a guard in a concentration camp. Old woman, Otto. People see the old woman and the old man shuffling in short sick steps and they don't imagine the crimes these people have committed! Do you understand my position?"

"I understand."

"I must have assurance."

"Your assurance is in your Jewish bones, Jules. You *feel* it, as I feel it—this is the chase. This is perhaps our last opportunity to catch a few—some—maybe many—and you know it."

Jules removed his glasses, dabbed his eyes, looking at Otto with that peculiar expression so common to myopics.

"My cigarette bothering you?" Otto inquired.

189

"No. I need new glasses."

"Why don't you get them?"

"My meager social security check does not permit such extravagances, Otto."

"Why are you saying such poor-mouth things?" Otto demanded irately. "I know and you know you can do that which you wish to do! Are you losing your spirit, Jules?"

The red-faced man slowly replaced his spectacles then sat gazing at Otto a long time before speaking. "I suppose I am," he said in Hebrew. "Losing my spirit. One cannot spend one's adult life in the pursuit of men such as these and not suffer. In the beginning, we were inundated with eager, intelligent, dedicated personnel. Money came from a thousand donors, the governments of the world jumped to give our requests priority. No longer, my friend. Now we are tired relics from a war three times removed from the present, and Vietnam undid more than the American resolve. I have been reduced to a beggar. No salary. No expenses. A tired old dinosaur sitting in this donated office playing detective with ghosts. My grandson comes over with his mother, my daughter. Raised in a kosher home was my daughter. The boy, now seventeen, is an honor student. Handsome, alert, a fine Jewish boy! But dating a gentile girl. He does not attend the synagogue because it is 'out of step' and when I mentioned Masada he thought it was a rotary engine."

Otto lit a cigarette, a reason to look away.

"They don't care any more, Otto. Nobody cares. If a proven Nazi murderer is living next door to a man these days, chances are he would not receive so much as a stone through his window! Nobody cares."

"I doubt that, Jules," Otto said. But he didn't doubt it.

In Hebrew, Jules spoke in whispery tones, "It is true, Otto. We are of another era. Old men talking old wars and old crimes. That is all."

A long silence settled over them, Otto's tobacco smoke curling upward toward the gray skylight, the room cold. Fully ten minutes passed before Otto spoke again.

"It's perhaps our last chase, Jules. I do not profess to know what is happening. I don't fully understand how this child has learned what she's learned or why she is doing whatever it is she's doing. But I know she is on to them. Two down. How many more to come? I do know this: Hans Luther Fiedler, the Jew dead in Chelmno, must surely rest easier knowing the Nazi who took his name has met a suitable end.

"The League needs a shot in the arm, you told me. A success. Maybe we get it with this. Maybe not. Maybe the girl has nothing to do with any of this—but maybe she does."

Jules sat, eyes closed.

"I can smell the spoor, Jules. So can you. Two old dogs gone stiff from kennel care—we smell the trail and the sap of youth is flowing again slowly, but flowing! We know they're out there, Jules. We can feel it! You can get the men, and the money, and if we fail how much worse can it be than it is sitting here surrounded by dusty yellowed papers and old photographs? Of course, if we succeeded—ah, well, what a final chase it will have been for two tired hunting hounds, eh?"

"To pay for the salaries, the expenses, this will break us financially, Otto."

"Do you smell the Nazi scent, Jules?" Otto leaned forward, voice lowering. "Can you sniff that excitement of the quarry running hard and far ahead? He thought he was secure, this old man of the wild, but we've picked up his trail again, haven't we?"

"My contacts are not what they were once," Jules said.

"We need only follow this child, Jules."

Jules nodded, eyes still closed.

"Begin surveillance at Christmas, Jules."

"Why Christmas?"

"The child must make excuses to get away from home. Currently, she is restricted to the house by her father. She will not be free of parental influence and school regimen until Christmas holidays. If she is going to make another move, that would be the most appropriate moment."

"What will following her accomplish? Suppose she proves to us that she is involved, what then?"

"Then, dear friend, Jules, we will know the stink in our nostrils is truly that of a fleeing swine, won't we? Armed with this knowledge, how difficult will it be to secure money then?"

Hands still clasped across his stomach, Jules opened his eyes.

"When are you leaving?" he asked, finally.

"Immediately."

"I will see what I can do, Otto."

"Good."

"No promises."

Otto turned at the door. "There never were any promises, Jules. I expect none now."

Otto watched Jules close his eyes again. He nodded at the woman with the bright red hair as she let him out. If he hurried, he could still make the next flight to Atlanta.

Otto rented a small apartment one block off Peachtree Street near the old Fox theater which had succumbed to the times and closed. Twenty years ago, patrons had listened to the largest organ in the South and thrilled to troupes of opera stars from New York's famed Met in that theater. The unlighted marquee was depressing, the entry dusty and littered. Next door was an apartment building, around the corner a quick-food cafe.

It took ten days to get a telephone installed, then Otto's call came from Jules in New York.

"We can do this for about thirty days, Otto. That is all. If there are no tangible results to report within this time, the effort must be abandoned. Do you understand? One shot only. So select your time with care. When will it be?"

"Christmas night and for the days following, Jules."

"You mentioned the child is being punished. You believe in spite of this, she will make some move again soon?"

"I hope so."

Jules spoke some distance removed from the telephone. He could barely be heard. Otto had to ask the man to repeat himself.

"I said," Jules started anew, "I pulled every string still available to me on this. I sent the bulk of the documents to our agent in Berlin. You remember Kruger?"

"Yes. A good man."

"He's nearly blind. But he said he will study the photographs as best he can."

"Excellent."

"Otto?" Jules faded away momentarily. "Otto?"

"Yes, Jules?"

"Where do you wish to have the team contact you Christmas Day?"

"At this number."

"You are not returning to Florida, Otto?"

"No. I'll stay here until this is completed." Otto subdued mounting excitement. "Did you have trouble getting good men, Jules? I need the best."

"They are the best, Otto."

The Roth home was redolent with the scent of evergreen, a huge tree dominating the den. Otto had been invited to share the holiday with them and he readily accepted. In the meantime, the small apartment was cluttered with the belongings of the four men hired by Jules. They checked their walkie-talkies, studied city maps and photographs of the family which Otto had secured, set up a shortwave radio.

Filled with sudden doubts, Otto was perceptive to every nuance of Pamela's voice and expression. It was inconceivable that anyone could dismiss two murders from the mind so completely. Even a professional assassin would surely have moments when

193

the subconscious flooded the conscious mind with mental images of a death scene. But the child would be expected to suffer even more of an alteration in mood, nightmares possibly, something that would suggest a disturbed series of thoughts.

If the child was distressed, she concealed it from Otto, her father and mother. Once her restriction was removed, a few days before Christmas, Pamela caught a bus downtown on the pretext of shopping. Upon her return each evening, it was obvious that was exactly what Pamela had done—shopped.

Janet was elated with Pamela's attitude. "Otto, have you noticed how she is picking up idioms of speech, the vernacular of her friends?"

"Most parents would derive small comfort from that," Otto had commented.

Janet agreed. "But when your child was born ancient, it's a relief to see her grow younger, Otto. Pamela was an adult at birth and only now is she becoming interested in youthful pursuits. Thank God for it."

Thank God. Yes. And was Otto to prove that this laughing carefree girl was an accomplice in the inhuman torture-murders he'd investigated? He had a keen eye for human failings, deviations in character. He began to worry that he had committed the League to a wild goose chase. Maybe he should call the whole thing off, wait and see. Every night he lay awake reexamining evidence. The conclusion was inescapable: the child was not aware of any murder. Yet, he felt the resolve rising even as he debated; the old "dog's nose" intuition had always served him well.

These young men sent by Jules were intense, quiet, in excellent physical condition. They went about their task with a detachment which suggested they were professionals. Otto's apartment became a scene reminiscent of the underground years of the war. On a day bed lay a pistol with a silencer. Radio equipment was connected to an aerial strung out the bathroom window like a clothes line. They were efficient and capable, but their reports brought only disheartening glimpses of a normal child doing normal things.

On the second day after Christmas, Pamela made her move.

She had left the house saying she had to go to the city and make exchanges on some of her gifts. She returned that evening shortly before dark.

"Did you get all your exchanges worked out?" Russell asked.

"Sure did, Papa!"

"How about a game of Scrabble later?" Otto called as Pamela continued upstairs.

"Not tonight, Uncle Otto. I'm bushed."

Otto saw Janet cast a worried glance toward the hall, then continue knitting. A few minutes later, Janet went upstairs. Otto departed for his clandestine apartment about ten, after a final nightcap with Russell. He arrived at the apartment an hour later.

"The girl went to the airport," one of the young men reported. He spoke with a Yiddish accent. "She bought a ticket, rented a locker and put the ticket inside."

"Ticket to where?" Otto questioned.

"Washington, D.C."

"Were you able to determine the flight or date?"

"New Year's Eve. Midmorning. The plane leaves at 10:20 and arrives 11:55, nonstop flight."

"I presume you have booked the same flight for one of you?" Otto said.

"Of course."

Otto rubbed his nose, smiled. "I think the chase is on."

The young Jew nodded, soberly. "She did something strange."

"Oh? What was that?"

"She changed."

"In what way?"

The operative groped for words. "Manner of walking, the way she handled herself. I had to get close behind to learn what flight she was taking."

"Trying to disguise herself then," Otto surmised.

"Her face seemed older, different. She wore the same clothes, but it was as if another person was in them. It was a complete transformation, Mr. Ebenstein. I don't believe a stranger would have thought this was the same person as the child, Pamela."

"Interesting," Otto said.

"It was," the operative explained, "as though she had studied a role, like an actress who becomes the part. Even her voice altered."

"In what way?"

"Deeper, rasping. Mature. And she spoke with a definite accent."

"Polish."

The young man's black eyebrows lifted. "Exactly," he said.

CHAPTER SEVENTEEN

PERHAPS IT WAS INTUITION, or a vague subconscious conviction that something was amiss, but whatever the impetus, Janet could not dismiss the sense of unease that gripped her. She had begun to doubt Otto's motives. The man was too available, too often a guest. She had watched him cement his relationship with Pamela, capturing the child's fancy with avuncular quips and tales. "Uncle" Otto was fast becoming a fixture around this house, as much at home as Eleanor or Harold. More so!

But it was not Otto's obvious adoration of Pamela which most upset Janet. It was the attachment which had formed between Otto and Russell. Russell was, inherently, a reclusive man who simply did not reveal himself to others. Yet, with Otto, he had undergone a metamorphosis. He went out of his way to make the brusque old German at home. The larder was now stocked with imported dark ales, links of Braunschweiger smoked sausages, a hoop of pungent cheese and cases of Otto's favorite Moselblümchen wine.

It was all a bit too much. It had happened too smoothly. Janet did not profess to understand the intricacies of Russell's deepest thoughts, but this was far beyond anything she would expect from her husband. He played endless hours of chess, pored over the Scrabble board, playing in German, speaking German with Otto more often than English. Otto had become a companion to Russell not only in their leisure hours but during the working day as well.

In their absence, Janet had searched Otto's room. Looking for what? She didn't know. But she searched anyway, her fingers feeling the tops of door frames, into dark corners of the closets, taking all the drawers from the bureau to look under and behind them. She went through his toiletries, clothing, everything! Of course, she had found nothing.

With Pamela gone for the day, still exchanging Christmas gifts and with Otto and Russell at the office, Janet made another thorough search of the child's room. She went so far as to remove paintings from the walls to examine the backs. She even brought up a stepladder and inspected the light fixtures. Still nothing.

Never had she invaded Russell's privacy. The dresser drawers which were his had always been his domain alone. She had never picked up his wallet nor inspected his trouser pockets. These were the "private" parts of a person's life and although it would never occur to her to think he was hiding anything, she searched them now.

She had discovered nothing to upset her, nothing to cause worry. Nevertheless she was plagued with dark thoughts about them individually and in collusion with one another. Was she ill? Mentally disturbed? Surely it would be better to be deluded than to succumb to the illness of suspicion she now suffered. It wasn't healthy to be obsessed with such doubts. It was affecting her life in unconscious ways, making her curt with Russell, snapping at the servants, actually avoiding conversation with Otto. It had to cease. She had to recognize the danger in catering to her paranoia and for God's sake have faith! She considered seeking the services of a psychiatrist—but that was a whim; he would only tell her to be logical, rational, sensible. She told herself these things already.

Then she found the key, completely by accident. After all the probing, the sneaking, the damned thing was tucked in Pamela's overnight bag in a small zippered pocket designed to hold cosmetics apart from the clothing.

It was one of those rental keys of the type found in lockers at bus and railway terminals. Drop in a coin and leave a bag for a few hours or days. Why would Pamela have occasion to use such a service? Janet glanced at her watch: an hour before lunch. Neither Pamela nor the men would return before late afternoon. With perspiring hands, she examined the key. Number 182; ATT. ATT? Atlanta—what? Airport?

She drove to the sprawling international airport, parked in a drizzling rain and went inside. The key had a blue enameled area with the number stamped on it. She told a porter she was looking for her locker and couldn't find it. He glanced at her key and instructed her to follow "the blue markers." Janet made her way across the terminal to a cluster of shops, restaurants, a bar and restrooms centrally located to serve the patrons using these gates for arrival or departure.

The locker was small. Janet slipped in the key, turned it. The door yielded. At first she thought it was empty. Then she saw the envelope—it had been placed all the way to the rear of the compartment. Janet opened it and groaned.

Eastern Airlines, Flight 278, round-trip ticket to Washington, D.C. In the same envelope, twenty crisp ten dollar bills. Also, a map of Washington, with a Georgetown address noted. She looked at the name on the ticket, tears stinging her eyes.

"Erika Krajewski?" Janet whispered. Who was that? Pamela using an assumed name? If so, why such an elaborate ruse as Krajewski?

Should she take the ticket? Confront Pamela? What then? This was evidence that Pamela was sneaking around, had bought a ticket—and where did she get the money? The Christmas gifts supposedly purchased in Europe had been dismissed with the offhand remark, "They haven't come yet." Did such gifts exist at all?

She must think. Sit down somewhere and think this through. Janet took the ticket, closed the locker, inserted a coin and removed the key to keep anyone else from renting it. She went into the coffee shop and found a vacant table. Drinking coffee from a Styrofoam cup, she made several notes on a napkin. The flight number, departure date, time, destination and the name, "Erika Krajewski."

Assume she did confront Pamela. What would she learn that she didn't already know? If Pamela admitted buying the ticket, she probably wouldn't reveal her reason. So far as Janet knew, the child had no friends or acquaintances near Washington. But what of this map, and the red penciled marking of a route with an "X" to mark the destination. Other check marks suggested the traveler had more than one stop enroute.

Janet took the map to a coin-operated copy machine and ran it through. She replaced the items in the locker, drove home and returned the key to Pamela's overnight case. The departure date was New Year's Eve. Four days away. Janet called her family attorney in Macon, Georgia.

"I want a flight round trip to Washington, D.C.," she instructed. "From Atlanta, leaving December thirtieth."

"Returning when, Mrs. Roth?"

"I don't know yet."

"Mrs. Roth you could call your local travel agent and arrange this."

"I'm calling you," Janet said, "because I want you to pay for it through your office. I also want a rental car waiting for me when I get there, and reservations at the motel nearest the airport. Dulles Airport."

"All right, Mrs. Roth. I'll bill it to your annuity account."

"Thank you."

She cradled the receiver, mood ascending. Very well, Pamela—Janet could play this game of subterfuge, too.

That evening over dinner, Pamela casually mentioned that she wanted to attend "A New Year's pajama party with some girl friends."

"Positively not," Russell said.

"Papa, why?" Pamela wailed.

"You have abused your privileges heretofore, this is why."

"Papa, I was on restriction for that."

"Nevertheless, you can't go."

"Papa!" Pamela's voice rose angrily, "You are being unfair to me. I served my restriction, didn't I? I was wrong and I admitted that. But now you are extending the period of punishment."

"Not the period."

"The terms then," Pamela said.

Russell took a deep breath, sat back and gazed at Janet. "What do you say to this, Janet?"

"I agree with Pamela."

Russell stared at Janet a long moment, then nodded. "Very well. I yield."

"Thank you, Papa." There was no elation in Pamela's tone. Throughout the exchange, Otto had continued ladling soup into his mouth, noisily sucking the liquid from his spoon. After several minutes with no conversation, Russell said, "I wish to apologize, Pamela. I was wrong. You are quite right. I have given the impression I do not trust you and nothing could be further from the truth. Will you forgive my hasty and improper reaction?"

Pamela reached for his hand, now smiling. "Sure, Papa."

Janet observed the two, seething inwardly. So cool, so collected, Pamela was really an accomplished liar! Sitting there now, her hand on her father's arm, reassuring him. Not a hint in her lovely eyes of the lie she was perpetrating. God, there was no telling how often the child had fooled them!

"Actually," Janet said impulsively, "I was considering going to Macon this coming weekend, myself."

"Then you and Uncle Otto will be alone," Pamela noted to her father.

"No," Otto said. "I also am going away for these holidays."

"Oh dear," Janet lamented. "Russell, will you be all right?"

"Certainly."

"Would you rather I wait until another weekend to go?" Janet gambled.

"No. I will be fine."

"You're sure?"

Russell looked at her with expressionless eyes, "I can take care of myself nicely, thank you."

The meal was completed in silence. Shortly thereafter, Otto retired to his suite upstairs and Pamela to her bedroom. Janet unconsciously stared at Russell as he smoked his pipe, reading a trade journal. He must have sensed her gaze; he turned abruptly to catch her looking at him.

"What is troubling you, Janet?"

"Nothing, Russell."

For an instant he appeared irritated, then returned to his magazine. Janet heard him grumble, "Worry, worry, worry."

It was snowing in Washington when Janet checked into the motor hotel overlooking Dulles airport. The rented car was parked, ready for her use. She reminded herself that Pamela's flight could be delayed, routed elsewhere, or canceled outright. Or somehow in the mob of people at the terminal, Janet might lose Pamela immediately after the child arrived—if she arrived.

She stood at the double-glass window gazing out into steadily falling snow, the airfield lights in the distance. She had had a pitcher of martinis delivered, and she stood here now doing something she never did—drinking alone.

If Pamela came and Janet lost her, or if the girl did not come at all, no matter. Janet had her copy of the map with the Georgetown address.

She sipped a martini, feeling a subdued exhilaration with her newfound role. She would bet anything the last people who would ever suspect her of counterplotting would be Pamela, Russell and Otto. Surprise! Janet's head was swimming slightly from the liquor. She tossed it down, winced, throat and stomach burning as the gin scorched her insides. She poured another drink, dropped in an olive, hesitated, dropped in a second one, and swiggled it with a gentle circular rocking motion. Yessir, surprise! Here she was, incognito, fifteen hours before Pamela's flight was to arrive, and Janet felt quite smug to have pulled it off thus far all by herself.

The following morning, imbued with an excitement she had never known, Janet picked at her breakfast in the hotel restaurant, impatient for the time to pass, then drove to the air terminal. She found a secluded area where she could watch the incoming flights. An airline agent had assured her it would be on time. Janet wore a new coat and a hat with a floppy brim over her face—out of character, but effective. In planning, she had reasoned that her rental automobile could be an encumbrance, since Pamela would surely take a taxi upon arrival. In either case, Janet was prepared. She too would hail a cab to follow Pamela. But her car was where she could reach it quickly, if need be.

Although she was here to intercept Pamela, fully expecting her when the child walked through the gate, Janet was stunned. It took will power not to rush forward and confront the girl angrily. Almost immediately, Janet's anger dissolved into dismay and rising dread.

That it was Pamela there could be no doubt. She wore her favorite slacks, carried the overnight tote bag, a scarf was thrown around her neck over her newest red plaid coat. The ski cap, the one the detective brought from Chattanooga, was firmly atop the girl's head. But within the clothing that was Pamela's, there moved a figure that shocked Janet. Her step purposeful, manner assured, Pamela might easily have been in her twenties! She waved away a porter, walking with long even strides out of the terminal, and lifted a hand to summon a taxi with the aplomb of a woman who had done this a thousand times!

In sudden fear of losing Pamela, Janet ran toward the exit and pushed through the emerging people. She found herself a scant few feet from her child as Pamela opened a taxi door to get in. Something dropped from the tote bag and the child turned to retrieve it as Janet shoved nearer in search of her own cab.

Their eyes met. Damn it! All right, the game was over. They were both caught dead to rights. All they could do now was wrangle over the concept of who had done what to whom. Janet sighed and moved toward Pamela. Then, totally taken aback, she saw Pamela turn easily, close the taxi door and instruct the driver.

"Pamela!" Hadn't the child recognized her? The hat and new coat, perhaps? Pamela's cab moved away as Janet reached it, calling, "Pamela! Pamela!"

A cab pulled up and Janet put an arm on the gentleman for whom the taxi was intended. "It's an emergency, forgive me, may I?"

She was in the vehicle now. "See that Yellow Cab ahead at the stop sign?"

"Yeah lady, I see."

"Follow it, please."

"After all these years," the cabbie marveled. "Okay. I'll do it!"

"Don't let them see us if you can help it," Janet implored.

"No problem."

Janet pulled the city map from her pocketbook, studied it, determined that they were following the marked route. The tires sang in slush, snow still falling softly.

"He's letting out his passenger," the driver said. Janet looked at her map.

"Is that a shopping center ahead?" she asked.

"Yes it is."

"Wait a few moments," Janet instructed. They peered through the sweep of windshield wipers, watching.

"Hey, the lady went to another cab," Janet's driver said. Janet leaned across the seat, staring.

"Follow him, please."

"All the way," the cabbie said gleefully.

Reading street signs, Janet followed the marking of the map. At the next "check" point, Pamela again got out of her taxi, walked about a block to another cab stand and took another vehicle.

"Acts like she expected to be followed," the cabbie remarked to Janet. "But she ain't looking behind herself too good, is she?"

"Apparently not. Do you think she's seen us?"

"If she has she don't care," the driver said. "She could've lost us easy in changing cabs had she wanted to. Here we go again." He pulled into traffic, tires whirring for an instant, gaining traction. The driver wiped his windshield with the back of a gloved hand. "Going toward Georgetown, looks like."

"Just keep following, please."

"That I'll do, Lady."

Through the township and into a hilly residential area they went, the streets uncleared here. Pamela's cab halted at the foot of a hill and there the child got out, carrying her tote bag, coat collar and scarf curled around her neck and face.

"She's not changing taxis this time, Lady. The nearest cab

stand is about a mile away. You want we should go directly there?"

"No. Let's sit here a few minutes. Can you pull forward so I can see where she's walking to?"

Pamela had begun climbing the city sidewalk, taking careful steps to avoid slipping. The snow was coming faster now, a screen that obscured Janet's vision. She asked the driver to go forward again.

"I doubt I can make that hill, Lady. Got no chains."

"I'll get out here then."

Janet tipped the driver ten dollars and left him grinning. "Just like the movies almost," he said.

A block ahead, barely visible, Pamela was trudging up the hill. Without a backward glance, she turned into a yard, pushing through knee-deep drifts. She disappeared from Janet's line of sight.

"Now we'll see what this is all about," Janet said aloud. She walked as fast as the uncertain footing allowed, making her way to the same house. She heard a motor, glanced up and saw a sedan crunch toward the middle of the street, skidding slightly as it maneuvered away from the far curb. Janet's foot twisted and she nearly fell; a sheet of ice glazed the entire walkway. She took tiny steps sidewise toward the street, grasping a small tree for support. The snow gave an eerie silence to the scene, devoid of movement except the automobile slowly sliding.

Hey! It was sliding toward her! The weight of the vehicle was pulling it downhill, wheels locked. The sedan's motor was a faint purr, fumes from the exhaust pipe misty proof that the engine was running! Janet eased away from the street again, back across the frozen sidewalk, toward a fenced yard. She realized it was snowing harder, blanketing the air with a veil that obscured everything except what was near at hand and the automobile, slowly, ever so slowly, slipping down the street.

Grabbing a wrought-iron fence for support, Janet lifted her feet high—she wore no boots and the melted snow had now soaked her shoes; this coupled with the freezing temperature had numbed her extremities. She pulled herself forward, shivering, still half a block to go before she would reach the house.

That was strange. The door of the sliding car was open on the side opposite the driver. Like a single wing of a wounded bird, feet scotched, the sedan continued to slip downhill, and—for heaven's sake! The windshield wipers were not moving! How could the driver possibly see with an inch of snow on the windshield—

The most irrational thought came to Janet's mind. As calmly as if she had been considering whether to prune this rose bush or that—she realized the car was coming for her. Actually the occupants of the car were coming for her. And she, like a snowbound beast, stood looking at the vehicle, its rear tires sliding as they were, a woolen-covered hand now visible on top of the open door.

When the car was thirty feet away, still moving, a ski-masked man appeared and jumped free. The figure ran on shoes which had cleats.

"Come with me, please," an accented voice muffled through the ski mask.

"I'll scream," Janet warned, stepping backward.

"Don't do that, Mrs. Roth. Come with me."

"My daughter is up there. I must go up and—"

"You can't go there, Mrs. Roth." He had her arm now, supporting, pulling, not as a threat so much as a guidance. The car door yawned, the vehicle still moving slowly.

"We are your friends, Mrs. Roth. There's someone here you know. Get inside please."

"Someone I know?"

"Get inside please. Quickly, please, Mrs. Roth."

Janet peered in, a hand was outstretched to her, the interior of the automobile darkened by snow blanketed windows.

"Get in please. Now!"

The man inside the automobile seized her wrist in a vise grip, pulling, the assailant outside shoving Janet onto the rear seat. The door slammed as the ski-masked man jumped in behind her. She felt the vehicle lurch, swerve, motor roaring now. From under the seat, a warm draft of heated air blew into her face as they held her down. The car waggled as the driver fought to correct the sliding.

"You're hurting me."

"Let her up, Muller."

Gentler hands helped her rise. She came up frightened, staring, unbelieving.

"Otto!"

CHAPTER EIGHTEEN

THE VEHICLE CAME TO A HALT at the foot of the hill. The man Otto had called "Muller" was out the instant it stopped. From up front came the crackle of a radio, a foreign language. The driver responded, then spoke to Otto in English:

"She is out."

"Already?" Otto said. "It hasn't been five minutes."

The radio sounded again, words Janet couldn't decipher.

"She's circling the block away from us," the driver reported.

"Otto," Janet questioned, "what are you doing here?"

"Perhaps he wasn't home," Otto said, absently.

"Otto! What's happening?"

"Janet, please wait to talk. Not now."

"Otto! Damn you, what's happening here?"

The driver said, "Muller is following on foot."

In Hebrew, Otto commanded, "Go to the house. See what happened. Tell them you are looking for your daughter. Make them think it is the girl."

The driver nodded, set the brake and a frigid gust of air swept all heat from inside as he stepped out. Otto was breathing heavily.

"Is Pamela here because of you, Otto?"

"I am here because of Pamela."

"Otto you lied to me. You followed her because of the things I told you. You used me. You used my hospitality. You said you wouldn't pursue this and you have!"

The radio buzzed, static erupting. A voice spoke in low tones. Otto grunted as he leaned over the front seat for the microphone. There was a quick exchange in Hebrew between Otto and the other man. Otto closed his eyes a long moment.

"What is it?" Janet demanded.

"We will go to my hotel room, Janet."

"Otto, damn you! Damn you! What is it?"

Otto grabbed her shoulders and spoke fiercely, "Do not become hysterical. This is not the time for that. Get up front. I will drive us back to my hotel."

"I'm going after Pamela."

"Where?" Otto snapped. "She is several blocks distant. Are you going to wander in the snow? Be sensible. Now get up front!"

Mutely, Janet moved into the front seat. Otto adjusted the bulk of his weight behind the steering wheel and backed away from the curb. The tires spun. He eased off on the accelerator and the vehicle crunched forward. Only now did he activate the wipers.

"You came to my home as a spy. You took advantage of my friendship, Otto. I told you I would not allow you to threaten my family."

"I am no threat."

"Then what are you doing here?"

"I am looking after Pamela."

"If you knew she was coming, why didn't you tell me? Tell Russell?"

"Did you tell Russell?"

Furious, frustrated, Janet glared out the window. The radio made periodic short crackling sounds, the transmissions too far away to be received now. Otto cut it off.

"What is Pamela doing here, Otto?" Janet's tone was more even.

"She came looking for one of the men she's uncovered."

"One of the men? You mean a German?"

"Not necessarily German."

"All right then, goddamn it, a Nazi! Will you stop being evasive!"

"Yes," Otto said, voice low, "a Nazi."

"Dear God."

Otto drove without further conversation. When he pulled into the parking lot of his hotel, Janet could see her own motel across the highway.

"I have a room over there," she said numbly.

"I know."

"I left a rental car at the airport."

"We will get it later." Otto offered her a hand over the slippery parking lot.

They rode an elevator to the fifth floor, walked a long carpeted hall. Otto grumbled something about "static electricity." The key in his hand sparked as he tried to unlock the door. Inside the room, several suitcases; maps and clothing were strewn over chairs and beds. A shortwave radio was set up near a window. The telephone was ringing. Otto answered in Hebrew.

"What happened?" Otto questioned.

"He was dead."

"You told me that. How?" Otto asked.

"I cannot be positive. Heart attack apparently. From the position of the body and hands, I would say the girl kicked him in the groin."

"Where is she now?" Otto queried.

"We are at the airport. She is evidently awaiting a flight out. I spoke with Jules. He wants us to abandon the case immediately."

"You must not do that," Otto said.

"I have my orders. We will pick up our things in a few minutes."

"I'll call Jules."

"If you wish. But we are coming to get our equipment now."

"Can you wait until I speak with Jules before leaving the girl?"

"No. I'm sorry. We have been given explicit orders to leave immediately."

Otto hung up, face clouded, and went to a bedside table where there was a half-filled bottle of Scotch. He poured a glass, offered a drink to Janet with a silent lift of the bottle. She shook her head. Otto took two large swallows before pawing through his suitcase for an address book.

He charged the call to his home phone in Florida. Then, with drink in hand and a cigarette between his lips, he listened to the phone ring on the receiving end, again and again.

"Yes."

"This is Otto, Jules."

"Yes, Otto."

"The men say they are leaving."

"That is correct."

In Hebrew, Otto protested, "I need them, Jules! You said thirty days!"

"Otto, Otto," Jules said, his whispery tone that of a scolding father, "you have involved my three best men in a serious matter. Did you speak to Muller about what happened?"

"Yes I did."

"You understand that everyone there is complicit, do you not?"

"I do not wish to argue a point of law, Jules! We are on the trail, I need these men!"

"Otto, the purpose of the League is not assassination. If you wish to seek vengeance, there are more rapid elements who will be happy to comply. But that is not now nor has it ever been our purpose. We strive to bring the criminal to justice, not render it! You have allowed a situation to develop that could be very dangerous to our entire organization. You have made accomplices of us all. In the commission of a crime that cannot be justified with any stretch of the imagination. How do I explain the expenditure of this money? Say that we 'got them'? Don't be ridiculous! It is over."

Throughout, Jules had not lifted his voice, not one hint of anger. Speaking as though far from the phone, his tone level, he was doing the only thing he could, and Otto knew it.

"There is a further complication," Jules said when Otto had not spoken.

"What is it?"

"An insurance investigator managed to gain access to everything related to the cases in Houston and Chattanooga. If I do not miss my bet, he will be there in Washington very soon."

"What company is it?"

"He identified himself as a representative of a company located in Berne, Switzerland. It is a box number only. There is no such agency, Otto."

"I see."

"Do you? You know what this man probably is."

"Yes."

"Then get out of there, Otto."

"We can intercept him when he arrives here, Jules."

"Otto!" Jules said, sharply, "This is not 1946! We cannot do such things with impunity any more. I cannot and will not intercept this man! Be wise. Protect your little girl. Get out of there!"

"Did you gain any more information?" Otto asked leadenly.

"From the materials? Kruger is not through with them."

"You will continue to help me in this respect?"

Jules sighed, a wavery exhalation. "Of course."

"Thank you. Good-bye."

The operatives had arrived and were quietly packing their belongings. "The woman does not understand Hebrew," Otto said, speaking of Janet. "Where specifically is the girl?"

Muller replied, also in Hebrew, "At the terminal. The weather is lifting. She should be on a flight out any time now."

"Your help has been invaluable," Otto said, without emotion. "I thank you."

213

The four men nodded, filed out, and closed the door. Otto stood in the center of the room, drank the last of his liquor and went to pour another. Damn. Out of cigarettes. He pulled open a dresser drawer, raked around a moment. He went to the telephone and called room service to order two cartons of his brand and another fifth of Scotch.

"There is trouble," Janet said.

"Yes," Otto confessed. "Trouble."

"Are you going to be honest with me? Tell the truth?"

Otto sat on the bed contemplating her in the now wilted floppy wide-brim hat. He shook his head and smiled.

"What?" Janet questioned.

"That hat."

She took it off. Otto was breathing with labored effort, the affliction of a heavy smoker, his obesity not easing the problem. When the cigarettes and liquor arrived, he closed the door, bolted and locked it. He spoke as he broke the seal on the Scotch.

"I wonder how strong you are, really," Otto said, tenderly. "In the war years I saw strong people grow weak and weak people become strong. I wonder with you, Janet."

"I don't know, Otto."

"Nor do I. I warned you I could only uncover facts, when you came to my house. Remember?"

"You said you would destroy those materials, Otto."

"I could not do that, Janet. There was too much there."

"What was there?"

"At least one Nazi tracked down. A hint of more."

"Russell?"

"No," Otto said, "that's a strange thing to me. Nothing whatsoever to implicate Russell. I thought there would be, but so far as I can determine, there is only one thing suspect about Russell."

"What is it?"

"He lied about his childhood. I had a voice analysis made of a tape on which he and I were conversing in German. The analyst said Russell comes from an educated, cultured background. He did not grow up on a poor farm, that much is certain. But this lie may be nothing more than a way to stop your inquiries. Or he may feel guilty for having survived when so many did not, and he eases his mind with this fantasy."

"Russell does not indulge in fantasy," Janet said.

"No. Probably not. But having an education is not a crime. There is nothing in Pamela's materials to suggest that her father was involved in anything relating to Nazism, except as a soldier. However, curiosity about her father apparently did unearth these others. She has an astounding capacity for logic and deduction. Plus her ability to use a man's speech patterns to trace his background. Ingenious. Brilliant."

"Otto, I want to know. I want your word that you will tell me. Everything."

"I do not see how I can avoid it," Otto said. "I cannot do this alone. My support has been withdrawn. The men are leaving."

"Leaving?" Janet stood. "What about Pamela?"

"She should be on her way home to Atlanta by now."

"I want to go home, Otto."

"I will make reservations for in the morning."

"Now, Otto. I want to go home now."

"You may do as you wish," Otto said. "But I am thinking how much time it will take to cover all that has happened. To discuss it. You see, Janet, it comes down to you and me. Perhaps you can help me unravel the largest mystery of all."

"What are you talking about?"

"Why Pamela is doing what she is doing. You see, I can understand how Pamela's inquisitive nature might involve her in such a project. She probably correctly guessed her father had been untruthful about his childhood and education. It would be normal for her to delve into the matter out of curiosity alone. But this has gone beyond normalcy."

Janet felt the tingle of rising fear.

"The girl used her time in Europe to verify things which she had only suspected. The trip was a windfall opportunity. She speaks several languages, she had unlimited railway privileges with a Eurailpass. She seized her chance and made the most of it. But when she returned, her quest became earnest, her actions aberrant."

Hands trembling, Janet pinned them between her knees, chest constricting, the fear rising, rising—

"According to the airlines, it is no problem to get a flight to and from Houston. This can be done many times of the day, flight time round trip is less than seven hours. That seems to be Pamela's only carefully planned, masterfully executed plot."

Janet's heart was battering her chest. "Fiedler? Doctor Fiedler?"

"You see, the police have uncovered no motive. Besides, who would suspect a fourteen-year-old girl?"

"My God in heaven!" Janet cried. "Are you telling me Pamela had something to do with Dr. Fiedler?"

"There is no proof. It seems to have been perfectly executed, as I say."

"Otto, I won't listen to this!"

The professor sipped long from his glass, eyes on Janet.

"She couldn't have!"

He watched Janet pace the room. "It would be madness. The news story said—torture."

She was shaking, voice aquiver, eyes darting, as her mind fought to grasp this, to comprehend, accept or reject. Otto waited, watching.

"She's a child—it would take strength—he was a—oh, God— *old* man—"

Stunned awareness. Janet burst into tears. From denials and alibis she turned to wild protestations and recriminations. Otto poured a drink, diluted it with water and urged her to sip the liquid.

216

"Chattanooga," Janet cried. "A camping trip! She got ill—caught a bus—" She looked at Otto.

"She made so many mistakes there," Otto commented. "She lost the hat. She had to take a taxi in a town where taxi drivers remember such things. I finally decided however, she had made more than one trip to the house, which is in a rural setting. I think perhaps she went on a bicycle the first time, perhaps left it to use in getting away."

"When could she have done this?" Janet reasoned.

"She was in Chattanooga for two days. Friday and Saturday. She came home Sunday on a bus. But finding that house! It is a country situation, no address, no street names. It would take instructions. I didn't see how she could ever find him."

"Of course she couldn't!" Janet said, sharply. "How would she know where to go?"

"I suspect Fiedler told her."

Janet began shaking her head slowly from side to side. "No," she said. "No."

"Coming here was an even greater hazard than the first two," Otto said, softly. "She did this in the face of rising parental suspicion. She had to pay for her ticket, get a map, check out the house, cover herself with an excuse to be gone a day or two, fly up and get back."

"How would she know these things? She changed cabs, had a marked map."

"She must have come before. Perhaps for a day. A single day is enough time to come, see and return."

"It takes money!"

"Yes. I was going to ask you about that, Janet. Does she have credit cards?"

"I took it away from her after she returned from Europe."

Janet jolted, physically. "She said she bought gifts—expensive gifts—with cash."

"These did not come?"

"No."

"All right," Otto exhaled , "there's the money."

"Fifteen hundred dollars."

"That's not much for all this running about," Otto said. "Does she have access to other money?"

"Her savings."

"Her own savings account?"

"Yes."

"She could withdraw from that without permission?"

"Yes."

Otto lit a cigarette. After a long silence, he said, "Drink your drink, Janet."

"It'll make me sick. I can't."

Another long silence.

"Who were these men, all of them? What did they do?"

Otto told what he knew of Hans Fiedler, the executed Jew, and the imposter murdered in Houston. He confessed that, as yet, they had not uncovered the true identity of the man killed in Tennessee.

"They are working on that," he said.

"Who?"

"An organization which has been chasing Nazis the world over."

"The men with you, who were here, they work for this organization?"

"Directly or indirectly."

"Why did they leave?"

Otto's voice altered, "Because the world no longer cares if Nazis exist. They could be implicated because they know a crime took place and did not report it."

Too stupefied to be shocked further, Janet said, "You mean murder."

"Yes."

"The man here?"

"She kicked him. Possibly to disable him. He died of a heart attack, apparently."

Janet sat, head hung. Otto sipped Scotch, smoked cigarettes, answered questions which came at increasingly longer intervals. He saw she was going to get through this. Janet had succumbed to a merciful form of consciousness common to traumatized creatures.

"I knew it, Otto."

"You knew what?"

"I knew there was something wrong. From the time Pamela was born, I knew it. Do you think such a thing is possible?"

"Reacting to subconscious fears, perhaps—"

"No. It was more than that. I knew something was in that child. I felt it then and nothing has ever happened to change my mind. It was like she had been put into my body and I was incidental."

"You mentioned that before."

"Something to do with Russell."

"Janet, let's try to confine ourselves to facts. The facts themselves are rather staggering."

"As though I were just a carrier. You understand, Otto?"

"No."

"Like," Janet's face twisted. "Like she had a mission—like Jesus must have been to his mother. I don't mean Pamela is a religious thing, I don't mean that at all. In fact, just the opposite. But she always did strange little things, Otto. Odd things. Like the showers. She is afraid of showers."

"I see," Otto said.

"Teensy things all her life. I worried and worried and I knew I had reason to worry, but I couldn't put a finger on it."

"Janet—"

"She was scared of the German language at first. Screamed hysterically when they held class. She overcame that when she was nine or so."

Janet paced the room with slow steps, a fist going into the opposite palm as though with force, but with very slow motion and light impact.

"Otto?"

"Yes?"

"What would be significant about orange marmalade?"

"Orange marmalade?"

"Yes, something about orange marmalade. Pamela has a phobia about it. She can't even eat with the stuff on the table. If she smells it, sees it, she gets sick to her stomach. She always has. What would there be about orange marmalade, Otto?"

His face was ashen.

"What, Otto?"

"It was the influence of something she read, possibly."

"No. This was before the reading started. What is it, Otto?"

"I can only speculate—"

"Then speculate!"

"They used marmalade. The Germans did. The *Nazis* did— they used marmalade as a reward."

He was trembling, fumbling to pour another drink. "Tell me, Otto."

"They starved them in the ghettos," Otto choked. "In Warsaw particularly. Weeks without bread or milk, months without meat. They offered marmalade to any who would come forward voluntarily to be relocated to work areas."

"What kind of work areas?"

"There were no work areas."

"Death camps?"

"Yes."

"Yes," Janet nodded. "Of course. Died for marmalade."

CHAPTER NINETEEN

EVEN HAD HE BEEN ALONE, Otto would not have slept. It was a bane of the elderly to sleep little and poorly. Since his retirement from teaching, he didn't allow such fitful nights to disturb him anymore. He slept when exhausted, napped usually, and no longer fell abed attempting to make slumber come. He sat now, side by side with his mirrored image across a vanity table: a glass of diminishing Scotch and a cigarette in the same hand, mouth agape, his lower lip hung in an imbecilic pose. It was not his own configuration which dominated his thoughts. And he had drunk himself sober.

Janet had fallen asleep on one of the two king-sized beds. Otto threw a blanket over her to compensate for loss of heat as the body succumbed to deepening levels of unconsciousness. Now and then, reality imposed on her subconscious, and she reflected dark thoughts by grinding her teeth, an unnerving sound in the silence of predawn.

Otto was not a dreamer. Awake or asleep, he did not fantasize. He'd once been an idealist, but that youthful state had long ago gone. There was a time when he prayed to God, trusted in divine intervention and persisted in the theological conviction that God's will would be done.

That had not been an emotional or purely monotheistic thought. He had sat many an hour on a stump in the woods, as a youth, and come to the conclusion there *had* to be a God. All religious arguments aside, Otto had deliberately, logically, become convinced that scientifically God *must* exist. It was the mathematical nature of all things that everything had a beginning as one. One universe, one galaxy, one planet, one continent, one species, ultimately and infinitely it all could be traced back to one cell, one atom. But somewhere, at some point, there was nothing and then there was something and that must have been God.

When he was only ten years old, Otto had—again logically—examined life. The genius of it all was awesome. Interlocking dependencies, this survives because of that, the sheer beauty of all matter—surely this could not be a cosmic accident. Life fell into certain patterns with certain laws. Whether one examined the neutron and protons of atoms, the planets around the sun, or the mystery of ever-expanding space, the laws did not deviate from the microcosm of cells to the macrocosm of the universe. It was quite logically, very simple, irrefutable—there had to be a God.

He had never indulged in the theological semantics of which religion or which God—these were inventions of man which surely God would overlook and understand. But in any instance, there was a God and what better lifetime pursuit could a being have than serving his fellow men in the name of that God? So Otto had become a rabbi. A good one. Devout, but realistic. He had entered medicine and later psychiatry as extensions of his rabbinical duties, a means of specializing in his quest to better serve mankind and God.

Otto had not lightly entered the rabbinate. Nor had he capriciously abandoned it. But when he was forced to equate God with Hitler, he shed his robes and had never considered taking them up again.

All right, so God would not intervene in the affairs of man. So be it. Granted then that God did not or would not come to the assistance of His people. Six million Jews went to their annihilation because God could not see fit to stop the carnage. Otto might have forgiven the deity out of deference to "man's will could not be God's fault."

But when men—not God—tried to assassinate Hitler, not once but several times, who saved the man? An explosive put on the same airplane was defective and Hitler was spared. At a rally where Hitler was to speak, a bomb was put in a column behind the podium and Hitler unexpectedly cut his speech short and left before it exploded killing others but not him. A radio-controlled bomb was placed in the very rostrum where Hitler would speak and this time they could not fail. But a few minutes before Hitler arrived, the man charged with setting off the device could wait no longer to relieve himself. He went into a public rest room, deposited his coin, shut the door. It took workmen with crowbars to get him out, and by that time *der Führer* had come and gone. His own officers placed a bomb that blew the pants off the man and still he survived! They shot at him, tried to poison him, again and again they failed as Hitler was spared by blind luck, poor timing and prescience. Who did he thank? He thanked God! It was "God's will," Hitler claimed, and "proof of divine destiny!"

In an American Negro minstrel song, a preacher is up a tree with a grizzly bear climbing the trunk. The preacher turns his eyes to the skies and fervently prays, "Oh, Lord, if you can't help me, for goodness sake don't help that bear!"

Otto could forgive a God who applied the same impartial nonalignment or the same unyielding rule of "let man's will be done." But he could not forgive a God who "helped the bear." Six million humans had gone to their untimely deaths, many by way of excruciating tortures and horrible suffering. It could have been halted with a fatal heart attack. If Adolf Hitler had died, it would all have stopped. But if God could not bring Himself to strike down Hitler with divine intervention—why did He save Hitler from death at the hands of other men? Was that mercy? Or madness? Who then was worse? Hitler for his obsession to exterminate a race, or God for protecting the man as he did so?

Never in history had one man, one single soul, been so personally responsible for a crime against humanity. So determined was Hitler, that he sacrificed military objectives to implement the destruction of the Jews. With direly needed military supplies halted on the way to the Russian front, Hitler permitted the *Schutzstaffel* to use the precious trains to transport Jews to their deaths. With his military advisors telling Hitler that highly specialized labor was being irretrievably lost from munitions factories by killing Jews, Hitler had them slain nonetheless. The German war effort actually suffered as Hitler relentlessly pursued the "final solution" to the Jewish "question." Had Hitler died, it would have ended. The army would have sued for peace. It would have been over and bad enough as it was. But "God" had saved Adolf Hitler until the allies were blocks from his bunker in Berlin. Many times, by all rights, the man should have died. For this, Otto could not forgive. And to live hating other men is destructive enough; but to live hating God is insanity. Hence Otto had come to the conclusion, with the same logical progression which first convinced him of God, that there was no God. He had believed that now for nearly thirty-five years.

Until tonight.

He had never given up inquiry, studying many if not most religions. He had examined their doctrines and found them all fundamentally the same. The "Golden Rule" for example, could be found in almost every religion. He had even toyed with the concept that man was the laboratory result of outer-space aliens, but this could in no way disprove or prove there was a God. Those aliens had a beginning, too, somewhere.

No, for Otto to believe in God again, he had to have a *logical* explanation of why God would allow a Hitler to be. He had to have a reasonable explanation based on more than faith. Blind faith was a ridiculous panacea for poverty, an unscientific excuse for aberrants, a hopelessly romantic balm for the desperate who could not help themselves. Otto no longer subscribed to the school of thought that anything, no matter what, was "God's will." To hell with that. Who could admire, much less worship, a cruel God who allowed a Hitler?

No. No. If Otto was to ever believe again, it was going to have to be more than a puerile theologian's weak argument based merely on faith. He wasn't buying the "God moves in mysterious ways" doctrine. If God wanted Otto Ebenstein's respect again, He'd damn well have to earn it, show just cause why Hitler had been allowed to develop, survive and slay as he had done.

After all these years, all these barren, godless, prayerless, unbelieving years, Otto got a brilliant flash of insight. At last, in the morass of minutiae in his mind, out of the holocaust and evil of man's inhumanity to man—Otto saw, understood, and now miraculously once again—believed in God. It had struck him with breath-taking logic. What had happened in a microsecond, that reacquisition of faith, was now taking him all night to examine and put in *logical* mental arguments to himself.

He had Janet to thank. And Pamela.

Half the world's peoples believed in reincarnation. Otto was too scientifically oriented to accept that. Like Judaism, or Christianity, it was too pat, unacceptably forgiving, like the desperate fool who saw all his misfortunes as "God's will."

But in truth that was precisely what it was. God's will. Only, not as theology applied it. Not quite what Eastern religions taught; almost Judeo-Christian, and yet neither! All the world's religions *almost* had it, yet none had grasped the truth.

Otto poured the last of the Scotch, lit another cigarette. He mentally counseled himself as though arguing with another being.

"Imagine yourself in a large room bigger than any room ever known to exist under a single roof. In this room are millions of tables and at each table sit souls we shall call 'people.' These people are playing a game. They have before them a series of marble-sized toys called planets. Each table has a different set of planets. But at this particular table is the marble 'earth.' As the people sit around this table, each second of time is but a second. To them. On the marble earth each of these seconds is, to the inhabitants of earth, seventy to a hundred years. Tick, a century; tick, two; tick, three; tick, four; tick, five centuries passed.

"Any of us at this table can play this game. When it is our turn we can go to earth at will. We may even elect what circumstances under which we wish to enter. That is, whether we are to be black, yellow, red, white, male, female, etc. From here, at this table, we see quite clearly that our period on marble earth will be, in fact, only one second or less. It is a fast game.

"But there's a catch. If we enter into this game, we go to marble earth, enter a womb at the point of conception, and somewhere between that instant and birth, we lose all conscious memory of this table and the true system of time. Why? Because to advance ourselves, to 'win' this game, we must rely on certain inherent genetic and philosophical attributes while down there on marble earth. We've done this many times already. Beginning players must take less developed forms: primitive tribesmen, cannibals, almost animal-like existences and it is up to our 'playing skills' as that being, to win a shot at the next most advanced position. Therefore, if we accumulate good points, during the microsecond existence of that play, the next time we may choose a higher station socially, mentally, philosophically, and yes, even theologically. That is, we carry forward in our programmed psyche some of the lessons from prior games.

"This may take millenniums or a few lifetimes, depending on how skillfully the player handles what some religions call 'karma.'

"Why do the beings on marble earth—or any of the other marbles like it—not know these answers? Because that would defeat the game, would it not? Because when life became unbearable, the population would slay their hungry children, their miserable

226

families and themselves, so they could escape this terrible, terrible existence and go back where everything is in perspective.

"Some do better than others. Some advance rapidly and with little failure. Others advance, fail, advance in the next existence, or set themselves back. The rules say, if you make an error, do wrong, you must correct this error in some future game. That is to say, if you hurt someone, you will be so hurt. If you murder someone, you will be so murdered. At precisely the point in your mental, emotional, financial and social status in that particular life as the person you so killed. If a gunman robs a grocer and shoots the grocer dead, the gunman may escape detection and prosecution during all of this lifetime. But in a future game, when the gunman is struggling to support a clubfooted child, a wife and two other children, fighting to exist as an honest, hardworking and honorable member of a society in which he lives, *another* player will enter and remove him from this life at the approximate point where he once deprived the grocer in a former lifetime.

"An eye for an eye. A tooth for a tooth. Nothing will interfere. A cunning, sly, powerful, dishonest player may enjoy wealth, position, anything he desires, and apparently escape retribution. But for every theft, every wrongdoing, he chalks up future scores against himself in the following lives he will play.

"Somewhere out there, a very unhappy soul once named Adolf Hitler faces the toll of the passing bell, the ringing of death's knell, at least 5,933,900 times, for that many Jews he annihilated in a period of less than one-fourth of one second in the marble-earth years of 1933–45.

"Why play the game at all? Because in time, eventually, by moving from marble to marble, table to table, all of this enormous room of games will have been played through with varying degrees of ascension, and the learned and wise souls will advance toward eternal happiness to sit with the Overseer, watching lesser players in their games. Out of millenniums of duress, eons of hardship, each successful soul accumulates greater understanding and compassion for other players. A soul has the prospect of constantly growing, evolving, expanding *ad infinitum.*"

It had taken Otto all of this night to put these thoughts to conscious words. He had come to his conclusion in a split second of insight, based not on the ephemeral arguments of theology, but on the universal and scientific laws of nature.

Otto drew on impeccable scientific sources. He had recently read a book by Dr. Wilder Penfield, a Canadian neurosurgeon who had devoted a lifetime to brain operations on sufferers of focal epilepsy. The operation involved going into the brain to remove damaged tissue which was causing "explosions" of electricity with results ranging from seizures so minor as to pass unnoticed, to convulsions. However, it was not the subject of epilepsy which prompted the world-famous surgeon to write his book, *The Mystery of the Mind.* In his book, Dr. Penfield noted that during these operations, the patient was always wide-awake. A local anesthesia was administered, the skull opened. Once inside, there was no pain, for the brain lacks that perception.

The surgeon must trace the precise location of defective tissue through a tedious operation, usually many hours long. This is done by probing the suspected area of affliction with an electrical prod which, when activated, produces certain sensations. If the electrical stimulation is on the part of the brain where speech originates, he may make noises, say something involuntarily, or even experience an inability to speak. An electrical impulse elsewhere could make the patient's hands, feet, fingers or other appendages move. By subjecting the patient to a series of verbal and visual tests during these electrical probes, the surgeon eventually isolates the damaged part of the brain, and can even determine what effects excising the tissue may produce in terms of long-range benefits or damage. In other words, the surgeon can reliably determine what his knife will do to the patient's ability to function, after the damaged area is removed.

During the course of these hundreds of carefully documented

cases, Dr. Penfield discovered one of the answers to a mystery that had intrigued scientists for thousands of years—the mechanics of memory. Penfield produced the most reliable data thus far to prove that the human mind is a continuous recorder. Whatever one's conscious perceptions at any given time, these perceptions become "recordings" which are stored in the brain for as long as the brain lives. In the course of stimulating the brain, as he searched for causes of focal epilepsy, trying to cure the patient of seizures suffered during attacks, Dr. Penfield's electrical probes produced some startling reactions!

Some patients experienced a "replay" of events which occurred at some time or another in their past. These events of themselves were often not momentous. But the very fact that the replay produced *unimportant* sequences of events suggested that *all* conscious perceptions are recorded during life.

One patient experienced a refrain of music, reliving again the moment when a piano was being played. The patient had been five at that instant, the music produced by a mother long dead and gone. Another patient relived walking on a street and he actually could read the billboards, smell odors from a bakery. These examples were not to be confused with *remembering* such events. The patients experienced a *reliving* of the moment and it was a continuous, ongoing experience, just as it was when it occurred. After the probe was removed, then the patient *remembered* the event—until this moment forgotten.

Thus Dr. Penfield discovered that the brain is a machine that records all perceptions without discrimination. He knew that the conscious mind could scan and recall much of the past. Psychologists knew that with the accumulation of experience, the brain scans and evaluates and makes an instant decision on a matter using the past recordings as a basis for analysis. But until Penfield proved it, man had only guessed that *all* events which we consciously perceive are recorded indelibly.

As a psychiatrist, Otto had been interested in these discoveries since most mental illnesses are rooted in the deep dark past where events occurred to distort the reality of a patient's world. The ability of a psychiatrist to uncover such events, and to help the patient relive them, was often the key to cure.

Penfield's book made the point that the brain is a "machine" and a "tool" and the two functions of conscious and subconscious are transcended by a *third* function that can only be described as the "soul." An unconscious person is not dead. Nor is the subconscious always functioning. Yet the brain is alive and vibrant, as electroencephalograms had proven.

People who had died—and been revived—reported that they "rose out of" their bodies and "observed the people" trying to save them. Such patients, brought back from the dead, said they experienced "great relief and a tremendous sense of peace." Some even resented the efforts being made to bring a heartbeat back to the body. Without exception, hundreds of these patients who had experienced death said, they had absolutely no fear of dying anymore. It was, they reported, a "good" state of being.

If a soul could return to a dead body, it was logical to assume it could go to another body—an embryo unborn and unclaimed.

From Dr. Penfield's discovery that all experiences are permanently recorded in the brain, Otto had gone to another medical report he had studied some time ago. In this, a biologist reported that in the basic building block of all life—the DNA of the individual cells—each cell is "prestamped" with certain experiences. In the simplest example, instinct in certain insects results in a highly evolved and extremely specialized action at a given point in the development of the creature. A paper wasp in a cell among many cells reaches a point in development when the wasp reaches up and cuts the paper covering his berth, thereby freeing himself. How does the wasp know to do this? A French entomologist, Jean Henri Fabre called it "the mindless miracle of instinct . . . not to be confused with intelligence." It can be so highly developed, this intuitive action, that a bee "instinctively" knows how to inform other bees in a hive of nectar, in which direction and how far, using a bodily dance to relay this information to fellow workers. Yet, as ingenious as instinct appears to be, it is, as Fabre noted, "mindless." If the wasp cuts the paper over his cell, he climbs out to unfold his wings and face a season of life. But if a second piece of paper is placed over the cell, after the same wasp has cut the original paper, he will remain there and starve. Instinct did not tell him to cut *two* pieces of paper. It only directed that the wasp cut one.

The mystery of how species relayed such specialized acts to future progeny evaded scientists until recently. When it was discovered that in the cells of the body of each newly hatched insect, fish, reptile, bird, mammal and perhaps even in plants, the cell is stamped with chemical instructions. From basic instructions to genes and chromosomes, which determine gender, coloration and conformation, to warnings which help a species to survive, the DNA (the cellular building blocks of the universe) tell a being what all his predecessors learned the hard way. Thus a squirrel which has never seen a hawk will "instinctively" freeze at the shadow of such a bird. The lucky squirrel can thank every squirrel that was ever born for that DNA message to "look out!"

There is a theory in psychiatry and the biological sciences, that every individual is the end result of every ancestor who was involved in producing him. Theoretically, from that first set of parents which evolved into today's man, this human under scrutiny carries trillions of messages accumulated along the way which give him his intuitive and instinctual responses. Intellect and societal pressures may override such cellular DNA messages, but they exist nonetheless. In theory, then, any traumatic, momentous, important event in the life of a single man carries over to the next generation. If the succeeding generations suffer similar traumas, the imprint is deepened to "instinct." If the threat occurs no more, or infrequently, the imprint wanes and disappears.

Otto had found this theory an acceptable premise for the reason

231

for mindless and universal fears. Primeval rites such as voodoo and black magic struck a chord in the most civilized men—the cellular warnings from a primitive past, surfacing in what modern man called "superstition."

Therefore, sitting here, sipping Scotch, smoking constantly, watching Janet sleep restlessly, Otto Ebenstein gained again something he thought had been lost forever—a faith in God. A faith in a system of a universe that could produce a Hitler and allow him to exist and wreak havoc on his fellow man. When the passing bell rang for each of the six million Jews, it rang but once each. For Hitler it must ring six million times to come. From that, Otto could draw comfort. And that would excuse God, who truly moved "in mysterious ways."

Pamela. Yes, Pamela. But it wasn't Pamela at all, was it? It was someone who refused to yield from a prior game, a soul in transit using Pamela's body and station, imposing as it were on Pamela's "game." Or, perhaps, this was Pamela's game. Otto couldn't believe that. The name Erika Krajewski, Polish, the obsession with things Nazi, the minutiae mentioned by Janet of the child's aversion to showers, marmalade, the German language—even Pamela's difference in appearance mentioned by Janet and the operatives who followed Pamela. The Polish-accented voice. Tiny pieces of a puzzle which fit together if Otto was thinking about this creature, Erika. God only knew what her story was. But Pamela, the sensitive, intelligent, perceptive child—Otto was convinced that the Pamela he knew had nothing whatsoever to do with the torture and murder he had investigated. That had been Erika, not Pamela. As to whether Pamela had been "imprinted" by something her father had done, or not, this was academic and unimportant.

The problem then became both simple and complex. Simply: why were such murders being perpetrated by a girl who appeared to be a normal teen-age child? Complex: how to stop it without losing the child Pamela in the fanatic grip of Erika. To punish

232

Erika, the authorities would be forced to punish Pamela who was, Otto now reasoned, totally innocent!

Therefore, Otto concluded, he must learn how far Erika intended to go. How many must die before she was avenged? He must protect Pamela until that quota was fulfilled, if possible. If Erika were here to annihilate all remaining Nazis, Otto would fail. But if there were a limited number—then, with her vengeance complete, Erika could go on to the next game and leave Pamela to this one.

Janet awoke as Otto sat on the side of the bed, a hand on her shoulder. She looked up at the red face, heavy jowls and blood-shot eyes. A fetid odor of liquor rode his breath. Otto smiled. He brushed back hair from her forehead.

"I have some good news," Otto said softly.

Reality sprang at her, awakening remembrance now and Janet began to tremble.

"I think you are right," Otto said.

"About what?"

"I think Pamela did not do these things, these crimes."

"Who then?"

"A Polish girl. A girl named Erika Krajewski."

"Do you mean that?"

"Yes. I have been up all night thinking it through. I am now convinced it is Erika, not Pamela. Erika is using your daughter."

"The madness here," Janet whispered, "is that I believe you. It cannot be Pamela. It cannot be."

"Get up now," Otto urged. "We must get your rental car returned and check out of your motel room. We will fly back to Atlanta. I think it is time for us to talk with Pamela. We are going to need her help to resolve it all."

CHAPTER TWENTY

MOROSELY, JANET GAZED OVER THE WING and through hazy clouds looking down at the crazy-quilt pattern of the landscape far below. Beside her, labored breathing a constant reminder of his presence, Otto drank one Scotch after another. Since lift-off in Washington, he had spoken twice: once to observe that stewardesses were "little more than airborne waitresses"; then to ask when Pamela had said she'd be home. It took extraordinary concentration for Janet to reassimilate a cognizance of time. Pamela had left for the pajama party Friday, December 31, arrived in Washington Saturday, January 1, and today was Sunday—she forced her mind to a conclusion.

"This afternoon," she said. Then, "What time is it?"

Without looking at his watch, Otto said, "We will arrive in Atlanta at 3:20."

"She should be home when we get there," Janet stated.

Otto crumpled a cigarette into an armrest ashtray already overflowing. He sighed heavily, shaking ice cubes in a plastic drinking vessel.

Before they left this morning, awaiting a flight out, they had come to an agreement on a course of action. Otto had suggested they confront Pamela with what they knew, assure her of their concern, and offer their help. If, as Otto predicted, Pamela persisted in denying it all, they should make arrangements for psychiatric examination. With unabated fear, Janet had listened as Otto spoke of God, a theory of reincarnation, and his terrifying conclusion: "It is not Pamela doing these things. It is the Polish girl, Erika."

That Janet had accepted this was, she now thought, a form of insanity itself. She embraced his outlandish suggestion as easily as she had once accepted the doctrines of the Methodist Church!

"There is hope," Otto had exulted. "We must satisfy this Polish girl. We must make her leave Pamela."

"You really believe this, Otto?"

His thick, tangled eyebrows had lifted, lowered. "As crazy as it sounds. I believe it."

Janet was ready to seize any chance, any hope, no matter how remote. Now, as they approached Atlanta, she recalled Otto's excited dissertation on his new concepts.

"This must be what the Bible means when it speaks of being reborn," Otto had said, eyes bright.

Her mind incapable of rational argument, willing to accept anything which would make sense out of madness, Janet had listened to Otto recount the horrors of Hitler's pogroms, the death camps, and his loss of faith.

"No compassionate God could permit such atrocities," Otto had concluded. "But I can believe God would permit a man to set the limits of his own hell."

He had paced the floor, the breakfast they'd ordered untouched as he spoke with the zeal of a fanatic. "If a bell tolled once each second for every Jew slain by Hitler in the death camps," Otto had reasoned, "it would ring 5,933,900 times, Janet. It would ring for 68 days, 16 hours, 18 minutes and 20 seconds continually! God did not damn Hitler and the others. They damned themselves to an eternity of retribution and suffering for all they've done to mankind. To make their hell all the more complete, far far out there, tens of thousands of lifetimes away they can earn their way free! Don't you see—this is the only way it can be. It must be true! It wasn't God's doing at all. It was man. Man did it to himself."

"But, Pamela—"

"Not Pamela," Otto said fiercely. "It is *not* Pamela. It is Erika. Pamela is the tool of Erika."

"Otto, I want to believe this. I want to—but—"

"It is true!" Otto had seized Janet's shoulders, his face twisted. "I tell you, and you must believe me, it is Pamela we must save at all costs. Save her from Erika."

"But how?"

Otto had walked the room, mumbling half sentences in English, lapsing into his native tongue, his manner only plunging Janet ever deeper into a depressing sense of futility.

The skies over Atlanta were clear, incredibly blue, and the sun was brilliant as they walked from the terminal to a taxi. In silence, they rode north. When they arrived at the house, Otto paid the driver and Janet fought nausea, stomach cramped, her legs weak.

"I'm afraid, Otto."

"Be strong. Come. Let's find Pamela."

But she wasn't there. When Janet found Russell, he was reading the Sunday newspaper, a cup of cold coffee beside him. He did not seem the least surprised that Janet had arrived with Otto.

"How was your family?" Russell questioned.

"I didn't go, Russell."

"Oh?"

"No. I decided to get off alone."

"I see." He turned to Otto. "And you, my friend? How did you see in this new year?"

"In Washington, Russell. It was snowing, too cold, and quite deserted."

236

Russell nodded. "Washington always is over a holiday. Well! Would either of you like a drink, or coffee?"

"Scotch, please," Otto said.

"Russell, have you seen Pamela?"

"She is not yet home."

"Has she telephoned?" Janet asked.

"No," Russell spoke from the bar, "should she have?"

"Not really."

Janet left the two men chatting amiably, Otto's ease and conversational exchanges maddening. Janet took a long, very hot shower.

By eight o'clock, Janet's concern was too obvious to conceal. Chiding her for "constant worry about nothing," Russell went to the telephone.

"What are you going to do, Russell?" Janet asked.

"Call to the family where Pamela went, of course."

"Don't do that."

"It is better that than to have you walking around wringing your hands and frowning as you are." Russell began dialing. Janet looked at Otto and his bland expression fueled her frustration.

"Russell, I don't think it is wise to call," Janet said.

He ignored her, standing with phone held to his ear by a hunched shoulder. "How do you do," Russell said into the receiver, "this is Pamela Roth's father. Can you tell me, has Pamela left for home yet? We wondered if perhaps she needed a ride."

Through slit eyes, every breath a liquid gurgle, Otto sat watching Russell. Janet's chest ached with taut muscles, her head beginning to throb.

"I see. Very well. Thank you." Russell hung up. Idly, he turned the coiled telephone cord to untangle it, then returned to his seat. He sipped his drink, eyes vacant a moment. Then he looked at Janet. Nobody had spoken.

"I assume you knew she was not there," Russell stated.

"Yes."

He pursed his lips a second, put his drink aside and with no indication of his thoughts, now looked at Otto.

"You too."

Otto nodded.

Russell took a deep breath, exhaled slowly. "For some time now I have had a disturbing feeling that I have been unable to dispel. At a loss to identify, furthermore. It is the feeling one experiences in a strange place where the people are not friendly, and yet no person has said anything unkind, no act of animosity has occurred. Yet there is this feeling. You have known such a feeling, Otto?"

"Many times," Otto said mechanically.

"I have had this disturbing feeling here in my own home," Russell said, quietly. "I wish someone would explain it for me."

Janet looked to Otto for instructions, but the professor was gazing steadily at Russell.

"Pamela did not go to the pajama party, Russell. Otto—" Janet's tone, an audible plea, made Russell look to their guest.

"Russell," Otto said in German, "I have disquieting news."

Instantly, Russell's face drained of color. His features set, he stared at Otto with studied calm.

Otto spoke again in German and Janet screamed, "Speak English, goddamn it!"

"I'm sorry, Janet." Otto continued, "The child went to Washington, and it was for this reason I was there. I had discovered she was going. I was there to intercept her."

Without looking away from Otto, Russell questioned Janet, "You went there also?"

"Yes."

In heavily accented English, Otto told Russell everything. He began with the day Janet came to Florida, the materials which she brought from Pamela. He made no effort to soften anything. In the methodical manner of a lecturing professor, he revealed his findings, his trip to Houston, the circumstances of Dr. Fiedler's death.

Throughout, his hands at rest on the arms of his chair, Russell listened with stoic forebearance, the expression on his face so devoid of emotion it scared Janet.

"After Chattanooga," Otto said, "I suspected there would be another such incident. I enlisted the aid of—" he spoke several sentences in German again.

For the first time, Russell's eyes darted aside. After a moment, he looked at Otto again and nodded.

Otto spoke in the monotone of a man imparting distasteful information, much as a policeman might explain the circumstances of a tragedy to a member of the family. It was the practiced report of a person who somehow keeps himself uninvolved despite his obvious involvement.

" . . . must have kicked him in the groin . . . heart attack . . . departed at once on foot . . . several taxi changes . . . to airport . . . "

Except for the one nod, Russell made no other move, said not one syllable as Otto brought the father to full awareness of his daughter's duplicity.

When Otto had finished the entire story, Russell went to the bar and poured another drink.

"Have the police been notified?"

"No," Otto said.

"You do not intend to report these crimes?" Russell questioned.

"No."

"Your men, they will not?"

"No," Otto said.

"And you, Janet?" Russell asked. His eyes were terrifyingly cold, detached.

"What?" Janet asked.

"What do you intend to do with this information now that you have it?"

"Russell, I am thinking about our child!"

"This is obvious," Russell said. "I am trying to ascertain in what manner are you thinking?"

"I want to protect her, to get her home again."

"Yes, well." Russell sipped his drink, looking at Otto again. "Yesterday is forever gone, eh Otto?"

"Yes."

"What was, even an hour ago, is no more," Russell said. "Now we have—how would one say? Turned a corner?"

"What can we do, Russell?" Janet whispered.

"I will have to think about this. She is sick, of course."

"Otto, tell Russell what you told me, about Erika."

"Erika?" Russell asked, "Who is this?"

Otto explained about the airline ticket, the name, his new theories of reincarnation.

Suddenly, Russell burst into laughter, a mirthless sound.

"Otto is a psychiatrist, Russell," Janet said, quickly. "He is a man who has studied the mind—he was a rabbi—he would know about such things!"

"You believe this, Janet?" Russell's smile was like his laugh, without humor.

"I can't believe Pamela is capable of murder, Russell!"

"No, of course not," Russell said, evenly. "But whether one wishes to believe that or not, she has apparently found herself capable of it. If all that you say is true, naturally."

"To hell with the semantics and theories," Janet exploded. "I don't give a damn about this game you two are playing. I care about one thing only—one thing! Pamela. Where is she, how is she, what tortured thoughts are going through that child's mind? Instead of playing human poker, let us think of what we can do about all this!"

"If my theory is correct," Otto said, "Pamela is unaware of these events."

"Psychotic, you mean," Russell stated.

"No. As I said. Erika."

"By whatever name you choose to call it," Russell's voice was sharper, "it is in the final analysis a psychosis, is it not? Schizophrenia, manic depressive, call it *Erika*, but the child is insane."

"Very well, assume that she is," Otto replied. "She is no less innocent even then. Pamela would still be unaware. She would still be the victim, if only of her own insanity."

"I find no comfort in that," Russell snapped.

"You should," Otto rejoined. "If we can eliminate this—Erika, we shall call it—and restore Pamela to herself, we can save the child."

"You fool," Russell stood, his voice conversational. "Both of you—fools."

"All right, all right," Janet said, "we must find her and send her to a doctor, put her in a hospital."

"Why did you not tell me what was happening, Janet?" Russell asked.

"I had hoped to stop it."

"And when it did not stop? Why didn't you come to your husband and tell him?"

"I didn't want to hurt you."

"Didn't want to hurt me? You come in from a holiday trip to inform me that my daughter may have murdered three men, yet you did not wish to hurt me with the information which might have prevented it all?"

"Russell, I had no way of knowing it would get out of hand."

"That is interesting," Russell said. "You saw my child pursuing a sick obsession. You connived with her, became a part of her madness. There must be a reason. What is it?"

"I told you, I didn't want to hurt you."

"Might I offer a counter thought?" Russell asked. "May I suggest you believed yourself what Pamela seemed to suspect. Is that not the reason, Janet?"

"Of course not!"

"You took everything to this—this man, and yet you could not bring it to me? Why else would you have taken such a move? Do you know what this man is? This Otto Ebenstein?"

Otto sat, impassionate, breathing heavily, face blank.

"He is a spoiler, Janet. He came here to uncover the Nazi he

241

thought me to be. Anything else he says is a lie. Is this not correct, Otto?"

Otto nodded.

"He has no emotions, this man," Russell seethed. "His guts were burned out long ago. He is a shell now. An old exterior surrounding a gutted body. He is a bitter anachronism, a piece of ash which somehow escaped the ovens! He has no love, no compassion, no warmth in his soul. He can never again so long as he lives trust anybody! He has been betrayed by neighbors, friends, loved ones. He has seen men eat men, and women tear limbs from their dead babies. He has witnessed a depravity of a type you cannot imagine! He is your friend? No, Janet. Otto Ebenstein has no friends and he knows it. What you accept as 'friend' he knows to be 'convenience.' He knows that you, like every other human he has known, would sell him to the gas chambers again for a slice of bread and a piece of meat. Otto—tell her. Is this not true?"

Otto nodded.

Throat locked, Janet trembled as Russell stood face-to-face with her. He turned, walked away. When next he spoke his tone was lower, more normal:

"Otto can be forgiven. I forgive you, Otto."

Otto's pig-like eyes stared, unblinking.

"He cannot be blamed for coming. He lives as he has lived for all the years since the war, in hopes of revenge. It is nothing more or less. Like every Jew, he harbors a deep hidden desire to torture as he has been tortured, to make death come with lingering agony as so many Jews agonized. But for Otto his torture has been the greatest, the longest, the most unbearable, because he somehow lived when others did not. He is not your friend, Janet. He is your enemy! He would see you die, Pamela die, see anybody die and never bat an eye if he thought he could get to one more Gestapo, one more SS officer, one more Nazi swine! He has used you, me, Pamela. Of course he doesn't want Pamela caught. She is doing what Otto and every other similar Jew has not the guts to do—

she is killing Nazis and doing it with excruciating care."

"Russell, you can't believe this," Janet pleaded.

"Tell her!" Russell commanded. Otto sat unmoving. "Tell her, Otto!" Russell suddenly seized Otto's shirt and shook him violently. "Tell her the truth!"

"Yes," Otto gurgled. "It is true."

"Of course it is," Russell said, shockingly calm now.

"What—my God—what—what can we do?" Janet cried.

Russell sat now, hands loosely clasped in his lap. He gazed at Otto without anger. "Yes, Otto, what can we do now?"

"I don't know."

"Hmm." Russell nodded slowly. "We could let her continue to kill until all are gone, perhaps. When all the murderers are murdered, maybe then Pamela will return to class at the Experimental High School and be a nice girl for graduation."

"I see now," Janet said, voice quivering. "I see it now."

"Do you?" Russell mocked.

"I think I do, Russell. Pamela is what she is because of you. Cell, soul and mind, by God you molded her."

"A shame she had no mother," Russell said.

"And like a fool I went to Otto for help. No different one of you from the other. Each of you suffering whatever twisted set of circumstances made you. Pamela, and now me, we're just two more victims caught innocently in-between."

"Now you hear, Otto?" Russell admonished. "Suddenly we are allies."

"I have run from one to the other, struggling to control and protect, acting like an idiot!" Janet said. "Russell the father and Otto the 'uncle' and not far dissimilar, either of you! Now you hear me, you two. You hear me and you better come up with answers. I don't care who is who or why. I no longer care whether Russell marched Otto's families into the ovens, or whether Otto kills a thousand escaped Nazi criminals! I care about Pamela. Only Pamela!

"I am going to call the police." Janet moved toward the telephone. Immediately, Russell and Otto were up. Russell moved to block her way.

"That would be a mistake, serving no good," Otto stated.

"We have had our moment of anger," Russell said. "Come sit down, Janet."

"It's almost eleven o'clock!" Janet cried. "Pamela isn't coming home, don't either of you see that? She is gone and this time she won't be back!"

"The police could not change that," Otto reasoned.

"Sit down, Janet." Russell held her arm, urging.

"It's because of you, Russell," Janet said, hoarsely. "Whether you are right or wrong, guilty or not, it is because of you. Pamela began all this in search of something related to you. Do you see that is true?"

"Yes."

"Do you love her, Russell?"

His face flushed. "You know that I do, Janet."

"If this is true, Russell, get her back."

"How can I do that, Janet?"

"I don't know. But I think you can. I think you are the key to this, Russell. You say you love Pamela. We shall see. If you are, as you say Otto is, a gutted human being, you will hold still, do nothing and hope for the best. But if you really love that child you will do what is necessary to save her."

"Janet, be realistic."

"You can do it, goddamn you! I know you can do it!"

Russell looked away. "I can only try. A man can only do certain—"

"You can do it if you love her, Russell! You know how; you can save your own child."

"Janet, in your mind, the world is orderly, so—"

"No logic, Russell! No Prussian philosophy. Save our daughter. Whatever it takes, save her."

Russell turned, speaking to Otto, "Can you help?"

"I don't know. I can call New York, ask. If we could determine the link that binds the three dead men, perhaps then we could learn where she has gone, who else she is after."

Russell nodded shortly. Walking toward the door he ordered, "Use our telephone, Otto, and call. I am going to the office. We will see what we can learn, working at it separately."

The front door closed and the ticking of a standing grandfather's clock became inordinately louder.

"What do you think, Otto?" Janet whispered.

"I don't know."

"Call New York, Otto. Please. Now."

Otto lifted the receiver, asked for information and patted his pocket for a cigarette.

"I forgot to tell him—" Otto halted.

"Tell him what?"

"About a man who—" Otto paused to give the operator a New York name. He scribbled a number, hung up a moment and then dialed.

"Who, Otto?"

"An investigator," Otto said. "An insurance—hello?"

Janet put an ashtray near Otto by the phone.

"Jules? Otto. Have you learned more about the insurance investigator from Switzerland?"

CHAPTER TWENTY-ONE

"IT IS SPECULATIVE ONLY, you understand," Jules said, his voice distant on the line. "The concept of an insurance investigator is actually brilliant, isn't it? Whether the death is natural or not can be officially determined with police assistance. Under the guise of filing claim, this investigator has access to much evidence, the authorities become therefore his unwitting accomplice. It is brilliant, Otto. Is it not?"

"Yes," Otto said. "Brilliant."

"Over the years a number of our operatives have been intercepted. You remember the men we lost in Brazil in the fifties? Most likely at the hands of this man, or another such man."

"I can see that."

"I telephoned our contact in Washington, told him to be on the alert for the arrival of this agent. I told him we needed fingerprints, photographs."

"Good, good," Otto said.

"Too late, Otto. He has been there already."

"Already?"

"The body was discovered at 3:30 this afternoon. He must have been right behind you. Very fortunate that we avoided involving the League. Otherwise, again it might have become the same murder for murder we had after the war, their operatives intercepting ours as then. We were lucky this time."

"What about Washington?" Otto persisted.

"Yes. My man there says the murder was reported and the insurance investigator was on the scene. Possibly he found the body, reported it and awaited police intervention before actually stepping into the matter. Very ingenious. Very smart."

"Then how did this agent know to be there?" Otto questioned.

"An intriguing thought. A terrifying thought in actuality, Otto. It suggests there is a viable network even now. We have suspected a loose connection might exist, but never any real proof of it."

"It does suggest that," Otto agreed.

"Further," Jules was suddenly louder as he spoke more directly into the telephone, "it suggests this agent knew of the association between Houston, Chattanooga and Washington; perhaps he went to Washington assuming this one would be alive, and with the hope of warning him. What do you think?"

"Could be."

"Yes. Ummmm. Of course then, this man will have a good idea who is next, won't he?"

"So it seems, Jules."

"Somewhere along the way he will be waiting, Otto. When the girl arrives he, or someone like him will be there. Therefore she must be stopped. For her safety."

"The girl did not come home, Jules."

A long silence. Then, calmly, "On her way to the next one, you think?"

"I assume as much."

247

"Too bad."

"Jules, can you help?"

"As I told you, Otto. Information, yes. Operatives, no."

"Even to catch this agent?"

"No. Identify him and we can handle it better elsewhere than here. In Switzerland, where he comes from, perhaps. At his home. Accidentally. Times have changed, Otto. Overt action no longer is permitted."

"For the sake of the girl, Jules."

"Otto, Otto—" spoken sadly.

"All right," Otto said brusquely, "have you spoken with Kruger?"

"I have."

"Anything?"

Jules sighed. The sound of rustling papers. He said, "This is extremely tenuous, Otto. Kruger can only say that he suspects the connection between them all is (a) Poland, (b) one of the camps, most probably Oswiecim since we know the real Hans Fiedler was there before going to Chelmno. Kruger says he thinks the Nazi pretender picked up Fiedler's identity from there. He says the girl's papers prove that Josef Braun Haas was transferred there because he supposedly died there."

"Anything else?"

"The bulk of the material the girl assimilated concerned an officer of the *Einsatzgruppen* assigned to Warsaw. His name was Frank Kingmann. Apparently, if Kruger is correct, Kingmann was first delegated to eliminate the *Untermenschen* in Lublin and Madagascar. Later Kingmann was liaison between the Polish camps, possibly with duties encompassing the transport of victims to the camps. He would, in this way, have some connection with Oswiecim if only remotely. However, according to Kruger, her papers show that Kingmann died on the Russian front during the purges."

"What else do you know of this Kingmann?"

"Nothing."

"Then we have no way of knowing where the girl may be going. It could be anywhere."

"That is correct. Whereas, obviously, their side more than likely can guess where. There is the problem, isn't it?"

"Jules!" Otto spoke angrily in Hebrew, "I need your help! This is League business and you know it."

Jules replied almost indifferently, "When you are prepared to identify a suspect, ready to place him under surveillance with the intentions of exposing him and bringing him to trial, then it is League business, Otto. This is not. You know better."

"Jules—I beg of you."

"It is always a hazard that one should become too involved to see the overall objective, Otto. I fear this has happened with you. Take my advice. Find the girl. Send her home. Keep her there."

"About the imposter, Fiedler," Otto said, "when did he go to Oswiecim?"

"Kruger says March 1, 1941. Whether to meet Himmler or with Himmler, Kruger isn't sure. But he believes this man, who assumed Fiedler's identity, may have been a part of the expansion plans which Hitler ordered for Auschwitz-Birkenau about that time."

"You refuse me manpower then," Otto stated, as though the question were still unresolved.

"Unequivocally, sadly, but yes, friend Otto. I am sorry. I cannot be a party to a vendetta."

"I will call again, Jules."

Jules disconnected without another word. For a few moments, Otto stood with eyes distant, then turned to Janet.

"Where is Oswiecim, Otto? What is it?"

"It is Polish. Their word. Auschwitz. The name 'Auschwitz' is the German term for the same place. In Poland."

"Who were you talking to?" Janet asked.

As though he hadn't heard, Otto questioned, "What is Russell's office number?"

He dialed as she recited the numerals. The phone rang several times and a man answered with the company name.

"Mr. Roth, please," Otto said.

"He won't be into the office until Monday, sir."

"He is there now," Otto insisted. "Please page him."

"I'm sorry sir, I am not allowed to do that on a holiday."

"You cannot page the owner of the business?" Otto snapped.

Janet reached for the receiver. "This is Janet Roth, I am calling for my husband, please."

A moment later she gave the phone to Otto again. Russell was on the line. Otto began speaking in German and Janet instantly became angry, demanding, "English!"

Otto continued speaking in German, very quickly, "There is a probable assassin with information to direct him to where Pamela may be going next. He evidently discovered the murder in Washington, which means he is very close. Do you understand?"

"Yes."

"Damn you, Otto! Speak English!" Janet screamed.

His tone unchanged, German still, Otto said, "Time therefore is of the essence, Russell."

"I see that."

"Do you have contacts in West Berlin?"

"A few," Russell said, curtly.

"Can you gain access to the secret files of the U. S. Document Center in West Berlin?"

"I don't know."

Janet was crying now, babbling, Otto ignoring her as he continued, voice level, "For thirty years they have been guarding thousands of documents involving World War II Nazis. The Document Center contains twenty-eight individual biographical collections, more than nine hundred rolls of microfilm identifying various Nazi officers, over a hundred rolls identifying Nazi judges, nearly four hundred fifty concerning the so-called People's Courts. As you know, the U. S. Government is protecting former Nazis who are again serving the state. If you could somehow get fingerprints and photographs from Houston, Chattanooga and Washington, and gain access to those files—perhaps we could determine the connection between these men."

"How do you propose I do this?" Russell demanded.

"I do not know how! I am reaching for straws. I called primarily to tell you of this agent who will, as you know, be after Pamela."

Russell hung up, leaving Otto with a humming line and a sobbing woman.

"You bastards," Janet screamed. "You bastards, both of you!"

"I am sorry I spoke so you could not understand, Janet."

"Hiding things from me even now, damn you both!"

"That is true to a small degree, Janet. I was also trying to keep anyone at Russell's office from understanding."

"Oh how easily lies come to you," Janet accused. "So smoothly and without expression. Such practiced and emotionless lies, Otto. Is the truth so foreign to you, to Russell? To everyone?"

"At the expense of sounding the philosopher, Janet," Otto said, "what is truth? I wish it were so easily defined."

Janet swung her arm from well down and behind her, bringing the flat of her palm hard against Otto's face. His head snapped back and he staggered slightly. Aghast, Janet stood with mouth open, stunned that she had done this.

"Otto—I—I didn't mean to do that."

"I have been struck before."

"Otto, I'm sorry. It was a reflex. Uncalled for. I'm sorry."

Otto nodded, jowls responding, eyes aqueous. "Would you do me a favor?"

"Yes," she said. "What?"

"I would like a scalding cup of tea, please. I'm too old for such late and long hours. I feel very cold. To the marrow of my bones I feel cold. Could you bear to have me go to bed now?"

"Yes, of course. I'll make the tea and bring it up."

Janet hurried toward the door and out. Only then did Otto lift a hand to touch the inflamed cheek.

When Janet went upstairs with the tea, Otto was asleep, lying fully clothed across his bed. She covered him with a blanket, returned to the den and there sat sipping the tea herself, liberally laced with rum and concentrated lime juice. She pulled her legs beneath her, the click-click-clicking of the upright hall clock the only sound in the room.

In an incredibly short period, her life and everything important to her had undergone irreversible transformation. Her sensibilities had been staggered, it was difficult to think a complete and lucid thought. She could not, she realized, even assign priorities in a logical manner. What had been her home was now this silent cell. What had been her friend, Otto, was now a frightening visage with incredibly terrifying potential to harm what was dear to Janet. Her husband, with whatever imperfections he suffered, was a stranger incapable of giving her the love and emotional security she so desperately needed at this moment. What she had trusted was now not to be trusted—these two men in her life. And her daughter. God only knew what her daughter had become. Janet did not presume to think that Pamela would ever again be a wide-eyed child.

Like the distant rumble and faint underfoot tremor of an impending earthquake which will destroy utterly, Janet's world was in a state of flux, liquid, insolvent. To whom could she turn? To whom did others turn when in troubled times? A friend? Even this word had changed in concept. As Russell accused and Otto concurred, "friend" was in truth "convenience." Illusory.

Nothing was stable. Nothing was permanent. In a mad world of insane inhabitants, here in this opulent and secure niche, she had somehow become prey and predator at one and the same time. From the depths of some inner source she found her mind dredging up unknown strengths, plotting, becoming as cold and calculating as her opponents. Were they her opponents, Otto, Russell—Pamela?

She sipped tea, listened to the tick-tock, heard the chimes strike six. Eleanor would be in the kitchen preparing breakfast for the master who would not be here. The maid, unaware of Janet's presence in the den, would shuffle about the kitchen with an eye to Mr. Roth's moment of departure. But Mr. Roth was gone. There was only Mrs. Roth and she wasn't hungry.

Janet had the detached sensation of a drugged brain, everything in the room disproportionately close or far, large or small, vivid or obscure. She became aware of irrelevant things: a dust mote waving in a shadowed corner where until now it had evaded notice and elimination. Janet stared at the oil painting hanging over the fireplace and suddenly realized she'd never truly *looked* at the picture before. It was quite good. A pastoral scene with sheep and a keeper.

"Merciful God!" Eleanor shrieked and clasped both hands to her bosom. "Mrs. Roth you're going to be the death of me yet!"

"I'm sorry, Eleanor." Janet was still unmoving.

"Lord, Mrs. Roth, my heart's at it a mile a minute. I was already conjuring dark thoughts."

"Oh? About what, Eleanor?"

"Mr. Roth is so punctual and this morning he's fifteen minutes overdue for his breakfast, Mrs. Roth."

"He isn't here, Eleanor. He had to go to the office late last night." Why was she explaining this to the maid? Why was she apologizing to the damned servants?

"Would you care for breakfast, Mrs. Roth?"

"No."

"Coffee then?"

Janet felt the oncoming signals of an imminent headache. "On second thought, Eleanor, I will take breakfast and coffee. Whatever you prepared for Mr. Roth will be fine."

Janet arose, gathered the teapot and cup, but her hands trembled so, she gave them to Eleanor. She walked into the hall and feeling eyes on her, turned to the stairs. Otto was up half a flight, freshly dressed, gazing down at her.

"Would you like breakfast?" Janet asked, leadenly.

"Thank you."

"In the kitchen then," Janet said, and walked on without him.

Russell arrived while Otto and Janet were still seated at the breakfast table. Otto smoked constantly, drinking yet more coffee. A man his age, Janet thought, would surely suffer from the extremes of his bad habits. But except for darkly circled eyes and the pallor of his skin, Otto seemed no different. It was Russell in whom the loss of sleep and change in routine was most apparent. He was haggard, unshaven, his voice hoarse as though bordering on a sore throat.

"There were six men, one of whom died naturally, three have been murdered, therefore two remain," Russell said. He sat next to Otto across the table from Janet in the breakfast booth.

"The tie between them?" Otto questioned.

"Each served in one capacity or another at a certain post in Cracow Province, Poland."

"Auschwitz," Otto stated.

Russell seemed unable to say it. He nodded.

"A unit, a squad, what was their connection?" Otto persisted.

"I am not sure. Except all were there and knew Dr. Fiedler. That is, the Fiedler killed in Houston."

"How reliable is this information?" Otto asked softly.

"It is reliable."

"Where did you get it?"

"What difference does it make?" Russell shouted. "Do you think only Jews have contacts in this world?"

"No, certainly not. Do you have faith in this information? We can ill afford an error in judgment. Time will not permit it."

"If I had not decided the information is correct, I would not be sitting here discussing it," Russell snapped.

"Very well." Otto methodically poured a precise amount of sugar into a fresh cup of coffee. "Now the important question: three are down. One is dead. Where are the other two?"

"One is in Connecticut," Russell rasped. "The other in Holcomb, Kansas."

Otto nodded, sipped coffee. "You have formulated a plan?"

"I shall take one, you the other," Russell said.

"Is there no younger man we can call upon?"

"No. I don't have anyone I can trust with this."

"But you trust me?"

Russell stared at Otto a moment, then poured himself a cup of coffee. His spoon grated on the bottom of the china vessel, stirring, stirring, stirring.

"You know what I will need," Otto said matter-of-factly.

"Whatever it is, we will get it."

"How soon can we leave?"

"You on the next flight to Wichita. A rental automobile will be waiting. You will still face a drive of 360 kilometers, more or less. Take warm clothing. It is below freezing there."

"I will need a weapon."

"It is upstairs on your bed. You know, of course, it must go in your locked suitcase and not on your person."

"Yes I know that."

"I want to go," Janet blurted. Both men looked at her, then began speaking to one another again.

"My curiosity," Otto commented, "did you manage to get into the files of the U. S. Document Center in West Berlin?"

"Yes."

"Ah. Then that is how you did it, getting this information?"

"Partially."

"Excellent. The League would give an arm and a leg for access to that source. It is strange that America, which championed the downfall of Nazism, would be the very nation to now protect the former Nazis in high places."

"It is a strange world," Russell said, acidly. "If you are to catch that flight, you will have to hurry, Otto."

"Excuse me then," Otto waited as Russell stood and let him out of the booth.

"I want to go, I said," Janet commanded.

"Not with me," Otto spoke offhand, leaving the room.

"Then with you, Russell," Janet said.

"No."

"You sonofabitch," Janet fumed.

"You will not go, Janet. For two reasons: first, because it might be a dangerous situation from which Otto, I, possibly both of us, shall not return."

"Are you serious?"

"Secondly, and primarily," Russell said, "because contrary to what you may think, I love you. Perhaps I have never said this enough, but now is an appropriate time to say—I love you and I have loved so few things in my life. But I love you deeply, completely, and I will not allow you to be endangered."

"Russell, I want to go anyway. I'll stay nearby, away from where it is you are going, but near. Please!"

"It is not something we shall debate, Janet."

She grabbed his arm, halting him at the kitchen door. "Russell," Janet whispered. "What has happened to us! What is going to become of us?"

He put the tips of his fingers against her cheek, "Life has always been—for me—" tears rose in his eyes. "It has always been thus with me, Janet. I do not profess to understand why."

For the first time in Janet's married life, she saw in Russell's eyes more than her own reflection. A shard of reflected light glistened. He drew her to him so tightly it left her breathless.

256

"All I ever loved was you, and Pamela," Russell's voice was muffled. "I would die for each of you. I would kill for either of you."

"Oh, Russell," Janet was crying.

"Call Harold, Janet," Russell regained composure, "tell him to drive Otto to the airport. Then hurry back. Soon I will need a ride there also."

"I'll take you, Russell."

"No." He pulled away.

"Please, Russell. Let me!"

"No. I want you here by the phone, should Pamela call. Now do as I ask, please. Call Harold."

"Russell—"

But he was walking with long strides up the hallway now, heels clicking on the hardwood flooring, poor lighting making a silhouette of him. It occurred to Janet, Russell had a certain military bearing. Every inch the officer.

CHAPTER TWENTY-TWO

OTTO HAD PREPARED for the weather. He'd purchased, and now wore, thermal "long johns." Despite two pairs of stockings, trousers, woolen shirt, sweater and overcoat, he was miserably cold. From Wichita, he'd driven the rented Buick 156 miles to the famous gunfighter's town of Dodge City. There he'd filled a new gallon thermos with scalding coffee, then continued west to Garden City and beyond six miles to Holcomb. Following Russell's directions, he'd proceeded due north to "a ninety-degree turn west, to another turn ninety-degrees north, thence four kilometers distant. The house is the only one visible."

The terrain was table flat. The paved road stretched away, perfectly straight, to the horizon, with geometrically patterned dirt access roads crisscrossing the plains. His only cover was provided by occasional snow fences, constructed of closely spaced wooden slats, barriers behind which drifts had formed.

Once the motor was cut, heat inside the vehicle dissipated quickly. Whistling winds gusting to forty miles per hour swept hoarfrost in a cutting swath. He sat now waiting for dawn, a mug of coffee clumsily held between gloved hands. He had demanded a white automobile and his hope was that it would not be readily seen by whomever else was out there waiting, watching. He'd gotten out of the car only briefly and only once. Scanning the pre-dawn horizon under a half moon with 12-x-50 binoculars, he could see lights burning at the wood frame farm dwelling. Behind the house stood two silos, a large barn, several sheds and a windmill with tail pinned and rotor frozen.

Back inside the vehicle he'd pampered himself by running the motor, but the heater never regained dominance against plunging temperatures.

Over the entire scene lay increments of snow frozen to a solid crusty sheet offering poor footing, deceptively covering any pot-holes or ravines. The safest approach to the domicile would be by this road and then up a long unpaved drive. There was positively no way the house could be reached under cover.

Through the frosted windows came the first rays of the rising sun as refracted light was prismatically affected by radial designs of ice flecks. A few more minutes. He stalled, poured another cup of coffee.

The wind had died. Absolute silence. Otto steadied himself, opening the car door. He stood, holding his breath to eliminate exhaled clouds. Through his binoculars, he first searched the horizon, then carefully observed the house. No sign of life. To his right, fiery bright and shimmering, the rising sun. He turned the field glasses to the farthest curve of the earth, moving clockwise, inching around, alert for any deviation in the scene.

He would never have seen it had not the sun been precisely where it was. A reflection stabbed across the barren landscape like a laser. He turned away, blinded momentarily. To ease his eyes, he put down the glasses a few moments, squinting in the direction of the glare. When next he adjusted the binoculars he identified the source and swore softly. A motorized camper. With the sun now off the windshield, Otto could even determine that it was one of the fiberglass body types, perfect for anyone who faced a long vigil against time and the elements. The swept lines of the motor home blended with the contours of the terrain and despite the fact the unit was in the open, as was Otto's car, it was extremely difficult to see. Had he not known exactly where to look now, he might well miss it.

A lost traveler? It was the beauty of such vehicles that they could halt anywhere; perhaps a weary driver had simply pulled over and gone to sleep in the heated home on wheels. Otto's instincts told him otherwise.

He drew on his war experiences, cupping the field glasses to avoid creating a telltale flash of reflected light that might betray him to the other vehicle. Otto got into the car again, leaving the front door open. He lit a cigarette and the smoke combined with the cold air seared his throat and lungs, stealing away the taste of tobacco. What to do? Sit here indefinitely? The camper was far better suited for that.

He decided against going forward on foot. He would feel more secure with his car close at hand. He slammed the car door. Turning the key, he heard the motor hesitate, then chug, chug, chug. Come on, damn it, come on—chug, chug, chug, ah! It roared to life. Thank God he had run the motor several times during his wait.

The tires had frozen to the ground and cracked like rifles as he began to roll. The heater wouldn't have time to warm the interior, but he had it on defrost anyway. He tried the wipers to no avail. The distance to the house closed slowly. Otto deliberately made the vehicle jump, hesitate, stall, leap forward and hesitate again. Finally, he allowed the motor to die, coasting to the side of the road twenty yards from the dirt drive which led to the farm dwelling.

"Better inside and warm," he said aloud, "than here and frozen." He got out, lifted the hood and with this as his pretext, studied the surroundings. Still no movement at the house. He left the hood up, circled the car, looked up and down the road. The camper was no longer visible to the naked eye. He threw a blanket over the thermos and binoculars, locked the doors and trudged toward the house, boots squeaking on frozen turf. In his pocket, heavy, loaded, Russell's Luger.

From the corner of his eye he caught a glimpse of the camper—moving. Otto hurried his pace. He stomped up the steps, rattled the glass in the front door by knocking, and turned slowly as though to see his whereabouts. The camper was coming down the highway, its roof appearing between drifts piled against snow fences.

"Answer the door, damn you," Otto whispered. He knocked again, harder. He went to a window and peered inside.

"Hello!" Otto called. He returned to the door, stealing a furtive glance at the camper which had now stopped. Otto could feel the telescope on him. He knocked again, calling, "Hello there!"

Through thin curtains he thought he saw somebody coming down the hall. Thump. Thump. Thump. The vibrations carried weakly to Otto, waiting nervously. He knocked again.

"*Ja, ja!* One moment!"

He tried to use the window as a mirror, but couldn't see the camper. As the door opened, a thought struck Otto like a hammer: the assassin had no idea who he was looking for! He would presume that Otto was—

"Come in, come in!" the old man stood in the middle of an aluminum "walker." It had been this that Otto heard thumping down the hall.

"Oh, oh, oh!" the man protested against the frigid draft. He wore a long flannel nightgown, heavy socks and slippers. "Shut it, shut it!"

Otto closed the door. Now he looked covertly for the camper. It was several hundred yards away, exhaust fumes rising from the rear.

"I've had car trouble I'm afraid," Otto said, turning.

The man was in his eighties. Sunken cheeks and flaccid lips over toothless gums. His eyes were that faded hue of the elderly, his head an uncertain bony structure atop a weak neck. His chin waggled. He grinned.

"Not many people come this way. Come in and warm yourself."

"I had trouble last night," Otto said, following the slow progress of his host. "I sat out there waiting for somebody to get up. I didn't want to awaken you."

"No mind, no mind, no matter," the old man rasped. "I just now put on water for boiling. You like oatmeal and butter?"

"No bother—" Otto protested.

"No, no, say, I get lonely out here. Only me in the house since the wife died. Me only. Just me. I have the cleaning lady, Arlene—Swedish girl I think—she comes three times a week. What is today?"

"Tuesday."

"Won't be coming today. You like oatmeal with butter?"

"I don't wish to be trouble."

"No, no trouble." The old man spoke in a high-pitched loud voice, as though Otto might be hard of hearing. "Just me in the house since my wife died. Me alone. I'll put on coffee. You could drink coffee, couldn't you?"

He stood before the stove, one waxen hand gripping the walker, spilling coffee grounds as he attempted to spoon them into a large, blue enameled pot.

"You like oatmeal with butter?"

"Yes."

"That's what I'm having. You like butter on your oatmeal do you?"

"Yes."

"Good. Good. Just sit down. I'll have it ready soon enough."

Otto walked to the kitchen window. The camper was beside his car now. Otto realized the old man was staring at him.

"You German?"

Otto nodded.

"Lots of German families around here. I come from Düsseldorf. Name's Schmidt. Franz Schmidt."

"How do you do, Franz. I am Otto."

"Jew."

"Yes," Otto said. "Jew."

"It doesn't matter to me. You like oatmeal with butter, do you?"

"Yes I do."

Otto moved his chair near a window giving him the best view of highway and drive.

"How about some coffee?"

"Yes," Otto said. "Coffee would be good."

"Not ready yet."

"When it's ready then."

"You'll have to wait until it's ready," Franz Schmidt said. He banged the enamelware pot with a spoon, "Hurry coffee, hurry along."

The old man turned, his support knocking aside a chair as he wheeled to face Otto. He began speaking German, "Like a pinch of salt in your coffee?"

"*Ja*," Otto said.

"Makes less bitter, the salt does," Schmidt said. He returned to English, "Say, what's your name anyway?"

"Otto. Otto Ebenstein."

"Otto. That's German."

"*Ja*. German."

"I'm German."

"Yes. You told me."

"From Düsseldorf. Are you Jew?"

"Yes."

"It's all right. Sit down, sit down. That's all behind us now. We're too old to fight over it. Sit down."

Otto remained seated, watching the camper. A figure rounded the van, stood looking at the house. He wore a ski mask, his breath snorting in plumes.

"How about some oatmeal with butter, Otto?"

"Thank you, Franz."

The old man stared at Otto. Voice low, he asked., "How do you know my name?"

"You told me your name. Franz Schmidt."

"Not Schmidt. Smith."

"Oh. I misunderstood."

"The American name. Smith."

"All right."

"Don't call me Schmidt again."

"No. I won't."

His face still intense, Franz asked, "Do you like oatmeal or not?"

"I do like it."

The camper was backing away from the car now.

"With butter or without?"

"With butter."

The motor home turned, maneuvering the space between fence posts, coming up the drive.

"Hurry coffee! Hurry!" Franz rapped the pot with a spoon again. "You want some coffee, don't you?"

"Yes," Otto said. He removed his coat, placing it over the back of his chair so that, folded, the Luger was easy to reach, if he must. He could hear a crunch of tires from outside, the rumble of a motor.

"Hurry coffee, hurry now. Otto wants coffee. You want coffee don't you, Otto?"

"Yes, I do." Otto put his hand back, casually, touching the butt

264

of the Luger. His heart pounded, his breath coming as though in rarefied air.

"I always put a pinch of salt in my coffee pot—"

A knock at the door.

"Makes less bitter that way. You put a pinch of salt in your coffee, Otto?"

"Sometimes."

The knock at the door became more insistent. If there were no answer—would he break in, gun in hand, committed to assault by mistake?

"One minute!" Otto yelled.

The old man turned, "What?"

"There's somebody at the door, Franz."

"At the door?"

"Yes, at the front door."

"Nobody comes out here."

The front door glass rattled, hammering, demanding!

"You should go to the door, Franz."

"It isn't Arlene. She doesn't come today."

Wham! Wham! Wham!

"One minute, coming!" Otto shouted.

"I can hear you," Franz snapped.

"Answer the door, Franz," Otto commanded.

Muttering, the old man stumped toward the hallway. "I don't have much oatmeal. Watch, Otto, he'll want oatmeal too."

Otto withdrew the Luger, hands shaking, cocked it, put it back in the pocket. He draped the coat across his lap, hand in the pocket. He had only to aim and fire.

"*Ja?*" Franz at the front door, partially visible from here.

"Do you have a telephone?" the voice.

"Shut the door, shut it, shut it!"

"Thank you."

"You like oatmeal with butter?"

Thump, thump, thump of the walker, coming down the hall.

"You like oatmeal with butter?" Franz repeated.

The man stepped through the door and his eyes locked with Otto's.

"Well? Well?" Franz shouted. "Do you like oatmeal?"

"Yes," the man was unsmiling. "I do."

"Goddamn it, Otto. What did I tell you?"

CHAPTER TWENTY-THREE

THE SKI MASK HAD LEFT AN IMPRESSION on a shiny bald pate. Steel-gray eyes set in a round face, nose red and lips discolored, he studied Otto. He was pulling off his gloves; hunter's gloves with the forefinger exposed for triggering a rifle.

"Smith," he said, the corners of his mouth pulling as though about to smile.

"No," Franz snapped. "No, no, no. That's my name!"

"Well," the newcomer said benevolently, "it is my name also. Perhaps we'd better go to first names then. Mine is Ralph."

"Franz," the old man said peevishly. He gestured at Otto. "He's Otto. A Jew."

Ralph ducked his head slightly. Embarrassment? Or covering a quickening alert?

"Nice camper," Otto said.

"Yes. Thanks."

"Goddamn it!" Franz shrilled. "Look it now! The coffee's boiled. Goddamn it! And I don't have enough oatmeal."

"None for me thanks," Ralph said.

"I guess you want some," Franz demanded of Otto.

"No. I would like coffee, if I may."

"Help yourself." The old man slopped oatmeal as he ladled it from a saucepan into a large bowl. He hobbled to the refrigerator and took out a dish of butter. He put this on the table and wheeled the walker, stumping into the hall. Otto, sitting, and the stranger still standing, contemplated one another.

"Shirley?" the old man was shouting. "That you, Shirley? No, don't hang up—this here is Smith out north of town. Franz Smith! Listen when you're through talking, call Andy and tell him there's a couple cars stranded out here near my place."

Otto watched for a reaction, but the stranger was placid, the hint of a smile still flirting at the corners of his lips.

"You live around here?" Ralph inquired.

"No. You?"

"No."

Franz returned and slammed two mugs on the table. He lurched between stove and the bare wooden table, delivering the enamel coffee pot.

"Wrecker's coming," Franz fumed. "Pour coffee. Sit down."

Otto hung his coat over the back of his chair, then sat with an arm dangled near the garment. Ralph removed his overcoat, draped it across his chair. He then turned the chair and straddled it with arms folded across the back, one hand close to the lapel of a jacket he still wore. Otto mentally cursed himself. So smart. Deftly, the newcomer had positioned himself to hide his chest and one hand. If he had a gun, it was there strapped under his arm—

"May I pour your coffee?" Otto asked, doing it.

"You had auto trouble?" Ralph asked.

"Yes."

"Such trouble in this kind of weather could kill a man," Ralph noted. His voice had a French inflection. He was forty, give or take a year or two. He had a slight paunch, appeared soft. Hardly what Otto would picture as a professional assassin. Nevertheless, Otto's heart pounded, the muscles in his neck and face so taut he didn't trust himself to try a casual smile.

Franz put butter into his bowl of oatmeal. He stabbed the mixture with a tablespoon, muttering. He scooped some of the steaming porridge and blew it. The stranger looked at Otto and discreetly tapped the side of his head with a finger. Otto nodded.

"You live here alone, old man?" Ralph asked.

"Me and the house. Wife's dead. Alone."

"Must be lonely," Ralph commented, standing. He walked to the back door, parted the curtains and looked out at the barn.

"Arlene isn't coming. You know Arlene?"

"No," Ralph said, pleasantly. He checked the pantry, a broom closet, walking to the hall to glance both ways. Throughout, he never truly lost sight of Otto.

The old man blew more oatmeal, unaware or uncaring that his guest was wandering about the house.

"Where's the telephone, old man?"

"Hallway. By the bedroom. I told Shirley to call a wrecker."

"Yes I heard you." Ralph opened a door and glanced into another room, then closed it.

"Mind if I smoke?" Otto asked at large.

"No, go ahead," Ralph replied.

Otto reached for his cigarettes and Ralph turned smoothly, his own hand going into his jacket. He stood waiting for Otto to withdraw a package.

"Would you care for one?" Otto offered.

"No. Thank you. Let me light that." Ralph withdrew matches and struck one, extending it between manicured fingers.

"Your coffee is growing cold," Otto commented.

"So it is, isn't it?" Ralph's gray eyes were steady, the constantly tugging muscle pulling the corner of his mouth giving him the appearance of a man always very near to laughter.

"What type work do you do?" Otto asked.

"Sales."

"Of what?"

"Insurance."

"Oh?" Otto adjusted his position, arm still over the back of his chair.

"Sit down goddamn it!" Franz ordered. "Goddamn it!"

Ralph sat, amiably. Otto sipped coffee, questioning, "Did you say you're on business?"

"No I didn't."

"What brings you this way then?"

"Going to Colorado. Skiing."

"Ah. Good weather for that."

"I hope so." The man had straddled the chair as before, right hand close to his chest. He still had not tasted the coffee.

"Old man, do you get many visitors out this way?"

"No. Not many."

The telephone rang and Franz sat upright, staring, swallowing. There was oatmeal on his chin. It rang again, very long. Franz stood, with effort, seized his walker and clumped out into the hall.

"And you?" Ralph asked Otto. "What brings you this way?"

"I took a bad turn from Wichita. I hoped to go north to the interstate and avoid the possibility of blocked roads."

"Yes, it's me, Shirley! What? What! All right, Shirley. Yes. I thank you. Arlene isn't here. I say—she isn't here! No I'm fine. Thank you for calling Andy. Thank you for calling Andy. I say—thank you! For calling Andy!"

The old man returned, muttering, "Deaf. Talks all the time. Shirley on the party line. She called a wrecker."

He sat and asked Ralph, "You going to drink that coffee?"

"Waiting for it to cool," Ralph said.

"Get me a cup then."

The corners of his lips tugging, the smile not quite ever developed, Ralph gazed at the elderly host with bemused eyes. "You have my cup," he said, without moving. Franz took it and with an oatmeal covered spoon stirred in sugar.

"How far distant are your neighbors, old man?"

Franz replied in German, "Fifteen kilometers north and Holcomb to the south."

Ralph turned to Otto, "You understand that?"

"Yes. I speak German."

Ralph nodded. "Do you get many visitors out this way?"

"No!"

"This must be your lucky day then."

Otto glanced out the window, following Ralph's gaze and then he saw what had prompted the remark. Down the highway, a heavy automobile was negotiating a U-turn.

"You have to use the telephone and get out of here," Franz snapped. "Arlene isn't coming. Use it and go."

"Franz," Otto reasoned, "did you not tell Shirley to call for a wrecker?"'

"Did I? Yes. I did."

Ralph was looking past Otto, out the window, at the car which had halted a quarter mile away.

"Busy place," Ralph said.

"Where was everybody when I needed them last night?" Otto countered mildly.

"That's not Arlene," Ralph concluded facetiously. A man had stepped from the vehicle and stood with hands cupped to his eyes.

"Popular item, binoculars," Ralph said.

Otto's mind whirled—who was the threat here? This sardonic visitor or the man outside? Or were the two of them together? A backup would have been wise for either of them, precluding surprise and reducing the chance for escape.

"Interesting," Ralph said softly. The car was now moving down the highway in reverse, away from the house.

271

"So remote and so busy," Ralph commented.

Otto touched the lump in his coat that was the Luger. He was trembling. He clamped the coffee mug with his other hand.

"The goddamn coffee's gone cold!" Franz shouted. He shoved his chair back, noisily. Neither Otto nor the other man made a move to help. The old man turned with a jerking motion, sloshing coffee from the spout of the pot as he wheeled to place it atop the stove.

"There is a proverb," Ralph said, conversationally. "A man who lives long is twice a child. I should not wish to live so long, personally."

If Franz heard, he gave no indication of comprehending. He stood at the stove, tapping the blue pot, muttering, urging the coffee to heat.

Otto reached for his cigarettes again and Ralph lunged abruptly, seizing Otto's wrist. He reached inside Otto's jacket, patted chest and armpits.

"Both your hands on the table, Otto, please."

"What is this?" Otto questioned.

"Do as I ask."

Ralph took a chrome .38 caliber pistol from behind him. It had been in his belt. Otto felt his heart sink. Ralph stood back from the window, looking at the far automobile, pistol pointed toward the ceiling.

"Now old man, I ask you once more, do you get many visitors? Has anyone been out to see you the last day or so? A stranger?"

Franz tapped his pot, "Hurry coffee."

"Franz," Ralph went over and put a hand on the old man's shoulder, gently persisting, "have you had strangers calling here recently?"

"Just me alone. Arlene isn't coming today."

"How senile are you, old fellow?" Ralph questioned, the tone of his voice and the impending smile giving a beneficence to his manner.

Like a steer about to be slaughtered, Otto sat, hands trembling atop the table, waiting for his throat to be cut. Better to die fighting than submissively! Try for the Luger, jump him, anything but this!

"You must understand me, Otto," Ralph said, as if reading Otto's thoughts. "It would be an error in judgment to move suddenly. You must sit with hands on the table. Hmm?"

"Are you going to rob us?" Otto bluffed.

"No. Your money is safe, Otto."

He was not yet sure that Otto was a threat. If this man suspected that, Otto would die instantly. But die eventually he would surely, Otto was positive of it. There was no chance the assassin would spare a witness. And had the old Nazi been in possession of his mental faculties, he too would have known his life was drawing to a close. The killer's only concern was to halt the chain of murders. Nobody would complain if a doddering old associate must be sacrificed to end the threat to themselves.

"Goodness gracious," Ralph said, "we are so popular today. What is going on here?"

Down at the highway, a delivery truck had stopped at the drive. A passenger was getting out. The vehicle pulled forward, shifting gears, leaving a bundled figure in the center of the road. The wind was lifting, sweeping rime and snow across the fields.

"Another guest coming, old man," Ralph said. "Is that Arlene?"

Franz poured coffee, spilling it, then replaced the pot on the stove. Ralph took the old man's arm and directed him to the window, gesturing with the pistol.

Head waggling, Franz demanded, "Who's that?"

"That's what I want you to tell me, old man. Who is that?"

"That's not Arlene!"

"Do you know her?" Ralph asked.

"Nobody comes out here! Who is that?"

Lips compressed, Ralph's tic was now more a nervous mannerism than the suggestion of good humor.

"Otto, I must ask you to stand and face the wall."

273

"What is this about?" Otto questioned.

"If you do not know, it does not matter," Ralph reponded. He tapped one of Otto's feet with the tip of a toe. "Legs spread, and lean against the wall, please."

Otto did this, submitting to a thorough search from boots to wrists. "Remain there, please." Hope evaporating, Otto saw the man going for the coat. The moment the Luger was discovered, it was all over. Otto would die in the next second.

Rap, rap, rap; gentle knocking at the door.

"Goddamn it, I only have coffee!" Franz shrieked.

"Answer the door, old man," Ralph said.

"No more guests. No more!"

"Answer the door, Franz," Ralph commanded, kindly.

"That's not Arlene!"

The knock came again, louder. It sounded as though the caller was kicking, rather than striking with knuckles.

"Go to the door, Franz. Go along now." Quietly, Ralph warned Otto, "Sit down. Say nothing."

Franz stumped down the hall. "Who is it?"

"Erika Krajewski!"

"Who?"

"Erika Krajewski!"

At the sound of the woman's voice, Ralph tensed, standing in the kitchen-hall door where he could watch both Otto and the old man.

How much good would it do Pamela to have Otto sit here and do nothing? In seconds, they would be dead and the assassin on his way. Ralph's only hesitation was an uncertainty as to who was his mark. With the assurance that his mission was fulfilled, he would act.

"May I come in, Herr Schmidt?" The voice came down the hall, deeper than Pamela's, heavily accented.

"Go away!" Franz yelled.

From a corner of his eye, Otto saw the unidentified vehicle coming fast—

"Come, come, Franz, you aren't going to leave the girl in the cold, are you?" Ralph said.

"That's not Arlene."

"Let her in," Ralph demanded, "we shall see who she is."

"Herr Schmidt! Please! I wish to speak with you."

"Go away, goddamn it!"

The car swerved, righted itself, and somehow avoided striking Otto's vehicle as it turned crazily and came up the drive.

"Herr Schmidt," the voice outside was pleading now, "Dr. Hans Fiedler sent me."

"Who?"

"Dr. Fiedler—Dr. Josef Braun Haas—"

Instantly, the assassin was aware.

"Doktor Haas?" Franz sounded pleased, his dementia flooding his thoughts with kindly remembrances. He was throwing back the bolt now, opening the door. Ralph took a half step backward into the kitchen, no longer concerned with Otto—this woman was the mark and he knew it now.

"Dr. Haas did you say?" Franz pulled open the door, his thin legs silhouetted beneath the flannel nightgown as the backlight of the doorway framed him. Ralph crouched, steadied his arm on the doorjamb, waiting for Franz to step aside so the woman could enter.

Outside a squeal of tires, but if the gunman heard he did not react, waiting, waiting, his finger white on the trigger. Otto! Goddamn you! Otto! Move! Move! The Luger!

His lungs locked, ears drumming, fear in every fiber of his body, Otto turned, fumbling, groping for the pocket and the butt of the gun. It was cocked. Aim. Fire. Hurry. Hurry.

"Come in, come in!" Franz at the front door, speaking German.

Arms leadened, shaking, the Luger obscene and heavy, Otto lifted it, grasping the weapon with both hands. Ralph was aiming, the hammer of the chrome plated revolver drawing back—

"Look out!" Otto screamed. He tried to steady the Luger, to point the wavering barrel. "Look out! Pamela! Look out!"

Somebody shouting. Footsteps on the front porch. Momentarily diverted, first by Otto's yell, then by the outside voice, the gunman hesitated, glanced back and, seeing Otto's gun, dove aside. Beyond Ralph's head the hardwood floor splintered. The Luger leaped and threw up Otto's arms. Gasping, he saw the killer roll over, come up, the looming muzzle of the chrome pistol steady and on target.

Otto fired again. Missed again. The assassin was taking care to do his job properly. Otto was soon to die—

Suddenly Pamela bolted past, knocking the gunman's arm as she ran through the door. The belch of flames and ringing concussion stunned Otto. Pamela dashed for the back door, again the gunman was bringing his hands down, arms straight, pointing, preparing to fire, aiming at Otto. Stupidly, panicked, immobile from fear, Otto saw the tunnel at the end of the weapon, his Luger weighted, refusing to rise and defend him—about to die—the bullet to come from that tunnel—

The roar of a shot, but not from the chrome pistol. Ralph was thrown against the wall, clawing, turning now to aim at the front door. The Luger was finally positioned and with great will Otto brought pressure against the trigger. The gun leaped! Smoke and noise and Ralph was sliding down the wall, crimson splotches, smears—

". . . only have coffee goddamn it . . . no oatmeal . . ."

"Otto, where is she?"

"Russell. How did you? Where did you—"

". . . Arlene's not coming . . ."

"Otto, where's Pamela?"

"Ran out. The back. Russell! There's a wrecker coming. They called for a wrecker."

Russell threw open the back door. Stinging gusts tore though the kitchen as he stood there looking out at the sheds, silo and barn.

"Shut the door! Shut the goddamned door! Shut it, shut it!"

Russell closed it, face ashen. He went to the corpse in the hall and took the pistol from Ralph's hand. Russell examined the weapon a second, stepped over the body and then lifted the gun to place it between the old man's eyes.

Franz continued speaking as though the dead man were not in the hall, the bullet holes were not in the walls, floor, ceiling—as though the pistol were not touching his forehead. He was saying something about "oatmeal" and "butter" when the hollow point shell jarred his head backward and dropped him like a sledge hammer.

Russell returned to the hall, wiped Ralph's weapon with a handkerchief and pressed the gun into Ralph's hand. He then put his own pistol in the old man's hand.

"Give me your Luger, Otto."

Otto watched as Russell cleaned the stock and tossed the weapon aside.

"We must find Pamela," Russell said.

Otto stood, stupidly. Russell shook him. "We must find Pamela, Otto. Hurry."

"There's a service wrecker coming, Russell."

"Later, Otto. Let us find the child now."

Otto threw on his coat, following Russell into cutting winds, needles of ice and snow stinging all exposed flesh. Stiffly, he ran toward the barn. It had grown darker, threatening more snow, the temperature plummeting.

"Pamela!" Russell's voice was almost lost in the howl of wind as he circled a silo, yelling, "Pamela!"

Visibility was a scant few yards and yet between gusts Otto could see to the horizon. In the distance were the winking red lights of an emergency vehicle. He opened a loosely hung barn door which creaked and banged, responding to variances of pressure as the wind put stress on the cavernous building. Otto stepped inside.

"Erika?" He spoke in Polish, "I am your friend, Erika. Come out now. You cannot stay here. People are coming."

Faintly, Russell's voice ebbed, returned, calling, "Pamela, baby, it's Papa! Pamela, where are you?"

Waiting for his eyes to adjust to the paucity of light, Otto heard a movement. He saw silt falling from overhead. He found a ladder, began climbing slowly.

"Erika, please allow me to help you. Come out. You cannot remain here. They will find you. We must go."

He reached the loft, wheezing, listening. A scrape from a dark corner. Otto moved that way, feeling for obstacles with his toe. "I am your friend, Erika. I understand you. I wish to help."

Another sound—a scurrying—rats? Otto turned slowly, his eyes seeing better now. "Erika, I am a Jew."

Something told him, warned him, and Otto wheeled. An indistinct form, armed with a pitchfork, stalking him.

"I am your friend, Erika," Otto still spoke Polish.

"Ja," the gutteral reply, "prove it."

He snatched at his gloves, fumbling with the overcoat, jacket, the buttons of one sleeve. She stepped nearer, pitchfork ready, rusty tines threatening.

"I am a Jew, Erika. I have been there, too, where you have been. I am your friend."

She took another step, her face shadowed, the weapon aimed for his chest. Damn these buttons! Otto snatched at them and the shirt tore. He grabbed his sleeve, pulling, lifting the fabric.

"See?" he said, holding his voice even. "You see this, Erika? This is proof—I am your friend." He exposed his arm, the telling tattoo.

"Many Jews abetted the death of their brothers," she accused. "This is proof of nothing."

"I came here for the same reason you did! To get Franz Schmidt!"

She halted, uncertainty evident only in the slight lowering of the pitchfork.

"I tell you—you cannot escape without me," Otto reasoned. "It will be too far, too cold, and they will find you even if you do not freeze. I have an automobile. I will take you away from here."

"And him?" she demanded.

"Who?"

"The murderer! Kingmann!"

CHAPTER TWENTY-FOUR

"KINGMANN?" Otto said.

"Who do you try to fool?" the girl scoffed. "You know him. He knows you."

"I know him only by another name."

Otto lowered his sleeve, speaking as he put on his gloves again. Already his fingers were numbed from exposure. "Erika, I am your only chance. The weather is becoming worse. You cannot walk away from here and survive. I have an automobile. I will take you out of this. Soon enough, people will be here. There is a wrecker coming now. If he discovers Schmidt and the other man dead, they will arrest you. I am your only chance."

"What of Kingmann."

"What of him?"

"He will kill me. Kill us both."

"No. I can send him away I think."

"Not now. He has seen me."

"He thinks you are someone else! Listen to the name he calls—"

"Pamela, darling. It is Papa. Come out, Pamela!"

Otto moved toward the ladder. "Wait here," he commanded.

There was no warmth in the barn, but upon stepping into the biting wind, Otto's body jolted. He hugged the wall, squinting south. The emergency vehicle was not far distant now.

"Russell!"

"Did you find her?"

"You must leave. Get away."

"Not until I find her. She is here somewhere."

"Don't be a fool!" Otto yelled. "Look!" he pointed at the approaching lights.

"I have to find her!"

"Damn it, man! How much good can you be to her if you are caught here? I will find her. I will handle the wrecker. If I become involved, I am an old man, my life is done! But you—you must think of Pamela. Run. Get away now!"

Russell hesitated, lips blue, then ran for his car. He spun the vehicle around and drove fast for the highway. Otto saw him turn south toward Holcomb.

"Erika!" Otto hollered through the barn door. "He's gone. Hurry! Someone is coming!"

She came down the ladder quickly, and together they raced across the yard and down the drive.

"Wait!" her cry was Polish.

"What is it?"

"My bag. I can't leave my bag."

"Where is it?"

"Inside the door in the hall. I dropped it."

The wrecker was near enough now to see the windshield wipers sweeping. "All right," Otto replied in Polish, "get the bag. Hurry."

He went to his car, slapping his hands for circulation, waiting. The wrecker pulled up and the driver cracked his window. "Got a call—you called?"

"Yes. I can't get my automobile started!" He saw Pamela round the house, going in the back door.

"Let me jump 'er off," the driver yelled. He wore ear muffs, fur-collared parka and a ski cap.

Pamela emerged through the front door, carefully closing it behind her, an airlines tote bag in hand. She trudged toward Otto, snow swirling around her.

"Try it now," the driver hollered. Otto twisted the key and the motor coughed, turned, turned, and roared!

"Goose 'er," the driver commanded. "Hold 'er down and give 'er plenty gas."

"How much do I owe you?" Otto asked. Why didn't Pamela hurry?

"Fifteen dollars. You see any other car?"

"You passed him. He got his started," Otto explained.

"Okay. I'll follow you back to Holcomb. You're lucky."

"How's that?" Otto questioned; he gestured to Pamela—come on!

"Old man Smith called Shirley Dobson, and she called me and that's a miracle! He's got hardening of the arteries in his brain and she's as bad—but I got the call anyhow."

Pamela slipped across the seat, under the steering wheel, to her side. She sat with her face covered. Otto slammed the door as the driver of the wrecker waited. Then, with the emergency vehicle following, Otto drove slowly toward town.

"Did you get everything?" Otto asked, seeing the bag.

"Ja. Everything."

When they reached the main highway, the driver of the wrecker left them with a wave. Immediately, a vehicle pulled in behind them and Otto recognized Russell's rental car.

He retraced his route to Dodge City. There was no way to hurry—the gusting wind and poor visibility prohibited it. And there was no reason for speed—it would be hours, days, before anyone discovered the bodies. The longer it stormed, the better.

With darkness, the headlights of the following car merged with other cars which had fallen into a line, seeking the safety of their numbers on this desolate and windswept road. The heater eventually lifted the temperature and Otto slipped off his heavy outer garments. He lit a cigarette, his silent companion's face dimly illuminated in the light of the dashboard.

"Are you hungry?" he asked.

"*Ja.*"

"And me. We will stop ahead."

"I do not wish to go inside," she said, her voice a husky whisper.

"No need," Otto replied amiably. "We will get food to go."

He had the thermos filled with hot coffee, ordered half a dozen hamburgers and french fried potatoes. The girl reached into her tote bag and withdrew several crumpled pieces of currency.

"I will pay," she said.

"No. I will pay."

"No," she said, forcefully. "How much? How do you say—in dollars? How much?"

"One dollar then," Otto relented.

He carefully selected a service station where he could refuel and they could take advantage of the rest rooms. It was one of those remote establishments, an oasis in a barren stretch, far removed from the next station and the nearest town.

Russell had pulled up at another service island. When Pamela went inside, still carrying her tote bag, he looked at Otto. Otto shook his head, negatively. When Pamela returned, Otto drove away. The girl glanced nervously at Russell's apparently empty vehicle.

"That resembled his automobile," she said in Polish.

"Whose automobile?"

283

"Kingmann."

"How would he know where we're going?"

After a long pause, the girl said, softly, *"Ja,* this is true."

The terrain became a series of rolling hills. The child gazed out her window into the night. At one point, she asked, "Where are we going?"

"Atlanta."

She adjusted her position, head resting on the back of the seat, face away from him. Otto noted her hand in the tote bag. The strap was wrapped around her other wrist.

Smoking constantly, debating how best to handle this child, Otto's mind operated on several levels simultaneously. What would be the best psychiatric approach, a worrisome thought. But heavy on his mind also, was the realization that Russell Roth was a man named Kingmann—and this child, Erika, knew him. She also feared him. Called him "murderer."

It was obvious to Otto, Russell had not gone to Connecticut to find the "other" Nazi. As a decoy, Russell had sent Otto into a trap to expose the assassin. Russell had known all along. How else could he have secured a source capable of revealing the ties between all the dead men? Yes, and then tell how to find Franz Schmidt with explicit instructions to a remote highland plains farm home?

Russell had known there was an assassin, even before Otto told him. He dared not call off the killer, or perhaps he didn't know how. But to save his child, Russell had divulged this information, using Otto to flush out the assassin without exposing himself.

The child turned, sighed in her sleep. Otto lit a cigarette from the butt of another. He pulled out his wallet and removed the picture he'd been carrying. It was Pamela's photo of the white, nondescript building. He put the snapshot on the dashboard.

She awoke speaking Polish. "Where are we?"

"Tennessee. There's coffee in the Thermos," Otto offered. "I think maybe two more hamburgers in the sack, if you want them.'

She ate the cold sandwiches. Otto tapped the photo atop the dashboard. "What is that place, Erika?"

She examined the photo, mouth halted in mid-chew. Putting it back, she continued eating.

"What is it?" Otto persisted.

"It is where they keep Zyklon-B."

"The gas?"

"Yes."

"Why was the photo taken of this building?"

"To show Kingmann."

"Show him what?"

"To see if he remembered."

"Why should he remember this place?"

She wiped her mouth with the back of a mud-spattered sleeve.

"Why should he remember this building, Erika?"

"Because he—" she sounded choked, "that was—"

"Yes?"

"That was where he shot—he shot—he shot—"

The child stared ahead, mouth agape, food on her tongue. She was shivering. "Erika?" Otto tried to break her thoughts. "Erika? May I have more coffee?"

"*Ja.*" Dully, absently.

"Erika. May I have more coffee, please?"

She nodded. But she never did pour the coffee.

The city came into view, rising like a cubistic impression among rolling hills. "Atlanta," Erika said. Her tone suggested she'd never seen it before, but knew this to be the place.

A steady rain fell, never completely stopping, yet seldom ever a satisfying downpour. Such weather was the deep South's melted version of the midwestern snowstorm they'd left in Kansas.

Otto had driven all these hours without relief, and now with an aching head, he still had reached no definite conclusions as how best he could handle this girl. What would snap her out of this? What key factor returned the child to "Pamela" when "Erika" was through? Home? This city? Did Erika quite deliberately yield to the mind that was the conscious entity, Pamela?

He had studied, and once seen, a mental patient who clicked from one role to another, a mysterious round robin within a single body, alternately gentle, tender and self-effacing, then suddenly violent and demanding. The patient had been the victim of an erratic system of chemical changes caused by a tumorous growth at the base of the hypothalamus. After an operation, the man became an understanding, responsible father and husband again.

What form of "surgery" would excise this Polish woman from the personality "Pamela"?

"I will get out here," she said.

Otto realized they were stopped; he'd been driving without conscious thought to the action. Traffic was jammed along the freeway.

"No," he said, too sharply. "Wait and I will take you someplace where you can be safe. There will be food and a bed—"

She opened the door, tote bag in hand. Otto grabbed her arm. "Erika. Let me take you with me."

Suddenly she turned and Otto was looking at the Luger he'd left in Kansas.

"I will get out here," she said, evenly.

He released his hold and she ran up an incline, crossed a guard rail.

"Otto!" Russell raced toward him from down the line of stalled cars. "Otto! Stop her!"

"No, Russell. No! She has a gun."

"I've got to catch her!"

"Do you want to make her guilty of murdering her own father? She has a pistol."

Horns were blowing. Russell gasped, eyes wild, "A gun?"

"Yes. The Luger."

"How did she get a gun?"

"At the farm house. She went back for her bag. She must've picked it up then."

The complaining motorists were producing a wailing cacophony behind them. "Let's go home, Russell. Pamela will be along soon."

"How do you know that?"

"I know," Otto said. "Believe me. She will be along."

Janet ran from the house and threw her arms around Russell, holding him tightly. Otto put both rental cars into the garage and shut the doors.

"Eleanor and Harold are gone," Janet was saying. "I told them to take off a week."

"Good," Russell acknowledged. "We are exhausted, hungry."

"Pamela?" Janet questioned.

"She will be along soon," Otto said. "Let us go in out of the rain."

"Is she all right?"

"Yes."

"Where is she then?"

"Here in Atlanta," Otto said. "Please, out of the rain."

"What happened?" Janet demanded.

"Janet, we have been two days without rest," Otto said. "We need food, now. Please, wait. Can you cook something for us?"

"Eggs, toast — "

"Good, good. We must make plans quickly."

"What kind of plans?" Russell snapped.

Otto shut the kitchen door, removed his coat and hung it on a peg inside.

"Answer me, please," Russell said, voice low.

"Very well, Russell," Otto stated. "It is Erika who will soon be here. She has a gun. She is coming to kill you."

"Oh, my God," Janet sank into a chair.

"I do not believe that," Russell said.

"The time for chicanery is past, Russell," Otto said. "I shall not try to prove a case here. Suffice it to say, when first the girl sees you she will draw that Luger and she will shoot to kill you."

"Why should my daughter do that?"

"Because it is not your daughter," Otto moved beside Janet, patting her back. "It is a Polish woman, a girl, named Erika Krajewski. And it is not Russell Roth she seeks. It is a man named Kingmann."

The blood drained from Russell's face.

"That is why she ran from you in Kansas," Otto said. "She knew Kingmann. She thought you had come to kill her."

"That is a lie, Janet," Russell countered without emotion.

"As I say," Otto continued, "we possibly do not have time to expound on the pieces of information I have learned. I will not squander precious minutes debating with you. But you are, or were, a Nazi, Russell. You are a man who is being hunted by Erika Krajewski. And as she was instrumental in the deaths of all the others, so will she kill you, without hesitation."

"More of that reincarnation drivel," Russell said, angrily.

"Russell!" Janet shouted. "Don't be a fool! No more lies. If not for yourself, think of Pamela."

"Ah, yes, Pamela this minute, Erika-somebody the next."

"It would be unforgivable if Erika shot you," Otto suggested, "and Pamela awoke to find a gun in her hand as she stands over the father she loves."

"You expect me to believe such—inanity!"

"Russell, please, please," Janet pleaded. "Whatever you are hiding from World War II—"

"Our lives have been destroyed," Russell said, brusquely. "For what? For a time and place so alien to all of us that it might as well have been another century! Look at me, Janet. To you and Pamela, I have been faithful husband and loving father. I am a prosperous, respected American businessman. I do not steal. I do not plunder. I am what you see. Is this not enough?"

"I don't know, Russell. Once, yes. I don't know now."

He massaged his eyes, wearily.

"Were you a Nazi, Russell? I must know. Tell me."

"Let us assume it is so, Janet. What then? Would you leave me? Revile me? Live with me despite your disgust? Would you pick and pick and pick for every gory detail? Could you ever stand to touch me again? Would we live apart under the same roof?"

"I don't know."

"You don't know," Russell said. "That is correct. You truly do not know. Very well, assume I am some horrible criminal escaped from a history of genocide. Let us say I personally drove men, women and children to the gas chambers. Do I look like a man who could do such a thing? Have you ever seen a shred of evidence, a single action from me, to suggest that I am such a man?"

"No, Russell."

"Don't you understand? *This* is what I am, Janet. What you see is what I am. What I have been—no matter what that may be—that is not the man standing here now. Are you going to despise Pamela for what she has apparently done?"

"Apparently?"

"We have no proof she has done anything wrong. Skipped school, perhaps. Ran away, yes! She was there in Washington and you saw her, but did you see her kill anyone, Janet?"

Weakly, "No."

"But let us *assume* Pamela has done these things—and we can only assume, we do not know. Assume she has and then tell me, can you forgive her that?"

"Yes. Of course."

"Yes," he mimicked her tone, "of course. Interesting. Now my question to you—if I were guilty of some similar deed in time of war—would you forgive me also, Janet?"

She looked away, eyes burning.

"I see," Russell said, softly.

"I want to," Janet reasoned. "I have prayed to God for help. I want to forget all this and have our lives again. Dear God, help us!"

"Over food you pray, you Christians," Russell said bitterly.

"For God men died in crusades; churches keep their parishioners destitute in the name of this god or that. You are so—so stupid, you people with religion. Did you know the Pope endorsed Hitler until it became popular to do otherwise?"

"That's not true!"

"It is true. When Hitler invaded Russia, the Pope issued a statement comparing the battle against Bolshevism to a religious clash of ideologies. Was the Pope right? Was Hitler right? Who was right? The Bible said the Jews would suffer. They did. Who was responsible? Hitler or God?"

"I don't want to hear that!" Janet shouted.

"I don't suppose you do," Russell rejoined.

"But," Otto said, "the point is well taken, isn't it?"

"Otto, not now—"

"No, no," Otto insisted. "Russell is correct to raise such points. From the side of the Nazi, or from the Jewish view, both present arguments and lay claim to God's will. Interesting isn't it, Russell?"

"Shut up, Otto."

"Consider again what I told you about reincarnation. Not a mystical, theological excuse for enduring long suffering, or as a means of explaining away life's constant failures—but as a means of continuing retribution: think about that."

"I'm going upstairs," Russell said.

"That would explain it all, you know," Otto stated.

"I find your theories as offensive as all the others, personally," Russell said.

The doorbell stopped them all. Pealing chimes which by tone and number told them it was the front entrance.

"Russell?" Janet whispered.

"No," Otto said, calmly. "Janet, you must answer. She won't know you."

"Won't know me?"

"Treat her as any stranger." Otto led her to the hallway. The bell sounded again, systematic gongs ringing through the house.

Janet went to the heavy wooden portal, peered through the one-way peep hole. She saw a knitted ski hat pulled low over the girl's head. Her coat collar was upturned against the drizzling rain, her face starkly pale. Wet hair clung to her cheeks and forehead.

Janet opened the door slowly; the girl put a hand in her tote bag, squinting through rain running over her eyebrows. Before Janet could speak, she heard the coarse, deep voice ask:

"Mrs. Roth?"

Breathless, "Yes?"

"My name is Erika. Is Mr. Roth home?"

CHAPTER TWENTY-FIVE

"HE ISN'T HERE AT THE MOMENT."

The configuration was the same: bone structure and nose—but this was only a visage of the child, Pamela. Those eyes, always so expressive and chameleonic, were now cold dark orbs in sallow flesh.

"May I come in out of the rain?"

"Yes. Please," Janet said. "Come inside."

"Do you expect him soon?" The voice was alien, accented.

"He—he's been out of town."

"I know." She kept a hand in the bag. "Do you expect him soon?"

"Come into the den," Janet suggested. "It's warmer there. Let me take your coat."

"No. Thank you."

Janet was shaking. She glanced toward the kitchen door at the far end of the hall. In the den, Pamela sat beside the fireplace, staring at burning gas logs.

"May I offer you hot tea?" Janet questioned.

"If it is no trouble." The girl studied Janet with an expression devoid of recognition. "He should be home soon. Shouldn't he?"

"I would think—Pamela?"

The girl blinked, long, lingering blinks, and stared again at the fire. "I'll get the tea," Janet said, hoarsely. "Excuse me."

When she entered the kitchen, she found Otto holding Russell's arm, restraining him.

"Russell—dear God—she's a stranger!"

"This is nonsense," Russell snapped. He snatched his arm free of Otto's grasp and strode down the hall.

"Russell!" Janet cried. He shook her off and walked into the den.

Pamela, forewarned by Janet's cry, stood at the fireplace, legs apart, both hands on the pistol.

"*Ja, Herr* Kingmann," she said. "*Ja,* at last."

"Pamela, put that down."

"Do you know me, *Herr* Kingmann? Do you remember?"

"Pamela," Russell took a step toward her and she tensed visibly. Otto slipped past him, circling wide.

"So many died," the girl's voice cracked. "Perhaps you do not recall only one among many—"

"Erika, may we speak of this, before you do something?" Otto questioned in Polish.

"Collaborator! You are no better than he!"

"It is not him who concerns me here," Otto said.

"Shut up, damn you!" Russell shouted. He took another step forward. To the girl he said, "Pamela, snap out of it. Enough! Put down the gun."

"Stay there, Russell," Otto warned.

"Do you remember? Erika Krajewski? Perhaps not the name. My face then, do you remember?"

Otto was close to the wall, inching nearer.

"The others did not remember either, Kingmann."

"Why do you call me Kingmann?" Russell asked.

"You are Kingmann," she stated matter-of-factly. Without looking at Otto, she said, in Polish, "Pig, you are going to die if you come a step nearer."

"Please," Janet pleaded, "don't shoot."

"Do you know this man?" the girl asked, her pistol leveled at Russell's chest. "Has he ever told you the things he has done?"

"Why are you doing this?" Janet begged.

"Tell her, Kingmann. Tell her why."

"I don't know why."

"You know."

"I've never heard the name Erika before."

"Auschwitz, remember? March, 1944. The war was lost and still you continued to kill—remember?"

"Are you saying you were there?" Russell demanded.

"I was there. You were there. Dr. Haas did not remember until I told him—"

"Pamela, darling," Russell halted in midstep as the Luger moved ominously, warning.

"They brought us in boxcars in bitter cold. Music played to calm us. 'Before we resettle you Jews, you must learn to work!'" Her tone was that of an actress recounting a scene, her words German. "'Everybody must work! We will not tolerate sloth. You will go now to be disinfected. Take off all clothing. Remove all jewelry.' Cut our hair . . . naked . . . cold . . . it is to disinfect, they said . . . breathe . . . take deep breaths . . . a way to disinfect . . ."

Russell's face was white. He held out a trembling hand. "Pamela, please, my baby, give Papa the gun."

"They beat us with whips and shocked us with electricity, pushing, pushing—"

"Please, my baby—"

"Into the showers! To be disinfected! We saw the bodies then.

We knew better. It was too late . . . pushing . . . pushing . . ."

Russell's outstretched hand quivered, lowered.

"So many," the girl croaked. "I was jammed between the legs and the bodies and my mother could not lift me up to breathe. Packed . . . so many . . . and the doors closed . . . people over our heads were watching through windows, some of them talking to one another as though we were only to take . . . showers . . . the showers . . ."

"Enough, Pamela!" Russell shouted. "Stop it!"

She was gasping, one hand to her throat now, speaking English between choking sobs, ". . . people smelled . . . choked . . . choked . . . screaming . . . trying to climb . . . crying . . . so many . . . so many . . . could not breathe . . . could not fall down . . . hurt my lungs . . . my mother's hand . . . the stench . . . the stink . . . the . . ."

"Pamela!" Russell screamed. "Pamela! Stop it!"

Sucking air between purple lips, words disjointed, the gun aimed, her inhalations a rale, gasping, ". . . feces . . . menstrual blood . . . Mama's fingernails cutting my arm . . . making sounds . . . making sounds . . ."

"Dear God what's happening to her?" Janet shrieked.

". . . so long . . . so long . . . so long . . . until nobody moved . . . so long before the doors opened . . . cold water . . . hoses . . ." She was quaking violently, eyes glazed, her fingers clamped to her throat, face livid. Russell stood like stone.

". . . took them out . . . stacked them . . . threw on top of one another . . . used hooks to get gold from the teeth . . ."

"Oh dear God," Janet wept. "Oh, please stop this!"

". . . tore their faces for the gold . . . found me . . . alive . . . took me to Doctor . . . Haas . . . did not let me die . . ."

Otto and Russell stood stock-still. Janet pushed past Russell toward the girl and Pamela jerked the gun toward Janet, more a move to warn than threaten.

"They asked you!" Pamela screamed. "Keep me alive, they asked you! They said it was God's will! For months . . . for months . . . I lived . . . saw terrible . . . terrible . . ."

"Pamela, baby," Janet was whispering. "Pamela, Erika, I'm sorry. I'm sorry, Darling."

"He killed," Pamela pointed at Russell, "shot . . . took me behind the Zyklon storage building and shot . . . they begged him not to do it and Kingmann refused. He said I must die. Took me behind the storage building and shot . . . himself he did this . . . with his gun . . . like this gun . . . shot . . . shot . . . shot . . ."

Otto lunged at the instant Janet reached out to touch the child. The Luger fired. Russell dived atop them all and locked the weapon in one hand, wrenching it from the screaming girl's grasp.

"Get blankets," Otto commanded of Janet, "belts, blankets, hurry!"

Pamela clawed at their eyes, kicking, biting, the two men shoving her to the floor by sheer weight, Russell's knee in the girl's stomach, Otto fully across her legs, her arms pinned.

"Filthy, dirty—" she was frothing at the mouth, her curses a mixture of Polish, German and English. She sank her teeth into Russell's wrist and he snatched free and slapped her hard across the face.

"Pamela! Snap out of it! Enough! Pamela!"

"Filthy *Schwein!* Dirty—"

Russell slapped her again, the full weight of his body behind the blow, and the girl's head slammed the floor. For an instant she was too stunned to move.

"Here," Janet dropped the blankets, several belts in her hand.

They rolled her, tightly, and bound the length of her body with belts—a restraining measure used with the mentally ill and violent.

"Call a doctor," Otto ordered.

"No," Russell countermanded.

"Call a doctor, goddamn you!" Otto snapped. Janet ran from the room.

"She will be all right," Russell seethed. "Give her a few minutes. She'll be all right." He stroked her face, "Yes, my darling. Soon enough, you will be all right again."

"You will kill me now," the girl said.

"Kill you?" Russell choked, tears welling up in his eyes. "Pamela, I love you. I love you. I would never hurt you. You are my baby. I would die for you."

"You will do it again."

"No, no. I will look after you. I will not let anyone harm you, I promise this, Pamela."

"Shoot me—"

"No. No. Pamela." Russell's voice came from deep in his chest, tears falling from his face to the blanket now encompassing the girl's body.

"I have—I have— "

"What, my baby?" Russell whispered. "What do you have?"

"Have—failed."

"Pamela, this will pass. Everything will be all right now."

"Killed them all—but one—"

The child closed her eyes, squeezing out tears. Russell patted her shoulder, loosened one of the belts slightly. He wept, shoulders heaving, whispering words which Janet and Otto could not hear. Then, Janet realized, the words were not English.

"The doctor is coming," Janet reported.

Otto still knelt at her legs, one hand on them to prevent a struggle. He nodded.

Janet walked over to her husband, lifted a hand as if to comfort him, then let it slowly fall to her side.

"She should sleep now, Mrs. Roth."

"Thank you, Doctor."

"Any idea what caused this?"

"No."

"She has a slight fever. Possibly from hysteria. I'll come back in the morning to check on her. Are you sure you won't want to put the child in a hospital?"

"No. My husband wants her kept here."

"As you wish. Well. Loosen the restraining straps as I showed you. Good night, Mrs. Roth. I'll find my way out."

Otto stood at the door. He walked with the physician the length of the hall, then down the stairs.

"Dr. Ebenstein, has this child been your patient?"

"I'm no longer a practicing psychiatrist," Otto said.

"Nevertheless, from your point of view, what happened to her?"

"Exhaustion, perhaps. As you said, hysteria."

"Would you care to offer a professional opinion as to what caused it?"

Otto stood with the front door open, a hand on the knob. "You have seen youngsters this age act similarly for a variety of reasons, have you not? Activity and tension at a sports event, perhaps—I agree with you, she will most probably be all right very soon."

The medical doctor nodded, shortly. "Good evening, Doctor."

Otto shut the door and returned to the den. Russell sat beside the fire, pipe in hand, a drink untouched on the coffee table. Beside the tumbler was the Luger.

"May I sit with you, Russell?"

Russell waved a hand at a chair. His eyes were reddened, cheeks inflamed. He had been crying again.

"Wicked weapon, the pistol," Otto mused, reaching for it.

"Leave it please."

"That is not the answer, Russell."

298

"Oh?" Russell's voice had a bemused lilt. "What is the answer, my all-knowing Nazi hunter."

"Such a thing must be someday explained to Pamela. What could anyone say? You must surely know the lifelong effect of a suicide in the family."

Russell sucked on the pipe stem, staring into the flames of the logs.

"An automobile accident would be the best way."

"But there is no debate that it must be done, obviously," Russell said.

"No."

"Kill another Nazi, eh, Otto?"

"If you don't, in my opinion, Erika will."

"And if I do, all will be roses in bloom again?"

"I cannot be positive. But I think so."

"My daughter—" Russell's voice broke. He turned his head away. In a moment he said, "My child isn't even here to tell me good-bye."

"No. She isn't."

Russell averted his eyes, tapping the pipe bowl against the hearth. He shoved the unburnt tobacco into the fireplace with one foot.

"Tell me, Otto—"

Such a long pause ensued, Otto asked, "What?"

"Tell me, in your theory of this—uh—this reborning business—what are my chances of coming back as a turtle? I should like to be a turtle, I think. A sea turtle."

"I don't think it works that way," Otto said.

"No. No, I suppose not."

"What are you going to do, Russell?"

"About what?"

"About the matter at hand."

"Hmm. Yes. Rush along to the next entity, is that it?"

"Something like that. But for the moment my concern is that child upstairs. We are faced with a decision, aren't we? Either we free her of this Polish girl, Erika—or make arrangements to have Pamela committed to an institution for psychiatric examination."

"My curiosity," Russell said, suddenly angry, "what would a psychiatrist say about all this, Otto? Would he embrace the doctrine of reincarnation, as you have?"

"In layman's terms," Otto said, evenly, "he would most likely diagnose it as a form of obsession which the child began as a lark, an obsession which manifested itself in a fantasy whereby she began to live the imagined role of the Polish girl, Erika. Any of us, reading a book, watching a movie, live a vicarious existence, for a few hours at least. The fine line between sanity and otherwise lies in returning to the present, to our own lives and identities. How many little boys swagger from a western film with an imaginary six-shooter on their hips? It is a normal fantasy. With Pamela, the psychiatrist would say, the personality became so engrossed with the horrors of Erika that Pamela was submerged into that role."

"Do you believe that a man named Kingmann shot and killed a Polish girl named Erika, after she survived the gas chambers?"

"Yes."

Russell nodded, eyes vacant, mind afar. He asked, absently, "Would you like a drink?"

"No."

After a moment, Russell said, "You think, then, an accident. An automobile accident?"

"Yes. It would be traumatic, but Pamela could overcome that."

Again, Russell nodded, his head continuing to go up and down, up and down, staring with sightless eyes.

"I suppose so," he said finally. "I have nothing more to keep me here. Believe me or not, I lived only for Pamela—and Janet."

"I believe that."

"I should put things in order," Russell said, brusquely. "But then, that is a hint that it was no accident."

"Yes."

"Interesting theory, this borning anew," Russell said, standing. "What did you call it? A continuing system of retribution? That makes it awesome, you know. I've been sitting here trying to recall just how many—sins—I must suffer for. I'm not sure I would want to come back."

"That is the surest proof to me that it is true," Otto stated. He too was standing now. He watched Russell swallow his drink in three large gulps.

"Look after my family, will you?" Russell said.

"For a price."

"What?"

"I will, but there is a price, Russell."

"Oh there is, my Jew friend? What is your price?"

"I want to know about the others, Russell."

"What others?"

"All of the others, Russell. All of them."

"What makes you think I know this?"

"You knew about Franz Schmidt. You knew the assassin was there. Perhaps you instructed him yourself, before you knew it would be Pamela he was after."

"No, I didn't do that. It's quite automatic. His task is to assure the remaining members that each death was either natural or isolated. That is all."

"So there is an organization."

"Nothing so sinister as a dormant party awaiting a chance to seize world control," Russell said, putting on his overcoat. "Nuclear weapons and all have precluded such a thing. No, this was a desperate last-ditch effort by a few to survive. Some were doctors, like yourself, or lawyers, professional men. They comprised the bulk of the *Einsatzgruppen* commanders. Were you aware of that?"

"Yes."

"I will drive you to my office, Otto." Russell watched Otto's face. "Perhaps you are afraid to ride with me?"

"Let's go, Russell."

They walked to the garage and Russell opened the doors, remarking casually, "Those rental cars must be turned in. I suppose Harold can do that when he returns." They got into Russell's Continental and drove away from the house.

"After the war," Russell said, "or more precisely, when we saw the war was lost, they assigned to me the task of creating a program we code-named 'Echo.' Echo was to be a system whereby any member could receive proper identification, hold property, have access to financial assistance. I shall not bore you with how it was conceived, but the implementation of it is something of particular interest to me."

The windshield wipers beat a cadence, approaching headlights glared brightly, then passed with the singing of tires on the rain-slick pavement. Otto half turned to better hear Russell's softly spoken words.

"At the time, in 1944, we had no idea what the world faced in this so-called Atomic Age. Computer science was a fledgling subject dealing mostly with theory. But Dr. Haas was approached by the Jewish physicist, Hans Fiedler, who was trying to buy his way out of dying. Many of the Jews did that, those who had the means. Actually, it was forbidden for any SS member to profit personally from the death of an inmate. In fact, over two hundred German officers and enlisted men were put on trial for that and similar infractions, most notably the commandant at Buchenwald, Karl Koch, who was convicted and executed for hiring out camp laborers to civilian employers. Privateering at the expense of the Jews was expressly forbidden. Himmler did not approve of becoming personally involved in the Final Solution."

The speedometer touched fifty, rose to sixty.

"When Haas came to me, he was excited about the prospects of

302

this tiny invention which the Jew, Fiedler, had called a 'transistorized component.' Haas had visions of the Reich using this man's ideas for computers to control the secret jet-propelled unmanned bombs being sent to England. I convinced him those papers might someday do more than gold to ensure our safety. Indeed, that is exactly what transpired."

Street lamps passed overhead, the rain a silvery veil surrounding each pool of illumination. Russell turned onto the main artery to downtown Atlanta.

"As it is, the computer made it possible for all of us, Otto. I set it up. Quite ingenious, actually. There is a television advertisement which states that a particular bakery's product is 'untouched by human hands.' So it is with the steadily declining membership of our diminishing organization. Each man's alias, background, family history, everything about him: computerized. Property changes hands, is deeded to and taken away from one or another of them. Money is regularly deposited in their bank accounts, thereby circumventing such things as social-security cards. The system has become a self-perpetuating entity, actually. The insurance man from Berne, whom we unfortunately shot in Kansas, is called for by the computer if a check fails to clear in sequence, or by any of a dozen indicators that the subject has met with death, or even if he is jailed. The system covers his immediate family in the event of a member's death. As it is, or was, I also became very wealthy from all this—while satisfying the original intent of the business and a world need at the same instant. It is a bit ironic, I suppose, to claim that 'God's will' be done. But that is precisely how I always felt about it."

The speedometer was touching eighty now and Russell was passing all traffic, throwing a swirling vortex of spray behind them.

"After we programmed the computers, sprinkling the data here and there in computer banks around the world, the system eliminated the deceased, adjusted the incomes; we have an automatic

303

escalator built in so that inflation does not overcome any of the members. I'm really rather proud of it all. Virtually nobody ever truly knew how it worked, before now, except me. Oh, Haas had an idea. But he lacked the expertise to fully grasp the genius behind it all."

"What of the others—the ones Erika got to?"

"I don't know," Russell said. "Men whose identity she tortured out of Haas, perhaps. People she met along the way, maybe. I don't know their connection to her. Except for Haas—that is, Hans Fiedler, I knew none of them personally."

The speedometer touched ninety—ninety-five—Otto put one hand casually on the dashboard. At this speed, they would not stand a chance—

"Ah," Russell said. "Here we are—"

They began to slow as he approached an exit, gently applying the brakes. He turned off the expressway, down a short street, then up the cobblestone drive to the office complex.

As they parked and Otto got out on shaky legs, Russell said, with amusement, "You see, Otto—we made it after all."

CHAPTER TWENTY-SIX

THEY SIGNED IN WITH A SECURITY GUARD, then walked a long hall, footsteps sounding hollow. Russell used a pass card to electronically unlock the double wooden door to his personal office. He went to a safe, worked a combination, opened it. From the vault he took a small loose-leaf booklet. Turning, he said mildly, "Why should I do this?"

"What?"

"Why should I do this?" Russell questioned. "No matter what has happened, why should I compound it by betraying associates and comrades-in-arms?"

"Because of Pamela."

"This won't help Pamela. It simply makes a traitor of me!"

Like a man emerging from shock, Russell gathered his resolve. "Why should I do it?" he reasoned. "It serves no purpose but the vengeance of Jews."

"You are doing it for Pamela, Russell."

"Ridiculous!" Russell said, savagely.

"Russell, when it was happening, they were like so many cattle. Ten thousand a day at Auschwitz alone. There was nothing to distinguish one from another. But now you know—your own child was among them. You executed your own daughter!"

The notebook quivered in Russell's hands.

"For thirty years you have had no misgivings, Russell. You did your duty. They were only a mass of faceless creatures. But, Russell, knowing you killed your own child! This is why you should do this. Because the others were a part and party to it all. Because, had it not been for them and others like them, your daughter would not have been there and it would not have happened.

"As foolish as it may sound, Russell—you are doing this for a moralistic reason, and it *is* for Pamela."

"For Erika."

"And Erika."

Russell closed his safe, spun the dials. He strode from the room and Otto followed to the elevators. They descended to a subbasement. Russell used his pass card to open a heavy insulated door.

"This is the master terminal," Russell noted. Otto watched him turn pages of the book, filled with numbers. Of these, Russell selected digits from each page.

"Nobody in the world knows the code but me," Russell said. The room reverberated with a slight humming of computers and the climate control. "If I had died, this would have gone with me. The combinations are committed to memory."

Russell sat at a keyboard. With one finger, he typed symbols into the terminal.

"Get a chair, Otto. This will take some time."

"May I smoke?"

"This equipment is so precious we are very diligent to keep it free of impurities. Even cigarette fumes would eventually be damaging."

Otto put away the cigarettes. Russell tapped, tapped, tapped the keyboard.

"I could erase it with a touch," he commented. "Or," he added a moment later, "recall it all."

He spoke as he typed: "I spread data through computer banks the world over. Hidden within our data. I'm feeding the computer a series of commands to scan. For the reasons of security, each of the responses we receive will have a code which must be eliminated to make it a working symbol. Throughout, the symbol that must be eliminated is Echo—'E.'"

"I understand."

Russell worked mechanically. "It would be an impossibility to recall this information without these two critical steps. The true names and current identities are never in one source. Government and private computers, the Federal Treasury, even NATO has been keeping us safe with their data banks. The system corrects itself. For example, when Franz Schmidt's next two pension checks arrive and are not cashed, the computer will signal an alert to the insurance office in Switzerland. Of course the insurance agent is dead in Kansas. When he does not respond to the computer's call, the machine will select from a predetermined list of men and will write a letter to them in numerical order, offering a job as sales representative of this company. Quite automatic."

"Ingenious, Russell."

"Yes."

Russell closed his book and pushed a button.

"Now then, Otto, I will have one of those cigarettes. It will be some minutes before we get a reply. Assuming I made no error."

Otto held a match and Russell puffed, inhaled deeply and sat gazing at the cigarette. "I always smoked a pipe because I felt cigarettes were injurious to one's health."

The computer began to "talk." Russell watched with detachment. Sensing the man's pride in his accomplishment, Otto said, "Quite ingenious."

"Yes."

At last, the data was in. Russell tore off the sheet.

"How many are there, Russell?"

"At one time, several thousand. I suspect only a few hundred now."

The laborious process began again, Russell carefully feeding in the new data and double-checking himself as he worked. An hour passed without conversation. Then, Russell stood, face drawn, exhaustion and stress taking a toll.

"It is done," he said.

"What now?"

"When I leave, you press this button. Thereafter it is automatic. Do not touch anything else during the entire time it takes. Let the machine run its course. It may be an hour or more. Be patient. Remember that the 'call' signal is going out to computers around the world. It will take time, even at the millionths of a second these machines transmit. Data must be selected, assimilated and transmitted. Do I make myself clear? Touch nothing after you push the start button."

"All right." Otto was breathless.

Russell turned to a telephone, dialed a number. "This is Roth. I am leaving Mr. Ebenstein in the master terminal room. When he is through, he will take certain classified data with him. He is to pass without delay. Have someone drive him where he wishes to go."

He hung up, then dialed again.

"How is Pamela?" Russell cupped a hand over his eyes. He cleared his throat. "At the office. Yes. He's here with me."

Otto had walked to the far side of the room, giving Russell an illusion of privacy. Russell said, voice low, "I called to say, I love you both. Tell Pamela when she awakens, will you?"

A long pause.

"Tell Pamela how much I love her."

After a hesitation, Russell said, "I am fine. I only wish to say—I love you and I love Pamela. That is all."

Russell turned to Otto, "She wants to speak to you."

308

"Hello, Janet."

"Is everything all right?"

"Yes."

"Otto, I want to apologize for things I've done and said."

"That isn't necessary, Janet."

"Promise to come back here before you leave."

"Very well. Do you wish to speak with Russell again?"

"No. I hear Pamela crying. She is still that other person, Otto."

"Can you handle her?"

"Yes. She's wrapped in that thing the doctor brought."

"Call if you need me." The phone hummed in Otto's ear. He hung up and met Russell's eyes.

"May I have another of your cigarettes?" Russell asked. Otto gave him three. Russell selected one, lit it.

"I have your word?" Russell said. "You will look after them?"

"I swear it."

Russell exhaled smoke. He walked to the door, paused, then left. Scarcely able to control himself, Otto sat at the computer. A glowing yellow button was marked "Start."

"Schwein!" The curse was coarse, deep. Janet sat with a hand on the restraining jacket. Pamela's upper lip was dappled with beads of perspiration, her eyes wild. She screamed in Polish and when Janet tried to soothe her, the girl sobbed, eyes tightly shut.

"My baby," Janet whispered. She wiped Pamela's forehead with a damp washcloth. "Please God, give back my baby—"

The speedometer rose steadily, windshield wipers sweeping with smooth strokes. Russell stared at the ribbon of concrete stretched ahead. He maneuvered the vehicle with one hand, his foot easing down on the accelerator. Seventy–eighty–ninety– trembling at one hundred—

Otto put out his cigarette, thinking: if she could come back only as one person, she could not have chosen more wisely. To punish this man, the one man who could pinpoint the others.

One-hundred-five–one-hundred-ten–one-hundred-fifteen; distant taillights suddenly became obstacles which Russell rounded with slight movements of the steering wheel. A flick of the wrist, a moment of distraction and the tires would hydroplane, the vehicle turning, vaulting, jump the median, head-on into—no! Not that way! He shoved the gas pedal to the floor. Coming up now—overpass—concrete—swerving, catapulting, screaming—Pamela! *Pamela! Pamela!*

"Mama!" Janet ran from the bathroom.

"*Mama!*"

The child had thrown herself from the bed and she lay face down on the floor, nose bleeding.

"Mama! Help me, Mama!"

"I'm here, Darling. I'm here!" Janet lifted the bundled form. She fumbled with canvas belts, webbing. Pamela was panting, face dripping nasal blood and perspiration.

"Oh, Mama! I had a dream." Sobbing without control, clutching Janet, "I dreamed—I dreamed that Papa—"

"Hush, baby," Janet consoled. "It's gone. Lie back, my darling."

Janet gently cleansed the child's nose and discarded the restraining jacket. When Pamela was breathing easily in deep sleep, Janet sank to her knees to thank God—and Erika.

Otto pushed the button. Instantly the computer responded:

KINGMANN, KURT ERDEL: COLONEL EINSATZ-GRUPPEN E.
ALIAS: ROTH, RUSSELL ELLIOT.
RES ADD: 14675 OLD SHELL ROAD, SANDY SPRINGS GA USA.

BUS ADD: PEACHTREE CIRCLE NW ATL GA USA/
INTELCON INC.
WIFE: MILLER, JANET DONNA
DAUGHTER:

The machine paused . . . chattering . . . chattering . . . chattering . . . had something gone amiss? Otto stayed an impulse to push the start button again . . . waiting . . . waiting . . .

Suddenly, the machine shifted, shifted, shifted, chattering. Then it began again . . .

. . . PAMELA. . . .